Copyright @Nathaniel Redcliffe. All rights reserved.
ISBN #: 9781796231229

This is a work of fiction. Names, characters, businesses, events and incidents that occur in the fictional town of Holders Bridge, are either the product of the author's imagination or used in a fictitious manner.

Dedicated to Rita Redcliffe (Our Valentine)

"I wonder who you think you are. You damn well think you're God or something? God give life, God taketh it away, not you. I think you are the Devil itself."
A mother whose daughter fell victim of Peter Sutcliffe (The Yorkshire Ripper,) 02/01/1981

Part 1 - Holders Bridge

Chapter 1

Jenny Woodfield woke up this morning not knowing it was going to be her last day on this earth. Jenny was only 17 years old and was in her last year at secondary school where she was very popular; especially with all the boys. Not only was she very pretty, she had round soft cheeks on her kind looking face, long smooth brown hair and soft green eyes. She kept very athletic by regular running, cycling, swimming and her weekly yoga sessions. Although Jenny's looks and her kind-hearted nature attracted the affection from many men and teenage boys, she would always gently turn them down because there's a boyfriend on the scene. An older boy from the college nearby who has the name of Mark Bell. Mark isn't quite intellectually equivalent to Jenny but she couldn't help falling for his sweetness, kindness and the fact that he had some maturity about him. There are times when Jenny wonders if she really is in love with Mark. Even though she thinks he is sweet and he makes her happy, somewhere in the back of her mind she ponders if it is the real thing or if they're just close friends. If it were time to dump him; Jenny's independent enough to not feel the pressure from society, and not force herself to be seen with a boyfriend. Currently, she remains loyal to him, doesn't even flirt with anyone else at parties. She regularly attends parties, but never drinks too much to get drunk, or uses any substances that could influence her mind or behaviour. No, she had seen what that stuff has done to her oldest and dearest friend, Chelsea Heart.

Today, Jenny is leaving the house for her morning run to prepare her for a hard day at school. Her lovely detached house rests on top of a hill so as the sun rises it shone over the top of the Woodfield's residence before descending onto the rest of the quiet and friendly street; Everlow Road. If there was a street in England that would resemble the American Suburbs, then Everlow Road would most certainly be it. She is wearing her running leggings that end at her ankles just before the running socks that are tucked into the professional/expensive, bright yellow, trail running trainers. To keep her warm, she put on her running jacket that is black on the front and back but pink on the inside of the long arm sleeves. Jenny protects herself from the sun by wearing a baseball cap which has her pony-tailed brown hair slotted out the back. After stretching, Jenny puts in her special headphones that have wires which are designed to withstand exercise. Song preferences consisted of something upbeat. Her run begins starting down the usual route, from her house down the hill of her street...

Shelly Jayne woke up this morning not knowing her friend and closest neighbour on Everlow Road was soon to be murdered. Shelly was older then Jenny, slightly taller and just as beautiful. Shelly is in her early 40's but looked much younger than her age. Despite the age gap between the pair, Shelly still attended the BBQs in the summer that are hosted by Jenny's parents, Raymond and Janet Woodfield. Shelly enjoyed talking to Jenny about books, music and make –up. Jenny was quite happy to reciprocate, due to her boyfriend not being interested in any of those things. If one or the other needed anything then they would just pop over to each other's houses without any questions asked. Shelly practically watched and babysat Jenny whilst she grew up from a little girl into the sensible young woman, she is today.

Shelly's long, light blonde hair brushes the shoulders of her pale green uniform with the collar that folds down away from her throat, which she wears for her early shift at the local coffee house. Shelly's tying her white apron around her skinny waist, and over the green skirt that ends at her knees. The remainder of her legs were covered by white tights. Shelly always wears flat white shoes, with the uniform which she deemed appropriate for work even though she really loved to wear high heels. Before Shelly leaves the house she always puts on her red lipstick, softens her eyes by placing light blue eye illuminator around her dark brown eyes. Shelly leaves the house quietly because she doesn't want to wake Richard, her husband. Just has Shelly approached her small white car Jenny ran past. Shelly waved to her and smiled because she didn't want to break Jenny's concentration, not that anyone could have. Jenny did acknowledge Shelly's presence and responded by waving back to her, for one last time.

Jenny's route took her off road and onto the dirt cycling path leading to the river bank. In the spring time, at this time of the morning, the path never looked so beautiful because on the left of the mud track you have the calm blue water and on the right you have a dandelion field, the cool breeze carries the dandelion heads into the air so that they hover over the path and float towards the clear blue sky. Jenny's route takes her away from the beauty of the river into a gloomy hollow where dead trees line the narrow path. Never her favourite part of the run, the eerie feeling she gets here is unsettling to her usually uplifting exercise regime and today of all days, the atmosphere feels more intense. The bare, skinny tree branches make Jenny feel more claustrophobic than usual. Not wanting to be vulnerable, she picked up the pace. The burning in her legs and the struggle to maintain her breathing doesn't seem to stop her from trying to escape into the open. With much relief, Jenny escapes the gloomy hollow and began to slow down to a jog like pace where she could take deeper breaths before she tackles the difficult terrain of a bowl. Most of the bowl is covered in long grass that grabs at the knees, but there are still parts of the track that are visible. The path dips and goes past a discarded refrigerator, then leads to a cul-de-sac. Jenny reached the top of the bowl and goes to turn right however something stops her. As she stands on top of the bowl, she notices someone coming down from the left-hand side. The figure is wearing a thick blue winter coat and dull grey work trousers. Jenny squints and leans her head forward to get a closer look. She walks to get a bit closer. The hooded figure has its hands in the coat pockets, looks up towards Jenny but between the woolly rims of the hood, there is no face, only darkness. Jenny is left vulnerable after sprinting out the narrow woods, running up hill and having a brief stop on top of the bowl, her legs have become jaded. She treads lightly down the bowl while maintaining a cautious eye on the figure, hoping to quickly walk past before restarting the run on the other side of the bowl. If she can get a bit closer than she might be able to recognise this person because here in the small town of Holders Bridge, everyone one knows everyone...

Moments later, Jenny's lifeless body lies wrapped in plastic in the middle of the path.

Chapter 2

Raymond and Janet Woodfield woke up that morning suspecting that their little girl made her way to school safely. Raymond is packing his brief case, ready for his day at work, Director of Finance of the town's main bank: Holders Bridge Trust. Mr Woodfield is a trusted member of the community which gives his business an edge over big, faceless, competition. Raymond was easily recognized among the community; not only was he a well-respected business man, everyone knows him by how he looks and dresses. In his fifties, he is tall, has fluffy, thick black hair above his thick, plucked eyebrows and his light blue eyes. He carries a bright white smile, which he'll show to anyone that walks past or comes close. His skin is always brown from tanning booths, making his whitened teeth even more blinding. He mainly wears a knitted green, sleeveless cardigan over a white shirt and red tie. He favours the horrendous beige trousers with thick black leather shoes that do not match at all.

Time has caused Raymond to fallout of love with his wife Janet. He's waiting for his daughter Jenny to pass her GCSE's, graduate college and turn 18 before he tells her that he is going to start the divorce proceedings. Although he doesn't love Janet anymore, he still thinks the world of Jenny and doesn't want to upset her, especially at the time of her hard work, studying and when she is just about to make something of herself. He yearns for retirement, setting his sights on the new red, 2017 Mercedes-Benz AMG Roadster with a soft-top, so he can pull the roof down to feel the breeze from the long, open, country roads whilst heading toward the unknown. Till then he must settle for the big, white, four seated, family friendly Hyundai that's sitting on his big drive way. Really, Raymond has fallen for the cliché of wanting a new sports car, to travel and to meet new people outside of the village where he's taken comfort and sheltered himself since birth. Before he begins his new life, he will leave the house to Janet and Jenny, making sure that they have enough money to last a long time and, so they can be "well off". Even now, has he is day-dreaming, his wife Janet is trying to talk to him.

"Do not forget you have that important meeting at two 'o clock at the town hall with the mayor and those oaths from the north about the loan and planning permission for the new hotel between Holders Bridge and the motorway" says Janet, whilst putting her pearl earrings in the mirror that rests on top of her white, expensive make up stand. "Quite frankly, I don't think the council will give them permission and I certainly hope you reconsider giving them a loan."

Raymond is still totally oblivious to anything that Janet is saying to him, he is just mindlessly placing various documents into the brief case that is sitting on top of their long dark green duvet which neatly covers the double bed.

"Raymond! Are you paying attention to me?"

"Yes, dear" said Ray, not fully knowing to what he has agreed to. He could have just agreed to one of Mr Scarborough's wife-swapping/keys-in-a-bowl nights for all he knows.

Janet was sure he wasn't paying attention, she's noticed he's been more and more distant recently but carries on regardless.

"I will pick up your suit from the dry cleaners at 11 and bring it round your office on the way to the supermarket"

That Raymond did listen to so he responds,

"Thank you, honey".

With the brief case packed and closed, Raymond makes his way out the house. Before he leaves the bedroom he kisses Janet on the cheek. Raymond smiles at her like he does at everyone to try and convince her, and maybe himself, that everything is still okay and that he is happy. As he walks out the room he shouts,

"I'll see you."

The half Raymond's secretary and half a stay at home housewife/mum doesn't even say goodbye in return. She is still putting the last pearl earring in her left ear. Using the mirror, she uses her fake, sharp, purple painted finger nails and tips to push up her curly red hair. She puts on her dark red lipstick, thick black eye liner around her dark blue eyes, dark blue eye shadow to hide the fact that she is in her late 40's but wishing to herself that the wrinkles on her face would disappear. She always wears her pearl earrings, her gold necklace and her favourite black chiffon blouse with the see-through arm sleeves. On her feet she wears black high heels to make herself feel taller because she is less than 5ft 5.

Just has Janet was about to seize the day and leave the house; the landline phone, which sat on the oak chest bed side cabinet, rang. Janet picked up the phone

"Hello?"

It was her friend Kelly saying "That her cousin Marian had heard from her friend Brad that he saw on the social media site that a body of a young woman has been found on the town's dirt track. Brutally murdered! He said! Poor girl, on the way to school! Can you *believe* something like that has happened? I'm just like… *oh my gaaad.*"

A mortified Janet had this dreadful, sinking feeling that it could be her daughter Jenny because she knows, for a fact, that she runs down the dirt track before school. Along with her stomach, her jaw dropped, the fingers in both of her hands clench into a claw shape, releasing the grasp of the phone. Her whole body trembles. Without thinking she ran towards the dirt track in her heals. The phone is left dangling from the cabinet.

Chapter 3

Jenny's teacher, Gail Brooke woke up this morning unaware that one of her favourite students has been murdered. Gail always preferred to be called be Brooke and when she teaches at Holders Bridge Primary School, she prefers her students to address her as such. She always believed the young adults are old enough to no longer use these formalities, and should be treated like the adult they'll soon become. However, that doesn't mean that she is their friend. She is their teacher and her upbringing on the council estate taught her to be strong when she needed to be. Brooke is tough but fair which made a lot of her students respect her. Some of the other uptight and stuck-up colleagues who can't handle their pupils as well as Brooke, do not like her. She is very pretty, with a few freckles on her nose and under her soft green eyes but not so many that they cover her whole face. Brooke also has a small cute birth mark on her left ear which looks like a mole but isn't. She is of medium height with a-not-too-skinny figure but not too over-weight either. Some men find her personality attractive, though others go crazy to see her legs because she always keeps them covered by wearing jeans; even though Brooke has nice legs and thighs, she hates wearing dresses but loves jeans and nice white trainers to match those jeans. When Brooke is invited to a party she still never wears a short dress that exposes her lower half, instead favouring a long, gypsy-esque, red dress that covers her flat shoes, Brooke detests high heels.

On this nice and sunny day, Brooke was leaving her mid terrace house on her not-so quiet street, which is full of parents maintaining a watchful eye on their offspring and their neighbour's kids. The older kids, all dressed in their school uniforms of black ties, blazers, trousers, shoes, and white shirts, stand in a group, all playing on their phones. Over the road from her is a field where some of the kids play football. On the pavement to Brooke's right hand side she noticed a group of young girls who are only around eight or nine years of age, wearing their adorable hair bands on top of their long hair, clothed in white dresses, black shoes and really thick white socks. To her surprise they were playing hope scotch which one of the adults drew on the ground with chalk. This was unexpected to Brooke because these days' children are normally glued to their laptops, computer games, or phones.

Mothers with prams and other people passing by were all saying "hi" or "good morning" to each other because in a tight and small street everyone knew each other. With the exception of the creepy Mr Dunscroft who keeps himself to himself and lives at the house on the end of the street, which always has the curtains shut. People notice that he peeps his head from underneath the curtain every day and when anyone catches him doing it he immediately hides behind them again. This doesn't bother Brooke because some people are private and just because they are that way, doesn't mean that he is hurting anyone. Having someone like Clive Dunscroft living behind closed curtains, being reserve or keeping his life private is deemed suspicious by the town folk. Thus, he is condemned to being the creepy loner that everyone talks about. He is a main target to many knock-a-door-runs played by the kids of the street because of his rumoured reputation. For instance; some of the kids believed he had a torture chamber in his sound-proof basement. In a way Brooke felt sorry for him but had to agree if someone was to look the part of being the "local, quiet, serial killer" of the village then it would defiantly be him. He gives strange vibes, looks constantly awkward, stiff but bent posture probably due to constantly looking at the ground when he moves.

Despite Brooke's sympathy for him, she admits how he looks and dresses doesn't help his own cause. The really thick rimmed glasses, the shirts that are his size but looks like it's made for a child emblazoned with either a picture of childhood toys, cartoon characters, a space rocket, or comic book characters. Which everyone thinks is bizarre because of his age. He is very tall, over 6ft 5 like a *Ramone,* but one that is overweight and going bald on top which he covers with a baseball cap. Brooke has a friend named Laura and she told her "that she saw him out the house once with his young boy, he held this boy far too close, and was holding his young lad's hand with such crushing capability." This makes Brooke suspect that he is a bit too over protective. She doesn't know much about the boy because she has never seen him, nor is he old enough to be at her school where she teaches.

Unexpectedly, Brooke is approached by a boy. He tugged on Brooke's jeans to grab her attention. Brooke looks down, gives him a friendly smile and asks in a friendly but a quite condescending tone "Are you ok? What is your name?"

The Boy pulls a broad grin at the very pretty teacher revealing all his missing teeth; he becomes very giddy and swings his body from side to side, as if he were going to ask her on a date, in a shy, awkward manner. Instead he sings to her a nursery rhyme...

"Beware, beware the man with no face.

He cannot see. He cannot hear.

He is the man with no face."

Beware, beware the man with no face.

He doesn't sleep, he cannot smile.

He is the man with no face."

The boy runs back to his friends and Brooke was left with a chill in her spine that she just couldn't shake, while she walked the rest of the way to school.

Chapter 4

Janet is walking at a quick pace down the dirt track, wondering her eyes aimlessly, not really sure what she is searching for but has a certainty that she'll know it when she sees it. The bottoms of her heels are constantly tripping over some small stones and the odd fallen twig from the branches placed on the trees on both sides of the path. Both of her arms are stretched out slightly, the wrinkly elbows inwards, forearms pointing skywards, hands in a claw-like position as if her sharp purple nails are about to cling onto something.

Up ahead, nosy neighbour's mill around. News travels fast here and the people are wondering if the rumours are true. The small town of Holders Bridge is about to have its first murder in 20 years. There standing in-between the herd of pedestrians and the-nearest-city-homicide-team is a line of yellow tape that runs from a tree on the right side of the dirt track onto a tree on the left. The local Sergeant, Simon Cole is standing there, enjoying the authority he has over the people. Simon is quite a small man, just over five and a half. He hates feeling small so he tries to broaden his shoulders and his arms by giving them a good hour of weight lifting daily to compensate for his height issues. Simon is also slowly approaching the big four zero, he has dark brown eyes, thick black hair with a big bald spot at the back of his head. He is dressed in his neatly pressed uniform, the dark green shirt tucked into his blue trousers, fitted with a black belt He also wears a dark blue tie, dark black boots and his badge which he polishes daily and hangs with pride over his heart. Nothing bad ever happens apart from a few men getting drunk and rowdy. A young woman in woolly hat takes out her phone to take a photo of the crime scene, before the picture was captured,

Simon grabbed the girls hand "No pictures at the crime scene."

Whilst everyone in the crowd are chatting amongst themselves, eagerly waiting on more information to whom has been murdered. There is one other man standing on his own, holding a smoke in his hand. He's on top of a small mud bank, leaning onto a tree trunk without any concern. He is known as the towns "hard-man", "black sheep", "trouble maker" Shane Crewball. Shane has black, shoulder length hair, a dark brown beard, and wears a black leather jacket, blue jeans with holes over his knee caps, brown boots one of which is held up against the tree he's leaning on. He is looking straight at Sergeant Simon Cole with his dark beady eyes and it isn't long till Simon notices him and begins to stare back. A stand-off was emerging. Shane just smiles to himself, takes a hit from his cigarette that was slowly burning away in his hand, exhaled the smoke like he was aiming it in the direction of Simon. Shane is not showing any interest to who is lying under the forensics team blanket on the ground. He is the first to give up on the staring competition, balances himself off the tree trunk, and walks off swinging his arms like he's the bigger man. Simon Cole never takes his eyes from the back of him until Shane disappears into the crowd.

Simon turns around and looks at all the forensic workers; whom are all wearing white hazmats suits that cover their full body and gas masks. They all are searching for clues, scouring the small, thin area and taking photos. Simon knows that all the information they find along with the actual body will be sent over to him but the rest of the team will be heading back to the city, where even more crimes were happening and taking the priority. Simon and his small team of officers will be left to solve the murder of Jenny Woodfield.

Simon heard someone shouting above all the din of those gathered around. The voice is shouting

"Move! Get out of my way!"

Simon quickly turns to see the commotion.

Janet Woodfield emerges, desperate to find out what has happened. Simon looks tragically shocked that she is here to bear witness the removal of her daughter's dead body.

One of the first thing Janet notice's is a body on the ground but it is covered by a long grey foil-type sheet. She has a horrific feeling that her gut instincts' were right, and it could be her daughter laying under it. Her jaw drops slightly and her chin begins to shake and asks Simon quietly "Simon, who is it?"

Simon remains silent and looks down.

Her voice gets franticly louder

"I said! Who is it!?"

Simon looks up to her and looks Janet in her wide, black mascaraed eyes and just simply says to her with a hint of remorse.

"I'm so sorry."

Janet crumples onto the ground, now with her legs around the left side of her waist and both hands pressed into the ground, she screams has loud has she could

"NOOOOOO! NOOOOO! NOOOOOO!" Then the words stop and she is simply yelling so loud has if it was an attempt to scream all the pain out of her body but it will never be enough. Two young male members of the crowd, who know Janet, pick her up from the ground by pulling her arms and attempt to remove her from the scene. They hold her up right but Janet is just looking up to the sky and screaming as loud has she possible can. Whilst she is yelling her body swings side to side but the two strapping young men do their best to keep her still.

Oh, the screaming, it seemed endless and the pitch of screeching was enough to make ears bleed, it was so overwhelming that all the people standing near wanted to cover their ears or just cover her mouth up. For the respect of Janet's grief all they can do is watch and listening to the intense sound of the screaming, the screaming that everyone will take home with them and cost days to forget. The screaming would not stop and she will continue to scream has loud as she possibly could, over and over until she can scream no more.

Chapter 5

Sun shines through the wide windows of Shelly's own coffee house that is named: "Goforcoffee" which is on Holders Bridges main shopping district. Goforcoffee is popular for the students of the local college to congregate, gossip, play on their phones and of course enjoy a cup of coffee. They tend to gather particularly in the corner of the shop where the comfy burgundy leather sofas are. In the middle of the room are your basic wooden tables and chairs under lots of dangling bright white lights. On the far-right hand side of the room is a long thin shelf attached to the wall at waist height, that have tiny purple flowers growing from small plant pots which seem to blend in well with the light woodwork and the bright green walls. Sat on one of the three long cushioned stools, sits the big time and famous comedian: Jack Mandolin. Mandolin was his stage name, Jack's real full name is Jack Mill but everyone, aside from his brother Frank, who calls him by his stage name. He is typing on his laptop, trying to come up with new material which he will test in his brother's own pub, "The Dive Bar". When Jack is back in town, it is a big deal and the few tickets for shows sell out quickly. So, during his time off stage, Jack tries his best to blend in with the public by not shaving the "patchy bum-fluff" around his face and wears a plain blue hoodie, blue jeans and white trainers, though he is no master of disguise, so his plans fail. Jack has thick curly hair on top of his head, shaven around the back and sides, brown eyes and is in his late twenties. Jack finished writing for the day so he closes his laptop and places it into his light green shoulder bag, stands up and walks over to the counter, keeping his head down in an attempt for nobody to see him. When he arrives to the cashier counter, he notices the owner/waitress Shelly Jayne. Jack looks up and gives her a big white smile "Shelly, it's good to see you again."

"I heard you was back in town Jackie boy" Shelly replied.

"I am doing another show at my brother's bar next week and can try and get you in, if you'd like to come."

"Oh, thank you for the offer but I've got the coffee house to run. I just had to lay off Anna because I can only afford to keep two waitresses now."

"I'm sorry to hear that."

"You're doing well for yourself, just done another world tour, you funny man. People have been constantly talking about you. The town was so looking forward for your return."

"It's good to be home though. Nice to see old friends and family."

"You've not forgotten your roots, it's a good thing, and most big shots would have left all us little people behind and never look back."

"How could I forget about you, Shelly?" Jack charmingly adds. "You should come with me, it'll do you some good to go out and see the world."

"That's awfully nice of you but my life is here, all my friends, my husband and my coffee house."

Jack looks disappointed but can't help but respect her loyalty. "I just would have liked to repay you for all the babysitting you've done for me when I was younger."

Shelly laughs, "My pleasure Jack. You need to find yourself a nice woman and settle down."

"I can't settle, you know me. Always on the road! Moving on from one city to the next!"

"You still end up back here though."

"Yeah" Jack pauses for a while before continuing "It's probably for your coffee, no one makes it has good has you."

Jack smiles and Shelly returns one back.

"That'll be £13, please."

"Sure" Jack proceeds by giving at an estimated £100 from his pocket which meant nothing to him.

"What's all this?" asks a very surprised Shelly.

"It's your tip."

"It's far too much. I can't take all this."

"You said yourself that you are struggling."

"I never said that! Me and my business are doing just fine without your charity," Shelly screams furiously at Jack.

Jack raises his hands has a symbol of retreating, "I'm sorry, I never meant to offend you."

Shelly realises that he has offered to help quite graciously only for her to slap it back in his face. "I'm sorry, I am just a bit tired" Shelly says apologetically.

"It's fine, honestly". Jack just gives a £20 note from the pile of money in his pocket. "You can keep the change though"

"Thank you, I hope I've not lost one of my best customers"

"Oh, who's that then?"

Shelly laughs. "Stop joking."

"Can I take a donut to go?"

"No you may not... You can take two without payment"

Shelly then grabs two thick, homemade donuts from the see-through warming cabinet and places them in a small white bag before handing them over to Jack.

"Thanks Shelly, I'll see you tomorrow."

"See you tomorrow."

As Jack walks out the door, Jenny Woodfield's boyfriend Mark Bell walks in. Mark is very handsome, well-mannered young man, he has a strong jawline, good cheekbones, lots of thick brown hair which is always gelled up, long eye lashes and dark thick eyebrows above dark brown eyes. He is around 5ft 9 and very athletic; his big arms, thick thighs and six pack show proof that he is so. Although, he should really spend less time at the gym and more time studying for his failing college course in sports therapy. He wears light white jogging bottoms, dark grey tracksuit jumper with the sleeves rolled up to his elbow and finally red running trainers with black soles. Even though lots of girls around Jenny's age, the girls at the college and a few cougars have thrown themselves at Mark, he remains only loyal to Jenny because he is deeply in love with her.

Mark pulls up a stool and leans on the cashier counter to lay his woes out like a drunk does at a bar.

A concerned Shelly asks "Is everything alright Mark?"

"No, have you seen Jenny?"

"Yes, I saw her running this morning before I drove to here."

Mark gives a big sigh, "She said she'd meet me at the bus stop so we can walk together on the way to her school."

"Maybe her dad took her."

"That guy scares me."

"You'd be the same if you had a daughter that beautiful. Speaking of daughters; do you still think about having children?"

"Well I do but Jenny is more focused on her career and her dream to be a doctor, she wants to wait till after she finishes her medical school and her fountain-ation years."

"I think you mean: Foundation years, dear"

"I want to be a Professional Personal Trainer too but I want a family with her more."

Mark shakes his head side to side struggling to get his head around what is happening.

"I think she knows how you feel, you're the only guy she really likes" Shelly reassures.

"It seems like she's hiding something from me lately."

"What do you think it is?"

"I don't know, it's like she's not offering *everything* to me."

"Do you mean sex?"

Mark cheeks turned red with embarrassment, but his politeness made him to continue to answer anyway; "We've still not done anything in a while. But it's not even that; it still feels like she is keeping something from me. Whatever it is, it's getting her down."

"Maybe you two should have a talk."

"I'm going to surprise her tonight!" Mark becomes so excited with the idea he slams his fist down on the counter top. "I'm going to buy her some flowers and chocolates. Yes. That would make her happy!"

"You're so sweet Mark, I wish my husband was just has thoughtful has you."

"How is Richard?"

"Same old. Same old."

The conversation between Mark and Shelly becomes interrupted has Simon Cole walks in.

"Shelly, I need to see you in the back." Simon demanded has he allows himself in the store room behind the counter.

A surprised but shocked Shelly agrees "Okay" but suspicion is raised in herself and within Mark. "Mark, Can you please look after the shop till I get back?"

"Sure but I've got college soon."

"I won't be too long, I promise."

Shelly loves her husband Richard very much but she and Simon were childhood sweethearts; they were in the same year of school together. It started when a very timid Simon Cole coughed up the courage to give the sweet and popular Shelly Jayne a candy that was in a shape of a love heart. Since then he and she became more than just close friends and Simon became her first kiss when they were 11 years old. However, when they left school Shelly fell for the rich, tall, handsome and successful Richard Dirking. This tormented Simon and made him feel small, so he left Holders Bridge for a while. After time away, he returned to the town a policeman with broader shoulders and upper body strength which helps him feel less insecure about people undermining his authority because of his height, and it might even give him more of an advantage if he ever gets into a brawl. Although he has great upper body strength, he lacks overall physical fitness, his hairy beer belly is evidence of his overindulgence and lack of cardio exercise. Secretly, he hopes criminals would not try to run away from him in case he can't keep up. He and Shelly got reacquainted and their friendship rekindled. After so many years, roughly three months ago, Shelly and Simon's love sparked again. Thus, an affair had begun. In the back room which is mainly for boxes of stock, Simon is pacing up and down anxiously with both his hands by his waist, looking unsure about his next move. Shelly walks in falsely believing that she and Simon were going to make love in the back room again, so she practically skips to Simon and presses both of her hands on his chest and goes in for the kiss. Simon pushes her away causing Shelly to feel worried and a slight hint of humiliation.

"Where were you around 6.30am this morning!?" Simon said sturdily.

"What?" asked a confused Shelly?

"I said: "Where were you around 6.30am this morning!?""

"Simon, you're scarring me."

"Answer the question, Shelly." He says more sternly.

"I was here, opening the coffee shop" Shelly was stressing over these accusations fallen upon her.

"Does the CCTV footage show you were here?"

"Yes, you know the camera is always on. I never just use it as a deterrent anymore, not since you told me about the burglary at the supermarket."

Simon breathes out his relief and becomes more relaxed. He embraces a puzzled Shelly in his arms.

"Thank God, I'm not here on a personal call. I'm here on real important, official police business. I know you were the first person to see Jenny this morning. You leave for work at the same time as her parents said she left the house for the run."

"Jenny? Why has something happened to her?"

Simon grabs both of Shelly's hands, kisses one of them and holds them both close to his chin while he drops his head down to stare at the floor, before telling her "Jenny's dead."

"Dead?"

"She was found this morning on the dirt trail"

Shelly breathes in a huge gasp of air and struggles to accumulate a sentence; "but, but I saw her. This morning. She can't be." Her stomach feels sick, Shelly leans over to vomit, placing one hand on her stomach cramp and the other on the wall for balance.

"I'm sorry."

Shelly hugs Simon tightly, places her head firmly on his chest to feel safer and more comforted from this tragedy. First it was only a few tears that poured slowly from her eyes but then she cried, hard all over Simon's freshly cleaned green shirt. Simon looked up away from Shelly because he believes seeing her cry will make him want to cry but right now he needs to be a rock for Shelly for she has lost more than just a neighbour, she has now lost a friend.

Chapter 6

On that dreadful morning, sat on her own in the back of the class room, sits Jenny Woodfield's BFF: Chelsea Heart. Ditching her usual mini-skirt, and the rebellious Marilyn Monroe shirt that reads; "I don't need your approval." For the dull black school uniform. Currently slouching on the grey school desk with her arms folded on top to form a pillow for her head, not paying the slightest attention to what her history teacher is telling her.

Chelsea's dark curly hair bounced when she lifted her head to look at her teacher with an annoyed gaze. Her blue eyes were even more piercing than usual because the overhead lighting made her pale skin even paler. She is not as clever has Jenny nor is she has athletic. Chelsea has slightly wider hips and a tad-more meat on her but that doesn't make her look any less attractive and it certainly never got in the way of the bond between them.

The Head Master's voice comes over the schools tannoy system "Chelsea Heart, please can you attend the teachers' lounge to see Officer Simon Cole. Thank you."

A disgruntled Chelsea stands up and slowly walks out the class room with both arms folded; "what now?" She asks under her breath.

Soon has she walks out the room the other kids start to gossip and spread rumours. Amanda, a pretty, pony-tailed blonde, one of the popular girls of the school, especially among the football team, whispers to one of the girls next to her

"I bet she's back on the coke. I hear she stole her daddy's life savings for some. She's trash." Amanda likes to bully girls like Chelsea to make her feel better about herself and to be more popular, but suffers from a traumatic case of... resting bitch face."

In the teachers' lounge sits Simon Cole waiting for Chelsea to arrive. Chelsea enters the room, stares at Simon but looks irritated to see him. A few months ago when Chelsea was on a cocaine binge, she felt as though Simon was picking on her. She knew he felt poorly that he couldn't stop the gangs and source of the cocaine supply, dealer Shane Crewball. Chelsea believed that Simon grew a personal vendetta against her, there were many times he charged her for possession, and if she was ever high or drunk at a party, Simon would purposely arrest her and her friends, (even just her once.) Giving the impression that he liked to humiliate her in front of her friends. There were other teenagers caught as well, no more than Chelsea though. In some words Chelsea was right; perhaps she was victimised at times and Simon actually needed to feel like he is doing his job by bringing the outbreak of drugs in Holders Bridge to a minimum. The powerlessness he suffers to actually "putting the cuffs on" Shane Crewball is a burning angst, Simon detests feeling small. Chelsea had never been to juvenile prison, she just had to pay many fines. Well, her parents paid the fees. Community service was served twice. She was caught stealing a car; thankfully the owners never pressed charges.

This time was different to all the other times because Simon is here to tell her the news of Jenny's murder. He thought it was best that he'd break it to her personally before the headmaster announces it over the tannoy system. Because she has been her best friend since childhood; she deserves better, better to find out face-to-face rather than being treated like just a fellow student.

Simon greets her as warming, as he can be "Chelsea, please take a seat. Do you want a cup of tea?"

Chelsea leaned her back against the wall, near the door. "No. Why are you here? I've been clean now for the last two months."

"Just take the seat" insists Simon.

Chelsea reluctantly sits down.

"Chelsea, I know me and you have never seen eye to eye..."

Simon pauses, like he cannot bring himself to tell Chelsea the news despite breaking it to everyone else so easily.

"Just say what you're going to say so I can get back to class."

"Chelsea, I just wanted to say how sorry I' am..."

She interrupts "Sorry for humiliating me! Harassing me! I don't know what you got against me! But you've got nothing on me now, pig!"

"I'm not here to arrest you."

"Then why are you here?"

"Jenny..."

Simon closes his eyes and inhales deeply to bulk up the courage to tell her the truth.

Chelsea is gowning inpatient and coming very eager to leave so much so that she shouts at him "Just tell me!"

Too much time has passed, to purposely delay her meeting with Simon, Chelsea snuck out to have a cigarette earlier.

The echoing sound of the tannoy system turning on echoes throughout the halls for everyone to hear.

The headmaster begins his announcement: "Students, boys, girls, friends, peers, teachers, and colleagues please can everyone stop what you're doing for a moment. Please, can I have a minute of your time? I must inform you that a student here at Holders Bridge Secondary School was murdered in the early hours of this morning. Jenny Woodfield body has been found on the dirt track near Summers Road. Everyone must attend the assembly this afternoon for a more thorough discussion. Your parents are being notified as we speak and hopefully every single one of them will be able to come and collect you. A counselling service will be provided immediately for anyone affected by this tragedy. Furthermore, I must ask all pupils, during this time, not to disturb Raymond and Janet Woodfield. If you're going to leave them flowers or a gift basket just leave it on their doorstep. I am sure they will appreciate how concerned you are as well has the love and support they'll receive from their neighbours and friends just has much has they'll appreciate the alone time that they need. Until the person responsible is caught, do not wonder off alone, walk home in pairs. If you have any information, please immediately give it to myself or Local Sergeant Simon Cole. Thank you for your time. Please continue with your studies."

A nauseated Chelsea slowly turns her head away from the tannoy system and stares at a self-loathing Simon, annoyed at himself for not doing what he set out to do, and tell Chelsea the news before finding out the truth just like she was everybody else.

Chelsea slowly stands up from her seat and walks over to the ashamed Sergeant until she stands over him "You was meant to tell me, wasn't you?"

"Yes."

"You was meant to tell me personally before the announcement. You have always been like a useless cop."

Simon remains silent.

She screams "Chicken-shit!" Just before slapping him hard on the cheek.

Simon right cheek is left with a red mark, still he does not flinch. Then Chelsea slaps him in the face again, and then again, again and so on. Chelsea's grief makes her irrational, as she continues to slap Simon across the cheek. After each slap, the pain receptors in Simon's face grew more accustomed to the blows of Chelsea's bare hand. As she adds further insults "You can't fucking do anything, can you!"

She still repeatedly slaps her tired 'n' naked hand across the smooth, freshly shaven skin on Simon Cole's face.

When the slapping stopped, the crying began.

Simon stood up to offer a supporting arm around her shoulder but Chelsea pushed him back.

"Don't you fucking touch me!" she screamed before running out the room.

Chapter 7

The eventful day has turned to night; the news of Jenny Woodfield's murder has spread into an outbreak, now the whole town of Holders Bridge knows. The illusion that people are living in the safest village in the world has now shattered; second guessing and rumours have spread among the small town. A group of hooded teenagers have gathered around Clive Dunscroft. Due to them half listening to gossip among the town and their parents. Suspicion has fallen on the town loner.

One of the delinquent boys uses spray paint to announce to the whole town that Clive Dunscroft is guilty by spraying "murderer" on the pavement just outside his house. Behind the weed filled front garden is Clive Dunscroft peeping out from behind his curtains and his thick rimmed glasses. Breathing intensely, his hands tremble and the fear only brings the urge to cry. Till little six year old, Bradley walks in from the kitchen wearing his blue pyjamas, carrying a bowl of cereal, mounted with an unhealthy amount sugar Bradley is mute, but he never needed to ask what was wrong. His facial expression said it all clearly. Seeing Bradley gives the strength Clive needs to remain strong so he closes the curtains sits Bradley on the settee, places his arm around Bradley as if it were to protect him from the trouble that lurks outside.

Just when Clive starts to feel safe, there is a loud splat-like type of noise hitting the front door. Bradley and Clive wonder what has just hit their front door. It goes again. Splat! Again and again, each more rapidly than the last. Clive goes in for a furtive look and finds that the boys are throwing eggs at his house. Clive is too weak to leave the house and confront the teenagers. All Clive can bring himself to do is cradle little Bradley in his arms and protect him as best as he can.

Chapter 8

Two minutes to midnight, the day draws to a close. Standing outside. Chelsea Heart has practically dragged out Mark Bell outside Jenny's house. Chelsea is wearing a black jumper to prevent the cold with a thin dark unitard to camouflage herself in the dark. While Mark is wearing his usual black jacket and his gormless facial expression that illustrates his confusion to why as Chelsea dragged him here, to the front garden of his dead girlfriends' house.

He asks "Chelsea, why are we here?"

"Because some fucker has murdered my best friend and your girlfriend. Aren't you angry about that?"

"Of course, but we're not going to find anything in her garden."

"We're going in her room, you moron."

Mark is dubious and unsettled about Chelsea's unclear motives.

"I don't think Janet and Ray want to be disturbed right now."

"That's why we're going to break in."

"We can't do that!" Shouts Mark

"Shhhh!" Chelsea shushes has she presses her hands over Marks mouth to keep him quiet. "What do you think you're doing? You're going to get us seen."

Mark takes a looks around the street encase someone did overhear him. "It's illegal."

"Come on, grow some balls."

Chelsea uses both her arms to pull Marks stocky but reluctant arm to the hedges on the side of the garden, so they have a better chance of remaining unseen. "Look it's up to me and you to find out who did this." Whispers Chelsea.

"We should let the police sort this out. It's only a small town, I'm sure Simon Cole will find out who did this," insists Mark.

"Simon Cole is a fucking idiot. He only arrests teenagers and pissheads. He's too much of a coward to catch any real criminals."

"I'm not sure, Chelsea" says a frightened Mark.

Chelsea looks Mark dead in the eyes before she asks, silently pleading but she has too much dignity to show that she's even remotely begging. "Look are you with me or not? Because one way or another, I'm going to find the piece of shit that killed my friend and I'm going to make him pay."

Mark was convinced that Chelsea has her heart set on finding out the killer, with or without him and he wouldn't forgive himself if anything were to happen to her "Yes." Short Pause. "I'm with you."

A pleased Chelsea smiles "Great."

"But how do we get in?"

"We are going to climb up to the window ledge by the drain pipe." As she speaks, she takes of her black jumper to reveal that she is wearing a slim fit, full body black leotard.

"What? Are you insane! We could fall."

"Do you mean to say you have never climbed up to Jenny's window in the middle of the night before? What kind of teenage boyfriend are you?"

"Not a creepy one," Mark replies. He thought it was only something that happens in movies... or in America.

"Come on, we're wasting time," she speaks quietly whilst climbing up the drain pipe, elegantly like a professional cat burglar.

She reaches the top of the ledge, pulls out a putty knife she has kept tucked in the side of her waist and proceeds by wedging the knife between the window and the lock. She wiggles the knife until the lock is broken. Chelsea climbs inside the open window, leans over from the indie, swings her arm back and forth in order to tell Mark to follow her up. Right now!

Mark follows his orders. He pursues Chelsea by climbing up the drain pipe. Even though Mark is muscly he struggles to lift his own body weight, there are a quite a few bangs as he pressed his feet against the wall, not being as stealthy as he hoped. When he threw his hand upwards to catch the higher tier of the drain pipe the whole thing shook. It was painful for Chelsea to view; it was like watching King Kong struggling to climb up the Eiffel Tower. Chelsea was praying that no one else can hear and no one is actually home. Mark eventually got to the ledge of the window. Chelsea struggled to pull him with all her strength ending up with Mark falling on top of her, slightly crushing her and making a loud thud on Jenny's bedroom floor. Mark rolls off her, Chelsea coughs but they instantly jump behind Jenny's big pink double bed in case Janet and Ray hear them break into the room. They both peek their heads up over the bed simultaneously, looking to see if somebody is going to march into the room, gratefully no one did or was going to.

Chelsea whispers "I don't think anyone's home."

"Where are they?"

"How am I supposed to know?" hissed Chelsea

They both stand up cautiously and begin to search the room. Jenny's rooms' wall was coated in peach coloured paint and posters of all her favourite bands and artists.

Chelsea sat by Jenny's desk which was a shelf for her globe and her laptop. Jenny had no password for her laptop. Chelsea looks through her documents but can't not see anything relevant, it's mainly just school homework.

"Have you found anything yet?" Mark asks.

"No but let me see if she has any hidden files."

Mark looks clueless to Chelsea's answer "*Hidden files?*"

"I'll show you."

Chelsea goes into settings, then ticks the box that says: "show hidden files". She clicked on "apply to all" and "ok" but unfortunately no other files came up. Mark looks surprised and said "I didn't know that but what would Jenny have to hide?"

An idea came to Chelsea. "Her journal!" Chelsea places her hands under her pillows on the left hand side of the bed but then turns to Mark and looks at him, as if something is amiss. She runs over to the draws of her desk and pulls open each one, rummages through each and every one. Chelsea asks herself "where is it?"

"Where's what?" asked a puzzled Mark.

Chelsea looks under the bed and jumps up saying "Her journal. Jenny had a secret Journal that no one knows about apart from me."

Mark stood still with shock, feeling like he's almost betrayed in some way about the news of a journal. "She didn't tell me." The exclusion caused sadness to grow within Mark. His face began to sulk and he laid his head on the right side of the bed, where Jenny normally slept. Close to the window and furthest side from the door. Chelsea tried to explain the best way she could and somehow wouldn't cause Marks feelings to get hurt. "Well I was the only other person to know about it. Me and Jenny were best friends since we were kids, I knew her a lot longer than you have. You never know; one day you two might have split up, young relationships normally do. So don't take anything personally and help me look for the damn thing!" She carried on searching until she noticed that Mark is rubbing his head up and down on Jenny's pillow. At first she thought "What on earth are you doing?" and "that's fucking weird" and just as she was about to open her mouth to say something to him, she realised, something she didn't quite take into consideration earlier today, that this boy, Mark, has just lost his girlfriend. One that he loved very dearly. He thought the world of her and this is probably the closest thing he'll ever get to being with her again. As Mark is carrying on caressing his head on Jenny's pillow with his eyes closed, like a dog scratching its nose on the arm of a chair. Chelsea rested herself beside him by laying on the bed facing him. She placed a comforting hand on his shoulder. He stopped and opened his eyes to gaze into hers. Just for a moment, has they both lay there, they are at peace. Not worrying about Jenny's murderer, a sense of calmness was in the air and their tired eyes become heavier and they are on the verge of falling asleep. Those precious few seconds become shattered when Chelsea asks "so who else could have known about the Journal?"

Mark sighed with disappointment because he was hoping to fall asleep and forget about his troubles just a while longer. "I don't know."

Chelsea leaps out of the bed and pulls out her mobile from her pocket. "I bet I know someone who has something to do with this. Shane Crewball, that scumbag did it!"

"We don't know that."

"If it wasn't him, I bet he'd know another piece of shit that does. I tell ya, he's got something to do with it. I can feel it."

"You're not going to call him are you?"

"Yeah, I'm going set up a meet, then we'll make him tell us everything he knows!"

"Shane Crewball? He's crazy. He'll kill us both and bury us in a ditch somewhere."

"Don't worry, I have a plan". Chelsea begins to scroll down her contacts list on her phone.

"He's dangerous, Chelsea. It's too risky."

"We can take him on his own."

"If he's on his own?"

"I'll get him on his own" Chelsea puts the phone against her ear.

"Chelsea, he'll kill us!"

"Too late it's ringing!" Shane must have answered the phone because Chelsea then turns down the pitch of the tone of her voice making her sound more serious "You there?" She puts on a hint of desperation along with her mellow tone "I'm really having a really rough day, I hear you're pitching some new gear...."

Chapter 9

It's closing time at The Dive Bar. The owner, brother of the famous comedian: Jack "Mandolin" Mills and lover of tight V-neck shirts, Frank Mill, is taking out the collection of many empty beer bottles leftover by his few customers of the night. Frank is a tough, working class, a number one grade shaved head with a face like a bull-dog but his loyalty to his friends, family and to his own business can't be matched by anyone else. After he left school, Frank started working at a warehouse before it closed. This is where he scrimped and saved until he finally fulfilled his dreams of owning his own pub. First, he wanted it to be a sports bar, after having enough of the drunk hooligans or "chavs", Frank decided he wanted a quieter, traditional, cask ale bar instead.

He threw the bin bag full of clanging bottles into the dustbin that was stored in the alleyway. Avoiding dregs that was leaking onto his white trainers. He noticed a man passed out on the floor. Not just passed out but also bare-bollock-naked.

"Could this have been a stag do prank?" Frank thought. "Perhaps he just got so drunk that he went streaking, got tired and then had a nap on the floor?" Frank hovered his hands over his nose and mouth to check that he was still breathing. This man must have been from out of town because he had never seen him before in his life. Frank was strong, so he easily turned this unconscious lad onto his side, even with his dead-body-weight. Now Frank Mills isn't gay nor has he ever fantasised about being with another man in bed, not that he sees anything wrong with that but the thought of having sex with another man never really turned him on. All the suddenly he couldn't help but stare at this naked man that was laying down in front of him. This man had short but thick black hair that showed no signs of receding, long eyelashes, perfect white teeth, cute short nose and a chiselled chin all making his face even more handsome. His hard, trim body looked like it has never seen an ounce of fat or sugar. His chest had just the right amount of chest hair while the rest of his body was bare. His hairy legs underneath his snake hips were long and the thing in between his legs also very long. Frank couldn't believe he was becoming so attracted to this strange, blacked out man. He could see a lot of woman would like him and could make any man's head turn. Frank soon snapped out of his gawking, he lifted the strangers' eyelids to see if his pupils were dilated. What he saw was quite a surprise; the man's eyes were dark, darker than he's ever seen before. Like an empty, deep well at night. "He must have took some pills" Frank guessed. He used his mobile to call for an ambulance.

Chapter 10

A cold shivery night lies ahead for Mark and Chelsea, as the pair wait on the outskirts of town by a corn field for Shane Crewball to arrive. They both withstand the piercing wind as they prepare to interrogate Shane for the death of Jenny. Mark is terrified about confronting the towns "hard man", he wants nothing more but to return home, go to bed and sleep for the rest of the week. Still he couldn't leave Chelsea on her own because she would face Shane with or without him.

Miss Heart is also cautious but her desire for revenge of her best friend's murder out-ways her uneasiness. She notices how twitchy Mark is, so she tries to toughen him up. "Mark, when Shane gets here you have to be firm, strong, don't let him see any weakness. Got it?"

Mark shakes his head "yes" but clearly didn't sound convincing enough to Chelsea.

"Seriously Mark, shit might go down and I need you to have my back."

"I've got your six."

"I've got your six?" repeats Chelsea. "What are you? You're not a fucking American marine, don't say that."

"I'm sorry" apologised a humiliated Mark.

Chelsea turns her back to Mark and folds her arms. She wishes that she didn't have such a wimp as a partner and could use some of the men from the gang she knocked around with back when she went drinking in the clubs in Holders Bridge. She could have asked Blake, the twenty-four year old she lost her virginity to because he was the closest "bad boy" she was into at the time. Chelsea was attracted to the bulking tribal tattooed arms, the coke, the night races, even the cheesy spoiler on the back of his car. She reconsidered asking Blake because she realised; what sort of twenty-two year old would have a 15 year old girlfriend? One that she couldn't depend on, that's who. Besides thanks to rehab, and the help of her friend Jenny, Chelsea no longer associates with them lot and vows to stay clean. She doesn't know which one of them to trust because anyone of them could inform Shane on her true intentions or kill her for him.

Despite Chelsea having turned her moody-arse back to him, Mark notices that she is shivering has she rubbing her arms to generate heat. Mark very kindly takes off his back jacket and places it over Chelsea's shoulders. She turned around to face Mark. "What are you doing?" She then threw his coat on the cold, wet grass. Mark kneeled down and picked it up and angrily flicked the grass of the jacket, "What's your problem?"

"This is the kinda shit I was on about earlier, you can't be so sweet when he gets here. You gotta be tough."

Mark remained quiet, he was exhausted and this only irritated him even more. "Jenny used to love it when I put my coat around her" he thought.

Walking alongside the farmers' fence was Shane Crewball. Making his way from his little caravan that's on the other side from the woods, which no one knows about.

"He's here, let me do the talking" said Chelsea.

Shane stood a fair distance from Chelsea and Mark, he laughs at the pair. He sees through the Marks fierce façade and notices the scared little boy that he really is. "So Chelsea, back for more. Back to spend daddy's hard-earned money."

"That's right, what have you got?

Shane pulls out an ounce of cocaine that's visibly seen through a small clear bag and waves it in his hand to entice Chelsea back into her addiction.

"For you, this is just a sweet sampler. Courtesy, of yours truly". He takes a bow to Chelsea. She'd be lying if she said that there was no temptation by the sight of seeing the stuff again, but it was Jenny that helped her get off the blow and it's Jenny's memory that holds back her urge tonight. "I need a hit, I lost my friend today, me and my friend want to party," lies Chelsea.

"I heard about your friend, such a shame really. She was a great piece of arse. Oh, the things I would have done to her." Shane licks his lips. Mark loses his cool, goes to punch him in his face and ruin the plan but Chelsea puts her hand out to stop him.

Shane noticed Marks attempt however.

"WOW! Easy boy! You don't wanna get hurt now, do ya?"

Chelsea changes the subject "You gonna hook us up or not?"

Shane smiles revealing his yellow and crooked teeth,

"Of course I'll hook you up, remember this is free, once you demolish this lot tonight, there's plenty more waiting for you afterwards."

Shane falls for Chelsea's bait and walks closer to hand over the ounce. Chelsea grabs him but the collar of his scruffy and smelly shirt and yells in his face, "It was you who murdered Jenny, wasn't it? Either that or you know who someone who did!? You're fucking tell me right now! "

"You dumb cunt!" screams Shane has he back hands Chelsea on her face, knocking her down to the floor. The fall did not only twist her ankle but smashed the phone she's set to record. Mark quickly pulls a trembling Chelsea up from the floor; she screamed from the pain on her way up and used her hand to bandage her cheek.

A frightened Mark bulks up the courage to confront him,

"You're a coward, hitting a girl like that."

"*Oooooh*, I want to carve into your pretty face" threatened Shane.

"We know you killed Jenny!" shouted Chelsea, through her clenched teeth.

"I can't believe you came here with no plan. I forgot, you're just kids. Come near me again and you're both dead."

Mark whispered in Chelsea's ear "Come on, let's go."

"I'm not going anywhere, until you tell me you did it! Or least tell me who did?"

"I don't know anything. Even If I did, I certainly wouldn't tell you."

"You're lying!"

Shane shrugs his shoulders; "You're just going to have to take my word for it, Chelsea. Leave my sight before things get much worse for you both."

Mark is just about to carry Chelsea home on his shoulders until Shane collars them; "Chelsea!"

Mark and Chelsea stop to listen to what he has to say just has Shane continues "Don't bother calling again, you won't get hold of me. And you..." Points to Mark. ".... Mark Bell, I know who you are. It won't take me long to find out even more about you. Like where you work and your daily routine. You'll never see it coming." Mark continues to carry Chelsea home, though they remain in silence. In Chelsea's mind, she was infuriated that her phone was broke, she never got the confession from Shane, though a glimmer of hope came from the words "daily routine." Sparking a fresh idea.

Shane watches them until they are far away enough before he can return to his caravan without being followed. When he returns, he will burn Jenny Woodfield's secret diary that he has hidden away…

Chapter 11

After a glass of wine and marking her students work, Gail Brooke retires for the night. It took her a lot longer than normal. Her mind was on something else; Jenny. The only student that she taught after school. What sort of creep would murder an incident teenage girl? In her home town too. She prays she didn't suffer and hopes that she was not raped as well.
After changing into her Pyjamas, she turned off the lights and slept under her duvet. It didn't take her long to fall asleep, the wine probably helped.
Brooke drifted into sleep, where she dreamt. It was no ordinary dream, it was like she is really there and she can feel the wind blowing by her and the hard ground he is running on. "Running?" Brooke questioned. "I don't go running." In a first person view, she is looking around at the unfamiliar part of the dirt track "Where am I?" She realised that her legs are running but it's not her. She's in someone else's body. She has become a passenger in someone else's body and suspects who. Brooke wonders her eyes, which is the only part of her body she can control, she takes glimpses of the swinging arms to try and get confirmation.
The vessels journey takes her up to a bowl-like shape in the ground, she notices a broken fridge that's been abandoned to her left. She carries on to her right. BANG! Out of nowhere! A hooded creature of some sort, JUMPS OUT! The darkness within the hood, where a face should be, blackens out Brooke's vision. She cannot see.
Her vision reappears and she has found herself outside of the body she was briefly within. There she was beneath some plastic bag, the cold, naked, still, twisted body of Jenny Woodfield. Just as Brooke suspected all along. To her surprise, Jenny's eye lids open wide to reveal her lifeless, brightly glazed eyes staring directly at Brooke. Her mouth opens wide, so wide,
so much that you can hear the bones in her jaw dislocate. Jenny screams! Screams! A distorted pitch higher than

none other. She stops screaming, closes her mouth and eyes.
To Brooke's horror she slowly reopens her mouth and her eyes again and whispers the song:

"Beware, beware the man with no face.

He cannot see. He cannot hear.

He is the man with no face."

Beware, beware the man with no face.

He doesn't sleep, he cannot smile.

He is the man with no face."

Brooke wakes up from her nightmare, drenched in sweat and fear. Could she be warning her? She recollects the song before from that little boy, this morning. The haunting has left her unable to sleep for the rest of the night or for the nights to come…

Part 2 – Carl "Bass" Sebastian

Chapter 12

In an estate not far from Sheffield City Centre, Private Paranormal Investigator Carl "Bass" Sebastian woke up after passing out on top of his settee. Groggy, hung-over, red eyed. Bass is tall, so his legs stick-out from the bottom of the settee, he slowly uses them to sit himself up but in the process, he spills an half empty whisky glass onto the floor. The remaining contents fall onto the floor, next to a half opened book on the Enfield Haunting in Brimsdown. Bass rubs his forehead in an attempt to get rid of his headache, but his pain is even more irritated by the early morning sunlight. He stomps over to his small window to sharply pull the blinds shut. Bass's bulky arms almost torn down the flimsy curtain rack that's perched on top of him. He sluggishly moves to the very thin kitchen in his tiny, one, bedroom flat. Pulled open the door to the fridge which would be completely bare apart from there's half a loaf of bread and some more whisky. Bass pours himself another drink, to perk himself up and for sharpening his senses. Feeling more refreshed after a nice, cold smooth gulp of whisky. Bass enters the bathroom. Too depressed to shower, he just uses the sink to splash cold water over his bald head and his sad red eyes. He looks up in the mirror in front of him and contemplates shaving off his stubble but in the end decides against it.

One of the oldest flip mobile phones still around, begins to ring in Bass's pocket. Carl reluctantly pulls it out of his pocket and stares at this unknown number that is displayed on the screen. Unsure either to answer the call, though he's not in the mood to talk to anybody, however it could be work. With one hand he flips open the phone

and presses it against his ear. Takes a deep breath.
"Hello" Bass answers. On the other side of the phone is a voice of a sobbing woman with a posh accent. "H-h-hello."

"Who is this?" Abruptly asks Bass

"My name is Janet Woodfield. Am I speaking to a Mr Carl Sebastian?"

"Yes you are. If you're trying to sell me something, I suggest that you hang up now."

"No, no I'm not trying to sell you anything. I require your services. At your utmost convenience."

"How can I help you, Mrs Woodfield?"

Bass can feel a hesitance over the phone, he knows what she is about to say next.

The voice of Janet replies "I need your help. I believe that my daughter's spirit may still be here."

"This certain thing may be best to talk about face to face."

"I will text you the address; you should also have already received full payment."

"How did you get my bank details?"

With some confusion she answers "It is on your website."

"Oh, yeah, I forgot that I had that. I got some IT apprentice to do it for me years ago."

"It did seem out of date. I am good at organising businesses and keeping up to date with any necessary affairs. I assist my husband with his work, perhaps he is quite similar to you in some aspects"

"He's a paranormal investigator too?" Jokes Bass

"No. He's a dinosaur."

"Dinosaur? I'm thirty eight."

"With respect Mr Sebastian. Could you please come down urgently? It's my daughter, Jenny; she was murdered, exactly one week ago today..."

There was a pause, Bass "I am sorry for your loss, Mrs. Woodfield."

"The police aren't getting closer to finding out the man responsible."

"You don't need to say any more, shall I meet you at the texted address?"

"That would be splendid, Mr, Sebastian."

"I'm on my way." Bass told before he hangs up the phone.

Bass dashes into the bedroom to pull out his duffel bag within his one tattered wardrobe, he throws the duffel bag onto his very low slung, bachelor style bed that might as well be on the floor. If it wasn't for his drunk one-night stands then he'd just have a mattress on the floor. Bass doesn't have any many clothes, all three sets fit into the duffel bag. All his clothes are bland, no stripes, no band names, no bright colours, nothing that could attract attention from others. They make him blend into the crowd. However, he does have a suit in a separate cover bag for attending the homes of the victims' families, in order to be more formal.

In the bottom of draw, which has one side off its hinges, Bass pulls out all of his equipment he needs. First the Infra-red night vision cameras, a torch, Electric Magnetic Field Detector that spikes rapidly in the areas where there have been ghosts. Next is a hand-held non-contact infrared Digital thermometer, which is used to record any sudden cold spots. Then the last few items to pack away are the motion detectors and a spirit box which is used to convert any high AM frequency noises from spirits or "white noise" into words.

That's it, all of Carl Sebastian's life in one bag, packed away before heading off to the next place. He'll only stay in a hotel or rent a cheap, small one bedroom flat in the next town, never making a home for himself because Bass knows that once the job is done then he will just do it all over again. Before leaving his flat behind for good, he pats down the outsides of his coat pockets to make sure he has his wallet, car keys and his lighter.

After dropping his key off in the manager's office, not telling him that he's left a settee, broken wardrobe and a bed. "It would be a nice surprise for the next loser, divorcee" thought Bass. He makes his way down the street, onward to the garage, where his cheap shoddy car is stored. He hates the idea of driving, he prefers walking or getting the train, but Holders Bridge is so far down south. Whilst walking down the estate, in the opposite direction, a group of rowdy young hoodies are taking up the complete pathway, playing grime music from their phones, jumping up and down, swinging their arms, laughing and just being disturbingly loud. An older grey-haired gentleman with glasses who's walking in front of Bass crosses the road to avoid any hassle. It's not something Bass wants to do though, "they're just kids" he tells himself while he stares directly at them in the eye. Determined to not cross the road because it would make him look "weak". The young miscreants stare at bass back, trying hard to look and act tough right back at him but their skinny and inferior shoulders just bounce right off his broad arms. Bass can feel their eyes on him has they turn to look at him, even spit on the ground has a sign of disrespect but Bass doesn't care he never turns back.

To drown out the sound of strangers, cars and just the outside world completely he puts in his headphones into his portable music device, to listen to some heavy metal music. Outside a shop is a very approachable, vibrant, twenty something, skinny, Indian lad who's wearing some sort of a charity shirt with a collection of leaflets. He's passing leaflets to by-passers with a friendly smile. Instantly he knows that he's going to approach him and he does so by standing right in front of Bass which instantly annoys him "for god sake, I've got my headphones in!" Bass mumbles bitterly has he throws out the ear buds within his ears. Not catching onto what he said, the polite charity rep continues anyway "Hello sir, please can I take a few minutes out of your spare time? To talk to you about how every day a tiger is being killed in the wild and there are only at an estimated of three thousand left."

"I'm sorry I can't talk to you."

"Why? Is it because you're hunter?"

"No, it's because I'm a white supremacist."

The frightened young lad from India quickly scurries away. Allowing Bass to be left alone to listen to his music. Carl doesn't actually have a racist bone in his body; he hates the ignorance of those who are. He was just purposely being mean to get the charity rep away from him.

Chapter 13

Simon Cole sits down with a warm cup of tea that Clive Dunscroft has just brewed for him. With his cold hands cupped around the sides, to keep them warm. "Thank you."

"I hear that you were made Chief Inspector, a congratulations is in order, I guess". Clive says, as he stands awkwardly over Simon.

"Yes they've placed me in charge, ME. Finally, I get the recognition I deserve, I can finally make some changes to this town."

Simon begins to shuffle on his seat awkwardly, worried why Clive is just stood over him watching him drinking his tea. Simon hopes that he's not drugged this. "Are you going to sit?"

"No."

Simon stands up because he already hates feeling small and wants some more ground to stand on.

"You know why I am here? People have been talking..."

"About me." Interrupts, Clive.

"Yes."

"How is the investigation going?"

"You know I can't talk about an on-going investigation."

"Is that why you are here because everyone else in this town thinks I'm a monster."

"No, it's not true."

"Where is my protection!? I'm getting death threats! People calling me names! Last week, kids were egging my house! Where was you then!?"

"I believe it wasn't you, I've known you long enough. You have to, I don't know, stop being so weird around everyone. Get out the house. I do care about you."

"But you don't care about me, you want me to keep my mouth shut. I know what you did."

Even though Clive is a lot taller than Simon, he walks closer to Clive in a threatening manner. Clive's invasion of personal space causes him to shake. Just as Simon looks up to stare into Clive's eyes, Clive puts his head down because even his thick rimmed glasses couldn't stop how uncomfortable eye contact makes him feel.

"Don't forget, it would implicate you too!" Simon says while prodding his index finger over Clive's Donald Duck T-shirt and into his fat stomach. "I am Chief Inspector now! I have true power and respect from the community! They would believe me more than you."

Clive slowly turns his head away.

Simon notices the childish, Disney character's shirt that he's wearing "For god's sake, Clive. You're an adult now. It's time you start being a real man and put on some real clothes."

"I think it may be best if you leave" Clive says quietly.

Simon purposely waits a few seconds to intimidate the timid giant a bit further before making his way to the living room door.

Just before Simon walks out, he praises "Thank you for the tea, it was lovely."

Simon stands outside the front door of his house, using a handkerchief to polish his police badge. Behind him, he can hear Clive rapidly locking three different locks on the door.

Clive was about to run into the living room and close the curtains but he spots little Bradley sat on top of the last few steps of the stairs, clutching the two wooden rails with his little hands. Clive notices he was using the rails to hide from Simon so to bring him comfort he kneels down, opens his arms to offer him a hug. Bradley needing to feel safe, quickly runs down the stairs, slamming his feet on every step and embraces a hug. Clive holds him very tight and offers reassurance him by saying "don't worry, he's gone now."

Chapter 14

Opposite The Fitness Ball Gym, a red Clio is parked. Sat inside, protecting herself from the light rain and wind, rests Chelsea Heart. Even though her eyes are fixed on the entrance to the building, every time she catches someone walking past the car, paranoia causes her to jump to see who the by passers are. The sound of running footsteps coming towards the vehicle, arouses Chelsea's suspicion. She turns and notices it's the person she's been waiting for. It's Mark Bell running in a waterproof, sport jacket, holding a gym bag. He throws off the dripping wet hood has he steps into the passenger seat of Chelsea's car. "I'm glad you've asked to go to the gym with me, the exercise will make you feel better."

"Actually, that's not why I've asked you here."

"You mean, you didn't ask me here to work on your bingo wings."

Chelsea's jaw dropped, "I never said I needed to work on my bingo wings!" she screams while deservingly punching Mark in the arm.

"Hey, what was that for?" whines Mark whilst rubbing his soon-to-be-bruised arm.

"Do you know who that Gym belongs to?

"No."

"Shane Crewball."

"Really? I didn't know that."

"You never saw it, Fitness BALL Gym, Shane Crew-BALL."

"No, I've never noticed it before."

Chelsea frowns at his cluelessness but Mark looks at Chelsea with his innocent, cute looking face, the sweet and the cute, lost-puppy expression wins her back over.

"I've been watching this place for the last week and I know that Shane only comes in to check on the place for an hour around five O'clock, when the place is jammed."

"Wait! You told me last week, that you was going to drop it! If you remember right, he said he was "going to carve my face."

"Well, I lied. Obviously. That creep murdered my best friend and I can't let it go."

Mark rests back on his seat, facing forward but not really looking. Knowing he'll regret what he's going to ask next. "What do you want me to do?"

"We'll pretend to go in for a work-out, then we'll sneak into his office and find some clues. Or find something else incriminating; like how he uses the gym for money laundering."

"I don't get you."

"Basically, evidence that proves he uses the gym's income books, to insert the cash he makes from selling coke."

"So we can get him arrested for that, instead of the murder of Jenny."

"Exactly."

"Chelsea, I think you've been watching too many films. We're gonna get caught!" worries Mark. "He'll see us on camera, we should disguise ourselves more." Mark pauses to think. "I know we'll dye our hair! I'll get some blonde tips and..."

Chelsea interrupts "How will dyeing your hair blonde make you unrecognisable?"

"Well I can't just walk in with a balaclava!"

"Look, we are just two people wanting to get fitter and healthier. You want to be a personal trainer, so you're practising, training me, for experience."

"That's a good idea."

"Now, let's get changed."

"Ok" Mark says before he starts stripping off in the car.

"Not in here! In the changing rooms!" Chelsea is quick to yell but then she couldn't stop herself from staring at his six-pack and his long fit legs leading from his tighty-whities. Chelsea bites her lip and plays with her hair on the side of her neck. She clears her throat and tells Mark "Put your clothes on, you look ridiculous. People will think we're going dogging." Chelsea steps out of the car, slamming the door behind her. Leaving a puzzled Mark, in the car, thinking: "What's wrong with taking a dog for a walk?"

Chapter 15

Meanwhile Carl "Bass" Sebastian takes his first steps in Holders Bridge Police Station. He sees only a few police men and women in such a small office, he believes such a small village won't need many police officers and President May probably thought the same while she was slowly cutting the police fund since she was Home Secretary in 2010. Bass walks up to the receptionist, a fiery red head who fell smitten to Bass's tall, rugged, bald look. "How can I help you, sir?" She asks with a big smile on her face. Bass doesn't smile back, he's far too serious but still manages a-bit-of-a-reply; "Who's in charge here?" Bass notices the rolled up sleeves on his plain blue but tight woolly jumper were beginning to roll down and he always has his sleeves rolled up. The receptionist watches the muscular arms has he rolls the sleeves back up. "*Hmmm*, his name is Simon Cole. Can you take a seat?"

"No. Just point me to his desk."

"I don't think I can do that. Although, I can tell you used to be a policeman."

"Really?" Bass is beginning to sulk; right now he's not interested in making conversation with her.

"Most people act nervous when they walk in but you look like you can just sit right at a desk. Hopefully one next to mine. Just a thought; have you still got your handcuffs?"

"This is urgent. It's about the Woodfield case."

"OK, it's the top right desk in the far corner, the short guy with a bald spot."

Bass walks off without saying a thank you. The receptionist turns around to have a look at his backside while he walks away.

Simon Cole's sat on his desk reading through case notes, when he notices a large figure heading towards him. Simon drops the notes onto his desk, leans back on his chair, acting in a natural, very lax manner. With folded arms, he looks up and down at Bass before asking him "can I help you?"

"My name is Carl Sebastian, I'm a Private Investigator." Purposely missing out the "Paranormal" section from his title in case the Law Enforcer believes he is crazy. "My friends call me "Bass" so you can still call me Carl."

"Why are you here?" asks Simon.

"Are you Simon Cole? In charge of the Woodfield investigation?"

"Yes I am Chief Inspector Simon Cole..."

Bass rolls his eyes, when he noticed how Simon overemphasises his title "Chief Inspector." With that and Simon's height, Bass could tell that "Chief Inspector Simon Cole" had a case of "small-man syndrome."

"...do you have any information about the Woodfield case?"

"That's what I was going to ask you. I need you to tell me everything you know so far and I want to see the body for myself."

Simon stands up, points his index finger on the top of his desk and begins to rant "Hang on a second! You cannot waltz in here and give me demands! I am the one in charge here! It is my, MY investigation! I'm the one in charge."

Bass raises his hands "OK, I get it, you're in charge but I believe we could help each other. I don't like it just as much as you. I've been employed by the mother; Janet Woodfield. She believes you need my expertise."

"Ha! Have you spoken to Janet Woodfield?"

"Not yet."

Simon Cole just chuckles to himself. Bass is curious to why, perhaps it's because she believes that her daughter's ghost still hovers around the village. So Bass must insist "What Janet is saying is true, then you need me, I was a Police Investigator before I became a Private Paranormal Investigator."

"Wait. Did you say "Paranormal Investigator"? This is a very serious time and Janet and Raymond Woodfield do not need any jokers like you sniffing around their daughter's murder."

"She's the one that called me."

"That may be true but she's clearly delusional and desperate to find out who killed her daughter. Not that I can blame her of course but she's grasping at straws. If you excuse me I have real police work to do."

"If you don't give me something I'll come back later, if you don't give me something later then I'll be back tomorrow and if you don't give me something then, I'll keep pestering you until I do."

"I will arrest you for interfering with a police investigation."

"I wouldn't do that, I still have friends at my old station." Bass lies.

Simon sighs, with his hands bitterly held against his waist, he turns to look at his desk for inspiration to find a bone that could be thrown at this dog. One that will keep Mr Sebastian busy and out the way.

While Simon was conjuring up a distraction, Bass looked over at the desk, the writing on the files were small for him to see but he saw a box of unusual fountain pens, one that looked like it was handcrafted single-handedly from wood. "They looked expensive and one appears to be out of the box" thought Bass. Chief Inspector Cole was struck by an idea "On the night of Jenny Woodfield's murder there was a man found unconscious outside of The Dive bar, owned by Frank Mill. He had no

Identification, he was stark-bollock naked and not one single person at the hospital knew him."

"Does it really matter if no one recognised him before?"

"This is a small town, we are a close community and everyone knows everyone."

"So you mean; you're a bunch of nosey bastards who wants to know everything about everyone because you don't really have much of a life of your own. Thanks for the tip."

Bass walks out the police station, knowing that the lead was just bogus; the man had probably just had too much to drink on a stag night or overdosed on something. He will check it out but it had fallen to the back of his priority list.

Chapter 16

Amongst the row of treadmills, there is one slightly inclined and slowly plodding along, is Chelsea Heart. Wearing a tight pink shirt, tracksuit bottoms and white trainers. Chelsea is using the long mirror in front of her to discreetly check out all the cameras in the room. There was one just between the entrance and the two exhausted skinny guys on two lateral arm raise machines. One clenching his aching narrow arms whimpering to the other "I don't think I can do anymore." "Me neither, I don't know why people enjoy coming here" the other replies. Suddenly, a beautiful, white blonde haired girl, with a narrow waist, both a curvy chest and lower backside enters the gym. A surge of energy bursts through the two young lads while simultaneously grabbing hold of the handles of the machine, began lifting and grunting like they've never done before, "...twelve! Thirteen!"

It's only a small gym, a narrow room and the other side, rests the second camera facing the mats which stop the heavier weights from damaging the floor. On the rubber gym mats is a small circle of meat-heads, there, Mark finishing his set of dead-lifts. Chelsea notices that sweat is pouring out of his head like a fountain, "my god, he's using this moment as an excuse to get his daily work-out in" while she's just there as a masquerade. Mark squats down to pick up his 20kg bar with a 20kg weight on each side. Chelsea is checking out Mark's arse every time he bends down. She has to tell herself "Stop it Chelsea, he is your best friend's boyfriend. Jenny may not be here but you're trashing her memory."

Chelsea jumps off the treadmill, grabs Mark and whispers "come on, it's time."

They leave the room full of equipment, going around the back of the podium, which stores the half-asleep receptionist, the pair sly across the changing room doors on the left in order to go right through the "Staff Only" doors. Chelsea is leading Mark down the restricted access corridor, keeping their heads down and picking up the pace whilst shuffling along the wall, trying to reach another set of double doors that lay ahead. Chelsea picks up the sound of approaching voices, "Quick, round here" she says in a rapid undertone. They crouch behind a corner of another corridor, praying that they won't get caught from the two talkative Personal Trainers; "... So, I said to Lisa that I've got a client five while six so I won't get there till seven..." The PT's were too distracted by the gossiping to notice the intruders. Just as they walk past; Chelsea steps back from the edge of the corridor and leans right into Marks sweaty body making her body instantly shudder "*aargh*, you're covered in sweat" murmurs Chelsea.

"What do you expect? I've just been working out" whispers Mark.

The cat-like thief's reached the set of double doors and stumble across an office door with a window. Chelsea looks through the window and sees an untidy desk, with filing cabinets in the corner of the room. "This could be it" suspects Chelsea. She tries the door handle but it's locked, as she surmised. She uses the bobby-pin from her hair to unlock the door leaving Mark very impressed and slightly worried "how did you do that?"

"Practice" she replied, not reassuring Mark however.

They both scurry through various documents, searching for anything that could be useful to proving Shane Crewballs' guilt. All they can find is a list of meeting appointments, letters. Chelsea opens up the filing cabinet and it's only full of client contracts. "What is it we're supposed to look for?" asks Mark.

"I doubt we'll find a document that reads "My Secret Plan to Kill Jenny" but there has to be something."

Mark starts to panic "We're going to jail for this."

Chelsea comes across his income book, she opens it up on the desk, "Here" she uses her finger as a marker along while she scrolls down a few random pages "Anything going out, reads ok. There's no random large amount of cash randomly appearing"

"How do you know this?" Mark asks.

"My dad's an accountant."

"He might be able to read this better then you?"

"We can't bring him into this; he's got enough on his plate. Maybe we will, when we have something more concrete. Come on let's keep on looking."

The search comes to a halt when they hear Shane's ruthless and belligerent voice howling down the corridor; ".... If that son-of-a-bitch pulls a stunt like that again. I'm going to break his fucking hand!"

Chelsea fills up with dread "No, he's early." She quickly puts the book back into place and out of hysteria struggles, to come up with an exit strategy.

"Out the window" Mark improvises. He lifts Chelsea up on his shoulders while she opens the window, she climbs out and Mark uses his own upper body strength to pull himself out.

The escapees run to the car parked on the other side of the street. Until Chelsea realised "We need to get our bags from the changing room!"

Mark and Chelsea took control over their breathing. Together they walked through the front door of the gym, trying to act calm and as casual Mark goes into the changing room, grabs his bag and heads towards the front doors then a voice comes from behind him "Mark." To his horror it was the last person he wanted it to be. Mark turned around and there stood Shane. Mark's heart leapt into his throat. Shane walks slowly up to Mark and puts one of his swinging arms around his shoulders causing a wave of unsettlement to run through his body.

Chelsea was just about to walk out the door of the changing room until she heard the sound of Shane's voice. She believed It would be too conspicuous if he were to see her and Mark together at the gym.

Meanwhile the smell of cigarette smoke from Shane's mouth was a bit too close for Mark's comfort. "Hey, Mark, last week I said something's I didn't mean. Emotions were high and all that. It's best we NEVER discuss those events again." Shane gives a wide though sinister smile.

"Don't worry, I understand" Mark bleats.

"Good" Shane pats Mark on the back freeing him from his lurking threatening clutch. "Listen! I have a limited time offer; £80 for the FULL year. How does that sound?"

"When I get some money, I think I'll get it."

"Good lad and tell all your friends!" Shane shouts whilst he walks away, back to his office.

Knowing that the coast-is-clear Chelsea walks out the changing room grabs a relived Mark by his arm and rushes him out of the gym.

Chapter 17

In the teachers' lounge at Holders Bridge Secondary School, Gail Brooke just poured herself a fresh hop drink from the coffee maker. Needing the sweet taste and the caffeine-pick-me-up from all the sleepless nights. First few nights it was the haunting visions from Jenny Woodfield that made her too scared to sleep. It was the unfamiliar bed at The Robinson Bed and Breakfast that kept her awake, the last two nights.

Cocky, tall and in a full blue suit, Brad strides towards the coffee machine, purposely waiting for Brooke so he can "accidentally" bump into her. "Hey Brooke. Did you have a nice weekend?" A dazed Brooke took a while before it registered that her colleague was talking to her. Not really in the mood to carry on a conversation, yet she's too polite to ignore him. "*Oh*, I'm sorry Brad. It was alright, thank you." she lied. It has been the worst few nights of her life. Scared to be awake, scared to be asleep and now too scared to return home. What makes it worse is that she can't talk to anybody about it, no one will ever believe her. Brad pulls a grin at her "It looks like you had a good weekend!" referring to the bags under her eyes. Brooke asks but with no real interest "Did you go to the Scarborough's house again?" Brad laughs "No, Me and my mate Dave found a rave a few miles out from here. We took a couple of E's and danced the night away." Brooke didn't find the topic inappropriate, he's meant to be a teacher and set a good example for the kids but he himself needs a little growing up to do. Even though she never says this out loud, but she's always hated his hair-do. Brad has both sides shaved off but there's a lot on the top, dyed blonde and combed over to the back. She believes that he's trying too hard to be a pretty boy. Not really in the mood to listen to Brad's usual antics, she puts on a fake smile and tries to slightly pull away from the conversation as politely as possible "That sounds great." Brad puts his hand on her shoulder stopping her from wandering off to ask; "Brooke, are you ok?"

"Yeah, I am just tired."

"I know things haven't been too good recently. I can't imagine losing a pupil. It must have been hard for you. So, if you want to talk about it? I know a great tapas restaurant on Carmondy Road? I would love to take you there Friday night?"

Brooke was touched by his concern, she thought he was being sweet. "Thanks, I have a lot on at the moment. Do you mind if I let you know?"

"Of course." He raises both his hands mid-air, "no pressure!" Brad breaks out a short burst of nervous laughter.

The sound of the tannoy system comes on. Brooke and Brad instantly knew it will be The Headmaster of the school.

"Attention! Gail Brooke, please return to your class room, you have a visitor. Thank you."

Brooke and Brad turned to each other and laughed.

Brad jokes "He has never been off that thing since he got it installed; he probably caresses it more than his wife."

Brooke realised "Was you here when he announced Jenny Woodfield's death, he did over the tannoy system!"

"Yeah but didn't he ask Simon Cole to talk to Chelsea face-to-face before?"

"But still, you would think that he would at least form a special assembly to tell the rest of the kids... or for me."

"It is a little strange."

Other things are starting to reoccur to Brooke "Do you believe that some people are starting to act a little strange as well?"

Brad frowns "What do you mean?"

Brooke, knowing that Brad doesn't understand decides that she's going to just drop it "It's ok, it's probably nothing."

Brad asks, changing the subject "Who's come to see you?"

"I am not sure. I best go and find out."

Brooke was just about to walk out the door when Brad shouts "Don't forget, Friday!"

Brooke doesn't respond just smiles, not fully giving an answer.

Brad pumps his fist in the air, believing that he's got her "in-the-bag."

Whilst the school were playing outside on their lunch break, the corridor was quiet. Brooke eventually reaches her office. She notices there is a strange man, using one of the kid's chairs to sit on the other side of her desk. He's bald, tall with strong arms, shame about the stubble. She likes her men to have a clean shave, beards are messy, unclean and like her father always says "they make people look more homeless."

Carl "Bass" Sebastian sitting across a teacher's desk for the first time in over twenty years. He turns around and sees a beautiful, blonde, with green eyes, few minor freckles and a distinctive birthmark on her left ear lobe.

"Hello" Brooke greets.

While she walks over to sit across from Bass. He discretely checks out her long legs and her slightly curved hips, but her trousers made it difficult.

"Hello, you must be Miss Gail Brooke my name is Carl Sebastian but people normally call me Bass."

"Bass? Like the fish?"

"Yes, it was a nickname I was given while I was a Police Investigator."

"Is that why you are here? I have answered all the questions to the police."

"I am not with the police; I'm a Private Paranormal Investigator."

Bass expected Brooke to laugh at him but she looked a little relieved.

"You hunt ghosts?"

"Yes. I know you're not going to believe me. It sounds crazy but I have been hired by Janet Woodfield-"

Brooke immediately jumps in and takes over the conversation. "I have seen her."

Bass leans in more intently, squinting his curious eyes "Who?"

"Jenny, Jenny Woodfield. The night she was murdered I dreamt that I was with her. In her body. Running down the dirt track. Then someone jumped out, a man in a hood. Only, there was no face. Just a black hole in the hood." The more Brooke goes on the more ridiculous it is sounding to her, let alone to this stranger.

Bass can see the desperation in Brooke's eyes. He knows that she wants him to believe her, in these experiences not many people with rational minds would want to tell these stories to anyone else because they know how ludicrous it sounds. There becomes a point when that person can no longer hide it. Bass adds some reassurance to Brooke just by adding "Go on."

She does, "Then I see her body." Words are becoming hard to come out. "Sort of... twisted" Then the tears began. "Pale."

Brooke is replaying the horror scene over in her head and is thinking of more words to describe the scene. Bass senses that she is struggling, so decides to stops her. "That's enough. I get the picture."

"It's not over" She adds. "There's a song."

"What song?"

She goes into the top draw of her desk and pulls out a blank A4 piece of paper and a marker pen. Quickly jotting down the song before handing it over to Bass.

Bass reads it out loud...

"Beware, beware the man with no face.

He cannot see. He cannot hear.

He is the man with no face.

Beware, beware the man with no face.

He doesn't sleep, he cannot smile.

He is the man with no face."

The case has piqued Bass' interest even more. He is more excited than frightened. "Are these visions reoccurring?"

"Yes. For four nights. Then on the fifth day. I woke up on the Friday morning, I had a shower. While I was getting dressed, I heard some kind of light scratching, like there were rats scattering within the walls. It was coming from downstairs. I quickly ran down the stairs and into the room. That's when she appeared to me again. In the corner of my living room, Jenny was there, scratching away, clawing off the wall paper, endlessly."

"What did you do?"

"I ran, I got out the house as fast I could. I've not been back since. I'm staying in The Robinson B'n'B."

"How much is the Robinson's Bed and Breakfast?"

After all that information Brooke had just shared, she thought to herself "of all the questions why have you just asked me this, THIS, off all things?" to clarify she asks; "Excuse me?"

"How much is the B'N'B? I need somewhere to stay during my time here. Can you get me a deal?"

"I guess so. That's not important right now!"

"Not right now but I'll need somewhere to sleep. Maybe we could split the cost and share a bed together?"

Brooke snaps, slams both hands on the desk "enough!" and walks over to the window, rubbing her pounding headache caused by the distress. "When will the visions stop?"

Bass doesn't comfort her, he doesn't know how to. He takes this opportunity to imitate a child, by raising his hand in the air, bouncing on the seat and talking like a know-it-all school boy; "ME, ME, ME, MISS I know this one!"

Brooke is not impressed.

Bass takes a more serious tone; "It's a bit cliché but they normally stop when the killer is caught or dead."

Brooke turns to look at Bass; "How long is that going to take it?"

"I don't know. However long it needs to."

"Why me? Why she doing this, to me?"

"I need to establish a connection between you two in order to figure that out. I want you to tell me more about Jenny. Your boss told me you were her teacher. He also told me that you taught her after school as well."

"Is that the connection?"

"Maybe. She doesn't mean to terrify you. I read about an Indian tribe, who believed that when a soul is taken by someone else, before their time, a piece of that soul is broken off, during the last few moments of his or hers dying agony. In this instance, it would be Jenny Woodfield. A part of Jenny's soul is showing you the last few moments of her dying agony."

"Is that what you believe, Bass?"

"Her ghost is manifesting itself from your dreams. That's why she was in your living room." Bass turns his head away from Brooke, like he normally does when he breaks bad news to anyone. "Her spirit is growing stronger. And because she's attached herself to you. She will soon be with you, everywhere you go. Your fancy-ass B'n'B won't protect you any longer."

In horror, Brooke puts both her hands over her mouth and practically falls on her chair. "Does she want to hurt me?"

"Where were you on the morning of the murder?"

"Wait! Are you accusing me?"

"She could haunt you for the rest of your days, unless you confess your guilt."

"I would never hurt Jenny! Like I said to Inspector Cole, "I was at home!"

"No Alibi? It's a bit suspicious."

"I would not lie to you or the police."

"Oh, grow up! Everybody lies! It's in our nature."

"That sounds depressing."

"That's because it's true."

Brooke and Bass stared at each other. Bass stands up and sees Brooke, with her head down sobbing quietly over the desk. An unusual feeling sinks into Bass, one that he hasn't felt towards a suspect or to anyone else, he feels a tad sorry for her. Empathy, he's read about it before, "Chances are that the killer is going to be the man, from the song. It says "The Man has no face." She could be warning you. So, don't go home with any strange men or with anyone you know."

Brooke laughs, "This is Holders Bridge, and everyone knows everyone."

"Yes but not everyone *knows everything* about everyone. People are always hiding something. Your closest friend or neighbour could be harbouring a cluster of secrets. Basically, don't trust anyone."

"If I had that attitude then I would be alone. "

"We are all alone in this world." Bass heads towards the direction of the door.

"Where are you going?" Brooke wonders.

"I still need to visit Janet and Raymond Woodfield." Bass would never tell her, that he's been purposely putting it off for a while. He tells himself that he needs a little more information before visiting the grieving relatives. He doesn't like to admit to himself the truth, and that he is just scared.

"I want to help you! With the investigation, I'm coming with you. I need to help, Jenny was more than just a pupil to me. I want to find out who did this! Stop these nightmares!"

"No, you can't."

"Why? Because it's going to be too dangerous?"

"No, it's because I just don't want you to."

"If you let me help, I'll get you mates-rates at the Robinson's Bed and Breakfast. I will also show you where it is."

It sounded like a good deal to Bass, he didn't actually know where anything is, in this town. He could let her drive because he hates it. But that would mean trusting her with the only valuable thing he's got. Plus with her hands behind the wheel, his life would be in this stranger's hands, he wouldn't be in control and he couldn't have that. "Fine, but we got to go now."

"Now! I have a class coming back from launch break in ten."

Bass gave an ultimatum; "Two options: stay here or you can ditch them."

With much reluctance, Brooke had to go for the latter.

Chapter 18

Driving down the wide streets of Holders Bridge, Bass is behind the wheel of his very affordable but reliable banger. Deciding to ditch the less accurate, satellite navigation system. He is now receiving instructions from a much perkier and chattier Brooke, much to Bass's annoyance.

"So how long have you been hunting ghosts?"

"A long time".

Even though Brooke has only asked two questions so far, the previous one was the third but that's two more than he could handle. He is currently withstanding them for now, he keeps the answers short and blunt.

"How do you kill the ghosts?"

"That's for me to worry about."

"How many have you killed? Well, is *killed* the correct terminology?"

"Plenty."

Brooke has been living in fear of these horrors she has witnessed the past week. She has read a selection of frightening books by many horror writers such as *Stephen King, Shirley Jackson, James Herbert, Bram Stoker* and more. She likes to keep an open mind on all genres, horror was not one of her favourites however she liked the characters, the thrill of being scared and it was ok because it wasn't true, just mere fiction. Now reaching the end of the denial phase, Brooke feels more intrigued and excited about the unknown. She has met Bass, a real ghost hunter with real stories to tell. Though, sensing Bass doesn't want to share. Perhaps if she got to know him more then he would open up about his supernatural adventures.

"Where do you come from?"

"England."

"I figured that but where were you born?"

Bass didn't want to answer the question. He knew if he answered with the truth, which is: *He hasn't got a clue where he was born.* It will only lead to follow-up questions. So he begins to lie; "Lincolnshire."

"Are you like me? Do you believe it doesn't really matter where you initially begin, it matters where we go afterwards?"

Bass was very impressed and throws her a glance of interest. "I do."

"Do you have brothers and sisters?"

Bass didn't want to give anymore quick fixes to her snooping; he pretends to not have heard the previous enquiry and follows on from the previous topic. "Well, I travel from town-to-town. When one job is finished, I go to the next. Always moving forward."

Brooke raises her eyebrows at Bass; "A lone ranger?"

Bass has reached the breaking point of his interrogation. "I'm going to put some music on. My MP3 player is attached to the radio player"

Brooke laughs "My word, this is an old car, you have even had to buy a special adapter to connect it to this radio player."

"Just choose a song."

Brooke flicks through the playlist, she squints at the tiny, dim lit screen of an old MP3 player. "All these songs are either really slow, easy listening to songs or sad ones that I know. Although there are some pretty fast, aggressive heavy metal bands. There is nothing in-between." She knows a lot of heavy metal bands, she does not like them in particular. A boy who studies under her that arrives to class with a hoodie full of death metal, doom metal, pirate metal, thrash metal bands and enjoys talking about them… A LOT.

"It depends what mood I'm in, sometimes I want to listen to something soft and then other times I want to listen to something angrier, that gets the heart pumping, the adrenaline going and the head banging."

Brooke is pleased that she finally found a topic that can get Bass talking, music! "How about this?" She picks out a song that she enjoys. The next second; *The Cranberries – Dreams* is being played through the speakers.

Now Brooke has established a common interest; she thinks it may be ok to ask some more questions about the poltergeist that's coming to haunt her. "So Bass, how did you discover the existence of spirits?"

"Hush. When the music plays, there'll be no talking."

"Are you joking? Surely, you cannot be serious?"

"Very. I love music and I'd rather listen to that then listen to you asking me a lot of questions or you rambling on about... Celebrity Sex Island or what other trash you women talk about that's on TV."

Brooke has never been so offended. She realises she might have hit a nerve by asking some personal questions, still there is no need for his attitude. "I cannot abide by any of that trash. It is demoralising to our future generation by teaching children that; all you need in life is to look good, you certainly have no need for education because you can just get drunk out of your wits and have various sex with strangers!"

"What future generation? It's proven that people are getting more stupider."

She fires back "It is pronounced: stupid. I am one of those who believe "Stupider" is not a real word, I would like all my pupils to follow my example." More irritated by Bass's comment she leans against the passenger door, with one clenched fist on the dash board the other leaning on her head rest, pointing towards Bass. As she yelled "You do not know me! Do not you dare believe that you have figured me out! I grew up on a council estate. My father taught me to be tough."

Bass waved his hands mid-air unenthusiastically "Oh, I'm shaking" he said sarcastically.

Brooke jumped back down on her seat with her arms folded, shaking her head. After a sigh, she calmed down. Even though she can't rationalize her view to the cantankerous driver, she carries on talking anyway "Some of my friends might enjoy watching the mind numbing, so-called "entertainment" like Celebrity Sex Island. I however do not. The difference between you and I; is I do not overly criticise their opinion. Not all women are the same. I grew up hanging out with other men-"

"Was you a prostitute?" Bass, badly jokes.

"No." She said, unamused. "Even though I still enjoy using make-up. Some of the boy bands my girlfriends enjoyed were too "mushy", as I described them. I was more of a tom-boy at school."

"So, you enjoyed wearing lots of denim and learned how to fix cars." Bass jokes wittingly.

Brooke looks over at Bass and he gives her a quick smile to let her know that the last sarcastic comment was meant to be taken lighter than all the other remarks. "Actually, my dad did teach me how to fix cars."

"See, I knew it."

There was a bit of silence has the song changes to the next and Bass takes a third exit on a roundabout.

Out of boredom, Brooke decides to have a look into the glove compartment. Inside she notices a small black journal. "What's this?" she asks herself whilst putting her hand inside the glove compartment. Bass shifts his eyes to his left to see what she's up to. He can see her inquisitive hand reaching out for the journal and instantly he slams the glove compartment door. Brooke just manages to pull her hand out but cuts it along the way. She cradles her slightly grazed hand with her other hand. "What the hell is wrong with you!?"

Bass remains silent.

"How did you get to be so rude?"

"It takes years of practice, don't think you can just start today."

"I hate you. I cannot wait until we resolve Jenny's murder."

Bass has no intentions of staying with her, once he's used her to get a cheap discount at the B'n'B, he'll be on his own again, just how he likes it. "This will teach you a lesson for prying into my personal things." He holds one hand of the steering wheel firmly while the other one grabs the music player. He loses a lot of concentration of the road while he bobs his head up from it and down towards the MP3 player. The next thing all Brooke can hear is a deafening sound of someone screaming down the microphones, a furious double bass that's keeping up with the tempo of the thunderous drum beats. Meanwhile someone is shredding the guitar solos at an alarmingly fast rate. Carl Sebastian is playing some Metal music, LOUD. Brooke plugs her fingers into her ears in an attempt to drown out the sound, sadly it does not work. "Can you turn it down?" She yells.

"Sorry I can't hear you." He could really. Filling up with excitement, Bass begins to slightly head-bang on his seat, along with him trying to emulate the drummer by continuously smacking his hand on a steering wheel continuously. Unfortunately, his passenger is not loving his taste in music. Brooke has to tolerate this, all the way to Janet and Raymond Woodfield's house.

Chapter 19

Bass and Brooke park the car outside The Woodfield's residence. Bass turns and looks at Brooke, after the ringing in her ears have stopped, she managed to hear Bass "You're stopping in the car."

That didn't sound like a question, Brooke thought. "What are you going to do? Lock me in the car?"

Bass got out and shut the door behind him. Just has he locks the door with his key fob. From within the car, Brooke screamed "There's no way you're leaving me in this car! If would rather break a window." Her claustrophobia outweighed her rational thinking, Brooke could easily open the door from the inside.

Bass can tell through the look in her eyes that she was serious. He had to admire her spunk, also he couldn't really afford to pay for the damage. Bass walked over to the passenger side door, he opened it in a gentlemanly-style. "After you, *me lady*."

Brooke is furious; she got out the car and walked to the front door of the house without saying a word. When realising she was standing alone outside the house, she briefly believed that he just ditched her and ran away, like a coward. She could see the car was shuffling; Bass was changing his clothes in the car. He's taken off his plain blue top, most girls notice the muscular arms but all Brooke can see his hairy beer belly. The next thing he buttons a white shirt. Bass was putting on his suit, the one he keeps in the boot of his car, the one he saves for formally meeting the grieving widows, in this case the grieving parents. He comes out the car still, knotting his tie around his neck. Brooke thought he did that very quickly, she sensed that it wasn't the first time he's had to have done that. Once he was ready, she rang the doorbell.

Janet Woodfield opened the door, recognising Brooke immediately though she looked inquisitive to whom she was with. "Hello, Brooke." Brooke noticed she was speaking in a lower tone then she normally would, that was hardly surprising, after what has recently happened to her.

"Hey Janet, it is good to see you. I wanted to wait a while before I came to visit. How have you been?"

Janet put her head down to the floor, she managed to muster one word "hard."

Brooke gave her a hug to bring her some comfort.

"Truthfully, I am sick to death of people coming round. Although it's good to see you."

"Jenny was a bright, kind, talented, beautiful girl. It was a great privilege to have been her teacher."

Bass is quietly wishing Brooke would shut her mouth. He wouldn't want to hear this, if it was he who had just lost a child, he wouldn't want to talk about it.

The kind words from Jenny's teacher had knocked Janet back a little. She believed it was nice thing to hear; now she is using her handkerchief, and carefully dotting it around her tearful eyes so that it doesn't ruin the mascara. She looks up at this handsome big lug that's with Brooke. "I'm sorry, Brooke, who is your friend?"

"We're not friends; Brooke here is just showing me the lay out of the land." Bass explained.

Brooke was slightly hurt that he immediately pointed out that they were not friends.

"My name is Carl Sebastian; we spoke on the phone yesterday." Bass uses both of his hands to softly cup one of Janet's smaller, frailer ones. "Mrs Woodfield, I am so sorry for your loss."

"Thank you, you best come inside. Would you both like a cup of tea?

Bass replies for them both "We would love one, thank you."

Brooke can't believe how polite he's being, did he change his personality in the car as well?

Once inside, Bass closes the door behind him. Janet pointed to the shoe rack, "Would you mind if you took off your shoes, please?"

Bass replies "Of course." He and Brooke do so. Bass put his shoes on the rack. He notices all the shoes were in size order. Smallest on the top, which would be for Janet, the middle shelf for would have been Jenny's shoes. The lower shelf must have been for Raymond's shoes. They weren't just in size order but also organised by colour. The brighter ones on the left side, darker side to the right.

Bass and Brooke walk into the big open lounge, on their way they could smell lots of polish as if an excessive amount has been used. By the giant window they could smell the recently used window cleaner. A sent of lemon was in the air, Bass assumes it would have been in the liquid that's used to mop the wooden floor with. The guests walk over to two brown settees both at a ninety-degree angle, in between them is a glass coffee table that looks as if it is in a perfect square. With four coasters fitted neatly to each corner of the table. Brooke believed that Janet has been keeping her mind occupied by cleaning, she heard from the neighbours; that she didn't take the news lightly. Which is understandable. Bass examined the settee before he sat down and he can bet any amount of the little money he had; that there was not one single crumb or hair anywhere around the area.

"Please, make yourselves comfortable. I shall brew a pot of tea" Janet welcomes, before leaving to go into the kitchen. Even though, neither Bass nor Brooke have seen the kitchen they can safely assume that it too is neat and spotless. Bass turned to look at three paintings on the wall; one of which is a small sailing boat on a rough sea. Second one is a wooden light house facing a sunny beach. The final one; a horse and carriage riding over the small stream instead of taking the bridge that runs over it, deciding to take the unclean and wilder route. Bass thought that one particular painting was fascinating, what else he found compelling was the fact the paintings were perfectly in line with each other. If one of them had a ruler he'd be able to prove it.

Janet came out the kitchen with a tray that carried a boiling hot tea pot, cold milk and sugar and three cups on sauces all in a triangle, with three separate teaspoons on the sauces, next to the cups, all pointing at the same direction and all at a forty-five-degree angle.

Janet places the tray on the coffee table, sits down and pours tea into the cups with one hand on the handle and the other on top of the lid. She serves over the warm sauces to her visitors.

"Your place looks immaculate, Janet" complements, Brooke.

"Thank you. I'm afraid, I must ask, why are you here Mr Sebastian?"

Bass begins to feel confused "Do you remember our conversation yesterday?"

"I'm sorry to say, I don't recall."

Bass is dreading on having to re-explain his occupation to her and tell her that her daughter's ghost hasn't fully "moved on." Bass puts his drink on the coaster and clears his throat "You called me here, believing that your daughter's spirit is still haunting the town."

Janet begins to feel confused "I said that?"

"Not in those exact words." Bass hates his own response, now he's worried that he's coming across has more crazy.

"My daughter is dead, Mr Sebastian. You're some sort, of clairvoyant? Psychic? Preying on some old woman's vulnerability while she weeps over the loss of her only daughter!"

"This is not a hoax. Mrs Woodfield. I'm a Private *Paranormal* Investigator." He purposely over emphasised "Paranormal" in hope he wouldn't need to explain himself any further.

"I don't believe, I would do such a thing."

"I hate to mention this here, but you even emailed me a statement confirming your payment."

"I do not believe in such superstition."

Brooke intervenes "I know this sounds unbelievable. It's all true; I've seen her, Janet. I've seen Jenny." Brooke gets all caught up in the moment and she puts down her drink of tea on the table rather than the saucer or coaster. Janet sees this, it infuriates her, and she stands up and screeches "*Nooooooo!* How could you just do that? Why?" She stares at Brooke with fiery eyes "Now, I'm going to get a wet tea clothe."

While Janet walks into the kitchen, Bass looks over to Brooke; "I knew I shouldn't have ever brought you."

Brooke was already at unease, slightly humiliated and now Bass has just made a harsh remark towards her, digging into the wound. Brooke and Bass were both distracted by a sound coming from upstairs and next thing they see is Raymond Woodfield came joyfully dancing down the stairs. Swinging his hips, jiving to himself, tapping his feet, clicking his fingers and singing cheerfully "... *Cause I'm Happy. Clap along, if you feel that clap along if you feel like a room without a roof. Because I'm happy!*" He stops singing when he notices, a now standing and concerned looking Brooke and Bass. Raymond throws his famous blinding white smile at the couple, "Howdy there! I am Raymond. Welcome to our wonderful home."

Brooke believes that he's overly cheerful for someone whose daughter has just been murdered.

Bass introduces himself; "my name is Carl Sebastian."

"It is sure swell to meet you my friend! Oh gosh! I just realised something, I would have loved to have stayed and chat with you folks, but I have to pick up Jenny from her running club!"

Brooke and Bass look at each other with wide eyes. Both thinking the same thing *"You can't mean your daughter?"*

Bass carefully approaches Raymond has he puts his shoes on. "Mr Woodfield-"

"Sorry old chum, can't have a chin-wag at this time, I must dash."

Raymond power walks out of the house. Both Bass and Brooke take a few seconds to absorb on what is happening. A voice comes from behind them, it's Janet Woodfield "Can you see what I have to put up with?"

Gail and Carl turn around and see a sombre Janet, she looked still and had a grave expression of her face, as if she has been locked in a wardrobe built for her size and realises that there's no way out.

"Where is he going?" Bass asks.

Janet walks over to the window, lifts up the net curtains. Bass and Brooke follow her. When all three look out the window and what they see is Raymond Woodfield sat in his car, not going anywhere, smiling to himself, putting all his tension into both hands gripping the steering wheel.

"He'll be there for a while" Janet told.

"I know you probably don't want us to but we just want to help. Can we take a look around her room?"

Janet doesn't say anything but nods her head to agree.

They could smell a vast amount of bleach as Brooke and Bass walk past the bathroom. They walk into Jenny's bedroom, Bass could tell that Janet and Raymond don't enter this room often, there is a bit of dust on top of her desk. Maybe they want to preserve her room for how it was, on the day she left or maybe they are too afraid to enter?

Brooke saw her homework on her desk, "I bet she would have gotten stars for all this work. I bet she would have gotten into Medical School, like she wanted. I bet she would have succeeded in becoming a Doctor."

Bass slams down a music magazine he was reading "Ye well, shit happens." Then he paused.

"Is that all you have to say." Brooke thought as she turns on Jenny's laptop.

Truthfully Carl Sebastian was sad about it too, he isn't going to show it. He was looking at all the posters of all the bands on the wall. Even though he thought some of the bands on the wall had too much of a generic pop-rock band sound. He liked the fact that Jenny had been really into music as well.

Brooke discovered on her laptop, the last known website she was a site called: www.RunningToGold.co.uk "Take a look at this."

"What is it?" Bass ran over to read the laptop screen over Brooke's shoulders.

"Do you know what this is?"

"It's called Running to Gold, I doubt it's specialised in selling Wheelchairs."

"Yes, Jenny was murdered when she went out for a run. It looks like she used The Running to Gold application on her phone and it has synchronised to the website. The map of her route, distance and times were all uploaded onto the website."

"Do you think we can get a GPS map of her last route?"

"Yeah thankfully, she clicked on the: *remember my password* option. It's probably the silliest things she has ever done, but a fortunate mistake."

After a few clicks on the mouse. It was there. A map outlining Jenny's running route.

"It looks like it ended here." Brooke pointed to the screen.

"It's probably where her phone was destroyed. Do you where this is?"

"I do but we should tell Simon Cole."

"I've met that moron, I bet he hasn't got a clue what he's doing. I wouldn't trust him with a bag of peas, not alone with this information."

Brooke had to laugh, she couldn't keep it in.

Bass decides "We'll tell him, in due time but for now keep it between us. Besides we don't know if we can trust him."

Bass and Brooke make their way down the stairs, towards the front door and Raymond Woodfield decides to swing back inside. Bass stops on the stairs, blocking the passage between Brooke and the exit. Feeling a potential danger from Raymond, regardless of that friendly smile. "Mr Woodfield, we're just leaving."

Raymond smiles, slowly begins to walk upstairs, keeping his light, clear eyes on Bass the whole time. Bass wants to retreats slowly but with Brooke only just behind him, he can't go anywhere. "I forgot, Jenny is at her friend Chelsea's house" He has a light chuckle to himself. "Silly me, how could I forget? I'm going to have a lay down before I pick her up."

Brooke tries not say anything that might feed into his delusion "A lay down, might be a good idea."

"Righty-o. See you in a bit folks." Raymond shouts cheerfully has he runs upstairs into his bedroom.

Bass whispers "Who's Chelsea?"

"Chelsea Heart, Jenny's best friend."

Bass added her to a mental priority list he's keeping in his head.

Brooke and Bass pick up the pace when it comes to getting out the house.

Outside the house, Brooke heads to the car. Bass shouts to her "Where you going? It's a nice day, let's take a walk."

"What the hell happened in there?" Brooke howls.

"When it comes to the supernatural death, people start to act a bit, *strange*."

"I can understand the Obsessive Cleaning Disorder but the father is living in a very unhealthy delusional fantasy. We need to get them both professional help."

"It effects the grieving more than most people. I can't explain it. A death cult in Uganda believe that if someone is taken before their time, it creates an unhealthy unnatural balance. I believe that it's true, and someone is murdered by an-other-worldly force then it will be worse. Something must enter the human psyche. I don't have all the answers, just theories and my own experience."

"What if the whole town gets infected?"

"Then there must be some really strong dark forces here."

This petrifies Brooke, she realises now more than ever, she is completely out of her depth. Over a week ago her biggest worry was: what should she could teach the kids in her English class. With only just getting used to the idea that ghosts exist, now she's hearing words like: "Other worlds" and "Dark forces". She looks up at Bass and realises that she needs him more than she would have liked. "This is all so much. If we kill whatever did this, would it rectify everything?"

"Not necessarily, it depends on the person as well. They have to be strong and save themselves."

"That sounds hard."

"Life is hard."

The pessimistic point of view from Bass still brings no closure to any of Brooke's worries. "I just need a minute."

"You're not getting one, the best thing to do is to just plough through it. Come on, we're wasting time."

Bass nudges Brooke along the way; as they start to walk down Jenny's old running route. On the way down Brooke noticed Bass was quiet. He was thinking "Has the death of daughter made Janet Woodfield so mad that she had simply forgot, the fact she had hired a Private Personal Investigator? Or has someone else impersonated her because they wanted him here?"

Chapter 20

Shelly Jayne is sat behind the counter in her very own and empty Goforcoffee shop. Waiting for the busiest time of the day when all the students finish for the day and commute to her shop for the rest of the evening. Lord knows, she need the money. It is not just the lord that knows though. A very tall, handsome, slim, stranger with slick black hair walked through the shop. At first, she thought it was her husband Richard but when this man came closer to her, with one hand in his pocket, swaying confidently, he was much better looking than Richard. This man through a cheeky white grin, slightly crooked but charming to Shelly, none the less.

Shelly pulls back her hair and smiles at this man "Can I help you?"

"No, I've come to help you." He says with a deep but soothing voice.

Shelly was merely puzzled, "Have you come to sell me something?"

"Your husband came to see me."

Shelly sighs "You're here to offer me a loan?"

"No. He told me how your little charming coffee shop was slowly going bankrupt."

"He shouldn't have done."

"It's a small town, people talk. I've heard it time and time again."

Shelly was cautious of the striking man, not feeling a trustworthy vibe. To Shelly, he's like a very experienced, elegant, smooth-talking sales-rep. "What is it you want?"

"Oh, I just like to help. I can see you don't trust me and that I very much understand. You don't like hand-outs, not even from your smart, successful and dashing husband."

He leans in and Shelly sees how dark this man's eyes were. She couldn't help but be lured into them, like falling for a bad boy. She knew it was wrong but it drove her wild, like it did to most women, in fact, all women.

The man was reading something from here, something you couldn't read from a book or body language. "You claim that you don't want your husband's help because you want to be independent. But the truth is that you don't trust him and you also don't love him. Not how you love someone else."

Shelly threw herself away from him, "Get out! Get out of my shop." She was scared because he was right.

"I'm sorry, I over stepped some boundaries. I meant what I said. I want to help."

"Why?"

"Because I want to return home. I've done something wrong, *a very long time ago*. I believe I've paid my penance."

Shelly's confusion only grew deeper, she just wanted this lunatic to leave before he hurts her.

"Sell your husband's Ferrari and give every single penny of it to the Salvation Army and then you'll slowly see your books incline." He knocks on the counter and smiles "Oh please, can I have an Espresso to go?"

Shelly doesn't say anything, she quickly makes him one in a plastic container, puts it on the counter. "That'll be two pound eighty."

The man in the dark, slim fitted, expensive suit puts three pound on the counter. "Keep the change." He drinks the entire sweltering hot Espresso, right in front of her, without coming up for air. Shelly thinks this man was insane. The blazing hot water would have scorched his entire mouth. The man grins, looking unaffected by the temperature of the fresh hot drink. He makes his way out of the door. "That was lovely, thank you. It would be a

90

shame to see you close. Don't forget to sell that Ferrari. Every penny and I mean every *single* penny must go to The Salvation Army. I can be found, upstairs at The Balconies Restaurant."

The man who left without leaving a name, leaves.

Shelly shivered. *"How could selling my husband's car and giving all the money to charity help increase my profits?"* Shelly thought. *"How could my husband make a deal like that, behind my back?"* She felt betrayed. They'll be some stern words with him later. *"Perhaps I could tell, Simon? No it has nothing to do with him. It only upsets him when I talk about Richard. Also he's got enough on his plate."* As the battle in her mind wages on, Shelly couldn't have stopped feeling like she had encountered the Devil himself.

Chapter 21

Gail Brooke and Carl Sebastian have been slowly exploring the dirt track, for what felt like hours, in pursuit of any overseen evidence, along the way.

Bass asks Brooke "Do you drink at The Dive Bar much?"

"Not particularly, what are you contemplating?"

"A man was found, passed out and naked. Apparently, he's not from around here."

"It is possible that, it could be a drunken ruffian. Is there any correlation between this and your stripper?"

"Not really, it was just a tip I got, I assume it was nothing."

"What did he look like?"

"I am not sure. The informant wasn't very helpful"

A thought came to Brooke; "There is a possibility, it could be Bartholomew Maithes."

"Who?" Bass frowns.

"Everyone calls him "Crazy Bart." I for one, find it unamusing. He suffers from Schizophrenia."

"Does he hears voices?"

"Unfortunately so, it is a congenital disorder."

"Where does he live?"

Brooke had an apologetic look on her face; "I have no idea. Put he sometimes appears around town."

"Do you know roughly what time? Or where?

"No, sorry."

Bass grunted "What use are you?"

Brooke was offended; she decided to carry on looking for clues on her own, in silence.

The Private Investigator added the suspect to his list of suspects.

Eventually they both reached The Bowl, the place where Jenny took her last few steps.

"This is where the GPS signal ended?" Bass asked.

"This must have been it, this must have been where she was killed. Her body was found a mile down the track, however."

"Have a look around; the killer might have dropped something here."

Bass walked over to the broken refrigerator, looking down at the grass along the way. He opened it up and there was nothing inside apart from displaced shelves.

Bass watched as to what Brooke was doing, she was scouring the area. When he knew she wasn't definitely looking his way, he pulls out the Electro Magnetic Field (EMF) Detector from the inside of his suit jacket. It was picking up a reading, meaning there had been some activity here.

"Have you found anything?" Brooke shouts from the other side of the Bowl.

"Not yet." Lies Bass, he doesn't think he needs to tell her about all his equipment, he tries to keep most of the information close to his chest.

"Anything could have been swept away by the wind. Or impounded by the police."

"I know, Simon Cole won't let me see any of the information for fear I'll "destroy" his case."

"You cannot blame him, not trusting an outsider who claims to be a Paranormal Detective."

"Maybe we should take a steady walk back, and have another careful look along the way."

Brooke agrees, she tells herself that; "The next time I walk out down the dirt track I shall be wearing my gardening jeans and cheap trainers, not my shoes and trousers."

"How about a small skimpy dress?"

"I despise like wearing dresses."

"That's a shame; I would have liked to have seen more of your legs."

"Do not be such a pervert. Can you keep those opinions to yourself?"

"I can't help it, I'm a red-blooded male."

As they walk further down the dirt track in silence, past the blooming trees. A cold shiver runs down Bass, not a cold spot caused by ghosts but an unnerving feeling has if he and Brooke are being watched. Bass rotates in a circle and he can see no one else around. Brooke notices Bass is standing still; "Is there something wrong?"

Bass walks up to Brooke and whispers in her ear "I think there is something watching us?"

"There's no one else here."

But there is something. Bass can feel it, his intuition leads him back to a Tree. He walks up to it, widens his arms and places his hands on its rough edges, almost giving it a hug. He gives the tree a pat-down, like the treatment you'd receive from an Airport Security Guard. He knocks on the bark, it sounds hollow. "Is this real?" Bass disputes.

"You believe that the tree is an imposter?"

It's even sounding implausible to Bass. "Something feels off, there's something in these woods." He walks off, though he never turns around to look back at his enemies, this time he cautiously did, in case it moved whilst they weren't looking. He can see is just a tree.

Now they are walking beside the water, still not spotted anything relevant along the way. Bass finds a bench, "Come on, and let's sit down for a bit."

"So much for not having a minute."

"Just look at this place." Bass says as he sits down. He grabs Brookes arm and pulls her down to sit next to him.

Bass is in awe of how the sun reflects on the surface smooth running water. Along the river bank the shining ray of sun light brings out the colour of the flowers, the bright red and pink Lobelia Cardinalis (Cardinal flowers), bright white Viburnum Shrubs that are on the borders on the bright green leaves. The attractive string of dark blue lobelia plants running along the ground.

Brooke concurs, "This place is beautiful."

"You know why? Because there is no one else here. Nature in its full glory, not been corrupted by the damaging hands of mankind."

Brooke grew scared of Bass at that moment. He has always been sarcastic, narcissistic but now she's worried that he could be a threat to other people. "If you hate people so much, why did you get a job that involves helping others?"

Bass turns to look at Brooke. "I might not like other people but that doesn't mean I want to see them killed." Well, maybe not everyone, he's met a few people in his lifetime he could quite happily strangle to death or smash their skulls in. That does not include innocent seventeen-year-old girls though.

This broody looking man, next to Brooke is only appearing to be more of an enigma to her.

"There aren't many Private Paranormal Investigators, there aren't many other Ghostbusters, not genuine ones anyway. So, someone's got to do it."

"I bet you prefer it as well because it is a different occupation to what everyone else does." Brooke suggests.

Bass couldn't argue, he always felt different to everyone else, an outsider. Perhaps he felt earning a living by doing something different, felt natural to him. Carl Sebastian being himself won't tell her how he feels. He'll just change the subject.

"How long of you been an English teacher?"

"Do you really care?"

"Not really."

A man on a house boat, waves delightedly to the couple on the bench. Of course Brooke waves back out of basic politeness. Bass is more ill-natured, by refusing to.

Bass turns his head to gaze down the river path to follow the man on the boat. He notices by the shallow end, a small group of people and what looks to be a priest, dunking their heads into the water. Every time someone's head was dunked, the priest shouted out "We bury the old life and we rise to walk in a new life."

Thinking that this mad priest is drowning people, Bass has to ask "What are they doing?"

"They are getting their sins washed away." Brooke replies.

"Isn't that more of an American thing?"

"It does not have to be."

"Why do people do it?"

"To make themselves feel better, boost their spiritual well-being. Are there any regrets or mistakes you like to feel atoned for?"

Bass has plenty; he's not going to tell a soul what they are though. "It'll make themselves feel better for a while but then they'll just go back to re-making the same mistakes as before."

"You are not a believer in second chances? Redemption?"

"No, people have to live with the choices that they've made."

"Maybe you have something to get off your chest?" Brooke leans her head to Bass broad shoulder. "You may even feel a little bit better."

"There's nothing to talk about." He lies. "I'm certainly not going to talk to a stranger about anything."

Brooke sits with her back straight.

Bass stands up; "I'm going to have a word with the priest; See if he knows anything about Jenny Woodfield."

He walks over. Brooke purposely waits a few seconds before she follows.

Father Paul is knee deep in the water, reading a passage from the bible to his flock of people, when he hears a calling from the sore. "Father! Father!"

Bass is on the shore, not getting his suit wet, watching as this elderly gentlemen, with grey hair, wearing a white priest robe and the white collar. Slowly making his way towards him.

"How can I help you my son? Do you wish to confess your sins as well?"

"I am not your son and I have nothing to confess. Is that what you're doing here? Selling lies to these sheep." Bass says bluntly, as he nods to the worshippers, with their soaking heads.

"Are you not a believer?"

"I don't believe in Heaven or Hell. I don't think there is a higher calling. I completely disagree with going to church; you take advantage of peoples needfulness for a sense of belonging, once you convince them to join your religion, you brain wash them, put the fear in god in them, in-order to control them..."

Father Paul, inhaled a slow deep breathe; the bible that he's cradling in two hands is now pulled up to his chest. "The church is a house of love."

Bass ignored, what he believed was tripe, carried on with his own ramblings; "...And I certainly don't believe what you are doing here is right."

Not many people have seen Father Paul lose his temper, because he's not normally an angry man, except this stranger, has just walked up to him and insulted his strongly held beliefs. Not being led into temptation, he remains calm, withdrawn from physical violence and inappropriate language. He recites a passage: "In Him we have redemption through His blood, the forgiveness of our trespasses, according to the riches of His grace." "That was in the New Testament, Ephesian, one, seven. No one is not worthy of being saved, we can all be rescued from the domain of darkness."

"You talk about saving people but how many deaths, or numbers of wars have been caused by religion?"

Brooke eventually decided to join in which rejoiced the frustrated Father.

"Bass, this is Father Paul."

"Hello, Gail."

"Please Father, I keep telling you to call me Brooke."

"I do apologise. Will we be seeing you on Sunday?"

"Yes. You will be seeing me on Saturday too."

Bass asks "What's happening on Saturday?"

Brooke and Father Paul give each other a glance before FP replies "Saturday is Jenny Woodfield's funeral. Her mother, Janet, has kindly asked me to the honourable task of giving the service."

Shit, that's only three days away, I still need to see the body Bass realises. Worried that time is running low, he needs to somehow get to Simon Cole so that he can see all his information. Trickery, deceit or violence, even. At the minute, he's still making enquiries, to what this a person, this charlatan knows. "Did you know Jenny Woodfield?"

"I am the one that baptized her."

"You lucky devil" Bass, mocking with his intentional pun.

Brooke squints her eyes at Father Paul has something occurs to her, "I thought she was an atheist?"

"She chose that path, not till further on in life."

"That made you, angry? *Vengeful*, even?" Bass interrogated.

"I have not killed anyone, Mr Bass. I was mortified when I heard the news, I was in the church preparing a ceremony I was going to give the children at The Primary School, Sister Burnett could vouch for me..."

I wonder why he felt the need to tell me his whereabouts and his alibi before I asked him, Bass enquired.

"...that's when I was struck down onto my knees. It has hit the community hard, lots of people, not just I. Especially Jack Mandolin."

"The comedian?" Bass asks.

Brooke responds "Yes, this is his home town. He came back to practise some new material for the tour. Instead he's now doing a charity concert in Jenny Woodfield's name. Do you think she were a fan?"

"Or he was a fan of her?" Bass suggested.

"A very kind and noble gesture, no doubt" said FP.

Bass doesn't believe that people are so selfless, "Why would a famous comedian care so much about one teenage girl's death?"

Brooke does recall "He did only arrive back home, the day before Jenny was murdered."

Bass grew more suspicious of this funny character. So much that he's pumped it from his mental priority list. Now it reads Jack Mandolin, Chelsea Heart and Bartholomew Maithes.

FP believes; "Good will to others does not go unnoticed in the eyes of others, nor the lords."

This was not an answer that Bass could accept. "There must be something more to it than that. I'd like a word with him myself When and where is the charity event?"

Brooke remembers "He's playing at his brother's pub, The Dive Bar, tonight as a warm up show."

"We're going to that then, Brooke."

Brooke puts her arm around Bass "It will give you a chance to meet some of the locals."

"I would rather have my prostate checked by *The Iron Giant*." retorts Bass.

Brooke smiled at him, not laughing at his witty reply but because she can gather he loathes socialising. She was right, this is something Bass was dreading, the idea of socialising, among the close community. Eventually, it was something he knew he had to do.

"Thank you, for your time Father" Brooke gives her gratitude to the elderly vicar. As she walks away with her arm linked with Bass.

"Right, we'll get to that Bed and Breakfast. You get me that discount, check in. Change, shower and then we'll meet at The Dive Bar."

"Do you know where it is?"

"No."

"When you leave the Bed and Breakfast, turn left, second right, you'll see the Goforcoffee shop and then it's at the end of that road."

Bass could have gone with Brooke, but he wants some time to himself, neck a couple of drinks before having to socialise with various people. Plus, he changed his mind about ditching her, after using her for the B'N'B discount, she could be his "back-up", an introduction to a few people. Besides, it was nice having someone beautiful to look at.

Chapter 22

The time read twenty to six pm, on the clock that appears to be a plate, with John Lennon's face printed on it. The sun was beginning to fall, the light descends through the windows of the Goforcoffee Shop. Sat on the cushioned stools are Chelsea Heart and Mark Bell, there's a hot drink of fresh coffee by the side of them though barely been touched, they're just on the wooden window shelf next to the tiny purple flowers, waiting to be cold. Chelsea has a text book in her hands, entitled: *The Full Body; Muscles, Bones and Palpations*.

Has Chelsea frowning face, read out the in-book questionnaire, her tone was growing slower, as if she, herself was struggling to follow the question. "Next question. What muscle, which sits underneath the Bicep Brachii, connects the Humerus to the Ulna and acts as the strongest flexor of the elbow?"

Mark was clicking his fingers, reciting through his memory bank, to what he had just been taught. "Ok, the Humerus is the upper arm bone and Ulna is the lower arm bone, I obviously know what a bicep and elbow is..."

Chelsea sips through her coffee that's become cooler. She can see Mark is grappling with the answer, his frustration caused him to grip his fingers into his thick black hair. His temporary tutor, Chelsea thought he was thinking so hard that all the veins on the side of his red balloon face will distend, it was quite comical.

"I just don't know" Marks exasperation caused him to slam his arms on the wooden side, causing both drinks and the plant pot to vibrate.

Chelsea looks through the answer book "It was The Brachialis Muscle."

Mark, with his left elbow on the side, buried his left hand into his forehead. "I'm never going to pass the written test."

Chelsea tried to raise his spirits. "I don't think the questions in the exam will be as hard as the ones in this book. I would have never guessed the answer, for a million years. You knew what the bones were that's more than I can do."

"I'm never going to become a Personal Trainer."

"Yes you are, Jenny didn't love you because you were a quitter. You can do this. Let's try an easier one." She slams her hand on Marks bulging triceps. Reading from the book she asks; "How many vertebrae's are there in a human spine?"

"Eight" He quickly responds.

"It's seven!" she quickly yells back, instantly crushing those raised spirits within a millisecond. Chelsea slams the text book. "This is ridiculous."

"It's my future, we're talking of."

"What about Jenny's future? I have discovered something on the internet..."

Mark gulps as he dreading about what's soon to follow.

"... A bug, like proper spy-shit. We can put one in Shane's office."

"Are you having me on? We almost got caught last time! I'm not going back there."

"We'll sneak through the window, we got in easily enough."

"Where are you going to get a surveillance bug?"

"Like I said: the internet. It's only two thousand pounds."

If Mark had been sipping on his coffee, the shock of the price would have caused him to choke on it and spew it back out. "Where would we find that sort of cash?"

Chelsea didn't have an answer; she considered stealing from her dad again. The impression she gathered was he might not be as lenient as before. She would be truly disowned, homeless, nowhere to turn because she has no one else.

Shelly Jayne, the beautiful, forty odd year old owner of the shop. In a good mood because her husband told her that she had permission to sell his Ferrari in order to save the Coffee Shop. He too mentioned that he was going away on a business trip for the next three nights in Paris. She not sure if he'll remain faithful whilst over there but that is ok, she's not going be either. Simon will be with her the next three nights. To express her joyfulness, she brings Chelsea and Mark a Sundae desert, topped with cream, walnuts, a cherry and two pink and brown creamed striped paper straws. "It's on the house. I think you two deserve it after what you've been through." She gives a soft, radiant smile. Marks eyes only glowed when he spots Chelsea's nice, white smile, her soft blue eyes lit-up and with the sun setting over her, they were clearer, kinder and carried a sparkle. Mark never noticed how blue they actually were before, they were always so angry and he had only noticed Jenny's. He not once gawped over her attractive friends, until now. Chelsea had noticed him staring at her, normally she would curse at the perverted, creepy gawkers. She herself found herself staring at his face, as the sun set over his, It outlined all his features; The cheek bones, chiselled chin, cute button nose, long dark eyelashes over his cute puppy-brown eyes. Both of them leaned into the sundae and drank from the straws, eyes still locked into each other's. So much so that Mark got cream on the end of his nose. Chelsea giggled with her hand over her mouth hoping some of the desert won't accidentally be spat out. Mark sees the cream at the end of the nose and wipes it off with his finger. He smiles. For a moment, they forgot about Jenny, Shane Crewball, and the pressures of stepping into the real-world. It was joyous to see Chelsea happy rather than so hostile. For the next hour, as Mark

elongates their slow walk home to Chelsea's doorstep,
they were being teenagers, like they were supposed to be.

Chapter 23

While Bass was checking himself into his room at The Robinson's Bed and Breakfast, on the first floor. Brooke entered her room on the ground floor. Her room had a very soft blue carpet which is kind to the soles of the feet. A white double bed with thick fluffy duvets and pillows, it faced a large bay window that can be sealed off by the purple curtains. The right-hand side is a TV stand, to the left side is a wardrobe with a mirror, there she'll change out of her trousers, shoes and her white teacher's blouse into something more casual. Jeans, black flat shoes, a red, hollow sleeve, lace V neckline, long sleeved, curved hemline blouse.

While Bass changes out of his suit in his room, it's similar to Brookes aside from the giant bay window, that's only for the ground floor rooms. Bass puts on his normal attire, plain black jumper that's a little bit too tight and with the sleeves rolled up, blue jeans, and plain brown shoes. Drinking the bottle of whiskey he ordered from the downstairs bar, hammering the clamorous Heavy Metal tunes, so much so, that his neighbour knocks on the wall, "Can you turn it down." Bass just ignores him. He needs to get psyched before going to a room full of people to question and the whiskey helps him to feel numb.

Brooke looks at the watch on her arm, realises it is ten minutes past seven and they agreed to meet there at seven thirty. She leaves the B'n'B, follows her own directions, on towards the first left on the dark streets and when she is about to make the second right, Brooke comes to a halt in order to not crash into Clive Dunscroft and little Bradley, who's in his hand. They seemed to be power walking around the corner but as soon as they both spotted Brooke, they too came to a standstill.

"Mr Dunscroft I'm so sorry. How are you?" Brooke apologises. He doesn't answer, he keeps his head down, and so the cap of his baseball hat covers his face. Brooke notices that Clive's body, stiff as it was, becoming very shifty. She looks at his shirt, there's a picture of an animated car, with eyes and a big friendly smiley face. An animated cartoon character for kids, presumably. The shirt also had some bizarre stains on, like clay or paint. He must have been doing arts and crafts, considered Brooke. She can tell he was very comfortable being in her presence. But why her? She has done nothing to him. Although she can understand how sceptical he is around other people while the whole town suspects him of being the murderer. Brooke notices a very young, shy, thumb sucking Bradley. She leans over to him, with both her hands on her knees, quite condescendingly and speaks to him as such. "And what is your name, little man?"

Clive answers for him, "He's mute, he's been like that since he was born." he says whilst he pushes a timid Bradley behind his leg. As if he is protecting him from her.

Brooke looks how over-protective he is over little Bradley. If he keeps treating him this way, he'll never be able to socialise (A bit like someone else she has met recently.) He will never be able to gain any independence, no confidence, forever afraid of the world and most of all; he will never get a girlfriend. "I am going to The Dive Bar to watch Jack Mandolin, if you would like to join?" She looks down at Bradley "a very funny guy and I might even buy you a coke?" She smiles in a way how naturally care-giving mothers smile at a new born baby. Again, Clive responded for him, "No... Thank you." There was an uneasy pause between the "No" and the "Thank you".

"Do you not think he should be able to play with the other children? Granted, there will not be many in a pub. You must know what I am aiming to express."

"He doesn't need anyone else." Clive's wide eyes and thick rimmed glasses stare at Brooke, his lips are slightly pouted, and his cheeks are puffy.

Brooke respects the boundaries of parents, she is not a mother herself so cannot judge how others raise their children. Brooke nods her head "Ok then." then proceeds by wiggling her fingers on her hand, a wave goodbye to Bradley. "Bye, Bye" She said, with that motherly smile again. Clive didn't move, not until Brooke had vanished around the corner.

Chapter 24

Carl Sebastian stumbled through the doors of The Dive Bar, fashionably late. Inside, Bass noticed the peculiar lay-out of The Dive bar; wooden flooring with a wooden bar. With many abstractions and illustrations on the roof and the wall, In the middle of the room, one example a manikin with a hulks hand, using an ironing board as a surf board. To the right hand side in between two wooden tables, that have beer barrels with cushions on as an excuse for seats, is an open coffin made out of a pink polka dot dress on the outside but on the inside is a painted white wall with what appears to be a gap in the middle. On the left is a painting of black cartoon music notes playing various hand held instruments. Dangling over the front door, above Bass, hangs a gigantic dream catcher. "Why can't there just be a *Weatherspoon's*? Or at least a proper bar-bar." Bass spoke to himself. His occupation of being a ghost hunter has made him see some weird things but this kind of weird, freaks him out. The "art" on the walls and roof were not the only cause of how unbearable the pub was to him. The room was heaving with many fans of the comedian; Jack Mandolin, who's on the ligneous stage, facing directly to the door. The amount of followers, and the raucous laughter from one stereotypical large, drunk Scottish guy is grating on the very marrow of Bass's bones. He thought the whiskey would make him less susceptible to the crowded room, but it had made him more agitated, very edgy and the feeling of needing to punch someone in the face. Bass moved very slowly to the bar, shoulder barging many of the town's locals as he passes them.

Taking centre stage, almost as if he is making it his own. Jack Mandolin is wearing a bright yellow patchy jacket, which helps gains the eyes of the audience as well as being comically appalling. He's currently got the attention of the crowd by the palm of his hands.

He is currently testing out a new routine, spinning left to right impersonating himself and a fictional wife.

"I said to my wife, who's a famous author, if I ever make it has a famous comedian, I would buy you a new car, a bigger house and give you everything you ever wanted."

Turns to the right, imitating the wife. "*N'aww* you're so sweet."

Back to the left, "Would I be your favourite celebrity?"

Role of The Wife "Well you wouldn't be my *favourite* celebrity."

Left side with a puzzled expression "Well, who would be your favourite?"

Spins to the right, counting fingers "Well, there's *Channing Tatum*."

"Naturally"

"*Ryan Gosling, Tom Hardy...*"

"I can see a pattern emerging here."

"*George Clooney, Hugh Jackman, Megan fox.*"

His eyes widen with excitement to the giggling audience.

Playing himself again "So I would be your *seventh* favourite celebrity."

Whirls to the right, with a condescending smile "Oh honey, I can't believe you think you're that high up."

Everyone in the room, except for Bass, is laughing.

Jack Mandolin, facing the left side, with his arms crossed, turning smug, he says "Well if you become successful with your published book, than you wouldn't be *my* favourite celebrity."

Reeling to the right with a death stare "And why wouldn't I be your favourite celebrity!?"

Jumps to the left, prancing on his feet, looking anguished and then flustered "Of course you would be my favourite celebrity, darling."

"Thanks babe, I love you."

Everyone in the room was laughing hard.

Jack Mandolins chuckle-some role playing came to an end. Much to Bass' delight, the comic takes centre stage; "Thank you everyone for coming. I hope you enjoyed the show. I will be doing a charity gig next week in the name of Jenny Woodfield. Tickets are available behind my brother's bar. It would mean a lot if you join me for that one special night. I know you'll have a good drink beforehand because, like we all do, we book tickets to shows and have a good tipple. "Oh, I booked tickets to see *Iron Maiden*, they're my favourite band, I cannot wait, and I wouldn't miss them for the world... But before we go we have to get ABSOLUTELY SHIT FACED." Thank you and good night." After a salute he walks off the stage has Jack Mandolin, then enters the welcoming crowd as Jack Mill.

Bass turns to Frank Mill, whose wiping glass, keeping a beady eye on this stranger from out-of-town.

"Whiskey" Bass demands.

"You're not from around here." Frank's tone is not friendly yet continues to pour him the house whiskey with ice.

"I'm sorry, I didn't realised I walked into *The Slaughtered Lamb*. Although it looks more re-vamped."

Not understanding The *American Werewolf in London* reference, Frank still knew this man was trying to offend him. "My girl does the illustrations, it's her idea. It's not really my scene but it makes her happy. I don't want you to think I'm sort of puff."

"I wouldn't care if you were."

Bass drinks the whiskey, it didn't give him that joyful, burning sensation that the strong-stuff brings. He, instead frowns at the glass with disgust.

"What's your name?"

"I'm Carl Sebastian, a Private Investigator. I was asked to help with the murder of Jenny Woodfield."

"Are you off the clock?" Frank nods to the glass whiskey.

"Medicinal purposes." Bass intentionally changes the subject. "You Frank Mill, the owner?"

"I am."

"You discovered an unconscious naked man on the day of the murder."

"What about it?"

Bass feels like Frank's being too defensive. "Who was he? My colleague believes it was a man called Bartholomew Maithes."

"No, I know Bartholomew. He has been seen streaking. He's completely cuckoo barking mad..."

That's a delicate way of putting it.

"... He's got some kind of schizophrenia, personality disorder or something. I don't know."

"Then who was the person you found?

Frank shrugs his shoulders. "He's not from around here."

"Can you at least describe him?"

Beautiful, Is what Frank wanted to say but if anyone else heard that, then the locals would start believing he's gay.

"Tall, black hair, slim, you could tell he works out, chiselled chin but it's his eyes." Bass leaned in on the now, subdued Frank. "His eyes were so *dark*." Rationale prevailed over the sombre "It was probably from drugs or something."

"Did you take him to the hospital?"

"Yeah, Holders Bridge hospital, only a tiny place."

"Thanks for your time, not the whiskey though, it's awful."

"I made that."

"Well... don't do it again. Give me one of your ciders."

"That was brewed by a farm not far from here."

"Good, southern scrumpy is the best kind."

Frank pours cider from a box in the fridge, into a fresh pint glass. "I like you, we get two kinds of people that come in here; those who like to drink and loudly talk too much. Then there's your kind, the kind who likes a stiff drink, drown his sorrows quietly. I always prefer that sort. If you do want to speak to Bart Maithes, the best way is to contact Julian Green, he's the head Mental Health Nurse for a private company called Staysafe."

Bass thought he'd still check out the schizophrenia patient however this tall, dark-eyed stranger seemed more important. He takes the refreshing drink of cold, sweet but slightly sour cider. "That's better." He slams a tenner on the bar, "I must ask; where was you on the morning of Jenny's murder?"

"I was here with my brother. Opening up the bar."

"You and your brother could easily vouch for each other. Unless you hate him because he's successful and you're not."

"I've fulfilled my dreams, I've always wanted to own a pub and now I do."

"Still is there another alibi?"

"My girlfriend was here, mopping the floor."

"Is she here?"

"No she's away, studying Art in London."

"If you can call this Art. It's a bit bizarre for my taste."

"Hey! That's my girlfriends work! Anymore word from you, about it and you're out of here." He threatens, whilst throwing a towel over his shoulder.

Bass takes his ultimatum seriously keeping his opinions to himself because he doesn't want to be barred from the only pub in Holders Bridge. Still doesn't apologise though, he just walks into the faceless crowd.

Nights like these, when Carl Sebastian goes out, all faces mould into one, not really looking at anybody, not engaging in eye contact. He does look for the biggest tart in the room and dances with her for a bit before taking her back for a quick one night stand. While he's working and not being the mood to get intimate with someone, everyone remains unadorned. Standing out in front of everyone and everything was Gail Brooke. She looked more ravishing than earlier today, which was hard to do. Still a shame she couldn't flaunt more of her legs though. It came as a surprising relief to Bass as he felt more at ease. She, however, looked furious "You are late!"

"I'm sorry, I was with my mistress, and she refused to untie me because I'd forgotten my safe word. It got rather embarrassing."

Bass threw her the least humours grin she had ever seen. Brooke had a bemused expression on her pretty face, something, she has a feeling; she will eventually be accustomed to.

"How can I depend on you? How can I trust you to have my back when the worst is going to happen?"

"You can't."

"I am not sure if I can do this with you anymore. I need some air."

Bass watches Brooke walk out the backdoor, by the stage which leads to an alleyway. Starting to feel a hint of guilt. He needs her, more than he actually knows.

Brooke stands outside in the dark alleyway, contemplating on hunting for Jenny's killer, alone and not having to deal with this sarcastic, selfish man any longer.

"Hi there, gorgeous."

Brooke had heard someone talk to her, assuming she was alone with her inward thoughts, it startled her. She turns around and sees a drunken Shane Crewball. With a bottle of something vile in his hand, the smell indicated it had a high percentage of alcohol inside. He's slouching on a chair, with his arm on top of another, trying to look relaxed and chilled, in reality he's wobbly. "You look *mighty* fine, Gail." His words were slurring.

"Shane, I knew you, when you lived on the estate, years ago. You were less of an arsehole then, simply a petrified little boy. That was all before you were running with Tyrone's crew, he was a big hitter in those times. Is this why you have chosen the life of a gangster? So you would not be so afraid?"

"I fucking love it, the rush you get, you can't beat it. The drugs, the violence and the respect. Now look at me!" Widens his arms. "I run this shitty little town now."

"You are nothing but a low-life thug, a mean bully, and a scum-bag. The only thing you run is that abysmal, germ-infested fitness centre."

Shane stands up and swaying closer to Brooke. Her father taught her to be tough, to stand up to the bullies. She also believes Shane isn't the menace as he likes to think. "I bet you like it though, a clean posh girl like you, wouldn't be seen with a dirty, scum-bag like me." While he talks, he walks so close to her, pushing her against the wall. She tries to squirm away but Shane puts both arms up on the wall on either side of her, trapping her. "I know deep down you want it." He licks the side of her cheek, from neck to her ear. She cringes when she feels the saliva from his tongue against her soft skin. She tries to push him away but not being strong enough, it was impossible. With both hands she knocked one of his arms off the wall, quickly goes to dash out but Shane pulls her back by the red top, stopping the possibility of escaping. Shane just laughs at her while she slaps both hands on his ashtray scented chest. "You might as well just enjoy it, baby. The more you struggle the more it'll hurt. Now why don't you and me go somewhere quiet?"

Every woman's worst fear, is about to happen. Brooke won't go down without a fight; her courage is superior to her terror.

"Hey!" A boisterous, deep, masculine voice came from behind Shane, this time; it's he who has lost the element of surprise. Turning around, standing there is a tall, muscular, bald, enraged man, Carl "Bass" Sebastian. "Get off her."

"What are you going to do about it? Do you know who I am?"

Bass, without the slightest hesitation punches Shane Crewball so hard in the nose, he falls over a chair. Brooke leaps into the arms of her saviour before standing behind him. Shane stands up, holding his broken nose, the leather jacket falling off the right shoulder, blood had quickly dripped onto the shirt. "When I find out who you are. I'm going to kill you, your friends and family."

"I don't have any friends or family."

Bass's reply became a shock to both Brooke and Shane. Shane was intimidated, even afraid of Bass but he doesn't say it, nor show it. He has his ruthless reputation to maintain.

Frank Mill comes running from the pub, gripping a baseball bat in his hand. "What's going off!?"

Shane gives Bass a sinister smile "This, this isn't over." Out of breath, too drunk to fight. Shane cowardly retreats away. Returning home, laughing frantically along the way.

Frank Mill was surprised to see that Bass has had a fight with Shane Crewball, most people are terrified of him. Even as someone who's strong as Frank is paying protection money.

The bar is closed early for the tonight. Leaving Jack Mill entertaining three of the most loyal, regular customers by telling the funniest stories that occurred to him over the tour. Frank Mill was behind the bar. While a shaken Brooke was sat down on the table, Bass leant down beside the traumatised woman "Are you ok?"

Brooke laughed but there was no humour in it, "Do you even care?"

"Of course I do. We might not be friends but that doesn't mean I want you to get hurt."

Brooke looked down and sees actual concern in his eyes.

"I did not know you could fight, well, your arms gave a good indication to your strength."

"I fought tougher man than him, back when I was at the orphanage, I had to fight a lot. First it was the other kids, then after a growth spurt; I was challenged by the local gypsy camp for bare-knuckle boxing." *I can't believe I've just told her this.* Bass stopped himself from talking, no one needed to know besides he didn't really want to reflect on cruel memories.

Brooke was hit with another surprise, "I didn't know you were an orphan, I am sorry." It explained his guard and mistrust towards others.

Brooke offered a comforting hand on Bass's thick and hairy forearm. In that moment Bass almost opened up more, he could have shared a little bit more information, he almost shared the fact that the hated to fight and purposely lost a few boxing matches so he wouldn't have to fight for a while. Approaching the possibility of sharing how he really felt, how alone and the unbelievable amount of angst he had to face in order to survive. Instead Bass pulled away his arm, rejecting Brookes nurturing offer.

The moment had passed when Frank shouted; "Brooke, I'll get you a whiskey, on the house."

"No, she's suffered enough." Bass shrieks back; "We'll have two pints of that cider."

"Coming right up." Frank pours two pints of cider and brings them over to the table.

Bass was starting to like Frank, almost feeling guilty about mocking his girlfriend's art work but he wouldn't admit it. "Who was that man?" Bass asks Brooke, referring to Shane.

"His name is Shane Crewball, he is the known drug supplier of the town. Targets vulnerable adults and children alike."

"And Simon Cole knows about this?"

"Yes, he has known for a long time but he has never been able to find evidence against him or arrest him."

"I'm guessing he doesn't really catch a lot of criminals."

"Only petty thieves, kids and drunks that leave my bar" Frank answers, whilst putting both pints of cider on the table.

"I guess, it's whatever makes him feel big and important."

"You have hit the nail on the head" Brooke says.

"Should we inform him about what happened tonight?" Frank questions.

"Would there be a point?" Bass, doubting the competency of The Chief Inspector.

Bass turns his head towards Jack Mill and the regulars who are in his complete grasp and exhaustingly laughing at the tales being told.

Frank comments "My brother, he's literally the happiest guy in the world."

Bass looks at Jack Mill while he's entertaining the rest of locked in guests, notices that he smiles a lot, a bit too much... *He's putting on a face, a mask of some sorts,* Bass gathers.

Jack Mill just finishing of a story, feeling staring eyes on him, and his intuition was correct when he notices Bass was looking at him, looking *through* him. He keeps smiling for his guests but on the inside he's trembling. Worry becomes a bullet in the brain, there's now only one thing stuck in the middle of Jack Mills mind... *Why does he keep staring at me? He can see right past my smile, he knows...*" Right excuse me gentlemen, if I can call you that." The three men, laughed, even though it wasn't that funny, they were very drunk. "I'm just going to the toilet, and I'll come back down and buy you all another round." The three men clang their pints together, cheering for the generous offer that's just been made, one of them shout's "That's why we love you, Jackie-boy." Representing how the whole towns feeling on the likeable comedian. Jack knows this all too well, yet he can't accept it. He runs upstairs to go the bathroom, just to get away from Bass eyeballing him.

"I'm going to ask him a few questions when he gets back." Bass behests.

"Can we please just go back to the B'n'B?" Brooke insists.

Bass was annoyed because there's still work to be done, more interrogation was needed, especially when he knows this "overly-friendly" guy is hiding something. Brooke's been through such an ordeal, she should be prioritized. "Ok, I'll walk you back." Looks at Frank "I will be back though."

"Understood." Frank said while he unbolts the pub doors to let Brooke and Bass out.

Concurrently, Jack Mill was in the bathroom of The Dive Bar, feeling like he's going to have a heart attack. He's clutching his tightening chest, digging in his fingertips into his ribcage, struggling to breathe. He looks at his reflection in the mirror, hating what he sees in it, hating what he's let himself become. Not feeling if he's able to return to the bar and putting on that happy face again. In due time he will do, fulfilling his promise of free beer to his guests with a friendly but fake smile.

Chapter 25

Brooke turned in for the night, after Bass kindly walked her to a room, like a gentleman, something else she never saw coming. She equates the bitter Private Paranormal Inspector to a flower that just keeps on giving. One that will prick you, if you get too close, she might add. Now in dressed her pink pyjamas, she turned off the lights, laid in her big soft, comfortable bed ready to sleep. Trying to put Shane Crewball's despicable act behind her, luckily she had a guardian angel near her. One that maybe a borderline alcoholic.

Still an hour had passed; she had not been able to sleep. Homesickness was the cause of the disruption. Brooke was longing for own actual bed in her actual home. Hopefully the hauntings will pass soon and she will be able to return. The digital clock reads twelve am, a new day, though Brooke still feels no sensation from this.

The closed purple curtains, opposing the bed begins to shuffle. A startled Brooke jumped up, staring at the detected movement. Possibly a draft seeped through the large bay window. The left one moved again. A scream! It came from a man, so it couldn't be the ghost of Jenny Woodfield. Brooke retreated to the back of the bed, as close to the head board as possible, pulling her knees into her bosom. Too petrified to move, her nonplussed eyes, fixated on the curtain, awaiting to see what terror lurked behind. There was a sound of faint heavy breathing, as if someone was taking the last few breaths too rapidly, when there's a bag over that someone's head and suffocating quickly. It worsens, Brooke can see what appears to be a man INSIDE the actual curtain, pressing outwards towards her. The outlined face within the curtain, moved to talk but no words came out. It cannot be possible, hoping she was a sleep and this was all a dream, *praying* this was a dream. But it was not a dream. The man withdrew back, so the whole of the blind looked level again. Now! An arm! The palest white arm appeared out of the gap in between the closed curtains, drops to the floor causing a thud. The sound alone would have woke her up, if she was having a nightmare. It was not, she's confined to a living nightmare. It was Jenny. The broken, twisted body was slowly creeping out the bottom of the curtains. She reached out her broken arms, dug her dirty finger nails into the soft blue carpet in order to pull her lifeless, naked corpse towards Brooke. As Jenny moved, Brooke could hear the stiff, broken, dislocated joints snap, with every slow move that she made, *click, snap, click*. Brooke could feel her own complexion turning white, mouth drying up causing her tongue to be a scratch pad. Perspiration leaked from Brooke's forehead and ran down alongside her tears. Jenny eventually reached the bed, putting both hands on the edge to pull herself up. The dirty, dry brown hair that covered most of her face appeared over the crest of the bed. She made a deeply uncomfortable gasp for air, with her broken neck, she would find it difficult to breathe. Brookes trembling body came immobilized, she wanted to scream but it was as if someone had ripped out her own voice box. Jenny's dirty, pale hand touched Brooke's warm knee, it was cold, *so cold* and unnatural. Brooke tightened her eyelids, has Jenny's frozen body loomed over hers. Jenny moved her blue lips towards Brooke as if she was going to kiss her on the mouth, Brooke could feel her frizzled brown hair on the side of her face as she turned away. "Please, don't hurt me." sobs Brooke. Jenny whispers in her ear...

"Beware, beware the man with no face.

He cannot see. He cannot hear.

He is the man with no face.

"Beware, beware the man with no face.

.He doesn't sleep, he cannot smile.

He is the man with no face."

Blackout.

Brooke woke up on the floor, drenched in sweat, urine and tears. Without showering, she sprinted out the room.

Chapter 26

With his shoes on, Bass is laid on his white bed, one of the comfiest he's ever been on. Finishing off the bottle of whiskey he started before leaving for The Dive Bar. A film is on the TV, one of Bass's favourites. Once settled, the plan is to watch the entire film, then hopefully the whiskey and fatigue will kick-in and he will be able to pass out. There was a loud, heavy, frenzy banging on the door. Bass, live-paused the film because he wanted to turn the noise down, plus he plans to finish it as well. Jumped out the bed, presuming that Shane Crewball had followed him back to the B'n'B.

"Bass, Let me in!" It was Brooke and she sounded hysterical and desperate. He rushed to open the door, Brooke pleaded "Please can I stay with you?"

"Yes."

She hugged him, Bass could feel her soaking wet clothes through his own. It made him feel nauseated because he could smell that her pyjamas were not only dripping with sweat but with something more disgusting. "Do you want to get in the shower?" It was more of a command than a polite offer.

"Yes, please."

"I'll get you a change of clothes whilst you do that."

"Thank you, oh, my door is still open."

"Don't worry, I'll lock it up."

While Brooke was getting the shower, Bass changed his wet clothes, grabbed his duffle bag and began walking to her room. Along the way he was thinking, under different circumstances he would have liked to join her. His mind begins to ponder, *why did she run to me? She must have plenty of real friends nearby? Was it because I was the closest around? Maybe it was because I saved her from being raped, now she feels like she can trust me? Can she trust me? I'm not the most reliable person myself.*

Bass entered the room and grabbed a spare pair of pyjamas from her draw. Proceeded by noticing the wet patches on the bed. Pulling out the EMF detector, it flashed from red to green implying there had been a ghost in the room. He felt a sudden drop in temperature; a chill ran through his spine, it was a cold spot. Quickly he pulled out his IR thermometer and it took a reading of minus ten degrees. It didn't last long; the room was warming up again. This also proved that there was a spirit from another world here. It also meant that the ghost is following Brooke now, wherever she goes. Question remains; *who is she warning Brooke about? Why is she connected to her? I bet Brooke is hiding something from me, everyone hides secrets.*

Bass locks up Brooke's old room and returns to his. There he gawps over Brooke, dripping wet, fresh out the shower, covering her hair with a towel and the other spare towel wrapped around her body. Bass normally would say something seedy or derisive but with the delicate state she's in, he remained pleasant and even politely looked away while she strips off to change.

"Have you done?"

"Yes, you can turn around now. I appreciate the integrity you have given."

"What is your connection to Jenny?" Bass directly asks.

"I told you, I was her teacher and nothing more."

"Yet, the only pupil you taught in your spare time?"

"I liked her; I suppose you could say we were friends."

"A close student and teacher relationship seems abnormal?"

"Nothing of asexual nature occurred, Bass."

Bass stares at her.

"Do you believe me?"

"I want to." A second after Bass said that, he knows that he has left himself vulnerable to her. She could abuse his kindness at any moment now.

"I have a hypothesis to why you are so restrained. You had an execrable childhood. Growing up in a care home. I surmised, I lived in a very unruly area whilst growing up on my estate. I can only imagine yours was worse."

"It's all in the past, life moves on."

"Well, if ever want to talk. You can talk to me."

Bass could hear sincerity in her voice nevertheless she doesn't need to know. In a Bass-style fashion, he changes topic, "Have you seen this film?" He poses to the paused film on the TV.

"I'm afraid not."

"It's called *The Perks of Being a Wallflower*, It's a classic, and I think you will like it."

After analysing the screen shot Brooke suggests "It will be just be another teenage drama drivel. Besides it's really late."

"If you fall asleep, I don't mind."

"Would you care if I slept beside you?"

"Go ahead."

Brooke snuggled next to Bass to use his chest as a pillow. This initially made Bass uncomfortable, when he's with a woman he just uses her for sex and now they are cuddling. Her heads on his chest and her hand is on his leg provided some warmth and comfort, he's not used to it, agitated and not at ease, almost pushing her off. Eventually Bass manages to feel more settled.

"So, what makes you declare this film to be a classic?"

"The soundtrack, in its own right."

"My idea of classic films are *The Intouchables, Gone with the Wind, Pride and Prejudice, The Pianist.*"

"Why don't you just watch it and find out?"

An hour and a half later, in a teenage girl's bedroom, a boy with depression and PTSD (Post Traumatic Stress Disorder) is telling a very pretty Emma Watson, his real feelings, that he's in love with her. He's always been in love with her and she deserves so much more than the past shitty relationships and the crappy ex-boyfriends. Tears stream through the teenagers eyes...

Brooke's feeling quite moved from the film, slightly uplifted and glued to the screen. Something brought her back into the real world. Her pillow, Bass's chest sunk in and then out deeply. She could feel the deep exhaled breathes that Bass was breathing throughout his nose. Looking up on his unshaven face, he was blinking rapidly and occasionally holding his eyes shut for some time. Realising what he's doing, *he's trying to stop himself from crying.* Was it because she was here? I bet he cries to a lot of films, when there is no one else around and there's no need to be so guarded. She best not say anything, if she did, he probably would chuck her out the room. Brooke will pretend not to notice and try to focus on the film before drifting off to sleep.

Chapter 27

Morning arrived; the sun woke Brooke, discovering to be alone in the bed. There was the sound of a shower running, Bass was in there. Blurred and tired eyes tried to focus on the digital clock beside her, eventually the numbers formed into Nine Thirty am. She collapsed back on the pillow, realising that a late night and six hours sleep was simply not enough. The shower stopped running, now it sounded like he's on the phone to someone, *who could it be?* He said it himself, that he "has no friends or family." *Could it be work related?* I'm surprised that little phone still works. Brooke noticed something else, Bass's little black journal is on the side next to the TV. Should she dare open it and read it? How much time does she have? Maybe a glimpse would not hurt. Brooke gently climbed out the bed, tip-toed across the room to where the Television stand is, he's still on the phone. Anxiously looking at the door and opening up the book to a random page...

What We Live For

Well I've travelled to so many lands
I've seen some places I thought I'd never go   -V1
Met a whole bunch of strangers
Some kind, some dirty, some clean

But when I get back home
I still see the same old faces   -V2
Filled with their own hopelessness
The despair, the anger, the fear

But we all want the same things
We want to live in a better world   -V3
We don't want backstabbers as friends
No pain, no hurt, no loss

I turned on the news today
I saw a group of politicians   -V4
They're creaming the honest good working man
More lies, more cheats, more costs

And I can't let things bring me down
You have to remind me to live because   -Bridge

It's what I live for!
It's not what I die for!
It's why I came!
It's why I'll leave!
It's what I do!

It's where I've been!   -Chorus
It's what I say!
It's what I think!
It's all I believe!
It's in the things I dismiss!
It's what I live for!

What I live for!
It's what we all live for   -The Closer
What we live for

My Uncle Went to Travel

My Uncle was a borderline agoraphobic
He thought leaving the house was Catastrophic
Realised today he had turned 65
Made him realise he had done nothing with his life
So a new passion for travelling he began to thrive

My Uncle went to work on many 3rd world lands
Determined that he'd feel real pain on hands
Rejoicing in the pleasures with his new companions
Because meeting people on a different ethnic
Soon made him realise; school boy dramas are so pathetic

My Uncle laid down on the cold desert floor
Looking up at the stars hoping to go on a little more
See the fear of the unknown had begun to excite him
Trying out unusual places to try different food and drink
Smoking new things to create nothing else to think

My Uncle came home with a fateful illness
His close friends asked: "why did you do you this?
See the doctors have not given him long to live
He replied: "I could have waited for death safely in my bed"
"But then I would have already been dead"

How can someone so shielded and irascible, write about being so free, so passionate towards life and love? What if he wants to be loved and free? This explains the writing, he writes about the parts of himself, which he cannot express in the open. It's the only way he knows how. It came to Brooke's attention, that Bass had been watching her whilst reading through his journal. After closing it, Brooke places it back on the stand.

Bass wanted to scream, expel Brooke out of the room and evict her from his life but he was engulfed with worry. He had not shown anyone his work before. *What does she think about it? Would she hate it?* Having to clear his throat to softly ask; "What do you think?"

Brooke paused for a few seconds before she responded "In my own opinion, has an English teacher. The poem lacks a curtain rhythm that poetry has. Albeit, it was deep, heartfelt, I enjoy anything about travelling. Have you ever left this country?"

"Once in Cambodia but I don't want to talk about it."

That's no surprise. "Why does the poem end with him dying? I can assume the answer."

"It's everyone's inevitable end. We are all going to die, I only hope that, I don't come back has a ghost, and be at true peace, vast asleep."

"I surmised you were going to say that. The song gave me a thrill, relatable lyrics and I can just imagine you on stage with an acoustic guitar while singing ardently."

"I wouldn't like to be in a band, I would be an absolute control-freak over the music."

"In conclusion; I believe you have done some good work and you should not be ashamed or feel self-conscious."

"Thank you, your honesty actually means a good-deal."

Brooke smiles at Bass, he inhales a deep breathe.

"Do you have anything about Pandas?" Brooke asks

"Pandas?" Bass frowns.

"They are so adorable, one of my favourite animals in this world"

"I thought an intelligent woman such as yourself wouldn't be so easily swooned by such creatures?"

"How could you not like them? Do you not agree, that they are cute?"

"Anyway, Brooke. I was just on the phone to Julian Green, a Mental Health Nurse. I've arranged to meet him so I can interview Bartholomew Maithes in the next hour. While you go to the hospital and check on the mysterious stranger with dark black eyes."

"Who?"

"Apparently a stranger was seen outside The Dive Bar, naked and passed out, on the day of Jenny's murder. It's probably nothing but thought we could check it out."

"Did he go into A and E?"

"I presume so."

"I suppose we can cover more ground if we split up."

"Exactly, then we could see Chelsea and Mark. Where do the kids hang out? Outside the local shop? Or at the park with a bottle of cider?"

"Goforcoffee, School finishes at three thirty, we can convene there at four thirty?" suggested Brooke.

"Good idea, hopefully, Jenny's boyfriend Mark will be there too and that will save us some time." *especially when Jenny's body is being buried in two days and still he's not examined it.*

"You could use the back up."

"Why? I've managed to survive on my own my entire life. I can handle a couple of moody teenagers."

"How can I put this more delicately? You need to be more like-able. You might get more information out of the locals, if you were to be hospitable."

"I'm not here to be anyone's friend, Brooke."

"A little effort can go a long way. Keep a flowing conversation; you might be able to discover more."

"This is why you're still around, come on, we need to go."

Chapter 28

It's Chelsea Hearts first day back at school, after having a week off for grieving, two days before the funeral. What a joke? Currently walking down the school corridor, feeling many eyeballs staring causing more resentment towards the "fake" people who surround her. That two-faced bitch, Amanda, has just invited her to a party tomorrow night, in honour of Jenny. *Amanda was not her friend, I was her friend. It's merely an excuse to get drunk while her parents are away.* Chelsea's thoughts turned to the past, remembering the times when Jenny always went to her friends parties and literally had to drag her unwilling friend along the way. Why? She would wonder off talking to everyone, never drinking too much. Whilst her anti-social friend would sit in the corner and purposely get too drunk alone before ditching the party to hang out with her older mates, and her boyfriend at the time; Blake. Jenny never liked that crowd, she always said they were trouble and had a bad influence on me. Of course she was right, but at the time, it was if they understood Chelsea more than anyone else. *I guess my best friend was just looking out for me. As she always did. I was the one holding her back. How do I repay her now? By having a crush on her boyfriend.*

During lessons, she would sit at her normal desk, as the teacher spoke, no words were to be heard. Chelsea's mind was somewhere else. *I'm literally the worst friend anyone could have, she would have been better off without me. Everyone's better off without me.*

Chapter 29

A man in his early thirty's, still fortunate by looking like he's still eighteen. A "man-child" some call it. Short ginger hair, matches his blue eyes and freckle's on his youthful face. In his hands, he's holding a set of keys, one of which is to open the door to flat number six, beside him. He's waiting for a Private Investigator to appear, *I hope he understood the directions I've sent him.* Julian Green thought. *Why does he want to interview Bartholomew? He doesn't have anything to do with the Jenny Woodfield murder.* The more Julian thinks the more concerned and anxious he becomes.

Bass walks up the one flight of stairs, trying to catch his breath, dreading about his fitness declining, too much drinking and smoking, that's what it will be. He's not eighteen anymore, not like this guy in front of him, wearing a cheap suit with no tie.

Julian greets the new arrival with a friendly smile and a handshake. "Hi there, I'm Julian Green, Leading Mental Health Practitioner of Staysafe. We spoke on the phone."

Bass doesn't accept the offer of the handshake, "I'm Bass."

Julian awkwardly retracts his hand, "Like the instrument?"

"Yes." Bass lies, cannot be bothered to explain the story of how his ex-colleagues at the station called him "Bass" because of his second name: se-BAS-sti-an. It's really like the fish.

"May I ask, what do you need with Mr Maithes?"

"It's confidential."

"Well due to the Mental Health Act, two thousand and seven, I will be speaking has his advocate. So any decisions will go through me."

"He's not of sound mind? Then why is he living in a flat on his own?"

"We at Staysafe support independent living. We have specially trained carers that check-up on our service users living independently regularly and an emergency response team on stand-by."

"Will we be needing the emergency response team?"

"Bartholomew has been making signs of increased progress. Taking his medication daily, admitting he knows the voices in his head aren't real and receiving Cognitive Behavioural Therapy."

"Has an ex-policeman, I know some knowledge of Mental Health."

"Although the murder of Jenny Woodfield had an effect on his behaviour."

"Did he know Jenny at all?"

"She had done some voluntary work for Staysafe, last summer, she served and cooked him meals."

"Is that safe for a young girl to do, alone?"

"She never stayed long, mainly just delivered food that she prepared at home, if he were to get violent, then I advised her to not interact and call us immediately."

"Has there been many violent incidents?"

Julian had an epiphany, albeit, a disturbing one, "One of my colleagues, was staying overnight, "sleep-in's" we call it. Around six in the morning he had an episode. It took four guys to restrain him, it lasted a good hour."

"When was this?"

"It was the morning Jenny Woodfield was murdered."

Bass's eyes lit-up, he couldn't have possibly committed the murder himself but how could he have known? "Let's go and have a talk to him."

Julian placed the keys into the lock and opened the door, an unbearable, nauseating smell crept out of the door causing the pair to cover their noses and mouth with their hands. The stench made Bass fear for the worst.

Inside a small, dark corridor, Bass noticed that mould was beginning to form in the wall. "That's one way to catch leprosy." That wasn't the first thing that stood out, Bass saw an unsettling amount of crosses hanging on the wall.

To the right of Julian, was the bathroom and he seen the source of the foulness, which clogged up their noses. The toilet has not been flushed for an aeon. A circle of flies hover around their enjoyable feast of piled up faeces that have risen over the actual seat. Darkness dominated the small flat as all the curtains and blinds remained sealed shut. There was some light escaping from beneath a closed door which gave some direction to where Bartholomew may be.

Bass and Julian entered the living room, brightly lit by candles, the melted wax fore-gathers on the rims of the handles before burning the dusty purple carpet.

Julian always known that he kept a Sign of The Cross in each room, but there was about a hundred hung up or drawn onto the wall.

Bass can see a skinny man, with long grey hair, wearing nothing but what looks like a ripped bed-sheet, tied around his waist to cover his modesty. Bony ribs pointed out of his hunched and spotty back. Bass approached this man with great vigilance, his heeded eyes were full of wariness but he spoke amiable; "Hello, Are you Bartholomew? My name is Bass and I am here with someone you know: Julian Green. We are here to help."

The elderly gentlemen turned around, he was murmuring something from beneath his long grey beard. Bass paced his steps before staying at a safe distance. Bass reads the tattoo across Bart's cadaverous chest it reads; "Jesus Is Our Saviour."

A cowardly Julian Green preserved a safe distance in the back of the room; he whispered to Bass "What's he saying?"

Bass didn't reply, he was too unsure himself, probably replying to the voices that communicated to Bart within his own mind.

"I'll go outside and discreetly make a call to the response team, take him to hospital, get him back on his medication and make sure he doesn't die of malnutrition." Julian jokes although there was no humour in it.

When Julian walks out the room, Bass is startled when Bartholomew looks at him directly in the eyes, no longer muttering something beneath his breathe, he spoke clear-as-day; "Carl..."

How did he know my first name?

"Carl Sebastian, You cannot let blood enter the garden."

Bass fell onto his knees, so he was at level with Bart, fidgety and confused. "What did you say?"

"Don't let blood enter the garden." Bart repeats.

Bass grabs his scrawny shoulder. "How do you know my name?"

Bass can feel the presence of Julian re-entering the room, he looks over his shoulder to confirm it was him and when he returns his apprehensive eyes onto the unfortunate Schizophrenic sufferer. Mr Maithes was reciting phrases, religious ones, possibility from the bible but it was unclear to Bass. Assured that he won't get much of a response from Bartholomew, The investigator decided to leave his questions for another day, when he will be more "with-it." Still not unsatisfied with his lack of answers; *did he really know that Jenny was going to be murdered that morning? Is that why he was in such a frenzy? Also where or WHAT is the garden? Maybe it was all just delusional ramblings from a mad-man. It's the only thing that makes sense."*

Julian Green locked the door behind himself and Carl. Placing the big selection of keys back into his trouser pocket. "The response team are on their way, we're going to take him to the hospital shortly."

Bass was pacing up and down the corridor furiously; "How could you let that happen?" placing the blame onto Julian.

"I don't know, our company; Staysafe isn't just placed in Holders Bridge, we cover two counties and Holders Bridge is just one small town within them two. We have a big area to cover and Holders Bridge is not always a priority."

"It's typical, young men and woman getting into jobs within Care but yet no one actually cares about anyone."

Rage built up within Julian, fortunately he knows how to place his anger in line, and he's had plenty of experience when it comes to confrontation. "I care a lot about the people in my charge, I admit, I will *personally* find out who's responsible for his care visits. He was doing so well."

"Yeah, until Jenny Woodfield was murdered."

"I believe the whole town is pretty shaken up about it."

"So I've heard. It's still no excuse, that man needs help, he needs to be put in a mental hospital. *You've* let him down." Bass jabs his finger into the smaller man's chest.

"Don't you think, I feel bad as it is?"

"You're just living proof to the fact that; people let you down. Even when people are at their most vulnerable." Bass reflected some of his personal issues while he accuses Julian even further.

Julian can see that Bass isn't just talking about people has a whole; he's coming from a personal experience.
"Maybe it is you, who needs help."

Bass storms off, clenching his fist "I don't need help." reassuring himself while charging off.

Chapter 30

It's a small town, everyone in Holders Bridge tries to get along with each other, so it's no surprise to Brooke when she can see A and E virtually empty. Apart from Mr Marshall, lying on a trolley, with a bandage over his head, he must have had another fall, the silly old fool. Brooke waved hello politely before spotting a nurse, a pretty, dark brunette in a white uniform with dark black tights, currently filling out some paperwork.

"Excuse me, nurse."

"Hello Brooke, how can I help?"

"Over a week ago, the night when Jenny Woodfield was murdered, a man was brought in, a possible overdose victim; I believe he stripped off all of his clothes."

"Oh yes, we do get a few people coming in for drunk and disorderly behaviour. He was different, and I don't mean to sound so unprofessional but..." The nurse whispered something that may have broken The Data Protection Act "... He had an enormous penis."

"That's... good to know" Brooke responded awkwardly.

"Oh yes, he was very handsome, tall as well."

"I am working with a Private Investigator to help solve the murder of Jenny Woodfield."

"Do you think this man was involved?"

"More than likely, it will be nothing, just checking up on a very thin lead."

"You have to see Dr Patil; he's at his secretaries' office."

"Can you take me to where he is? If you have the time."

"Yep, please follow me."

"It is very much appreciated, thank you."

The nurse led Brooke to a grey lift, "I'm afraid it's on the other side of the hospital, the quickest way is to take the basement."

The woman entered the lift, it descends to the basement and when the doors open to a long, pitch-black corridor.

"Are the lights broken?" Brooke has had enough nightmares in the dark; she remained guarded as she cautiously steps out of the lift. A small light on the wall instantly flicked on, which briefly frolicked Brooke.

"They work by motion sensor, in order to save the hospital some money."

"I bet this corridor gets a little spooky at night?"

"It's creepy, I would go outside and take the long way round, but I can't wear my uniform outside, it's policy."

The girls walk along the corridor, with a light switching on, once every three to four steps they take along the way. Eventually they reach the opposing lift doors.

"They don't last very long." The Nurse pointed out. Brooke can see what she meant; all the lights in the corridor were off by the time the lift doors shut.

The Nurse has taken Brooke to the secretary's office, there among the female's behind their computers is an Indian registrar, leant over the wooden desk, with one hand behind the back of his rolled-up-sleeved, red shirt and the other hand is placed on top of the workspace for balance. "Dr Patil, this is Gail Brooke. She wants to ask you a few questions about that naked, sexy, man that rolled up last week. The one with the extraordinary dark eyes." The Nurse turns to Brooke; "I have to get back to work. Are you ok getting out?"

"Yes, thank you for your help." Brooke acknowledges the Nurse's time before she proceeds to her duties.

"Yes, Well I can't really break patient confidentiality" He remonstrates whilst sitting himself up and using his index finger to push back his glasses.

"You are obliged to, if it involves a murder."

"Are you a police woman?"

"No, I am with a Private Investigator. I just would like to know more about this newcomer, this unfamiliar stranger, who mysteriously appeared, completely bare. On the day Jenny Woodfield was murdered."

Dr Patil took Brooke to one side away from potential busybodies.

"I do not see the link but there is something, something, strange about him." The Doctor said with a lower tone as if he didn't want anyone else to hear. The quieter she got, the more Brooke was lured in. "You know how most people, passed out, unclothed, outside a bar, would be under the influence of drink, hallucinogenic drugs or narcotics?" The Doctor was whispering by now.

"Yes." Brooke replied, questioning where the Doctor was going with this.

"Well his toxic report came back negative."

"Are you suggesting that he decided to take a nap whilst fully nude at his own comprehension?"

"It gets more bizarre; I sent a sample of his blood to the Pathology Lab and somehow his blood doesn't belong to any group. It is not A positive, B negative, or anything. The machine comes up with an error message, every time."

"This cannot be plausible. Notwithstanding the fact, that, I have seen some far-out incidences recently. Have you tried another machine?"

"I did, I sent it off to another hospital the following day and the results came back the same, just an error code."

"Where is he now?"

"I don't know, on that night, I went to get the consultant, I could not find him. So I came back to phone the on-call doctor for a second opinion and the guy disappeared."

I have to tell Bass. "Does anyone else know about this?"

"No, I've not recorded anything, I'm worried people will laugh at me for incompetence, casual gossip within this town, tends to go along way here."

"I know that feeling, all too well."

"He's probably just a drifter, no one else has seen him before and it may be unlikely I will see him again. So please, can you keep it quiet?"

"For now but I cannot keep a promise. Not if it helps solving a murder."

"I completely understand."

"Your valuable time is much is appreciated Dr Patil." She credits before walking out the room and heading back to the lift.

The symmetrical polar grey doors slide apart. The darkness of the basement corridor still kept Gail vigilant. Brooke had a minute strain of claustrophobia within her, although the tunnel itself isn't that small, the thought of being trapped underground was terrifying. The silence was nerve-racking and the gloom was fearsome. Although aware the lights will come on when she starts moving, the difference between this time and the last; is the fact, she is on her own. So she thought...

She moved quite quickly towards the other end of the eerie tunnel, every two steps or so a small light on the wall would be summoned by her movement. Why have I chosen to go back out this way? She asked herself, out loud. The pace was picking up, turning on the small row of lights quicker and quicker each time. The sound of her own short breathes and the footsteps resonating off the walls, the echo brings triumph over the silence but didn't change the uncanny atmosphere. Brooke tried not to think about the possibilities of being buried down here. "You are a big girl now, no need to be so deliberating." The lifts that will ascend her appeared before her eyes. Brooke senses something moving behind her, she becomes stationary. Leaping into a U-turn, praying to be wrong, and praying that the mixture of the claustrophobic darkness was playing tricks on her mind. Yet there was *something* there, one of the lights was switched on at the other end of the corridor, it would have flickered off by now because all the rest are off, and she can only walk in one direction. Either there is an electrical fault and the motion sensor had broken, or the ghost has returned again and is standing in front of that one particular light. If it was Jenny's ghost then she should be able to see her, like Bass said, if Jenny is back from the dead, it is to warn her, not to cause her harm. Though there is nothing there. Brooke had stood in the same place maintaining a watchful eye for too long that the light beside her had caused to flicker. Just before the English Teacher continued the process of escaping; on the opposite end of the supposedly "empty" tunnel a second light came on, then the third light. This confirmed something was moving, and it was coming towards Brooke. She fled to the lifts, constantly hitting the call-button with the palm of her hand. "Come on!" She violently screamed at the lift. It was arriving, slowly, as the fear caused her heart to beat and her mind to race, time had slowed down. Spinning her head around again, the trail of lights approaching Brooke were appearing, the fifth one flickered on, then the upcoming two. The following light turned on, quicker than its predecessors. Brooke practically fell into the thinnest opening gap of the doors. The ninth and tenth light practically at the same time, so did the eleventh and twelfth, meaning whatever was coming after her, is moving faster. Brooke was punching the close-doors button with her the side of her sweaty fist. Then smacked the next level up. Brooke, hunched, panting rapidly, grasping one hand on a rail, staring helplessly between the gaps of the leisurely closing doors. The "Nothing" was flicking on the lights within milliseconds, one after the other at an alarming rate. Whatever it is, it's running down the corridor. When the last light is shown, it will mean, whatever's chasing Brooke will be in the lift with her. Just before the doors fully sealed shut, Gail has a glimpse of Jenny's face between the doors.

Brooke makes it out to the ground floor, collapsing out of the lift, disturbed and traumatised, trying to gather her own breathes and thoughts, has her blood pressure begins to descend. She slowly walks out, taking short pauses after each step. Fortunately there is no one else around, to see her, the graciousness of the nurses and probing locals will soon rush to her aid. Then she would have to try and explain what happened, not even Brooke will be able to do such a thing. She needs Bass, now longing to feel safer, securer and for someone that may actually believe the events that just occurred.

Chapter 31

Clouds have claimed victory over the glowing warmth of the sun. The outsides exterior exhibits the insides of Jack Mill and his own dark thoughts His buried *secret* has declared victory of his internal geniality and clouded his warmth. Conflict is the cause of his recent insomnia. His heavy head dangles over the wooden bar inside his brothers' bar, The Dive, feeling as ugly as the gargoyle-like position he's hunched in. Frank Mill comes back from changing the barrel. His little brother straightens himself and puts on a big smile.

"Do you want another drink?" The landlord asked.

"Yes, lager please?" The comedian replies.

Frank Mill pours Jack a "freebie".

"Frank, I don't think I'll be able to do the charity show for Jenny Woodfield."

Frank's concern widened, not for his little brothers sake but one for his business. He would lose a lot of money if the charity night gets cancelled. "Why not? The town needs a good laugh, especially since it's the night after Jenny Woodfield's funeral."

"Exactly, it's too soon, some customers might not be in the mood to have a laugh..." Lord knows, he isn't in a laughable mood. The jokes he's recently thought of feel too forced, unfunny, and unwilling. Some have even grew darker, as if he's gradually moving into black-comedy territory and that's not his style. "... I'm not really in the mood to do this show. I don't feel funny."

Frank leans over the counter to look at his brother in his eyes, completely missing the despondency inside them. "Look, this isn't a time to be so soft, I know you probably don't *feel* like it, but this whole town needs you, I need you to do this. We all do things we don't want to do, but we have to man-up, that's what we Mills do."

Frank walks away to mingle to a table of four older gentlemen, sitting in the corner of the room. Leaving his brother to dwell upon the emotional blackmail, that's laid upon him. Jack hated how his big brother used the word "I" when he said "I need you." THE PRESSURE. The famous comedian is stuck in turmoil, too uncertain he's able to perform. Why should the burden fall upon him? Why is it his responsibility to enliven the whole town? Is everyone quickly wanting these dark times to elapse? It's unfair, he's no saviour of the people, not when he can't even diminish his own pain. Jack Mill finds some easement in getting merry.

Chapter 32

Bass is staring at the woman sat opposite him, struggling to accumulate a sentence that would offer consolation. Brookes head bowed, her expressionless face looking into the cup of black coffee. Strands of her knotted hair broke loose and now dangling by the side of her soft cheek. After she recalled the day's events, stillness was the atmosphere. Goforcoffee was quiet, the young lad behind the counter was half asleep, unprepared for the upcoming rush hour of students that were already making their move.

"Have you heard of a place called The Garden?" Bass asked, hoping to gain more insight as well as breaking the silence.

"Are you referring to a Garden Centre of some sort?"

"No. At least, I don't believe so. I saw Bartholomew Maithes, apparently his condition deteriorated since the day of Jenny Woodfield's murder. He told me, and I quote. "Don't let blood enter the garden." Can you make sense of that?"

"I am afraid not."

"There's no Garden in Holders Bridge?"

"Mainly farms or a park which is conjoined to the side of the dirt track."

Bass shook his head unbelieving the possibility of the options. "Perhaps it was just mere ramblings of a madman"

A few people enter the door, the sound of teenagers roaring into the coffee shop, talking aloud, crashing against the tranquillity, Causing both Bass and Brooke to look up.

"Are they here?" Bass's referring to Chelsea and Mark.

Brooke is navigating her search from her seat. "I cannot see either one of them."

"I imagine you're good with faces, I'm not, and I once introduced myself to the same person at least three different times."

"I am actually surprised that you even introduced yourself."

"It was for work purposes. Is there anything I need to know about Mark or Chelsea?"

"Chelsea has only just recently cleansed herself from a cocaine addiction and has now taken the path of sobriety. She has always been a feisty girl, strong, wilful but a misfit. The attitude had taken a turn-for-the-worse when her mum became ill."

"It's her own fault for misusing it."

"Her mum was dying, Bass." Brooke expressed.

"Everyone loses people they love, you don't see everyone else taking a bump to get over it. I suppose I am lucky in that respective."

"How?" Brooke asks.

"Well, I'm not really close to anyone, so, I don't have to grieve. The sad truth is that... everybody leaves."

Brooke grew concern for her companion, though she understands him a little more, stranded by his parents, guessing, from such a young age has caused deep routed trust issues. He will never get close to anyone because of the fear of being abandoned again. His attitude pushes people away before he has the chance of getting close to anyone. "Easier to hurt than to be hurt" Gail thought.

"Tell me about Mark Bell." Bass stirs away from his personal issues.

"He is such a lovely boy, very handsome, avid on his fitness, although dim. He and Jenny were such a cute couple."

"Do you think he hurt her? Physically?"

"No, Mark would not hurt a fly, literally speaking. He never killed a spider, always through them out of the house."

"That doesn't necessarily mean he wouldn't hurt his girlfriend." Bass stated.

Chelsea and Mark walk through the door, shoulder to shoulder. Bass and Brooke watched their journey from getting a coffee from the counter and then taking it to their usual spot, the stools by the window. Brooke noticed that whilst the teens were waiting for the drinks to be poured, both of the youths hands were almost touching, like a magnetic pull, one which they were resisting.

Bass told Brooke to give it a minute before heading towards Mark and Chelsea. When they did, Chelsea was just informing Mark about the party that's "supposed" to be held in Jenny's honour and her much reluctant attendance.

"Mark and Jenny, this is my friend, Bass." Brooke introduces.

"*Friend.*" No one has ever referred to me as that." Bass mused to himself.

Chelsea giggled, "*Pfft.* Like the fish? Lame."

Bass retaliated "You must be Chelsea Heart. Aren't you a little young to have a coke addiction?"

Chelsea tensed her shoulders, her thin eyebrows pointed as she grew defensive "Excuse me. Who are you again? What I do is not any of your business."

Mark felt awkward and started fidgeting on his seat.

"Doing dust is a lot of fun though." Bass oddly nods his head for approval.

152

Brooke through Bass a look of disapproving frown.

"What!? It's all good, in moderation." Bass replied to Brooke then he turned to Chelsea. "However you never took it in moderation did you?"

Chelsea leaned back, her fierce eyes staring daggers towards this arsehole standing over her.

"Where did you get it from?" Bass demanded.

Chelsea leaned forward towards Bass's ungroomed face and said quietly behind her jaws "Go and fuck yourself."

Brooke intervenes "Now, let us start over. Chelsea we are only here to help. Myself and *Carl* are doing our own investigation into Jenny's murder. We were wondering if you would be able to help us." She speaks politely, maintaining peace.

Chelsea relaxes slightly although crossing her arms and giving Bass an inquisitive guise "Are you some-kind of detective."

"Yes a private one." Bass will refuse to mention who hired him.

"Wow." Marks lower jaw dropped with such amazement.

"If you want to know who killed Jenny? It was Shane Crewball. That's the guy who did it." Chelsea conjectures.

Bass turns to Brooke "Is that the creep who attacked you last night? In The Dive Bar."

The spark of interest caused Chelsea's eyebrows to rise along with her eye lids.

"Yes it was. But nobody in this town knows exactly where he lives. He covers his tracks, remarkably well." Brooke answers.

"Simon Cole has been trying to catch him for years; he's responsible for the coke flowing through Holders Bridge."

"Are you certain that he committed the crime for murder?" Brooke questioned.

Bass can't believe what she just said; "You're not defending this scum bag are you?"

"We have to be certain, we need concrete evidence, before we condemn this man."

Mark spoke out "I heard that he cut a man's hand off, just for going to his gym without paying."

"Then did he go out drinking with *Robert De Niro* and *Joe Pesci*?" Bass mocked, for Marks tone made the story sound like a silly unbelievable rumour.

"Of course he did it" Chelsea bawls. "Everyone knows it! I pleaded. No. I begged, on my knees, for Cole to arrest him." A pause followed. "But that joke can't do anything."

Mark aided Chelsea "We confronted Shane Crewball ourselves, he said nowt. We broke into his gym, trying to find clues-"

Brooke adjourns "You cannot break into his property. Do you realise how dangerous he is? Let alone the illegal implications?"

Bass supports her "You can't go around playing Fred and Daphne."

Mark looks puzzled "Why am I Fred?"

"Because you're too pretty to be Shaggy!"

Mark smirks, almost like he's bragging "You think I'm pretty?"

"Don't be so vain and self-absorbed." Bass, now yelling. He stopped to notice something else; he saw how Marks eyes were quite dark. Recalling what Frank, The Landlord of The Dive said, about the naked man, who was found unconscious, on the night of Jenny's murder. This streaker had the darkest eyes that he's ever seen in his life. The P.I saw how dark Marks eyes are, he imagines under the influence of drugs and poor street lighting in the night, may cause his eyes to be darker. "Mark, do you ever go drinking at The Dive bar?" Bass asks.

Mark has a slow reaction before answering "I don't really drink that much, I have been in, like."

"Did you go in on the night of Jenny's murder? You know, to blow off some steam. It would be quite understandable, given the circumstance."

Mark was just about to answer but Chelsea quickly rebuts "He was with me; that was when we both faced Shane."

Bass doesn't say anything in return; he suspects she could be covering for him, or for each other. "Where were you both on the morning of the murder?"

Chelsea and Mark both turned and faced each other, concurrently they returned their heads back to Bass. Chelsea spoke first "At home, in bed." Mark followed "Having breakfast with me parents."

Brooke asked "Can your parents both confirm this?"

"*Duh*, they already told the police. And you would have known this, if you had spoken to them" When Chelsea says "Them" it sounds like "em."

Bass returns to his interrogation towards Mark. "Did you and Jenny have any arguments?"

Mark begins to interlock his fingers, with both one elbow on the stool, the other on the window ledge. After shrugging his shoulders, he replies "No more than any other couple."

"None that got out-of-hand? Physically?"

Mark gasped, the very idea, the notion "I would never hurt Jenny. I loved her." He can feel his eyes began to well-up.

155

Bass sighed then looked towards the counter and the door that leads to the store room, unable to handle seeing another man cry.

The owner, Shelly Jayne and Simon Cole came out of the back room, having a very short "fumble" in the store room, insensitive to the half-asleep boy behind the counter for when it's the busiest time of day. Simon was straightening his shirt, tucking it back in his trousers. Shelly is checking out her reflection in the surface of the coffee machine, making sure her hair is neat and her newly painted make-up isn't smothered. The adulterer and the Chief Inspector noticed someone was watching, Shelly had never seen him before yet Simon had, The Private Paranormal Investigator he met the day before. He grinned waiting for this moment, the time when their paths met once more. Shelly put on a big smile, it unintentionally revealed embarrassment although the intent was to show that nothing happened or was happening. She noticed that Mark was wiping his eyes with a sleeve of his tracksuit jacket. Her caring side, a motherly instinct, took over and marched over to protect the teenagers, believing they were being harassed by this stranger.

"What's going on here? What have you said to this young man? Can't you see they're still grieving? Why don't you just leave them alone?" With every question Shelly enraged, came a crabby finger being pointed at Bass.

Simon strutted over with his hands in his belt, like a wannabe cowboy.

"It's *Officer Dibble*." Bass addressed Simon, by referring him as the cartoon policeman in Top Cat.

The kids were clueless to the reference, making Bass feel old.

"Look who's here, the Ghostbuster."

"Ghostbuster?" Chelsea questioned, her pale face looking confound.

"That's right, I've been doing some digging, your friend here, is not just a Private Investigator, he's a "Private *Paranormal* Investigator" a strange out-of-town weird-o, that doesn't need to be here, just scaring people for no reason. He's a joke..."

Bass felt humiliated but he remained calmed, over the years he's became accustomed to masking his emotions, maintaining a great poker-face, so he thought.

"... Me and some of the guys from the station read your book-"

"I hope it wasn't on the top shelf." Bass's criticising the Chiefs height.

"We all thought it was very funny, the way you tackled all those monsters and ghouls."

"I didn't think you would like it... there's no pictures."

Chelsea burst out laughing "Are you serious?"

On the other hand a very gullible Mark looks petrified "There's ghosts?" he gulped.

Brooke placed a hand on Bass's shoulder, "You never told me you had a book published."

"You never asked." snaps Bass, despite that he feels like he gained, somewhat, support from the teachers hand.

"What exactly are you doing here?" there was some reproach in Shelly's tone.

Bass couldn't speak nor find the right words, he didn't want to worsen the situation, not wanting to magnify the irrationality, inflame the folk's anger. If he said that Jenny's ghost was real, he would be crowned as the town's jester. Jenny's mourning school chums next to him would be furious over either one of the two things. The first; Jenny's soul is not laid to rest, not in a better place, if there were such a thing. The second thing; they would believe he is a pretender, using the murder of a teenager for his own profit. Brooke, beside Bass, wanted to scream that she even saw her ghost, how it plagues her days and nights. But too, was on the same wave-length as her partner. Choosing to carry on the burden because her friends, families, neighbours and Bass would be better off by keeping the truth hidden.

Their saviour came through the sound of a police radio. The Chief Inspector took the call in private, when it finished, he returned to insult Bass even further. "Trouble, down east, a kid's bike has been stolen. Probably by a ghost." Simon waves his arms by his shoulders, terribly impersonating a ghost "*Wooooo*".

"*Go get 'em tiger*" Bass says in an acidulous, slightly high pitch voice, badly impersonating a woman, *Mary-Jane Watson* to be exact.

Bass watches Simon walk out. Brooke noticed Bass looks more despondent than before.

Shelly returns to behind the counter to serve fresh customers.

Chelsea gets off her seat and drags Mark up with her by his hand "come on, let's go Mark."

Mark pleats, in a whiny, quite comically tone; "But what about the ghosts?"

Brooke blocks Chelsea's escape; "Promise me you will stay away from Shane Crewball."

Chelsea's blank expression, along with the deafening silence gave no promises to Brooke.

"If you do..." Bass pulls out his wallet from his pocket, opens it, pulls out a card and gives it to Chelsea "...If you ever get into trouble, don't be afraid to call me."

Brooke was impressed by Bass's protective side, even attracted to it.

She snapped it from his hands "I hate Simon Cole, he's as smart as an Orangutan. If I were to call someone, it would probably be you rather than him. That is, IF, I were to, I don't need your help."

"Don't pretend you've got it rough, you're not that hard."

"How would you know? You don't know anything about me?"

Bass grabs Chelsea white arm, sending a warning signal, a shock-wave through the rest of her body. With some might, he pulls the stroppy teenage girl a few feet away from Brooke and Mark.

"I know you live in a nice area, go to a nice school, and probably have a nice daddy with some nice friends to match. So don't walk around like you have nothing to lose." He was cautioning her, over how Shane Crewball could have Mark, her father and any other friend killed. Also comparing his background to hers, for he, was raised with no parents, gained no friends in his care home. To be brought up truly alone, in a rough estate, fighting to survive. Of course Chelsea knows none of this, sure a loner at heart, possessed a rebels spirit. Nevertheless she has people, an only child with a big house, and no comprehension to what it's like to have NOTHING. Chelsea grimaces, completely ignoring Bass and charges out, deserting Mark.

While Bass was admonishing Miss Heart, Mark was having a quiet word with Brooke over a personal issue. "Gail-"

"Please, call me Brooke."

"*Ahh*, I'm sorry, I forgot..." Mark apologises politely. "...Say, there's someone, who, *erm*, like-like's, someone but it's your girlfriends' friend. Even though, that someone's girlfriend is no longer here. She, *err... moved*. Would it be ok to ask them out?"

It didn't take much for Brooke to cotton-on what he was babbling on about, she smiles to how cute he's acting. "You are so sweet, if you want to ask out Chelsea, then, I personally suggest, that you would patiently wait a fortnight to wash over the remnants of Jenny's funeral."

Mark's bewildered, like a cat looking towards headlights. "*Wha-*"

"I would wait two weeks till after the funeral. If it still does not feel like the right time, then cease the offer of a date, till the time is right."

After watching Chelsea leave abruptly, Bass walks over to his companion and Mark, eavesdropping on the second half of their conversation.

"No one cares about your school-boy/playground drama." Bass, audaciously commented towards Mark predicament.

A petulant Mark shoulder-barged the unfavourable "Ghost Hunter" as he bailed out.

"There was no need to be so brusque." Brooke commented.

"Remember, he is a suspect, not your friend." Bass whispered.

Bass walked over to finish off his chat with Shelly.

Shelly, saw the oath, lethargically walk over to her, jumping the que of customers, suddenly feeling obliged to justify her part-time lover, Simon. "He's a good man, you don't know him. You don't get the pressure he's under. The last time there was a murder in Holders Bridge, it remained unsolved."

Bass wondered why she felt like she needed to defend the Chief Inspector, he also spotted a handcrafted, wooden, fountain pen, resting in-between Shelly's fingers, the missing one from Simon Cole's collection, something, he's guessing, doesn't give to just anybody. Yet he remained on topic; "How long ago was that?"

"Twenty years. Simon's a good man, he just doesn't want history to repeat itself. The whole town hated Sam Peterborough, who was the Chief Inspector at the time, for his failure to capture the culprit. You see, we never get any murders here, we're a strong community. Myself and my husband, Richard, have travelled to many cities for his business. Those places never take care of their own. So you can imagine the outrage I had, the whole town had, when someone had committed such a dreadful act towards a neighbour of ours. Especially to my sweet friend; Jenny."

All Bass registered from her rant, was the fact she was married to someone else yet it looked like herself and the Chief Inspector were playing "nooky" in the backroom. A fact he could perhaps use towards his advantage? Not caring about how high she placed her friends and neighbours on a pedestal. If she wants to carry on the illusion of living in a perfect town, where the people are really not out for themselves, that's her problem. "What happened to Sam Peterborough? Did the council force him to take early retirement?"

"No, he killed himself; he couldn't handle the shame any longer."

Bass didn't feel remorse, for he had not known the man. "Who was the person who got killed? Was it another teenage girl?"

"No, a retired man in his fifties, Billy Lane, they called him."

"Could you tell me more?"

"He was a miner, from the nearest pit village, he retired here because he said he wanted to live out the rest of his days somewhere quiet, peaceful, and beautiful. It's all I really know. The person, who knew him the most, was our vicar, Father Paul."

"Thank you." The Private Investigator concluded that this murder isn't relevant to the current one. Interesting enough to follow at some point during the investigation. "You mentioned Jenny was your friend..."

"She was my neighbour; I even saw her running, before..." Shelly paused, thoughts turning inwards "... before the incident."

"You were the last person to see her alive?"

"I was here, opening up, when it actually happened. Simon has already seen the CCTV footage. I would never hurt her, she's my friend." Shelly gulps "WAS my friend."

"Are you not thirty years older than her?" He was only guessing, giving the small tell telling signs of ageing behind her blue eye illuminator, and around her red lipstick, wrinkles had just began to appear. Parts of her body behind her green uniform and apron, we're not as firm has a younger woman's body, still no-less attractive.

"I am in my forties; I used to babysit her before I bought my own coffee shop."

"You own the place? I heard whispers that this place was going under? Is that true? I know what it's like going it alone; I left the police force to become a Private Paranormal Investigator. My own business struggles at times. You think you can succeed but blind optimism gets crushed by the cruel weight of reality."

"That's a depressing thought, Mr-" Shelly paused for Bass to tell his names.

"Sebastian, Carl Sebastian but my friends call me Bass."

"Mr Sebastian. My business did struggle for a while but an investment came through. My books are steadily coming through. As if by magic." Magic, had nothing to with it, she wonders, fearfully, she's made a deal with some sort of crossroads demon... or worse.

"Which investment?" Bass wondered.

"A small independent coffee company my husband recommended. It's all boring stuff."

"What does your husband do?"

"Richard, is an investment banker, he goes away on business a lot, makes a lot of money, has a lot of hands to shake. Etcetera"

Bass wonders if she's just with him for the money and is secretly in love with Simon because it's obviously not for his looks. "Was Richard in town on the morning of Jenny's murder?"

"No, he was at a meeting somewhere in Edinburgh, I can't remember." She was lying to protect him, When Shelly left the house, and her husband was still in bed, alone, with no alibi. Even though there's no love, she still cares about him.

Bass suspects, the slight change in her soft voice, indicates that this is a lie. He doesn't press, he'll find the truth soon, or the arrogant nature will make him presume so.

"Are you working tomorrow? It's just; I may have some more questions?"

"Sorry, I'm off tomorrow, chores to do around the house."

A plan fabricated in Bass's head.

"Can I help you with anything else?"

"No." Bass returns to Brooke, the only person he trusts.

"What did she say?" Brooke asked, now sat down on a stool, with one leg resting over the other, looking eager to leave.

"How about I tell you, over dinner?"

"Are you asking me out on a date?" Brooke smiles.

"No, I'm just hungry and quite fancy a sit-down meal before bed, I've not eaten all day."

This disgruntled Brooke. Though it baffled her because she found his pessimism and ego irritating, she still secretly wants him to say: "Yes, I'm taking you out." Brooke tried to respond as distantly as Bass does. "It depends on what you have an appetite for?"

"I'm the tourist; you know this town better than I."

"How about we get changed at the B'N'B and then we may act accordingly?"

"Good thinking, Batman."

Chapter 33

Night time has begun, Brooke is sitting in her car, parked outside The Robinsons Bed and Breakfast, waiting for her escort to come down. Bass walks out the front door, struggling to walk over the pebble stoned front drive in his shoes. Brooke thought her "*non-date*" looked very handsome in his suit trousers and white shirt with the sleeves rolled up. 'Tis a pity about his messy stubble and the beer belly, still does not look big enough to start popping buttons anytime soon. Bass entered the passenger seat of her car, he thought his date for evening looked gorgeous. She was wearing a lovely long purple dress that reached to her shoes, small silver sparkling earrings, and her blonde hair perfect tied back with in a bow. Black eye shadow around her soft green eyes, the contrast between the two, seems to create a perfect mixture. He wondered if she bulked up the courage to go back to her house to grab her things.

Brooke can smell a hint of whiskey behind his aftershave. She considers the possibility of him drinking beforehand, maybe to settle the nerves.

"You look stunning, Brooke." Bass complimented.

Brooke was charmed; "I suspect that is the first nice thing you have ever said to me."

"I bet it isn't. Shame you're not wearing a short dress though."

"Pervert." Brooke sounded as if she were disgusted. "Have you decided on where we are going to eat?"

"I told you, I'm a tourist in these parts. You choose."

"No, you decide."

"Ok. How about Chinese?"

"No, I am not really in the mood for Chinese."

"How about a curry?"

"I normally love an Indian but it does not agree with me. I believe we have a lot more work to do tomorrow."

"Ok, does Holders Bridge have a Thai restaurant?"

"No, there is only on Thai place here and it is not that great."

"Fish and chips?"

Brooke hums "No, not that."

Bass is becoming annoyed, his tone louder, "How about an Italian?"

"Too many carbs."

Bass now gritting his teeth, sighed with frustration; "Why don't you choose then?"

"No, I am letting you decide on where we are eating."

"Mexican!?"

"No, it coincides with the reasons for not having an Indian."

Bass now ready to smash his head against the dash board. "Just pick a damn restaurant."

"The Lockwood is a nice restaurant."

"Right! We're going there. Start the car." Bass screamed the command.

Chapter 34

The waiter in a bow tie, just brought Bass a bottle of lager and a separate pint glass, that would have been unutilized, if it were not for the stunning blonde sat opposite him. Across the navy blue table cloth and the folded white napkins, Brooke has just sipped her sweet, fruity, red, gin and raspberry juice from her round glass.

Bass never thanked the waiter for his service, he was too eager to hear the rest of Brooke's story, once she had finished supping.

"... so, then she told Gaz that I was sleeping with his brother. Obviously, a barefaced lie, a tall-tale manufactured by such an envious cretin. I am not that type of girl."

"What did you do next?" Bass queried.

"I smacked that bitch to next week." Brooke grinned, proudly.

Bass is perplexed that he was so fascinated by her story, normally he doesn't give a rats-ass about people's personal problems. He seemed to be lured in by her past accounts and astonished by her little mischievous side. "Gail Brooke, I can't believe you just swore, I bet there's a little devil in you."

"Well, in the estate you had to stand up for yourself-"

"Naturally."

"Once, a girl on my street had stolen my bike. I ran home crying. She was parading my little pink stabilized bicycle on my street, even in front of my house. My father saw me; I told him what had happened. I expected him to go and get it back for me, He told me to "go and get it back." Even at that age, I knew what he had meant, I hit her, pulled her hair, tackled her to the concrete below. I strolled my pink bike back to my house, feeling awfully guilty to what I had done, expected to get into trouble from my parents. But my father patted me on my crown and said "Well done girl, don't let anyone take something that is yours." With my new opponent squatting in her so-called house near mine, I was so fearful of her returning reprisal. I was unable to sleep that night, pondering if she and her comrades were manifesting some scheme to beat-me-up after school. However the girl respected me, eventually we became good friends."

"Where is she now?"

"I heard she went to jail, for reasons I am unaware of."

"I bet she doesn't speak as good English as you." Bass said whilst gently pouring his bottled beer into his glass.

"We do not have to be defined by where we come from."

"I agree. I too went through a similar thing; I got a plastic fire fighter lorry for my seventh birthday, the other kids in my dorm, beat me and took it."

Bass inhaled deeply, he felt so shameful for being too young, too weak, small and powerless. Embarrassed that he wasn't tough enough to fight for what was his, unlike his companion, who he hopes thinks no-less of him. He wants to be seen as strong, not someone who she needs to feel pity for, although she does. Brooke has so much commiseration for her ill-fated friend and proceeds to ask; "Is that why you do not possess much belongings?"

He was surprised she had noticed that; "I suppose so. Anyway! Like you said, it doesn't matter where you come from. Sure, I had a shit-hand dealt to me when I was young, but I couldn't grow up to be a low-life thief, murderer or a wife-beating drunk, like what other damaged people do. I wanted to grow up to be a policeman, to stop those arse-holes. Maybe, even take out my anger on some scum bags, who enjoy hurting smaller people. As the times changed that became harder to do. The worlds all too P.C. now." Bass engulfed half of his pint.

Brooke thought it was his way of saying he would like to protect people, those who were afraid and frightened like he were whilst growing up. Another question dawned on her; "How did you get from being a policeman to becoming a Private Paranormal Investigator?"

"I was partnered with a man named Mathew Horde. You can tell straight away, he didn't want a partner. Nobody else in the department liked him, he was a loner..."

"Like someone else I know" Brooke chuckled to herself.

"... I thought; that's fine by me. I don't really want to work with anyone. I noticed he was doing some *strange* stuff; he was looking for things that nobody else was searching for? Smelling things a lot, had all sorts of different gadgets that he purchased himself. He was looking for supernatural evidence. If there was proof that it was more of a natural cause then he wouldn't be interested. He taught me a few things; I carried on his work after he was killed by a vampire."

If Brooke was having a sip of her Gin then she would have spat out the contents from her mouth. "Did you just say *Vampire*?"

"Yes, they too exist, not in the way horror films portray them. They have a virus, one that's hereditary as well as infectious. It places people in a permanent half-life status by practically slowing down their organs. They need blood to keep the heart pumping not for food, they still need that, and yes, they CAN eat garlic bread. They can go near crosses and have a reflection in the mirror."

"Really?"

"They're made up of matter, why not. However they can't go in the sun, their body's dreadful immune system sees all sun-sensitizing drugs as an antigen. They are easy to kill; it doesn't need to be a steak through the heart."

"How would you destroy a ghost?"

"Fire, fire is what kills the ghosts. There might be other ways, ways that the fire brigade won't have to be called out, but that's the only one I know."

"What other mythical creatures and monsters be extant? Werewolves? Shape shifters?"

"I've not seen any of those, *yet,* I once crossed paths with a possessed doll, there was a witch inside, and it slowly tried to possess the boy who owned it."

"How did you manage to stop it from happening?"

"I set fire to the doll."

"What if a fellow-human was possessed by someone or something? Surely you cannot burn him, or her, alive?"

"I guess, it depends who that person is." Bass smiles.

Brooke laughs at his joke, *well*, she hopes he was joking. "You never answered my question."

"Truth be told, I don't know, might have to call for back-up on that one."

Brooke believed if she had not seen the ghost of Jenny Woodfield, she wouldn't have believed any of this. Then again, she and Bass would have never met. "Thank you."

Bass looks confused, "For what?"

"For answering some of my questions. I can tell how uneasy you are, when talking about yourself or mentioning your work."

A thought occurred to Bass, she was right, he doesn't tell anyone anything. Until now, it just flowed out, it felt nice. Nice to have someone he can actually discuss his past and vocation with, without fear of ridicule. The waiter returns to serve their meals...

Bass washed down the chicken and basil risotto, he had just eaten, with a second drink. Tiredness started to originate. He waited patiently for Brooke to finish her lobster salad before asking the waiter for the bill. Once the waiter arrived with what he ordered, Bass gasped in horror, his eyes pinned open and almost going into cardiac arrest after reading how unpleasantly expensive the amount was due. He placed his hand into his pocket to pull out his wallet. He through the right amount of notes to pay off his debt. Brooke looked up at him, "How much do I owe?"

"Don't you worry about it, dinner is on me."

"No, I would like to pay for what I owe."

"Money's not an issue."

"It is the principle, I insist on paying for my half."

Bass was impressed, "All previous dates I've been on, the girls have never even glanced at the case of the bill, let alone offer to pay. I got to admit Brooke, independence is an attractive quality." He withdrew half the English Sterling he placed and handed the bill over to Brooke, she then filled in the remaining gap. Closed the black leather book, before handing it back, to the smartly dressed steward.

"How many girlfriends have you had?" Brooke asked Bass.

"None. I've never been in a full time relationship. I'm always skipping from one town to the next, if you get my drift?"

Brooke had a troubling supposition; "So when you are finished here, in Holders Bridge, are you not going to stay?"

Bass never contemplated the idea before. "I haven't made my mind up" in regards to Brooke, the notion makes its way into likelihood.

"So, you never have been in love with anyone?"

"I don't think it exists, it's something we all like to believe is real. The thing we read about in books, watch in films, or listen to in music, that kind of deep; I-will love-you-forever, you're always on my mind, sort-of-love, is a fairy-tale. It just isn't plausible..." Bass levels his hand, mid-air, about eye-level. "The Chain of Connections goes from: Stranger..." he lowers his hand, to indicate he's going down a list of some-kind "...to Third-Party Colleague, Colleague, then to Friend, Friend to Close Friend; the kind that says I love you more than a friend, but not enough to date you."

Surely, he cannot categorise how people connect to others, or how they feel towards others, Brooke silently disputed.

"Then the sixth level of connections is; LOVING someone. The kind you date, have sex with, make good nostalgic memories with, spouts of mania occur, but that kind-of love wears off, like everything else, it diminishes. You get bored, or you slowly resent them for the rest of your life because you can't do what you want, when you want anymore. People still cling onto each other because they're too afraid to be on their own, too insecure, too scared to be independent, and because they were never attracted to them in the first place, they slowly build up resentment. Some people just use them for their lifestyle; the fancy house, money, flashy cars and other material possessions; yet, they still sleep with other people because they're not really happy."

"It is ambiguous for someone who has never been in a relationship." Brooke stated.

"I admit, I have never got past the colleague stage. But you can't look me in the eyes and say I'm wrong."

"There is a seventh level, a deeper connection. The kind of love where you REALLY love someone, the "fairy-tale kind." Where you sob your heart-out for days, after you break up with them. The one which motivates you remain faithful. The type, which places your partners interests first, above all else. Meeting that person who is determined to keep you happy, is the greatest sensation of all time."

"Did you love someone that way?" Bass enquires

"Yes, he was a terrible boyfriend."

Bass shrugged his shoulders, "Then, what was the point?"

"Yes, I fell madly in love with an arsehole-of-a-boyfriend, when I was young and naive. I firmly believe that I can feel that way about someone again, nonetheless, this time will be with a person who has mutual feelings. Thus, we can truly be in a team."

Bass admitted to himself, that she had a valid argument. He hoped for her sake that she was right. "I always believed the seventh step was the dangerous kind of love, the I-LOVE-YOU-SO-MUCH, and THAT-IF-YOU-EVER-LEAVE, I-WILL-KILL-MYSELF-OR-MURDER-YOU. The dangerously obsessive kind."

"You cannot try to delineate relationships between two individuals." Brooke perspective unaltered. "I have heard you say a lot of strange, unimaginable things tonight, but this one is the most unbelievable yet. Perhaps your scepticism comes from the quantity of music you listen to. I have seen the amount of sad slow songs, on your playlist, they all sing about heartbreak, loss, or not being able to be with someone due to self-doubt."

"I enjoy listening to them because the lyrics are real, and relatable to everyone."

"Maybe you just like to feel sorry for yourself. What about the songs about loss? Have you lost people?"

"I haven't been able to save everyone, no."

Brooke did not detect any remorse from his gruff tone; "What were their names?"

"Does it matter? They were clients; these things are going to happen."

"What if you fail to save me?"

Bass become furious, his agitated chest caused heavy breathing "I'm tired, let's go."

Brooke was vexed as well; it had been a lovely night, now ruined by his woeful state of melancholy.

The drive back to the Bed and Breakfast is short, but it will feel like they are both driving to the other side of the country.

Chapter 35

The night woke up many creatures, including the foxes, owls, even the small, adorable Dormouse, who preys the berries on the branches of the over-hanging tree, which shades the little pond in the garden of the Robinsons Bed and Breakfast.

Bass woke up on his settee, the one that should still be in the ragged ends of his last residence, Sheffield. A migraine too powerful to notice he is somewhere else. His throat and body craved water, he half opened his eyes to see that the kitchen light, around the corner, is already turned on. His head is so dizzy, that when he stood up, the whole room swayed from side to side. The motion sends him toppling against the walls. Walking in a drunken stupor, he makes it to the kitchen, using both his arms to rest on the door-way. Worn out, exhausted, muddled and thirsty, causing what he soon notices to be more mystifying...

To the left of the kitchen, is your usual white worktop that rests on top of cheap cupboards, cooker, an old washing machine, etc. To the right of Bass, is a long, square, wooden dining table and sat facing the wall is Carl Sebastian, *another version* of Bass, a sorrowful, woeful looking self, dressed in the darkest suit ever made. Sitting down, facing the wall, clutching a knife and fork in each hand. The cutlery is wielded on both sides of an empty plate. In order to return some perception, the Bass by the kitchens entrance, swipes his hand from his wrinkled forehead down to his chin, pulling down the rugged skin from his cheeks along with it. The agitated Bass looks at the miserable version of himself, observing something red on his chin, like some-kind of spilt tomato sauce. Sat facing towards the curious, stood-up version of Bass, sits Gail Brooke, she is unconscious, probably because she has been scalped, there is a bowl indicating where her brain should have been.

The good version of Bass, becomes protective, enraged for he now knows what's happened. The crestfallen version of himself, has literally ate away her mind and is far too sad and defeated to care. He has to get in there to save her from himself. Bass, in all his heartache, outrage, bangs on the walls side of the passage but he can't get in, a force is stopping him from entering the kitchen. He screams with all his might but not even sound can penetrate this barrier.

He wakes up.

Drenched in sweat, leaping from the chair he once slept in. Bass tripped up from the small blanket that's fallen on the floor. He had to make sure Brooke was alright. There she was, fast asleep, in the double bed. Like a guardian angel, he watched over her. "*This is probably the best night's sleep she's gotten in over a week. I best not wake her.*" Bass viewed. He needed a drink, first water then something stronger, for he won't sleep, not until his body gives in, during the early hours of the morning.

Chapter 36

Grey clouds reigned the sky, as it would do for the duration of the day. Bass left in the morning, before Brooke woke up. Following the hunch he felt since yesterday, now lurking in the parked car, near the police station, watching and waiting for Simon Cole to leave. Eventually he did, Bass trailed him to the butchers, most likely for a personal errand. Then pursued him to warn off a couple of teenagers outside a shop. His intuition eventually pursued The Chief Inspector to the assumed location; Shelly Jayne's house. Bass recalled her saying; she had the day off today, he had an inkling, Simon was going to "pop round", like the milkman would.

He watched the Inspector go in the house and waits patiently for the entanglement to finish. Bass was left alone with his thoughts and his phone. He sent Brooke a text message saying that he's sorry, easier through message rather than in person. He proceeded by asking Brooke to be more productive, by going to the local library to research any supernatural events that may or may not have occurred Holders Bridge. Also to explore old books, newspaper articles, the internet to search multiple paranormal websites and blogs. Something very selfish of the Private Paranormal Investigator, it's a job he loathes; his lack of concentration causes his mind to go blank very easily. She replied with a short, brief message; "Ok." It came as some relief to Bass; yet, Brooke still remained on his mind. *Has she really forgive him? Does he scare her? What about that dream last night?* He concluded to repress his depressive judgements, just on more, may push her away... *Then again, why am I so concerned with what Brooke thinks of me? Who is she to me?*

Casting his mind back, during the stake out, by the butchers, he saw someone that is similar to Brooke, the giddy feeling he gained, like a school boy. *Perhaps they could have done the job together.* Then recalling the disappointment, to find out it wasn't her. The same thing happened later, and this woman didn't even resemble Brooke. *Why am I seeing Brooke everywhere or hoping to see her? This can't be a healthy. Why should I care? After all, when I've finished here, I'll move on to the next place, leaving her and this town behind... right?*

His trail of thoughts was broken when he notices Shelly accompanying Simon out the front door. "There's no way he lasted two hours, after five minutes, he probably spent the rest of it crying, like a loser." Bass discriminates his "man-hood".

Simon adjusted his belt after dusting off his badge, walks towards his car. Bass vaults out of his car to block Simon's pathway, disquieting the Chief Inspector. "I think the whole town and the press might be interested to learn, the lead investigator to Jenny Woodfield's murder is having an affair with a suspect. Not just any suspect; the last person to have seen Jenny alive."

Simon knew what he was insinuating, but he detests being bullied, "You cannot stand there and blackmail me. DO YOU KNOW WHO I AM!?"

"I don't care who you are. You're going to give me what I want. Otherwise I'll start talking." Bass threatens.

"No one would believe you, an outsider, this town respects me-"

"Well, you don't want the town to lose respect for you."

"You have no proof."

"I have pictures." Bass lies.

Simon knows this isn't true, he bursts into laughter. "You don't have a photo of me."

"You do know how much this town loves to gossip?"

Simon spits on the ground, as a sign of respect. He straps his hands on the side of his wide hips, looking like he's contemplating his options. "What is it you want?"

Sounding reluctant, Bass thought "I want to see Jenny Woodfield's body and to read the corridor's report."

"Done."

"I also want everything you have on the investigation."

"No way, I can't do that." Simon protests.

"I just want to read it all, see all the evidence you have and read the interviews and statements you have."

"Ok, but I'll be with you, watching you."

"Deal."

Simon huffed a heavy exertion, "Follow my car back to the station, and then meet me in my office."

Bass watched him sulk off into his car, once the police car drove away, then will he.

Chapter 37

Simon Cole is sat on a spare chair, with his arms folded, begrudging and scrutinizing Bass while he reads his case notes and interviews on his chair, HIS CHAIR, HIS DESK. *How dare he? He was The Chief Inspector and he should get the respect he deserved.*

Bass read through the interviews of locals, finding nothing of any interest or relevance. Until he found out who discovered the body; *Father Paul*, who just so happened to be wondering out there, ten miles away from his church? "Did you know about this? What was Father Paul doing out there?"

"Praying." Caustically said Simon.

"This is serious; did you not find it at least suspicious?"

"What's the old man going to do? He's a man of the cloth."

"So? It doesn't mean that you should trust him."

"He wouldn't have called the police, if he had done it himself."

"You don't know that."

"He was just walking his dog. It's right there on the report."

Bass, thought he would interview the priest, to see if he really is a man of god. "You found no evidence? Not even her clothes?"

"There was nothing" There was a hint of embarrassment in his voice.

Bass surmised, Cole didn't want to appear incompetent; "I admit, me and Brooke walked Jenny's running route and we didn't see anything either."

This came as some relief to Simon, who's now observing Bass with his right elbow pointing down on the arm rest, his right index finger is digging into his temple. "Janet Woodfield told me Jenny was wearing her running gear."

"Then, where could it be?"

"God knows."

"Where's your morgue?"

"It's on the building, on the opposite side of the hospital, two streets down from here. You'll need my keys to access her cold chamber, top draw."

Bass follows the instructions, places the silver ring of keys in his pocket.

"Do you want me to come with you?" Simon offered.

"I'd rather receive a head massage from *Edward Scissorhands*." Bass crudely said in response, before walking out.

After reaching the building; Carl Sebastian was instructed by a short, cute nurse to go into the lift to take the next floor up. After doing so, the small lift ascends calmly before shaking, the entire grey box constantly rattles, Bass's now unsteady on his feet, quickly grips the hand rails by the mirror. Fear told him that the wires above were going to snap and he will plummet to his death. The whole of this metal tomb trembled violently and endlessly, it's screeching on the walls, unsettling. Even with his eyes pinned shut; he can tell the lights were flickering. Now on his knees, his breathing out of control, hugging the handrail, and pulverizing his teeth. Getting ready to fall...

The lift stops, still on the mucky floor, with his arms wrapped around the rail support, Bass opens up one eye. Only to discover an empty corridor lay out in front of him, on the other end is a door that's ajar. The humiliated feeling worsens, after stumbling upon used chewing-gum stuck onto the inside of his hairy arm; thankful to have kept his sleeves rolled up. Still alert, placing wary steps along the corridor, heading towards an unwelcoming door; a freakish sound was literally buzzing in and around Bass's large ears. For it sounded as if there was a swarm of bees, their uncanny noise reverberates throughout the hall. Bass scans the area, peculiarly; there was not one insect insight. *Perhaps there is a bee's nest in the vents or walls,* conjectured the Investigator. Still, it felt as if one landed on his cheek, with a slap, it would hurry-it away. Nothing was there, nothing to ward off, nothing on his cheek but a slight red mark. *It must have escaped.*

Bass entered the opened room, only more obscurity was revealed, for he sighted a room full of clocks, UNTOLD CLOCKS. So many different types: on the walls, the floor and some hanging from the ceiling. To which none of them were working, the second hands all frozen. He first saw a grandfather clock in the corner of the room; the time had stopped at seven thirty. A gold cartel clock on the wall stopped at nine seventeen. On the floor was a floral clock that had no numbers on. A binary clock that didn't make much sense Bass anyway. In the middle of the room, on the worn out/ slightly torn up green carpet, a disturbing dolls head clock that stopped at ten o'clock. A carriage clock with Chinese numerals stopped at what he could guess was; two thirty-five. A striking clock with Arabic numbers that stopped what may have been seven fifty-two. A cuckoo clock with the rooster hanging off the balance, it's tiny, wooden, painted face, looks as if it's lost the will to live or driven insane by not returning to its home, is Bass's concept. A digital clock flashing at eight thirty-three but the unearthly one he distinguished is how the sand in the hour glass is stuck half way.

Where the fuck am I? He had to leave; *it must be a practical joke. It had to.* Simon Cole has set this out, to freak him out. He hasn't got time for his games, where's the morgue. That dumb nurse must have sent him the wrong way.

Bass storms back to the lift, disregarding the sound of the invisible bees that resonates off the walls. Carl oscillates back and forth from re-entering The Death Machine that is a lift. "Where's the stairs when you need them?" After bulking up the courage, he stepped inside. Whilst traversing back down to the ground floor, Bass is terrified the lift was going to break again.

Once taking a heavenly step onto the solid, stable, ground floor, he found the nurse again; she personally escorted him (via the stairs) to the morgue. Exactly where she said; one floor up. *It must be in a different part of the building? What an unusual layout. What an unusual joke.* Bass told himself, overruling the most experienced, surreal moment by materializing a newer, more logical viewpoint.

Bass took the time to acknowledge the nurses time and effort to assist him because he never thanking her. In the cold, lifeless, hushed, morgue, alone, In front of him are three sealed cold chambers, only one of which has a padlock on. Bass moves closer to read the card in the middle of the silver door. In red felt tip pen, it reads...

JENNY WOODFIELD

D077994567236

D.O.B. 25/02/2001.

Bass unlocked the padlock, dropped it on the floor, heedlessly. After opening the silver door, he pulled out the long sliding drawer by the handle. Under the white sheet, Bass examined what is Jenny's body, just the body, she was not fully dead, not while her spirit still roams the earth. Straight away, the Y shape stitches on her pale body, from the autopsy, stood out before anything else. If there was anything else; no bruising on her body, the coroner report confirmed that she died from suffocation then from a broken neck. Also the tendons and ligaments in her arms, shoulders, legs, and spinal vertebrates were either fractured or broken. Thankfully, it was the neck that went first. She was strong, healthy, young and athletic. It must have acquired some great strength to snap her. So there should be some bruising on her skin, why isn't there any? They can't have snapped on their own, something must have done this, something unnatural. It doesn't make sense. Bass guessed, Simon Cole already knew, he's probably rejected the fact, claimed it to be untrue because he doesn't know what to make of it, after-all ghosts don't exist, do they?

Chapter 38

The libraries ready to close for the day. Even though Brooke had enjoyed reading about the history of Holders Bridge, there was nothing in the realms of the supernatural. No ghost stories, no conspiracy theories. Just an ordinary, run-of-the-mill, small, restful, town, in the south of England. As she prepares to leave the library and wonders why she has had no contact from Bass.

***

After making the funeral arrangements, all by herself, Janet Woodfield has spent the day glued to the TV screen, too scared to move, encase she drops something on her immaculate floor or makes a crease in the settee... or in the black dress she's wearing, ready for tomorrow.

***

Father Paul was in his church, making sure everything was in place for the funeral and rehearsing his words for the following day. Only having his German Shepard; Bruce, to keep him company.

***

Shane Crewball has been out of town for the last two days, with some "muscle" to collect his next *package*.

***

Jack Mill has been in bed all day, unable to move.

***

When the town have finished work for the day, they returned home to be with their families. In preparation for the funeral tomorrow; those people also include Clive Dunscroft and Little Bradley.

***

Frank Mill is serving customers at his bar, as usual. In between pouring the punters their pints, he's defrosting food for the finger buffet and wrapping up fresh sandwiches. Tomorrow afternoon will bring in a lot of customers, for The Dive bar will hold Jenny Woodfield's wake.

***

Meanwhile Chelsea Heart was at Amber's house; for a party "supposedly" in memory of Jenny Woodfield. People who Chelsea never even knew or talked to, would come up and hug her, offering her beverages, forgetfully omitting the past addiction. Chelsea believed their overbearing condolences were fake; they are only giving her attention because she was the closest person to Jenny. It's to make themselves feel better, less guilty, rather than have any regards towards her mourning friend. The party was loud, Chelsea hated the type of music, it was either grime, newer R'N'B stuff, with so little melody, it was nearly impossible to dance to, and someone talking nonsense in low-key. Other songs included someone attempting to rap over someone else's' tune, mixed in with a drawn-out bass, that would shake the walls. Walking from one crowded room to another, searching for Mark, at least then there will be someone to talk to. Underage pupils would talk about Chelsea, indiscreetly; one girl in a short dressed and low-cut top practically just put her hand in front of her mouth, telling her boyfriend, about the coke addict, as if Chelsea wouldn't notice. Then that same girl would smile, ear to ear. Chelsea wouldn't reciprocate; she didn't like her, and would rather brand this tart an "idiot" than give a false impression.

Rooms were becoming cramped with raunchy teenagers, drunk on vodka-pops. A lot of naive young fools, drank far too much, too quickly. Someone's passed out on the cream sofa. One girl had vomit down her black top. "Idiots" Chelsea again labelled her fellow school attendees. If she were to drink with her own friend, they would have enjoyed the whole night, listened to some good rock tunes, talked, not pass-out so early. Chelsea lent against the kitchen sink with her glass of full-fat-coke. Watching two fornicating youths near the fridge, hands all over each other, their kissing, so sloppy, far too much tongue, it was nearly laughable. The uncomfortable feeling of being an outsider was beginning to take its toll, rolling her eyes, *tutting*, unable to stay in the kitchen any longer. Shimmying through the thinnest gap between gate-crashers, college boys and teenage girls, she could feel eye's on her, paranoia was sinking in. *"Why am I even here?"*

She recognised Marks football team but he was nowhere in sight.

Chelsea took a drink of her coke, it was so sweet, and it tasted good, TOO GOOD. Chelsea lifted the glass to her nose, to sniff its contents... there was vodka in it. She had been spiked. Some bastard has done it on purpose, either for a joke or to "loosen her up." Chelsea knew what she must do, pour it down the sink... but it did taste good... no, think of the promise you made to Jenny... *Jenny.*

She's been so busy trying to solve her murder, there had been so little time to grief, the funerals tomorrow, TOMORROW.

How am I going to be able to get through it? When I can't even get through tonight?

Chelsea doubted herself, her mind folded inwards, into her own little world, she completely forgets about the other people in the room.

My best friend.

Water started to seep through her eyes, she can feel the whiter side of her eyes turn to red. She's the shit-friend, the screw up, while Jenny had a whole future ahead of her. It's the first time she cried since the news.

Why does Chelsea Heart get to live and Jenny, have to be taken away? If anyone were to deserve it, it would have been me.

Chelsea used her hand to clutch her light head and shook it side to side, like she's disagreeing.

Jeez, how much of this vodka have I had?

NOT ENOUGH.

She rushed to the kitchen, stealing everyone else drinks, whatever she can get her hands on, necking the entire loot, in order to completely blank out the mind...

Mark Bell eventually arrived at the party, once leaving the gym, the dinner at his parents' house was nowhere near ready, and he fretted during the wait, craving to line the stomach but didn't want to leave Chelsea alone at the party for too long. At his arrival, he was greeted by his drunk, affectionate, football teammates. There was a lot of; "*Ahh,* bro, proppa sad, b'owt Jenny, dude" and "You need owt, just gotta ask, innit." but there are some of his closer friends who gave him a hug and said, a simple; "I am so sorry for your loss, mate." Some of the girls wanted to give him a hug to bring comfort. Two different girls had other ideas to "comfort him." Mark declined them all.

"Thank you, guys. Have you seen Chelsea?" Mark repeatedly asked.

Until someone mentioned that some guy named Blake swung by and picked her up.

To his consternation, Mark knew where they were going and what they were going to do.

No Chelsea, don't give in, you've been doing so well. Please, think of the promise you made to Jenny. Mark implored.

Should he call the police? No, they would arrest Chelsea. His friends look too drunk and aren't as tough as they like to appear, they're still kids themselves. There was one number, he got from Chelsea...

Chapter 39

Bass was with Brooke; sharing the day's events. The only two occupants of the small dining room, in the Bed and Breakfast, sat opposite each other, over a candle lit small dining table, with a white knitted table cloth dangling down, almost touching the couples knees. "I could have spent the day reading and jotting-down the numbers of the clocks... but it would be too *time* consuming." Bass, making a dad joke.

Brooke laughed at how bad it was; "That was awful."

"That's why it's funny." Bass smiled.

Brooke thought he had a nice smile, it's a shame he doesn't do it much. "You should do a warm up act for Jack Mill, on his concert that is in Jenny's name?"

Bass resisted "There's no way, you'll get me on a stage. I kind of disagree with doing a gig just for one person."

"It is to bring the community together, to prove that we are united and strong. No one can push us down, we are one."

"Where's all the charity concerts for the hundreds of people that get murdered everywhere else?"

Brooke couldn't find an answer.

"We are not really "all one" really, we are all alone." It was a doleful sound from Bass.

Brooke changed the topic, wanting to keep the conversation light; "What do you fancy eating? We could share some spaghetti?"

"Like, lady and the tramp?"

"Can I be portrayed as a lady? I am not even wearing my dress tonight. I just wanted to be comfier in my jeans."

Bass was pleased that Brooke was so comfortable enough around him; she could wear her normal attire.

"I do believe that you do look like a tramp, you have not made the same effort as yesterday. The sleeves are still rolled up on your jumper and you lack the ability to shave."

Bass chuckles, his eyes lit up and so did Brooke's. The candle light made her green eyes sparkle. He was drawn into them, she too returned the gaze. Both completely lost in each other, speechless. A light burned bright inside Bass, it was a feeling he had never felt before, and he couldn't reject it, not this. A hint of pressure built up around his eye sockets. A warm, tight, feeling burst through the middle of his rib cage, making it hard to breathe. Both bodies became motionless, knowing that they should drop their gaze soon, neither one of them could. The light inside Carl burnt bright, slightly hurting, weakening his defences, and oppressive in a way. He felt as if, all of his insides just dropped onto the floor. Nevertheless he wanted more, he wanted her, needed her...

The phone rings.

Tension now broke, Bass exerted a heavy sigh, with frustration he yanked the phone from the pocket, slammed it on the table. It was an unrecognisable number, might be more work. Could it be something to do with this case? He answered "Hello.... Mark!?" His face expressed confusion. "Slow down... Where is she?"

Brooke detected panic in Bass's voice.

"I'm on my way." Bass hung up the phone, looked towards Brooke, "I have to go."

The panic from Bass transferred to Brooke, making her distressed; "Who is it? What is happening?"

"It's Chelsea."

"I knew that girl would get herself into trouble."

Bass stood up, necked the whiskey that was in place, for Dutch courage. "It's not Shane Crewball. She's fallen off the wagon and I'm meeting Mark to get her from her ex-boyfriend or something. Do you know where Sapp Road is?

Brooke rushed up onto her feet.

"Quickly."

Chapter 40

In a disorganised bedroom, on the edge of town, Chelsea Heart's bent over a smooth wooden desk, using a rolled-up twenty pound note to snort a line of coke; the rush, one that was sorely missed. Exciting, agitated, literally buzzing from this ambivalent feeling. Her mid-twenty year old, ex, Blake, is sat on top of his un-ironed, stained, blue single bed, his back against, the wall, though having to hunch forward because the flap of his baseball cap is pointing towards the back. His left leg rubs on top of the right, the material of his tight, skinny, black jeans rubbing.

"Don't you ever take your fucking shoes before you go to bed" Chelsea's repeatedly nodding her head, like she's agreeing to anything/whatever, while dancing to herself and scratching the nasal base.

"No, girl, shut your gob and get over here." Blake demanded, pointing his finger to the small vacant space on the bed, beside him.

Chelsea necked a bottle of cheap beer, to temporary quench the recycling dehydration. Climbing next to the gangster, she always thought tattoos were sexy, including his tribal one that ran from his neck towards his muscular right arm. It was clearly shown for he was only wearing a small, tight, black vest, a rugged stubble also tantalizes however his looked funny, it was a very thin beard that ran from ear to ear, crossing over the chin but no hairs on his cheek or neck. Chelsea didn't like it, having said that, the drugs and alcohol in her system made her lustful. She wanted it, rough, fast, hard; thrown about, even a slap in the face.

There was chaotic banging on the front door; killing the mood. The spooning pair on the small bed looked towards the commotion.

"CHELSEA, OPEN UP."

"Mark?" Chelsea jolted.

"Come on, let me in, I'm here to take you home."

"I'm gonna knock this cunt out." Blake flounced to the front door, the uncontrollable rage and adrenaline caused veins to pop out of his neck, shoulders and the steroid influenced muscles in his arms. A perturbed Chelsea is following behind. "Please don't hurt him, he's just a boy." He ignored her plea, recalling many accounts in the past, where she could never contain his troublesome temper.

One half of the door window was boarded up by wood, Chelsea could see a blurry Mark from behind the other. He could just make out a bleary image of her and Blake, in return. He hit the door repeatedly "Chelsea!" Mark shouted with grave concern.

Blake hauled the door open to scream in the smaller face of smaller Mark. "What do you think ya playing at!? You better leave now or I swear to god, I'm going to hit you." Blake looked like he was ready to use his curled hands, his scrunched angry face made Mark think of the word "Juggernaut" for some reason.

Mark wiped the spit from his face, looked over Blake's shoulder, under his shiny silver ear ring, to talk over the ex-boyfriend to Chelsea. He can see how dilated her eyes are. "Chelsea, we need to go, it's Jenny's funeral tomorrow."

"She's not going with you, pipsqueak." Blake told her saviour.

"You made a promise, how can you break it? Don't you care?" Mark evoked.

The use of emotional-blackmail antagonized Chelsea; she spouted so rapidly, it came out as one sentence, not even stopping for air, knowing she should have stopped talking but unable to help herself. "Piss off Mark I mean who the fuck are you anyway you're not even a real man you couldn't look after Jenny and you certainly can't protect me from Shane Crewball or anyone else at least

Blake is a man a man who is strong and knows how to please me you sure as hell couldn't please Jenny cause yeah us girls talk I bet you wouldn't even choke me like if I asked."

Blake is now feeling ten times more masculine.

"No, I wouldn't choke you, I could never hurt you." Mark replied.

The honest, sweet answer dumbfounded Chelsea, who's bouncing on the spot.

Blake blustered "See, she doesn't want you, so get lost."

Mark punched Blake on the side of his face. Chelsea gasped with astonishment, she spoke with her hands over her open-mouth; "Mark, I didn't think you had it in you."

Blake, erected quickly, his face red with blind fury, attempts to return a blow. Mark leaps back, lands steadily on his sober quick, light, feet. Blake's right swing resulted in accidentally hitting the door frame. Mark put his weaker side, the left side forward, bringing his stronger side towards the back, in order to perform a striking right hook. Blake was a bull-seeing-red, his state of enmity was relentless, he through countless jabs towards Mark, there was so many fists in the air, some unmethodical and aimless, he blocked and/or dodged most of them, till Blake lowered his elbow to parry a critical punch in Marks stomach. Mark bent forward, cradling his stomach, winded, beat. Blake felt the sense of victory and just as he was about to waltz back inside, to have his wicked-way with his gal...

A car slammed its breaks, inches away from colliding into the spoiler on Blake's car.

Carl Sebastian and Gail Brooke fling out the doors.

Blake dashes inside to bring out a bat, clutching the weapon with both hands, preparing the instrument to be used effectively by placing it mid-swing. Bass sees this yob, trotting towards him, so he instantly feels the need to poke fun; "Put that down and put your hat the right way round, you're not in a nineties boy band."

Brooke ran towards a red and bruised Mark, who is coughing his-guts-up. Whilst stroking his back, she looks up towards Chelsea, who looks scandalized by Mark's condition.

Blake flung the bat towards Bass's head, with some might; Bass caught the receiving end of the bat with his bare hand. Bounding behind his rival, bringing the bat with him, he began chocking Blake with his own weapon. Now struggling to breathe, his legs kicking in the air, Blake tried to use both his hands to pull away the bat from his crushing throat.

Brooke turned to Bass, terrified that he is going to kill him; "Bass!" She calls. "Stop it."

He continues to squeeze the life out of the thug.

"I said, stop it." Brooke yells, so loud all the street can here.

Neighbours had slowly begun to disperse from their homes to witness the drama.

Bass lets him go, Blake falls to the floor, now sat on the floor, kneeling against the brick wall, regaining his breathe and strength.

Brooke turned and saw the new found street audience, "Shall we go home." Brooke whispered to Mark.

Mark stood up, took deep breaths, pushed out his chest, gave an ultimatum "Chelsea, I'm going to drive home, come with me now or that's it, I won't see you ever again."

Chelsea ran to Marks side, she placed a hand on his broad shoulder, goes to jump into his arms, then last minute. Deciding, it's probably best not to hug him right now. She retracted her hand, looking remorseful and regretful.

Mark escorted Chelsea to his car. Brooke was apprehensive about Bass's tactics for pacifying his anger. She held the unwavering view; he was going to KILL Blake and confident he wouldn't feel guilty.

Bass felt a blow at the back of his head, when he hit the ground, in a semi-conscious state, he was transported *somewhere else...*

Chapter 41

Mark and Chelsea got into his dads, blue, low two seater, BMW Z3, convertible. They drove home, Chelsea crying eyes were looking out the window, towards the passing bright orange street lamps.

She looks towards the subdued driver, it appeared as if he were fully concentrating on the road but it was transparent to Chelsea, his mind was elsewhere. "Mark, talk to me."

Tears trickled down his face "Chelsea. I don't know what to say, I've never been good at words."

"I'm sorry; it's all I do, let people down. It's all I'm good at. I've failed you, Jenny, my dad-"

"You're dad doesn't need to know about this, you can sleep at mine."

"Thank you." She smiles, not that she feels like deserving his kindness. "I didn't mean what I said, earlier."

"So I didn't please Jenny in bed, it's probably why we never slept together much."

"You did, Jenny told me; she was lucky to have lost her virginity to you. It's true. I wish, I could have had a boyfriend who's as sweet, as loyal, as caring, as you. I choose arseholes, like you've just seen."

"The thing is, I like you Chelsea."

Chelsea moved closer to Mark, as much as her seat belt would let her. "I like you too, I know it's awkward, you being my best friends' boyfriend, an' all."

Mark turned to face Chelsea in the eyes, "Chelsea, I don't know what I would do, if you left me as well." There was something subjugating in Marks voice.

To Chelsea he sounded domineering; she had never seen a controlling side to him before.

Chapter 42

Carl Sebastian woke up on an echo of freshly cut grass. His head was pulsating, he groaned while awaking from the half-asleep, drowsy state. He pushed his sizeable hand out the smooth, bright green grass, so he can elevate himself up back up onto his rocky feet. It appeared Bass was at an astronomical sized, National Trust Garden, as far as the eye can see. Bass realised it was sunny, but just a few seconds a go it was night. How long had he been out? That Blake must have sucker-punched him, a cowardly attack from such a weasel. He doesn't mind being hit, but it should have been while facing him, eye to eye. The question remains... *How did he end up out here?*

Bass discovered an undulating path, he thought he'd best follow it and gather his bearings. It may lead back to Holders Bridge. Paying attention of the long trek, he perceived that not one bit of tall grass loomed over the edges of the path, so many miles of grass. Additionally, the previously past tree's never dropped a leaf onto the earth, he looked up at the shadowing branches, the leaves were greener than he'd ever seen, as if they never die here...

No, it can't be, it doesn't exist...

It must have taken many men to have preserved it so effectively.

Bass went off trail, trampling over the low-cut smooth green. There was a perfect circle of a plot of soil, in the middle was a flower, a single dark blue tulip, wrapped around a wooden pole. The next perfect plot of soil, in a sublime circle was an individual pink camellia, twirled around another wooden pole. Bass was very good at recognising flowers because when he was younger, one the carers, Mrs Fuller, had a great green thumb, a true flower enthusiast. While all the other miscreant kids in his home, were playing football, he would assist her in garden, absolutely loathed participating in team sports, besides helping her with the allotment was great escapism. Bass saw lots of other immaculate, dug up lands of soil, kindred to these two, he was self-confident that there would be different flowers in each one.

Bass could feel the warmth of the sun, even though he was not sweating, surprisingly, not with his jumper on. Looking up to the sky, there was no cloud in sight, neither was the sun...

Am I really... dead?

Bewilderingly, Bass slapped his own bare arm, feeling the pain

No, still here.

Assuming, if heaven is here, no pain shall be felt.

Bass walked, for what felt like miles, he came across, a pond, the clearest of blue waters, not an ounce of pollution or limescale insight. He saw many types of fish swimming in harmony. By the bank are a family of ducks, lovable, cute ducklings under their mothers' wing rubbing their adorable heads against the mothers' fur. Bass began to overthink; to him, they were not living in fear of predators, they could have even waddled towards Bass defensively, and accompany him without fear of being prey. They've managed to maintain an innocence that the adult world could not uphold. Conceivably it was an irrational notion, if it were feasible, it was to be here, in this garden.

"The Garden, Don't let blood enter the garden." Bartholomew Maithes voice came inside Bass's head, reciting an old memory.

"Hello there!" A welcoming voice came from behind Bass.

The Private Paranormal Investigator turned around and saw, stereotypically, a gardener. He's wearing a long white shirt, blue overalls, and black boots. The Gardener ran towards Bass, giving him a friendly white smile and tight hug. Bass tensed up, he didn't like being hugged from strange men. "Ok, let go." Bass ordered.

The Gardener looked like Bass, as if they were lost, reacquainted friends. "It's good to see you." He smiled again.

Bass appeared more estranged; "Who are you?" he asked.

"I am The Gardener."

Bass briefly scanned his uniform, "I can see that. Do you work here?"

"I sure do, I am very lucky to be chosen."

"Am I dead? Is this... *heaven*?"

"No, but what you call *Heaven,* what others call *Moksha,* what others call *Nirvana,* isn't far from here."

Bass felt he had to ask a question, one mankind has been asking, since the beginning of time; "Is God real?"

Gardener raised a beam but with no teeth, "what some call *God,* What some have called *Ahura Mazda,* What some call *Jah*, What some call-"

"Ok! I get it." Bass interrupts.

"The bringer of life; It is bigger and greater then what the human mind can comprehend."

"If you could please be a little more vague? It would be helpful." Bass said sarcastically.

Gardener laughed and patted his visitor on the back.

"Why am I here?"

The Gardeners cheerful grin turned into more weighty, as if he was about to say something momentous; "Two dark forces have entered the small town you're currently occupying, Holders Bridge."

"Two? Let me guess they're both *Conservatives*."

"One stronger than the other. One there is nothing you can do about. The other has conjured powers from Great Mother Earth, *Nature,* you'd call it. Causing an unbalance, a theory which we both agree on."

Bass had to concur, "The disruption emphasises people's preternatural side. The locals and the grieving begin to experience more abnormal behaviour. Which I've seen with my own eyes here, and elsewhere."

"Voids between worlds and different realities have become narrow. You need to destroy the dark force that stole the life from Jenny Woodfield. Bring some order back to Earth."

"Why can't you or the "big man" do it yourselves? Are you too busy planning new diseases to kill people?"

"That's natures job not ours. I don't know who killed Jenny Woodfield and our Lord can't see who's done it."

"What!? Even God can't see this thing?" Too unconvincing, even to Bass, and all he's witnessed.

"It's too unnatural. But I have faith that you will solve it."

Bass had begun to feel the pressure, never has he felt so discomfit about a job. "Why have you asked me? I'm just one man. My life will just be as meaningless in Heaven, as it is on Earth."

"Don't you believe you have a purpose? Maybe not every single person has a plan bestowed upon them. It doesn't mean that you don't have a purpose. You have love, free will-"

"Do you know what human beings do with free will, over populate the earth, drain it's resources, steal, hurt others, murder each other, we're all better off dead."

"Do you believe that's true?"

Bass believed it was a rhetorical question; the friendly Gardener knew that he didn't. "Do you know about all the horrible things I've said about God? The blasphemy?"

"We are aware of your sacrilege. You had every right to be angry, abandoned by your mother and father like that."

"You don't get to talk about that." Bass was prickly about the subject. He paced up and down, walking back and forth, stroking the stubble on his chin, giving him an inquisitive appearance. Working out in his head, all the facts he'd just been given and trying to solve what his next step is.

"You cannot tell anyone about this place, not even *Gail Brooke*." His eyes widened when he mentioned her name.

How did he know about her as well? "Have you been spying on me?"

"I had to, the almighty said so. See, I needed to know if you keep a secret, if humanity knew the truth, would interfere with their lives, their choices, their course in life, would the amount of suicides incline?"

"I won't say anything; it feels like a big burden though."

"When you go back, this will feel like a dream."

"I have to ask; I've been walking for miles. How big is this place?"

"As wide as eternity."

"What a day to forget my *Fitbit*." Bass, using humour as a coping mechanism. "Do I get anything for this?"

"Satisfaction of bringing justice to Jenny Woodfield's' murder? Letting her soul ascend into what you call... *Heaven?* Allowing her parents and friends to sleep easy at night?"

"You still didn't need to summon me here. I was already on the case."

"Also this..." The Gardener points to nowhere in the field.

Bass reflected on a door that appeared from thin air. Just a dark brown, solid oak, wooden door with a golden knob, leading nowhere, literally nothing, was on the other side. He asked oneself, if it was worth opening or not?

"If I open this, will I go to my own personalised heaven?" *Not as if any friends or family will be there waiting for him.*

"No. This is *your* door." The Gardener told.

Bass was perplexed to have immediately understood, what he had meant; "If I open this door, floods of anguish and sorrow will flood over me."

"It will also mean; *you can let somebody else in.*"

Bass is unprepared to validate his own feelings, unfit to be more in touch with his emotions, unready to let someone into his life, refusing to *feel* the pain. The doubtfulness turned into ferocity, "Fuck you." He screamed before punching the door. The solid oak should have either broken or split his knuckles... it felt... *soft...* like a pillow... It WAS a pillow?

Carl Sebastian woke up in his bed, with a fist digging into the pillow beside him. He was back in Robinsons B'n'B, lying under the duvet covers, still in his clothes. Brooke stood by the bed with a tray of tea in her hands, leering at Bass with such fright...

Chapter 43

It was noon time; the skies were just as dull and grim as the day before. A line of cars were tailing the leading funeral car from Father Paul's church, back to the Dive Bar. Thunder roared in the sky, not a drop of rain appeared. Though, the cautioned gatherers were pulling umbrellas out at the ready. Standing out in a row along the street, backs against cobbled stone walls, leading away from the house of worship, many mourners were peering through the windows of the torpid moving vehicles. Gatherers were wishing they could express their sympathy towards Janet Woodfield, in the leading car, all on her own, Raymond not in sight, deciding to forsake his own daughter's funeral.

"He probably couldn't cope" "His mind had snapped" "The past few days; Raymond had been searching, in and out of the town, looking for Jenny." "He believes she's still alive somewhere." These are just a few of the things; the town have been talking about. Furthermore; whispers of concern, spread for Janet, "How does she cope on her own?" "Is she shutting everybody out? This is the time where isolation cannot be the healthiest decision." "Apparently Father Paul told Miss Jacobs, that she spent all day, yesterday, cleaning the entire church. He tried to persuade her to go home but she would not leave. Janet told the Father that she wanted it clean for today."

Carl Sebastian walked into the Dive Bar; grabbing a drink (or three) before the funeral party arrive. Only Frank Mill was inside, taking off the foil from the spread he laid out on a table.

"Bass. A cider?" Frank was surprised to see him here, and not attending the funeral. Although his suit and the fresh shave on his gloomy mug, indicated otherwise.

"You're not attending the funeral?" Bass enquired.

Frank went behind the bar to serve him his drink. "Neither are you."

"I never knew her." Bass said while climbing on the stool, opposing the bar man.

"Ditto. Don't detectives go to the funeral, you know, to see if the killers there."

"I don't, I think it's disrespectful. The last thing the family wants to see, is the investigator. It gives a horrible reminder that their loved one was murdered. Funerals are meant to be a celebration of life, so I've been told."

Frank now suspects this gloomy man has never been to a funeral, giving his customer the requested drink.

Bass notices in the left corner, by the entrance, there is a large portrait of Jenny, different types of bouquet flowers, small framed photos of the deceased with her mum and dad. Another photo is of Jenny and Chelsea when they were toddlers, in a swimming pool during one hot summer's day. A recent one of her and Mark with their arms around each other. Middle left shelf, was Polaroid photo of Shelly and Jenny in a lovely summers dress, taken at a BBQ. Then a collection of Polaroid's throughout her years, starting from when she was a baby, ending with her recent school photo.

"What's with the shrine?"

"It's tradition, here in Holders Bridge. Whenever someone is cremated, the ashes are sent back to wake, to be on top of that stand. Everyone will line up to individually pay their respects, one by one."

"That's a bit weird." Bass bluntly said.

Frank was offended "If you don't like it, feel free to leave."

"Sorry *my fuhrer*. I would, if I could." Bass finished his drink, points to his empty glass "another."

The funeral cars halted outside the pub. The Funeral Director stepped out to open the door for Janet Woodfield, in a gentlemanly style. She stepped out, placing a gloved hand on the drivers arm. Bass noticed she was all in black, with a veil hiding her face, though it could not mask her grief.

Frank Mill poured a free glass of brandy, in preparation to her entrance.

Janet stepped inside first, the Funeral Director walked in, holding an urn. The man placed it on top of the stand of photographs.

The F.D. turned to the bereaved mother before leaving "If there's anything you need, do not hesitate to ask."

"Thank you, Charles."

The driver/Funeral Director was in fact called Charles, Bass detected.

Janet leisurely approached Bass. Looking through the thin black veil, Bass could see Janet's purple eye shadow, dark red lipstick and her curious expression.

"What are you still doing here, Mr Sebastian?"

"I've just come to pay my respects, I am so sorry for your loss, Mrs Woodfield."

"No."

Bass fell stunned.

"...You are still on your witch hunt. Like I have told you before, I never paid for your services."

Frank Mill overheard "I thought, you said Mrs Woodfield hired you?"

Bass was just as muddled over Frank, for it was HER voice on her phone and someone had paid him. "I've started my enquiries. I'd like to see this through to the end, if that's ok with you?"

"Carry on, Mr Sebastian. Have you found him yet?"

"Was it definitely a man? Frank interfered.

Bass looked over at the barman with a mistrustful view, *is he beginning to get nervous?* "Well we've found evidence that suggest it was."

He lied to see if Frank grew twitchy.

"Oh right, I thought it would be. We don't have to talk about this right now. I have poured you a brandy, Mrs Woodfield. On the house."

"Thank you." Janet took the curvy glass, not lifting the veil to have a drink; she took it straight to the far end table, to sit on her own.

Bass watched Frank's body language, he didn't detect anything abnormal.

Others joined the wake, Chelsea was first in line of many, to kneel before Jenny Woodfield's ashes. Wearing a black dress that reached by her knee caps. She could feel her bony knee's pressing on the wooden floor. She didn't say anything, inside she was urging to say "I'm sorry, I've let you down again." and "I miss you" but unable to say anything out loud. Chelsea never cried during the funeral, she felt numb. This was a stupid tradition, a pointless one, Jenny's gone, there's no bringing her back, why does everyone have to bend-the-knee to some earn and a bunch of photographs that resembled a life that once was. A whole bunch of idiots, including Mark and her dad, were queuing up down the street to do the same thing. Chelsea didn't really look at all the pictures, only half glancing at the ones herself was in. Craving a drink, knowing full well she can't have a sip, it was liking having an itch inside her chest, one that can't be scratched, the bodies urge was becoming too tempting, and not that Frank would serve her anyway. She needed to distract herself, after noticing Bass, Chelsea thought a conversation might take her mind off the itch. She got back up on her feet and walked over to him, it's a shame he shaved, and she liked the stubble. "Hey there."

Bass finishes his pint before Chelsea could see, its sweet contents, "its *Lindsey Lohan*." he jokes, but it was humourless.

"I just wanted to say thank you, for last night, and that I'm sorry."

"You were upset over your best friend, don't worry. If it happens again, you'll have to get some other mug to help you out. There's only a number of times, I can allow you to keep feeling sorry for yourself, if this keeps on recurring, then you're on your own. So, I recommend you keep on the right track and stay on it." Tough love, that's what Bass believes.

Chelsea hung her head in shame. "Ok." feeling it was harsh, but fair.

Chelsea noticed Mark approaching the shrine. He's not wore his suit for a long time, in fact, he's been piling on the muscle since, it was very tight on him. Mark tried to bend down but if he did so, the grey trousers would rip. The boyfriend tried to lean on his left leg first, stooping one half of his stiff upper body, he bent his right knee to drop the right side of his ungiven body.

"Is he having a stroke?" Bass asked Chelsea, in his usual, mocking fashion.

Chelsea laughed at Mark.

"Has he got a pink tie on? Does he know it's meant to be black?" Bass noticed.

After many indiscreet rigid movements, Mark finally managed to shuffle downwards onto his knees. There he saw a picture of him with his arms around Jenny; he recalled where it was taken, when they went hiking along the moors. How they laughed, how they took a long kiss on the lips before the photo was taken, how the wind blew strands of hair over her kind face. The memory brought tears to surge from his dark brown eyes.

Chelsea had sat next to him, whilst the water flooded from his eyes, throughout the service. It caused her to feel guilty *Why didn't I cry? Should I have done?*

Simon Cole ditched his uniform for his dark black, freshly ironed suit. He looked across the room towards Shelly, even though she was talking to other people, her forlorn eyes kept glancing to Simon. He thought Richard would have come back to town, to comfort her, on this day, but I guess not. Shelly walked out, her eyes focusing on Simon as she moves, maybe she expects him to follow but he needs to stay.

The pub was gradually becoming overrun. Gail Brooke didn't bend down on her knees in front of Jenny's ashes, she took a slight bow, Jenny wouldn't have liked people kneeling before her, and she believed that we were all equal.

Bass jumped out of his seat when he saw Brooke. He thought she was attractive in her long, dark, Polyester, pencil cut skirt, with chevron pattern around the V-neck. Bass assumed that she had shoes under the remnants of her dress, for he had remembered that she hated high-heels. He also noticed Brooke had puffy eyes and a red nose, she'd been crying, understandable, given the circumstance. Bass hugged Brooke tightly; she rested her head on his left pectoral. He could feel her neatly knotted blonde hair on his chin. They both closed their eyes, relishing in each other's comfort. Brooke leant back, looked up towards Bass, there's something different about him. "You shaved." she noticed.

"Well, I thought I would make the effort."

Brooke smiled, wondering if he did that just for her, after the comment she made last night; about him looking like a tramp and she preferred men that shaved.

"I'm sorry about this morning." Bass apologised. "I had the strangest dream."

"You were screaming in your sleep. What was it about?"

Bass paused "I can't remember."

The English teacher suspected he was lying, it was probably something from his past, and he didn't want to talk about. "I am going to get a drink. Would you like anything?"

"Cider, please. I'll get you one on the next round."

When Brooke walked away, swerving around people. Bass noticed Chelsea grinning at him.

"What?"

"You like her."

"Well, you like Mark." Bass retorts, childishly.

Brooke was at the hard-pressed bar, whilst waiting to be served by Frank, she noticed Clive Dunscroft, sat on his own, drinking a juice box through a straw. He had not brought Bradley with him; he probably thought he is too young to attend the funeral, and still protecting him from the issues of death.

Frank Mill approached Clive, whispered in his ear "it's probably best you leave, before some of the others get here."

Clive finished slurping his juice and protested "I have as much right to be here, as everyone else."

"Half the town think you've killed Jenny, you being here will just cause trouble. So I'm telling you, you're not welcome here."

After being served by a blonde waitress, Brooke turned her attention back to Clive, only to discover he had left.

The comedian Jack Mill glanced around the room, giving icy stares to his praising fans; *none of these people are my friends. I don't belong here.* Low-spirited thoughts sunk its claws into every orifice of the happy-go-lucky chaps' brain. To distract himself from the lack of belonging, he began to catch-up with an old acquaintance Michael Dunn; an overweight man in his fifties who's scratching his tie with the greasy palms from his chubby hands. "It's good to see you again, Jacky-boy. Shame it was under such circumstances."

"It's great to see you again." Jack shouts with enthusiasm. Though underneath the gracious smile, Jack is actually thinking; *Great, it's this fat fucker, look at him, with that shabby blue' n' white striped shirt, and that long greasy white hair, and pornstar 'tash. It's a funeral! You scruffy bastard, have some decorum.* "So, how are the kids?" *Why have I just asked that? I don't give two shits about his kids.*

"The kids are great thanks. Days like today put things into perspective; Seventeen is no age, poor Jenny had a whole life in front of her, never going to prom, missing out on all the possible adventures, never watching the final season of *Game of Thrones* ...

Jack is still displaying a false beam, and is nodding to his head to show interest. Underneath his eyes he's screaming; *Shut the fuck up, already.*

"...I couldn't imagine losing my two little girls."

I don't know if I would care if anyone else died. Jacks being tormented by his own beliefs... *Of course, I would care. I should care... but, I don't know if I do.*

The reunion was disrupted by Carl Sebastian placing a firm hand on The Comedians shoulder. Causing Jack to jump out-of-his-skin.

"Do you mind if I have a chat with your friend?" Bass asks Michael.

"Of course, I'll see you soon." Michael dispersed, knowing Bass's tone was heavily insistent.

"Can I help you?" Jack simpered.

Telling the comedian's smile was fake, "My name is Carl Sebastian. You are the comedian, from this very town."

"Are you a fan?"

"No, I think you are as funny as genocide."

"Did you know Jenny Woodfield?"

"Unfortunately, I've never met her but I hate losing a fan of mine, I treat all fans like family."

"Cut the crap. Where were you on the day of her murder?"

The comedian stuttered struggled to recollect his memories.

Bass studied the man, as he was awkwardly shuffling, scratching his hair.

"I was at my mums; I haven't seen her in such a long time."

"Really? Because your brother told me you were with him, and his girlfriend."

Jack was panicking; the anxiety had given him terrible memory loss. Now, over worrying, he's appearing too suspicious, making him look more suspicious. "Yes, yes, yes. That is right. I was here with them, then I went to Goforcoffee."

Bass doubted the truth, hearing the story being changed, only built mistrust.

Jack forces gawky laughter, the nervous sweat stuck caused a wet patch on his neat pink shirt, "I remembered, I've actually got to be somewhere." He flees.

Bass was about to halt the cowards escape, but then he's distracted when Gail Brooke returns with his pint.

Janet Woodfield places her hands flat on the table, all at once, she separates her fingers, so her dark red polished nails are spread out as far as they can go. "This place is filthy." She says with disgust, behind her gritted teeth. She goes behind the bar, startling Frank Mill; "Mrs Woodfield" he calls.

She ignores him; too busy dashing through the cabinets, finding all the cleaning supplies. "Janet" he calls out, again. Janet Woodfield begins to dust the tables and chairs rigorously and placing beer mats at a ninety degree angle and the corners of every table.

Frank Mill had to serve his overwhelming amount of punters and decides to let her get on with it.

The room falls silent, as everyone stops and stares at Raymond Woodfield as he makes his way through the door as jolly as he can be. In his normal attire, he gives everyone his infamous bright white smile. "Hello everyone."

"Where's he been?" was the first question that came to everybody's head. Janet turned around and took one glimpse at him before turning back around, dismissing his appearance.

"So who was the unfortunate soul to pass away?" Raymond asked everyone in the room.

The question made all whole town feel awkward, there was shuffling among the unpleasantness, many remained silent, expecting someone else to answer.

"Come on folks! Who's going to tell me? Who died? I don't think I would know 'em."

"It's your daughter." Bass answered.

Now everyone's head turned towards him. Half the town now frightened of the altercation that may erupt, the other half angry because they felt that Bass was being inconsiderate. This outspoken outsider hasn't got the right to tell him, especially, like this.

Bass had overheard; though he doesn't care. The Private Paranormal Investigator believed; if they really cared about this man, then they would have told him the truth instead of letting him carry on a dangerous delusion.

Raymond laughed out loud and hard "Jenny's not here, silly."

"I am sorry but it is real." Brooke apologetically succoured.

Raymond laughed again, Sending shivers to the nearest locals. Now wiggling his right index finger at Brooke, "You, you" as if Jenny's father was convinced her and Bass are playing a trick. Frightened guests are now edging towards the door.

Raymond stopped and turned towards the big portrait of Jenny, slowly moving his head towards the urn. *No... It's not true... it can't be... it won't be.... but it is.* Raymond's hands reached up to the sky, trudging towards the shrine. His eyes wide and his mouth dropped open; his tanned, brown hands are making their way to the top of the stand. Inches away from grabbing the urn, he pulls his closed hands back to his green cardigan, hesitating. Then out and in; his actions are repeated; the mind is torn between accepting and refusing the truth. He stretches out his arms again, heavenward, he picks up the urn.

Everyone else in the bar watches with dismay, alarmed by what he'll do next.

Raymond rests his head against the white doves on the ceramic work and closes his eyes, like a boy sleeping on the body of a teddy bear. A tear drops from his closed eyes and he begins to sniffle.

The atmosphere in The Dive bar dies down, everyone's apprehension as dissolved into concern. People moved closer to Mr Woodfield to offer some tenderness.

"Why?" He wept softly before opening his eyes, looked at all the people in the room. "I've been a fool and I can't express my apologies to you all." The shame of recent actions caused by his denial has caused embarrassment and sorrow. He feel's alone. He inhales deeply before stating "I'm going to put this right." He zips out the door, leaving people bewildered to where he's going to go.

Shane Crewball enters The Dive bar, in his normal dregs, just missing Raymond's take-off. "What's his problem?" He jokes with bad taste.

Nobody in the room wanted this man here but his fearful reputation as caused the towns-folk to be tight-lipped. Gatherers swarm out.

Bass walks right to him "What are you doing here? Nobody wants you here."

"Whoa man, I've just come to show my respects 'as all."

Chelsea smashes a bottle on the table, forming a dangerous weapon. Mark grabs her arm. "Get off me." She kicks, screams, swinging her glass blade aimlessly in the air. No matter how hard she tries, she can't escape from Marks grasp.

Mark forms a barricade of himself, hoping she won't stab him in the process.

"You killed Jenny! You bastard! I'm going to kill you!" Never as she had an appetite for Shane's blood, she's always been angry at the suspect but for him to gate-crash Jenny's wake, caused her to snap.

Simon Cole impedes "Chelsea stop. It wasn't him. Shane didn't kill Jenny."

Chelsea regains her composure, struggling to comprehend what The Inspector had announced. "What are you talking about?"

"There were witnesses placing Shane opening the gym."

She dropped the broken bottle but turned her hatred towards Cole "You knew, all this time, you didn't say anything. After me, begging you to arrest him, you still never said anything."

"I couldn't discuss an open investigation, I'm telling you now because I don't want to arrest you for attempted murder. Not today"

Bass stormed towards The Chief Inspector, pointed his finger in Simons shoulder, "You also knew about the body, you laughed at my work but you failed to mention that you knew there was no marks on her body." He talked quietly but there was much aggression in his tone.

"Keep your voice down. You don't want others hearing this nonsense."

"You're not welcome here." Mark declared to Shane.

"Fuck you snowflake, Jenny didn't even love you, she was in love with her..." Shane pointed to someone else in the room.

Mark followed the direction from his broken finger nail towards... Gail Brooke.

"That's the connection." Bass spoke out loud.

Brooke protested "He is lying, Mark. It is surely a delusion, this creep as manifested."

"Then why couldn't she stop talking about you, probably ranted on for ages, how she looks forward to your visits."

It was piercing revelation to Mark. *This explained the niggling feeling of loving her more than she loved him.* "The reasons why they've never had much *intimacy,* the thing that has been on Jenny's mind for so long. I bet she was debating on leaving him because she was secretly into other girls."

Janet Woodfield overheard, stopped cleaning to hiss at the quarrellers. "My daughter was not a lesbian! She was a clean girl." She scowled at Brooke and repeats; "A *cllllleeeaaan* girl." Janet goes upstairs to clean the bathrooms.

"I should check up on her, try and convince her to have a lie-down". Frank suggested, before he followed her up the stairs.

By now, most of the locals vacated to their homes.

Bass turned to Brooke "This is the connection, that's why she chose you to haunt. She was in love with you."

Chelsea already baffled bewildered "What are you both talking about? Haunting who?"

Brooke and Bass slide their eyes towards each other.

Chelsea pushes Bass, with his size; he isn't knocked further than an inch. "Is this true? You claim to be a Paranormal Investigator, you're here because Jenny's ghost is haunting Brooke."

Brooke gently holds the furious teens hand; "I know it seems implausible. I would not be convinced either. But I have seen her ghost, for a whole week, Jenny has been warning me of the murderer in town."

"You're full of shit, the pair of you." Chelsea screeches.

"I've had enough with your bratty attitude. Where's your father?" Bass wondered.

"He didn't stay because he hates me. Everybody hates me."

"That's not true." Mark objects.

"Don't listen to this guy." Shane, points to Mark. "I don't know why you are all blaming me. What about the boyfriend? Jenny said that Mark was so angry, about her wanting to leave Holders Bridge to pursue her Medical career, they had the worst argument ever, he got so mad, she thought he was going to hit her..."

Bass grabbed Mark by the collar, "I thought you said, you and Jenny have had any nasty rows. You lied to me."

A petrified Mark became dumb.

Simon broke Bass's grip of Marks shirt, "Don't you grab him like that."

Even Chelsea, looked as if she was harbouring reservations towards her friend, while he was defending himself; "Yes, I wanted to stay here, in Holders Bridge and she wanted to leave. We got into an argument, I did get mad, but I'd still, NEVER would hurt her."

Brooke questions Shane "How would you know all this?"

Something is registered within Chelsea's mind, *how would Shane knew her secrets and feelings, unless...*"Her hidden diary, you have Jenny's hidden diary. The one that's been missing from her room."

Shane, sweats with nervousness, *SHIT, I've gave it away... anyway, she can't prove it, I've destroyed the evidence.* "I haven't got a clue what you're on about, love. I aint stole, no, teenage girls diary. I don't wanna read about period pains and shit."

"You have it, you killed her and then took her diary!" Chelsea accuses.

Bass yells at Simon "We need to arrest him!"

"On what grounds? We have no proof that he has the diary."

"He just said it, in front of all these people." Bass roared.

"No he hasn't."

"Do your fucking job?" Bass's voice is growing louder, with his temper to match.

Brooke notice the smirk on Shane Crewball's face, she bets he's adoring being under the illusion of being an untouchable. "I bet he's burnt it. He is a moron but he can clear his tracks."

"Charge him on the grounds of conspiracy." Bass demands in a frenzy.

"With no evidence, it's got to be the right person, I am the one with the responsibility and the weight falls on me. I can't be seen to be a laughing stock." Simon delineates.

The shouting match between the ex-policeman and the current Chief Inspector is getting thunderous.

"Do you really care what people think, over the murder of an innocent girl?"

The room's tension escalated.

"If I arrest the wrong person, Shane is going to sue the town. I will be demoted." Simon's now red in his little face.

Shane, who's finding all this amusing, puts his hands up in the air "Ok guys, I can see this is all becoming a bit too tense." He smiles. "If I were, hypothetically speaking had her book. She would have given it to me."

"Why would she give it to you?" Chelsea asks.

"She believed I was lonely, "misunderstood", that I just needed someone to give me a chance..."

When Marks fuse was blown, he went to punch Shane, till he heard his grey suit jacket and shirt rip.

Shane laughed at him, "You guys, it's been emotional but I really should go." He said with a joyful tone.

"You're a scum bag, who sells drugs to kids and rapes women, you deserve to be alone." Bass boldly mentions.

Shane flaps his hands, the sound of his leather sleeve hitting against the rest of his jacket, forms a slight clapping sound. "What are you going to do?" He walks out, carefree.

Chelsea's craze became immensely deep. She felt the need to hit something, claw, bite, MURDER something. The breathing grew rapid, deep. Her red eyes narrowed above her trembling body, when a tearful Mark hugged Chelsea, the fury softened.

Simon walked out with his head hanging low.

The remaining few locals dispersed, chatting among on themselves. Wondering what's really going off, forming their ideas along the way.

Brooke leaped into Bass's arms, which he happily embraced.

Chelsea looked over to Marks broad shoulder and asked "Brooke, is it true? What you've been saying, about Jenny's spirit?"

"Yes." She replied.

Brooke took Chelsea to a table; there she told her everything that has happened so far.

Bass still wondered "IF, and that is a big IF, Shane Crewball never murdered Jenny Woodfield, than who did?" turning his suspicion onto Mark. Who returned the glance "I'm sorry I lied, I thought I'd get into trouble, the fight got nasty, but really, I would never hurt her, she was the world to me."

Could it have been a crime of passion? The, I love you so much; I'd kill you if you leave. The final chain on the list of connections; "Well, clearly you were not the world to her. She obviously preferred the rug" Bass insulted, to see what reaction he'd get, also felt the need to hurt someone else.

"You know, maybe it's you who deserves to be alone." Mark committed before he trails out in a dismal mood.

Bass was hurt, because he knew Mark was right.

221

Part 3 - Broken Bass

Chapter 44

During the schools dinner break, sat crying by the brick wall of the playground, is an overweight seven year-old boy, in a shirt and shorts, they are practically hand-me-down-rags, big bulky shoes, white socks. Sobbing his eyes out into the palm of his soft hands. The other children are still playing on the playground, purposely excluding the "Minger" or "The Scrounger." A teacher, with long dark hair, Mrs Amy, kneels down next to the child to try and console the young lad. "Carl."
The young Carl Sebastian, lifts his red face and snotty nose from his hands, to look up at the pretty, kind, teacher.
Carl shouts out his blubbering; "All the other kids are mean to me, they call me names like "Orphan" and say things like; "nobody wants me." It's because they don't, nobody wants me." He slams his forehead into his chubby arms that are sat on his knee caps.
Mrs Amy carried much pity for Carl, but she believes there's nothing she could do. She places both hands on his mushy shoulders, in this moment, she believed that offering some tough love might be more suitable, for her sentimental and meek student. "Carl, Listen to me." She shakes his body, though it doesn't cause a response.
"Look at me." She told firmly.
A sobbing Carl lift's his head again.
With a sturdy hand, the Teacher wiped the tears from his plump face, "You have to stop all this crying. I know you are sensitive, I know you are very smart. You've expressed it through all the poems, which you've written for me."
The snivelling face on Carl reverts into a smile. "You really like 'em?"
"I do, very much so. You have great potential. One day you will meet a lucky girl, your age that will cherish the

things you have wrote for her. Until then, why don't you keep the romantic, "soppy" poems to yourself?"

The seven year old was heart-broken; *did she not care for the poems he wrote for her? She was the only friend he had.*

"Also, if the other kids are mean to you, hit them back. What they give to you, you give them back twice as much. I shouldn't be saying this; however, I have no authority during out-of-school-hours, so hit the biggest bully, once you knock him down, the rest will follow."

"What if I can't?" screams the young boy.

"You have to Carl, just until you get adopted by a loving family, who will buy you some new clothes, bathe you, and adore you with affection. This will build your confidence up. Till that time comes, you have to be brave and be tough."

Bass agreed. He remained in hope that he will one day be adopted by a new Mummy and Daddy, not knowing that day will never come. He followed his teachers advice and "toughened up." It didn't happen overnight, but eventually his sensitive heart turned to stone, then he'll know what it's like to be a Man; cold and callous.

Something is happening... Bass is in a young boy's body, he looks down and recognises the horrendous charity shoes. The stumpy, hairless legs and recalls the school playground. He's entered the body of his younger-self, in his own memory. *Although...* the sky is black... the memory has merged into a night terror. A football slowly rolls to a halt. All the other children on the playground appear to be rigid, mannequins, and like mannequins, **they have no faces**. Despite not having any eyes, Bass knew they were staring at him. Even though not one had a mouth, all the children on the playground began to sing...

"Beware, beware the man with no face.
He cannot see. He cannot hear.
He is the man with no face.
Beware, beware the man with no face.

He doesn't sleep, he cannot smile.
He is the man with no face."

Bass could feel something small drop on his shoulder, he slowly moved his pudgy head to his right side, only to notice a maggot wriggling on his shirt. A second one fell, to worm amongst its predecessor. Bass peeked up to the sky, to find, Jenny Woodfield's pale corpse leaning over him, spewing live maggots from her mouth, as well as them foaming, in her eye sockets.

Chapter 45

Bass's eyes pinned open, to see Brooke's eyes staring back at him, instantly alleviating his stress. Both are now lying in the same bed, facing each other. Brooke's head lifted from her pillow, her blonde hair swayed as she tucked her right hand beneath her cheek. She could see the foreboding trouble in his eyes. "This may be the second night; I have seen you shout in your sleep. Is there anything you would like to tell me? Perhaps, some angst will unfetter?"

Bass, only half understood what Brooke meant, yet he replied anyway; "I saw Jenny Woodfield."

"Jenny? Why would she be haunting you?"

"Maybe it's because of our connection?"

Brooke looked surprised; "Do we have a connection?"

"I like to think so. Brooke, I'm sorry for being so distance at times, I'm sorry for my own defensive guard, and I'm sorry for all the cruel things I've said, and will say. I don't know how else to be. But, from now on, I will never lie to you and will never keep anything from you. Does that sound weird?"

Brooke smiles "It sounds sweet." She moved in closer to Bass.

Bass watched the wrinkles of the beds white linen wave towards him, as Brooke curls her legs to his. Their chests now touching, faces closer than ever, their body heat started to transfer from one to another. Brooke wanted Bass to make a move.

With his strong right hand, Bass stroked along Brookes curved and bare left hand side, from the black bra strap to the edge of her matching underwear. He wanted to kiss Brooke, though he felt like he would be taking advantage, with only just returning from her friends' funeral, she could be in a vulnerable state. Also he didn't want to ruin their good working relationship, or so he told himself.

"There is something I need to tell you."

Brooke appeared more curious. "What is it?"

"Do not freak out, after we confronted Blake, I passed out and I was taken to The Garden. I believe The Garden is where man and woman first walked before being banished to earth."

"Do you really believe that? You are not the religious sort." Brooke stated.

"I believe what I see; I never thought it existed till now. While I was there, a Gardener told me; there were dark forces in Holders Bridge, bringing an unnatural balance and in order to correct it, we must find Jenny's killer. This is what I've always suspected beforehand."

"Do you mean Heaven exists?"

"It is some kind of afterlife, something bigger than our notion of Heaven."

"Does this mean God is real?"

"I haven't seen it for myself but the word God is just simply a word for something our minds will not be able to comprehend." Bass paused, "Do you believe me?"

"I have always believed, Bass, I am a catholic girl since birth."

"You never mentioned your religious beliefs before."

"I find religion to be a personal experience; it brought me solace during bleak times. Such as; my father's passing."

"I didn't know, I'm sorry for your loss."

"It was some time ago, though it never gets easier."

Bass wishes he could summon the words that would cheer her up.

"At least we get to see our loved ones again." Brooke says positively.

"I don't know, The Gardener never said anything about that." Bass doubts.

"Are you not a believer now?" Brooke asks.

"Frankly, I'm more confused and angry."

"Why are you so angry?"
"I thought when we die, it'll be a deep sleep, a peaceful rest, true peace. And this so called "living" will come to an end."

"So it is self-directed hatred."

"If anyone else would know the truth, it would bring them joy or closure of some-kind. But not me, am I so damaged?" Bass wanted to cry, he resisted knowing Brooke was watching.

"Carl Sebastian, remember anything broken, can be fixed." Brooke amended.

Bass relished in her words, though he never spoke, he was thankful.

Rain started to hit the window, opposite the bed, making frequent but gentle tapping sounds

Brooke rolled over onto the other side "such a romantic sound."

Bass agreed, whilst putting his arm around her stomach.

The both laid in silence, listening to the light raindrops tapping against the thin window pane.

Bass broke the silence "There's just one more thing bothering me."

Brooke lifted an ear up, as if it would increase her hearing.

"If heaven, or not-heaven, wherever does exist… Does Hell?"

Chapter 46

Raymond Woodfield walked down the street, to the people passing by; it looked as if he was walking aimlessly in the rain to clear his head. The walk was not undirected, for he knew where to go; The Balconies Restaurant. The night's rain followed through into the morning, making a mess of his black hair and the green cardigan. The sleeves of his white shirt are transparent. Puddled water seeped into his black shoes. Raymond is too distracted to pay attention to the downpour, recalling his adventures last week, his denial of his daughter's death had took him to St Ives, Cornwall. The annual family holiday location, he assumed Jenny would be there, hiding from her wrathful boyfriend, they had such a horrible argument about their future, and how she wanted to leave Holders Bridge. She cried in his arms for what seemed like an hour. *How I do miss holding her...*

On his way to St. Ives, he stopped off at the occasional pub to talk to the locals, of the different villages and to enjoy a glass of port. Normally Mr Woodfield condemns drink driving, yet he couldn't help himself. He greeted the strangers with a different name. He referred to himself as Mr James Hippleton, to be a different man, a man with no history. At one pub near Yeovil, he met a strange man, claiming to have cured his cancer by setting fire to his own bookies. "Are you madman?" Raymond demanded to know. This man was clearly a deranged drunken piss-artist. Raymond had met pathological liars before, during his work at the bank. This man was literally celebrating every day of his life, two months ago, the Doctor had told him he had three months left to live and that day he had claimed to have been cured. "I still don't understand how becoming a pyromaniac would destroy your cancerous cells? There is no correlation between your health and your business."

He replied, "He had made a deal."

Raymond had enough of his gibberish and left the lunatic to his own devices.

"Not far now." Raymond told himself, as he walked past the barbers.

Three days ago, his renunciation had led him all the way to Peak District at National Park, hoping to find his daughter and her boyfriend to have gone wild camping, a brutal six hour drive for nothing. He walked among the mountains all night, to find nothing. He had to return home the following day, back to his home town for this funeral. He knew deep inside, it was his daughter's body that was in a box, one that will be cremated to mere ash. Raymond had refused to accept it. Prolonging his return by going to a bar where he would meet more locals, under the name; James Hippleton. He met a couple in their forties, Janice and Rob. They had been trying hard for a baby, sadly age was not on their side, and time was against them. He had made a deal; Rob was a steel worker, he too had made a deal, he had to send some steel work to the poorest regions of the globe. Risky business, not only there's a possibility of being fired, but jail time was on the line. Well, Raymond had noticed Rob was drinking lots of alcohol in a celebratory mood and Janice was just on pop. Raymond considered it was a coincidence more than anything else, he raised a glass to the happy couple, and bid a merry farewell before departing.

This morning, while having a cup of coffee at Goforcoffee, Shelly Jayne, told him of her story, saving her own business by selling her husband's car, and giving all the money to charity. She told him that this man can be found here, in Holders Bridge, at the Balcony Restaurant. Could it be just one individual making these "deals" or is it all non-related? However, there is one thing Raymond wants, he's willing to trade anything for it, *anything*...

Raymond embraced the warmth of the restaurant. He swiped his hand across his wet hair, sprinkles of unwanted rain water dropped onto the thin green carpet below. With the same hand, he used it on the gold hand rail to balance himself up the stairs. The whole place was noiseless, unsure if the place is open at TEN A.M, he still continued to climb. The stairwell lead him to a white door, the hallway was still hushed, when Mr Woodfield opened the door, sound poured out, the more the door opened, the louder the room became. The music being played sounded like a classical nineteen thirties orchestra, the trombones, the plucking of the double bass, piano keys, violins and the crackling sound that could only come from an old recording studio and classic vinyl. Jenny's father scanned the room before sitting down. Most of the occupants were of the elderly kind, many faces he doesn't recognise, all sat in square booths around the room. There was only one round table, singled out, in the middle of the room, on top of what appears to be a dance floor. A young, pretty waitress approached Raymond with such a radiant smile. Raymond gazed on her skimpy dress, and her long skinny legs, he had to remind himself that he had a daughter her age, before drooling any further. "Can I help you young man?" The brown haired waitress offered.

Raymond was startled by the flattery "No, thank you, Miss. I am not quite sure what it is, I am doing here."

"Right this way."

She escorted him to the round table, in the middle of the room. Where a small candle was lit in a tiny glass and a tall, handsome stranger sat comfortably, facing the door.

Along the way, he noticed the oldies around the room, never once looked at him when he entered or walked across the room. They were too deep in their newspapers or their own conversations. It was quite a nice feeling, not have watchful eyes stare at him.

The lovely waitress pulled the chair out for Mr Woodfield. "I will be back with your drink, Mr Woodfield."

Raymond flashed his bright white smile and the young woman, "Thank you." She left, while he was unaware that he never told her his name or what he likes to drink.

The handsome man smiled a charming grin "Mr Woodfield, It's lovely to meet you" He offered a friendly handshake.

Raymond shook his hand, with a soft grip while examining the deboniars clothes; the expensive, stylish suite, a dark purple tie, burgundy shirt, confident appearance, revealed he is successful, confident, and probably has the gift of the gab. He probably likes to "win", as well as take risks. Albeit his dark eyes, spell mistrust; "What is your name?"

The man smiled but never replied.

The beautiful waitress returned with her bright smile and a Martini with an olive inside the appropriate tall curved glass. She placed it in front of her customer.

"Is that a real Martini? The one that's *James Bond's* preference."

"It is. I hope you'll enjoy It." said the beautiful young lady before she walked away.

"I have always wanted to try one of these, but never took the moment to actually ordered one."

The refined gentlemen opposite smiled again, this time the smile indicated that he somehow always knew.

Mr Woodfield adored the sweet taste the drink had to offer.

"It's on me. It's the least I can offer, I can't imagine what it's like to lose our only daughter."

Mr Woodfield placed the drink gently back onto the table, "Are you the person, I am here to see?"

"I don't know, am I?"

"I've heard about these deals, you are making?"

"Have you now."

"The extraordinary things you have done for others, things that are not humanly possible. I have to know..." Raymond paused "Could you bring my daughter back from the dead?"

"I can."

Raymond heart jumped into his throat, excited and anxious, he had to know more "What do I have to do?"

"I can only swap *a life for a life*." He held up his index finger, to indicate the figure one.

Worry replaced the grieving fathers' excitement. "What do you mean?" He asked even though he already knew what he meant.

"Kill Shane Crewball and your daughter will come back to you."

"I don't know if I can."

"Why not?" The dashing, well suited man leaned forward, closer to Raymond. "Shane Crewball is proverbial stain that marks your little town. Your daughter is innocent, beautiful and had a whole future ahead of her. She dedicated herself to a career to help others while Shane Crewball devotes his life to hurt others." The man looked less handsome now, with his tongue slowly pushing through the middle of his clenched teeth.

The dashing man's' eyes were darker than before, more luring to Raymond, drawing him into temptation. "Did he kill my daughter?"

"No." The debonair straightened himself out, cleared his throat, and then checked to see if his tie wasn't crooked.

"Then I can't do it, it will condemn my soul."

"Not necessarily, just repent, it's so easy."

"But Jenny would never forgive me; she would find out, she would hate me."

"At least she would be alive."

Tears came down from Mr Woodfield's eyes, he broke down on the table, sobbing uncontrollably, digging his wet eyes into his palms. "I'm sorry, I'm weak, I couldn't protect me daughter, now I can't do anything to bring her back. I'm a failure has a husband and father."

The charming man stood up and moved across to rub Mr Woodfield's shoulders, looking concern for his guest, "Raymond, you are not a failure, you are just a man. A good man." He emphasised the word "Good."

Raymond, felt embarrassed, humiliated that he's just cried in front of this stranger, in the middle of the restaurant. "I'm sorry."

The man returned to his seat, opposite Raymond. "If it's any consideration, you are doing the right thing. And you're welcome back anytime; you will have to buy your own drinks though." The enticer ended with a good-hearted joke before unveiled another grin.

"I apologise for wasting your time, thank you for the offer." Raymond slowly walked out the room, along the way out, he noticed not one elderly person in their booths, have turned any attention towards him.

Chapter 47

Bass steps on the crack of the pavement tile, while he makes his way to the newsagents, having his headphones in to ward off any conversations from by-passers. This morning's theme includes soft, romantic, melodic, piano songs. The key focus of the uplifting lyrics is; love and not being alone. There was a slight spring in Carl Sebastian's step, he hadn't even noticed. A tall red head, in a winter coat and leopard-print scarf, had noticed, so she smiled at him. Bass, uncharacteristic-like, returned the smile. Other locals who know of Bass, though never met him, believe he is now giving a less-hostile vibe. Despite the rain finishing, the freezing gale winds, the sun was shining, brightening up the houses red bricks. The barbers white entrance was more dynamic, the shops painted blue colours more vibrant and the grey surface on the apartments above were not-so depressing. Had the influence of a positive, euphonic, happier song, changed his cognitive thought process? Perhaps, it was the beautiful blonde, who recommended the song over breakfast?

Outside the newsagents, Chelsea Heart, was pacing up and down, hugging herself for warmth. Bass believed she looked cold, and if she were similar to him, then he knew that Chelsea wouldn't mention her disposition to anyone else. The Private Investigator was startled when she approached him, "Bass" she yelled.

"Had she been waiting for me?" He thought, unable to tell if it's his Detectives intuition or paranoia.

"Chelsea, what are you doing out here?" Bass asked, casually.

"Can you buy me a packet of fags? I'm not allowed in there since I've been band for shop lifting."

"Isn't there anywhere else you could have gone?"

"Not where they won't tell my father."

"How long have you stood here?"

"I've just got here."

"Shouldn't you be at school?"

"It's Sunday. Are you going to help me or not?"

Bass paused, contemplating, "Money first." he demanded with his hand held out.

Chelsea gave him ten pounds from her pocket.

He placed it in his jeans pocket before entering.

Inside the shop; Bass noticed it was empty, apart from the kind, Syrian man who smiled at him who welcomed him with a friendly smile, "Hello, my friend."

"I'm not your friend" Bass almost commented out loud, but then he considered; it could appear to be a racist remark, plus there was no need to upset this man's feelings.

Browsing down the aisles, down the cereal section, Bass had to laugh at the cheaper, knock-off cereals that imitated the bigger brands: *Cocomoms, Wheated Shreds, Frostier Flakes.* The sunnier Private Inspector was craving chocolate, his sweet tooth had not been satisfied in a while, the cravings were stronger when he was in a good mood, and it had been a while since he was in a pleasant mood. Further along, Bass reached "Aisle of Random Crap" pointless, cheap objects that no one ever buys, such as *A One Direction Stapler, A Lizzie McGuire sticker book.* "Do kids these days know, who she is?" Bass chuckled to himself. Amongst the shelves is a Singing Bass Fish on a wooden plaque. Bass pressed the button, the fishes head lifted up but before it sang its jolly tune, it froze. The Bass had broken in Carl Sebastian's hand. *"There's a metaphor in here, somewhere."* Among the junk; a small, cute, cuddly Panda Bear toy stands out.

Bass recalled the time when Brooke mentioned; how much she loved Pandas, and how adorable they were. He knew this cuddly bear would make her happy, and so, with no hesitation, without glimpsing at the price tag, he grabbed it.

Bass bought the Panda Bear, chocolate and a pack of cigarettes from the very polite man behind the counter before returning outside.

Back in the cold, Bass gave Chelsea her exact change.

"Thank you." she said.

Bass took out two cigarettes from the packet, and placed them behind his pocket before giving her the rest of the packet; "compensation."

Chelsea looked surprised "I didn't think you smoked."

"I tend to enjoy one every now and then. I treat myself to one after I solve a case. Or when I'm really drunk."

"I see."

"Can I ask you a few questions about Mark?"

"Why?" She asked, curiously.

"Do you think he would hurt Jenny Woodfield?"

"I never thought he would, he's been so clingy, recently. He's called me at least ten times, left me a dozen messengers. I'm ghosting him."

"You're *toasting* him?"

"GHOSTING, it means ignoring. I remember; once Jenny came to me crying, she cried easily, so I never took no notice before. Mark was so jealous of this other guy, it was this other lad who came onto Jenny, Jenny politely turned him down. Mark blamed her for some reason. Even though Jenny would never cheat on Mark with another man, of course, now we know why."

Chelsea placed the cigarette in-between her dark red lips. Bass took the lighter from his pocket and lit the cigarette for her. She inhaled deeply into her lungs.

"Do you believe what Shane Crewball said?" Bass asked.

"I do, I've read her diary; Jenny mentioned Mrs Brooke, a lot."

Bass was surprised. "Did you sworn to keep her secret? Is that why you never told anyone else?"

"She never knew I read it. One night; Jenny picked me up from Blake's house; I was in a right-state. I was steaming. I slept on her floor, she was writing in a diary, I'd never seen it before. When she fell asleep, I put my hand under her pillow to get it. I blocked out most parts, including her love for Gail. Because, all I remember reading was a part; it said "as much as I love Chelsea, she's been my best mate since childhood, but I wish sometimes we weren't friends."

Bass could see the regret written on her kind, pale complexion "That's cold; I assume you were a handful. So it's true about Brooke?"

"I just don't know why she wouldn't tell me. We told each other everything."

"Maybe she would have done, in time. It could have been down to shame? Embarrassment? You saw how strange her mum reacted, it could have been due to her parents' approval?"

"Janet and Raymond aren't bigots, I've known them for a long time."

"We never really know someone."

Chelsea has another drag; "They're not homophobic, I can tell you that, for sure. I don't get why they've been so strange recently."

"It's because of Jenny's unnatural death."

"Miss Brooke tried to tell me, I couldn't really follow it all. But it's the Ghosts, isn't it?"

"Something like that, her untimely death, Jenny's ghost warning Brooke of her killer, has caused an unbalance in nature, making the grieving to react *strange.*"

"This town has been acting proper weird recently."

To Bass, it sounds like Chelsea's becoming more convinced. "Do you know anyone who would want to hurt her?"

Chelsea pauses for a while to think about the question, "No, everyone loved her. She was kind; always went out the way to help others, loyal to a fault. All she wanted to do is be a doctor and stay fit."

"Perhaps that's why?"

"I don't understand." Chelsea asks with a puzzled expression on her face.

"Maybe, it was nothing personal, maybe the killer wanted to murder someone, someone who everybody likes, something that resembles innocence and kill something that is *good.*"

Chapter 48

Bartholomew Maithes is walking down the street with is shopping in his hand. Being in a more conscious state, Bartholomew had managed to change into a fresh pair of clothes; a grey hoodie, jeans, an old pair of grey pump-trainers to go outside his flat and see life. More alert than he had been in the previous days, enough to know, the sofa behind the shop window, was not really talking to him, it was his sickness. "Praise Jesus" he told himself, thankful the good days The Lord offered. With Jesus and The Holy Father on his side, he has faith he will make it through each day.

The street is getting busier, everyone knows Bart, aware of his condition and noticing today is one of his good days, they all smile and wave hello at him. However they maintain a fair distance encase he snaps, and his jittery head unease's others. Sometimes he talks to himself, he'd spout a word such as; "nope" when he hears the voices, he knows are not real.

Bart noticed an innocent, smiling, little girl, wearing a thick woolly hat, glove and a puffy pink coat. She waves at him and her smile shows her missing teeth. Bartholomew crouches with one hand resting on his knee, his shopping bag dangling from the wrist, he gives a friendly wave in return, and his smile shows his missing teeth. The little girls laughs, the mother smiles politely at Bart while simultaneously pulling her daughter inwards for protection. Bartholomew detects he's beginning to scare others, "Bless you and your child, ma'am" he wished, before making his way back home, his neck twitching along the way.

The voices, were getting louder, there were many, too incoherent to understand, Bartholomew dropped his bag to clamp his hands over his ears, to drown out the sound, an apple rolled onto the pavement. Passers-by thought poor Bart was just having another episode. Voices were getting louder, never have they been so loud before, they were screaming at him, but they were too many for him to understand. "Stop" He cried out.

Then the voices did stop, they all stopped to point Bartholomew in the same direction, towards a man...

This man, very tall, very handsome, covering his expensive suit with a long fancy overall-coat. He walked with such charisma, has he placed his hand to wipe the edge of his coat, and he raised his thick eyebrow over his dark, dark eyes. Bartholomew eyes sprung open, his body trembled before him, and his draw dropped in fear, for he knew what he was...

"HE'S THE DEVIL! THE DEVIL IS HERE! EVERYBODY!!" Bartholomew warned.

People around him fled to a safer distance.

"CAN'T YOU ALL SEE HIM, HE'S HERE!" He points, and screams but no one else could see him.

Bartholomew tried his best to warn everyone, he franticly jumped and screamed, so everyone could see the danger. He just wanted to do his best to protect everyone, but the more frantic he got, the more frightening he came across. "THE DEVIL IS HERE! EVERYONE RUN FOR YOUR LIVES." A few people did. Bartholomew hurled himself to a crowd of people, to do the one thing; God had just told him to do, kill the devil. Has he pushed and shoved through a gazing crowd, he accidentally knocked over a pram. Scream rained over the street, from a horrified mother.

Around the corner Carl Sebastian heard the commotion, he ran towards the danger to investigate.

Chapter 49

The police have just arrested Bartholomew Maithes; Carl Sebastian has just giving his statement to a police officer. Bass had to have a smoke to calm the shakes; the adrenaline is still pumping through his veins. He had just spent the last ten minutes restraining Bartholomew from hurting himself or anyone else. Physiologically speaking, the inhale of the nicotine made him feel better already. His mood dropped when Chief Inspector Simon Cole approached him, Bass sighed then mocked, "I'm sorry; I don't have any spare change."

"Sarcasm is the lowest form of wit." Simon returned.

"I thought you were."

"I need to take a statement from you."

"I've already giving it; just ask your deputy."

"You're going to give me one."

"Why?"

"Because I am the Chief Inspector and you're going to do it, because I've told you to." Simon stomped his authority.

Bass laughed at him, "You'd just dismiss it, like you dismissed Jenny's body. You know there was something wrong but you ignored it."

"There is a logical explanation, to why there is no marks, no bruises-"

Bass interrupts, "Not even a trace of DNA found on her body, no skin tags underneath her nails, no hairs, and no blood. Someone as athletic as Jenny wouldn't have gone down without a fight."

"The killer must have been a professional."

"So ninjas are to blame?" Bass said sarcastically.

"There's no such thing as ghosts." Simon stated. Then he immediately felt embarrassed by what he shouted, worried the other locals heard.

"Remember, when we first met and I asked you if people are acting strange, well, can't you see that they are?"

"Holders Bridge, is a quiet, normal, little town, I think you need to check yourself into a Mental Hospital, maybe you'll share rooms with Bart?"

"He saw something, I need to know what it was. I have to ask him some questions, like right now." Bass demanded.

"He's heavily sedated, right now."

"Which hospital is he going to?"

"You don't have the liberty to know that information."

"What? You can't do this! I need answers, damn it!" Bass furiously spouted in Simons face.

"Don't worry, he'll be given the special help that he needs, he'll be cared for and looked after."

"Have you interviewed him? What did he say?"

"Like I said, he's heavily sedated."

"Do you plan to question him?"

"I do, but what he says won't be of any use, he's crazy."

"He's not crazy, not entirely, he saw someone, some-THING, you got to find out who?"

"He said he saw the devil."

"What does he look like?"

"He's red and has two pointy horns." The Chief Inspector ridiculed.

"Look, I wouldn't have believed it either but I've seen a lot of strange things in this town and now I'm open to any suggestions."

"A lot of strange things have happened since you came along, why don't you go back to what-ever shit-hole you crawled out of?"

"I'm not going anywhere."

Simon had to admire his determination, "I thought so. If you want to know where Bart is going, then beg."

"Excuse me" Bass said, even though he heard him clearly.

"I want you to grovel, on your knees and then I'll tell you"

"Fuck you." Bass told, he was too proud to ever submit to this puny little man.

"I guess you'll never hear what Bart has to say."

"I'll tell everyone about you and Shelly Jayne."

"No one will believe you, everyone knows you're insane, rude, antisocial, sociopath, who doesn't care about anyone." Simon notices a Panda Bear toy stuffed in his rivals' back-pocket, *he does care for someone, Gail Brooke*, he assumes. "Who's that for? Someone special?" Nodding towards the direction of the cuddly toy.

"Yeah, your mum."

"Very original, I have someone in my life too; we wouldn't do anything to lose them, would we?"

"Can I ask, why?"

Simon looks confused "What are you on about now?"

"Why did you and Shelly have sex in a closet? One in her coffee shop? A public place? You could have done it anywhere that's more discrete."

Simon smiles "The possibility of being caught; it arouses us."

Bass thought he was strange, but it kind-of made sense, at the same time.

Simon returned to the main topic "Carl, I don't like you, it's obvious that you don't like me. I want to catch the bastard that killed Jenny too. Please, please, stay out of my way. Let the real policeman do their job. Don't fuck things up for me. A man did this, A MAN, do you really believe The Devil himself murdered Jenny Woodfield?"

Bass replied "It's a possibility."

"I still need that statement." Simon ordered

"Oh yes, I will be right back." Bass said, though he intentionally never returned.

Chapter 50

Jack Mill is sat on his brothers red settee, with a note pad and pen in hand. Trying to materialize some new jokes for tonight's charity show. The pad remains blank. Writers block? No, something more serious... depression. He's been smiling so much for so long, it had simply ran out. His life-span has a whole, corresponds to the time in a day; It starts of great, fresh, Jack becomes an opportunist, the world's his oyster, he can be and/or do anything. Then it gradually deteriorates.

"I can't think of anything." Jack tells himself. "Am I really that dull, boring and unimaginative to create something new? Have I spoken so much, I am now dumb?"

Jack constantly jabs the pen onto the paper, leaving lots of blue dots on the top of his sheet.

He decided to cover his eyes and jot down the first thing that comes to his mind, without thinking he imprinted the sentence...

NOTHING MAKES ME HAPPY.

He can't face going on stage tonight, how he wished his brother would listen to his pleas. "Don't make me go on that stage." He begged, but he uses his business as emotional blackmail. Frank would say "I would lose out on a lot of customers, the money will come in handy." Then he would plea for him to carry on with his performance. Of course Jack would do it, he doesn't want to let his big-bro down.

Jack makes his way to the small kitchen, to brew a coffee, "A sugar rush would ignite a flame" he thought.

He looked up on the lights above; he remembered that a light bulb needs replacing. Also the burglar alarm needed replacing, and the kitchen sink needs re-sealing. Jack went to get some milk from the fridge, sadly it was bare.

"I don't need all this right now." He sighed.

He needed to go to the shop, "another job!" These simple jobs piled on the pressure of the weight that's dragging him down. That's how Jack describes his depression: *A Weight*. Placed on the back of him, all the time, pulling him down. Some days it's heavier than others, lately, it has been unbearable. Even though his list of jobs are simple DIY jobs and his brother thinks he's just being lazy. Really, The Comedian feels like they're too much. He might as well be given the twelve challenges of Hercules. Now, Jack feels unable to do anything because he's useless... *worthless*.

The youngest of the Mill brothers, recalled the time he was working on the building site, he started off keen, enthusiastic, willing to learn but he couldn't follow the instructions the others gave him. Everything he did or tried to do, went wrong. Later, Jack tried to work in IT; again he couldn't install the simplest of software. The instructors told him what to do, the lack of an attention-span caused Jack to lose focus, and his mind drifted elsewhere mid-way through the instructors guide. He never lasted long at the jobs he worked. So, he decided to work for himself; never having to let anybody else down, and to never feel so unworkable again. The question was; what job could he do for himself?

After week of unemployment, staggering through the streets of London, he found a bar that had an open-mic night. Under the influence of his "Dutch-courage," Jack told everyone all his incompetent stories. It brought a laugh from an audience, there and then, he had found his calling. Over time, Jack has slowly lost the pleasure of doing stand-up comedy, "Why am I losing interest in the things I love?" The answer was easy; like everything else. How thick, pure, unprinted snow turns to thaw. How fresh fruit will turn sour. How beauty will turn to age. Everything deteriorates.

Chapter 51

Chelsea Heart was stuffed, after having a massive steak dinner with lots of vegetables. Mark's body however absorbed the protein, calories, vitamins it needed, and could eat again very soon. A weary Chelsea sat on the edge of Marks blue bed, clenching her stomach while Mark was tidying his room, transferring the crinkled clothes from the floor into his brown Cayuga drawers.

"Thank you, for dinner. It was nice." Chelsea complimented.

"I'm glad you liked it. Thanks for coming as well. I got proper worried when you wasn't texting me back."

"Sorry, I was in one of my, I-wanna-be-alone kind-a moods." Chelsea puts on a big smile.

"I understand, I'm still pretty bummed n'all."

"Can you do me a MASSIVE favour?"

"Yes, anything." Mark leaps onto the bed, beside Chelsea, like a loyal Labrador puppy.

"Can you go to the shop and buy me a packet of cigs?" Chelsea asks before reaching into her pocket to pull out another tenner.

"You know smoking's really bad for you, you'll have no stamina and-"

Chelsea stops him "Please, Mark" She rubs his muscly arm, flirtatiously while giving a pleading expression on her face.

Typical man, Mark falls for her act, "OK, I'll be back in ten mins." Mark, pockets her money and puts on his back leather jacket.

"Thanks and could you get some Ice cream as well, not the one from the local shop but the one from the fridge in Goforcoffee, please." Chelsea gives a white grateful smile, jiggling her body with excitement before leaning back on the bed, with one exposed pale thigh on top of the other.

"OK, see you soon." Mark says before walking out the bedroom.

Chelsea looked as if she was going to hurl, her tongue pressed against her lower lip, sickened by the little, nicey-nice, innocent girl act she just put on to manipulate Mark. Now he had gone, Chelsea searched for his room, to look for evidence, suspecting he had something to do with Jenny's death. Her gut tells her that it wasn't Mark, she had just watched him spend twenty minutes trying to open a can of chickpeas with a left-handed tin opener, despite the lid already having a finger-pull leaver. He doesn't have the brains to organise such a brutal assault and not leave any evidence. For all that, Chelsea suspicion was aroused when he suddenly became too clingy and needy towards her, also the fact that Mark had never told her, the police or Bass about how much he screamed at Jenny for wanting to leave Holders Bridge. Looking back, Chelsea remembered he could get quite possessive over Jenny when she talked to other guys, although she wouldn't cheat on him, she was merely being polite.

Chelsea looked through his three doored closet that matched the drawers. She scavenged through the pockets of all his neatly folded jeans that were on the base. There was nothing expect a used tissue, *"Yuck."* Chelsea grimaces. She looked through his surprisingly expensive, brand, tracksuit bottoms and jacket pockets. Still, nothing was inside.

Underneath the narrow side of the room, where the roof slants, is a computer desk, with an old bulky monitor and computer tower. "How old is this thing?" Chelsea asked herself, while tapping the back-end of the bulky PC monitor. There was nothing on the computer except for lots of porn addresses in his browser and viruses. "This is what you've been doing the last week. Get *ad-blocker*, idiot." Chelsea laughs to herself.

Chelsea spotted his gym duffel bag, lobs-out his sweaty gym clothes, there was his college books, inside. She flicked through the pages, it was all homework, with lots of spelling mistakes inside. On the back cover of the book is a drawing, an attempt of a drawing, of Jenny. It looks horrific, a toddler would have done a better job. Jenny's right eye was bigger than the left and is higher than the other. Her cute button nose, is now tripled in size. Her hair long brown hair is now a very long tally-chart. Despite the disaster of a portrait, Mark really did love her and now she regrets the accusation. Chelsea looked up and Mark was there watching, bewildered and appalled.

"Mark." a startled Chelsea says out loud. She carefully places the book on the computer desk.

"I didn't know what Ice Cream flavour you wanted, so I thought I'd come and ask." He through the packet of cigarettes on the bed; "Why are going through my things? Are you spying on me?"

"It's not what it looks like."

"I know what this is; I might not be the sharpest *batarang* in the *utility belt* or fastest canoe on the stream..."

"Where are you getting your metaphors from?"

"...You think I killed Jenny?" Mark feels betrayed, again. "First Jenny kept a secret diary from me, saying she loved her teacher and now you, you used me, you didn't want to have dinner with me, you were looking for clues."

"I had to be sure, I was looking for evidence, to prove you were lying to me the whole time, like how you never told me about the horrible row you had. Maybe, it was cause I wanted to prove myself wrong. I like to think it was the latter."

"What does that mean?"

"I wanted to prove that you would never hurt Jenny, and I was an idiot, just for even thinking it."

"No. What does "latter" mean?"

"*Oh,* the last one"

"The last what?"

"Never mind."

Mark begins to cry, he's hurt "I think you should go."

Chelsea's guilt makes her do something she doesn't normally do, beg. "Mark, please."

"Go!" Mark yells.

Chelsea slowly walks out the room, with her head down in shame. She pauses by the side of Mark. He can't bring himself to look her in the eye, he doesn't want her to see him cry. Chelsea already knew, he can see his face go red, she can hear the sniffling and the quiet whimpering.

"I am sorry, Mark." Chelsea says before stepping out, the door slams behind her.

Chapter 52

Shane Crewball approached The Balcony Restaurant, with a semi-automatic handgun in his pocket. He's only prepared to use it, if he has to. This is a visit to warn, not to kill. This is not the first time, he had to intimidate some new soldier, coming onto his turf. Shane's pretty confident he'll make him "step off." It was a false sense of confidence, brought on by the hit he just bumped in the office of his gym. He's been hearing rumours of this guy who makes these "special deals." Well there's only one guy who the people in Holders Bridge should turn to for deals, and that's Shane Crewball.

His heart is pounding, bouncing off the floor, ready to fight; he swipes the messy beard with the sleeve of his leather jacket. His trigger happy hand wavers close to his pocket, eagerly ready to "put one through some arseholes head."

Inside, he runs up the green carpet stairs, his other hand used on the gold hand rail, to push his body up. His overly long hair flapped on the back of his cigarette scented jacket. He stormed through the open door, on the upper level, barging past the beautiful waitress friendly welcome. He wasn't sure who to look for, now he does, a tall dude sat in the middle of the room, on his own by a small lit candle. *Fucking idiot sat in the open. He's making so easy for me to take him out.* Shane looked around the room to see, if this man had any of "boys" with him. All he noticed was a bunch of stupid old people, jabbering away at shit.

Shane sat opposite the tall guy, who's wearing a fancy-ass suit. Trying to act calm and casual but his body can't stop shuffling, full of adrenaline, too agitated, too bustling. On the other side of the table, the dark eyed man was as cool as a cucumber. He knew why Shane was here, he smirked, mocking his efforts of trying to frighten him. The steady handed debonair watched Shane

Crewball, wriggle, wave his long hair and heard him sniff a lot through his nostrils, probably needed to have a little something, to reach a nerve to confront him. The handsome dark eyed man, interlocked his fingers, and leant over the table. "I know why you are here. Can I offer you a drink?"

"No." Shane refused. He smiled, revealing his yellow stained teeth.

The handsome man, smiled back only to show off his perfect, white teeth.

"I know you are new here, so I'll give you the benefit of the doubt. But there is something you should know; this is my town." Shane warned.

"But this isn't *your* town." The other man informed, while stroking his tie in such a suave manner.

"What you're doing here, has got to stop, I'm asking you nicely. You only get this once. If I find out, you're continuing your business here, and then we'll have a problem. You don't want a problem with me."

"Actually, Shane I do have a problem with you..."

Shane deeply inhales, fluttering his hand over the automatic.

"... You are a murderer, a rapist, a liar and a thief. You sell drugs to vulnerable children. You couldn't make it has a gangster in the big city, so you came to this charming little town and put fear into the hearts of some good people. The worst part is, you enjoyed all of it."

"You can't prove shit, if you have heard of me, then you should know, not to fuck with me."

"I also know you stole Jenny Woodfield's belongings."

"It's not like she's going to need them."

"It's pretty poor stealing a dead girl's jewellery... and diary."

"I couldn't give two-shits about that slut. She's just another dumb bitch who got herself killed."

The well-proportioned man slams both his fists on the round table, has he stands up.

Shane, to defend himself, pulls out the handgun and pulls the trigger numerous of time... *Click. Click. Click.* The gun jammed. Shane turned the black handpiece to its side, looking discouraged towards his defence.

"Was you going to shoot me in a room full of people?" The man laughed.

"How are you doing this?" Shane's body began to tremble, his heart was pumping fast, not due to drugs, but the fear.

After realising the place fell silent, Shane scanned the room, all the elderly gentleman and ladies sat around the edges of the room, were now unvarying, all their unblinking eyes were impaling on Shane.

Shane hadn't been this terrified in years, not since h was first recruited by a gang. He wanted to run but he was transfixed onto his chair. Shane returned to the man, opposite whose eyes were totally black.

"There is a certain place, where people like you, belong." The man said.

The pygmy flame from the candle burst into an explosive, roaring inferno that shot up skywards. It died within an instant, causing the room to fall pitch black.

Once the gangster, leapt up from his chair, his arms wavering in the dark, searching for something to hold onto or an exit. Eventually his beady eyes adjusted to the darkness, only to reveal all the elderly couples and singles around the room, were actually shadows. The shadows were rigid at first, but then began to dance, and whisper in tongues, a language Shane never heard before.

They took delight in tormenting another wretched soul. When the room and candle lights returned; It was if nothing had altered, the elderly gentlemen and women were talking amongst themselves or reading a newspaper. The crackling thirties orchestra played as the vinyl span round again. The beautiful waitress collected glasses from the tables. The suave debonair returned to his regular seat. Though, Shane Crewball had disappeared, never to be seen on this earth again.

Chapter 53

Carl Sebastian and Gail Brooke were sat in the dining room at The Robinson's Bed and Breakfast.

Facing opposite sides, they were both grabbing some dinner, before they go take a steady walk to Jack Mandolin's charity comedy night. Brooke has a little companion next to her bowl of soup, a little cuddly Panda Bear toy.

Bass's gift had made Brooke's day, her smile made his.

"Thank you so much for my little bear, he's adorable."

"Anytime." Bass smiled before tucking into his lasagne and chips. "Have you got a name yet for the little fellow?"

"I have yet to decide on one."

"Would he like some lasagne?" Bass places some meat and cheese onto his folk and goes to feed the toy.

Brooke slaps his hairy wrist away "He is a vegan." she adds.

"Because Pandas are herbivores?"

"Actually, they are Omnivores." Brooke corrects with a slightly smug grin.

"I'm sorry I didn't go to fancy all girl, posh school."

"I would find it peculiar, if you did attend an all-girl secondary school."

They both laugh.

Bass supped his pint, "Well I've told you about my day. What have you been up to?"

"Well, I went to see Father Paul, to question him, over Billy Lane, to see if his murder coincides with Jenny Woodfield's. Unfortunately he vacated the church for the day."

"I thought it was strange, he wasn't at the wake. You shouldn't have gone on your own. I'll interrogate him tomorrow."

"Do you mean to question? Not to *interrogate.*"

"Same difference."

Brooke took a sip of glass of her sparkly wine. "You appear to be in a cheerful mood."

"I've been miserable for such a long time, maybe I don't want to be miserable anymore."

Brooke was curious to know if it was because of her, "Any reason in particular?"

"Maybe it's the beer?" Bass jokes, dismissing the question.

Brooke rolls up her sleeve of her blouse to rest her right elbow rudely onto the table, she rest pretty face on her hand, an index finger on her soft cheek, the rest of her fingers are curved under her chin. Her beautiful blonde hair dangles down the side of her kind face. Bass looks at her arresting green eyes, captivated by her beauty, lured in by the sultry gaze again, something he couldn't get used to, nor desired to. He peered amongst her exposed left ear. "I've been meaning to ask you, is that a birthmark or a mole on your ear?"

Brooke scratched her left ear lobe with her nail, where Bass had noticed, "I was born with it, I surmise it is a mark, rather than a mole."

"It doesn't matter, Brooke, you're still the most beautiful woman I have ever met. So please forgive me if you catch me, staring at you every now and then."

Brooke heart melted, so charmed by his compliment. She had noticed, he's changed, more different now, compared to when they had first met.

Bass, struck an idea, something he wanted to do for a long time but never met the right person to ask. Until now, he found the right place for it as well. "Brooke, come with me to the back of the B'N'B."

"Why? Where are we going?"

"There's something I've always wanted to do, meet me in the garden of the hotel in fifteen minutes." Bass said has elevated himself off his seat.

Brooke had never witnessed him so exuberant before, he feverishly jolted up to the room. She smiled, curious and excited to discover what laden plans Bass is preparing.

Gail Brooke gently walked out through the back patio doors, stepped onto the short grass in her flat shoes, wet grassed seeped water into her bare feet and onto the underpinning legs of her trousers. The blouse she wore, was not enough to maintain warmth. So she rubbed her bare arms with her hands. On the other side of the garden, in his usual, creased funeral suit is Carl Sebastian. By his left, is the little home-made fish pond lit up by blue and green LED pond lights. Above Bass's sweaty forehead are string of garden lights, hung up on the tree that foreshadows the pond. To the right side of his sweaty palm, are speakers attached to his portable music device.

Brooke was fascinated, engrossed by the all the effort and grandeur. "Did you all do this, for me?"

"Well, the lights and pond were already here." Bass answers honestly. "However, I think it's the perfect spot."

"What for?" Brooke asks.

Bass hit's play on the music device.

The soft, delicate guitar chords from *David Gray's-We Could Fall in Love Again,* began to play. Brooke moved closer to Bass, just as the musician gently sang the fragile words, about someone yearning for his soulmate, desperately believing they can soon rekindle their love.

"I've always wanted to slow dance to this song, I've just never met anyone, who I'd thought would."

Bass offered his hand, his heart was pounding fast, he was praying that she wouldn't reject him, or think he's an absolute weirdo, and laugh at him.

Brooke thought it was so romantic, spontaneous and bold. Presuming not many people, get to see his softer side, she feels pretty special. Brooke takes his hand.

A thankful Bass, uses his right hand to interconnect his fingers with Brooke's left hand. He places the other hand, on her slightly curved waist and pulls her in. The other hand now moves to hold the middle of Brooke's back. Brooke's right arm is now wrapped across her man's broad shoulders. The pair slowly swayed their hips in motion to the song. Brooke looked up to Carl's dark green eyes, they abandoned their previous dismay, now they seem clearer. "I wish it were not so cold outside."

Carl Sebastian looks into her light soft green eyes, "We're not outside; we're in a ballroom..."

The two place their foreheads together. "...close your eyes, imagine what I am."

Has the sound of the smooth saxophone is playing, *they did,* statistically impossible, but Gail Brooke and Carl Sebastian defied the impossible and jointly imagined the same surroundings, the exact same clothes on each other. In an empty school gym hall, a disco ball reflected small round lights that span on the surface of purple drapes that cover the room. Bass was no longer wearing his old suit, he was in a fresh, tuxedo, ironed white shirt, a bow tie around his collar, black blazer, trousers and shoes. They both visualized Brooke wearing her favourite long purple dress; her blonde hair was neatly tied in a bow, just like she wore on their first dinner date. With their eyes shut, in their envision, hand in hand, gently jiving their hips, slow dancing on the dance floor, their feet avoiding confetti and balloons. Bass did see something, Brooke never envisaged, a wooden door with a gold handle, he'd seen it before, in the garden, only this time, the door opened.

The song ended, bringing the pair back to reality, yet still close together and their hands never departed.

Brooke, released the hold of Bass's hip; took his hand, leading her man across the back patio, through The Robinson's Bed and Breakfast dining room, leading him upstairs. Bass tread behind Brooke, he was nervous, knowing what was going to happen, his heart began to pound, the sweat started to break and his stomach rumbled. Even though Bass had made love before, he had never slept with someone he cared about so much. With not wanting to disappoint, once they entered their bedroom, the telltale-signs of worry began to show. So he conquered his body by dominating hers. Bass held Brooke against the wall, he kissed her for the first time. Brooke's left thigh sprouted into the air, he brushed his lips delicately against hers and leaving an impressionable peck on her lips once they finished. Brooke's hands ran up his muscular arms but before she could caress any further parts of his body; Bass restrained her hands. His large left hand had pinned her right hand on the wall, he tenderly brushed the fingertips of his right hand across the inside of Brooke's left arm until their fingertips linked. Brooke knew he was taking control of her body, but the warm sensation told her to submit. He raised both of her hands over her head, causing Brookes' legs jelly. His left hand held Brookes' arms in place, the other hand ran down her side, breast to thigh. Carl Sebastian moved his lips close to Gail's, she wanted him to kiss her, this time more passionately, so animalistic-ally, that it would become difficult to breathe. Though she could not, for his lips were close but not close enough, teasing her. Bass moved in to kiss the right side of her neck; Brooke closed her eyes and gasped into the air. He carefully worked up the right side of her neck, gradually reaching up to gently bite her earlobe. Now, Bass had allowed her to kiss him the way she desired to.

Brooke was stroking his broad shoulder blades when Bass tore the top of her blouse, causing a button to fling onto the floor. Pulling the blouse over her head, he proceeded to snap off the bra strap hook. Brooke unknotted his tie and pushed off his jacket. Bass held both of his rough hands on the side of her upper-body; along the way he purposely used his thumb to flick an erect nibble on her round circular breast. After deciding that it was her turn to take charge; Brooke loosened his belt and pants before pushing her man onto the bed. Carl laughed whilst taking that surprisingly-light bounce on the white sheets. The seductress curved her back in luscious manner to slowly take off her trousers. Climbing on top of her man-mountain, the soft hands slid up Bass's collar line before ripping buttons off the white shirt. Placing her hands on his hairy pectorals to balance herself; Brooke slowly steered her tense warm body on top of Bass. He held her backside, as the man looked up at this beautiful woman groaning on top of him, her beautiful, messy blonde hair wavered over her shoulders and fulfilled face.

After a while, Bass grabbed Brooke by her cosy, hot curved back to pull her towards him. As he swung round to sit on the edge of the bed; Brooke was now sat on top of his tree-trunk thighs. Knowing what he was going to do next, she wrapped her long smooth legs around his waist, fused her arms behind his muscular back. Carl Sebastian carried his girl across the room to sit her down on top of the hotels smooth desk. Bass carried on the same flavour as before by vibrating his hips affectionately. To release the tension, Brooke gently gnawed on his shoulder bone. It wasn't as rough as Bass normally prefers, though it does not matter, it was still the best. For tonight, his broken soul had embedded into hers.

Chapter 54

Jack Mandolin, put on his yellow patchy jacket, to act the part of The Comedian. Noticing that it appears to have loosened, he's unknowingly lost weight. He's walking down the street towards the Dive bar, for tonight is the night of the charity comedy gig, all in Jenny Woodfield's name. The *weight* on his back is too exhausting, the heaviest that it has ever been, and he's tired. Jack's eye lids are weighty; every muscle in his face wants to drop onto the floor, forcing his head to constantly look downwards.

As The Comedian ponderously enters The Dive Bar, the rowdy room turns quiet. Everyone is now sitting solidly still in their seats, frozen in darkness. There is only one light in the room; one red spotlight shining on a microphone that's standing in the middle of an empty stage, the red light is meant to indicate a welcoming, but it is a warning. Jack knows he shouldn't go on, every fibre in his being, is screaming "DON'T GO ON STAGE."

In his brown shoes, Jack takes one step on the wooden stage, the tap echoes throughout the room. He turned rigidly to face the microphone. There was a round of applause, The Comedian did not hear a thing, he's not really here, and he's crawled into the emptiness within.

The audience waited for a joke, and waited, and waited. Has the silence had grown; the crowd suspect something is wrong.

Jack Mill, younger brother of Frank Mill found the strength to lift his head, though not a smile. He spotted his big brother behind the bar.

Frank Mill was raising his hand, encouraging him to speak out; he didn't want his little bro to scare off his customers.

Jack Mill talked into the microphone; "I'm the biggest liar without even lying to anyone."

The crowd laugh.

"Don't laugh. This isn't a joke, I've manipulated you all into thinking I am one of the happiest people in the world! Well I'm not! I'm so far from fucking happy."

Tears begin to stroll down from his eyes

"But you don't care about me! None of you do! Well if you want to know I cried last night and on the way here. Because I know: you use me to distract you from your meaningless lives. I cling onto *you* because it's better than realising; there's nothing else out there for anyone. So I just want to say; FUCK YOU ALL."

A bottle is thrown on the wall, just behind The Comedian, shattering all around his back though he never flinches.

An angry audience storm out, shoving chairs, and even tables along the way.

Frank Mill stares resentfully at his brother, angry and confused.

Jack Mill slowly walks upstairs, anguish ran through his body, alongside his blood stream, knowing he couldn't cry it out, he simply had to *bleed* it out...

Chapter 55

Bass woke up beside Brooke, with the biggest smile on his face. He shuffled closer to her, his naked body closer to hers. Bass watched as Brooke opened her soft green eyes. She smiled when she saw him. Closed her eyes again, inhaled deeply through her nose as she stretched out her exhausted body.

"Good Morning." Bass grinned.

"Morning. Last night was impeccable."

"You weren't so bad yourself."

Brooke opened her eyes to Bass crawling on top of her, ready to go again. Brooke bit her lower lip with much excitement. She rubbed his bald head, while kissing his lips softly.

The phone rang.

"Who could that be?"

"Leave it." Bass, sighed with frustration.

"It could be important, we already missed the charity concert, last night."

Bass slumped to the side of the bed, he was left laying fully nude, because Brooke used the duvet to wrap around her body.

Brooke put down the phone, looking mortified.

"What is it?" Bass asks.

"The comedian Jack Mandolin had a break down at the concert last night. Shortly after, he attempted suicide."

"Where is he now?"

"At the hospital."

"Let's get over there." Bass said, springing from the mattress and throwing on yesterday's unwashed clothes.

Brooke and Bass arrived at the hospital, they respectfully entered a single room. Laying in a hospital bed, with the sides up, rests Jack Mill. On the comedians left is a large coloured man and to his right, is someone Bass has met before; The ginger haired, man-child, Julian Green.

The first thing Brooke saw was Jack Mills surprised faced, then the hospital gown, and the bandages wrapped around his right wrist.

Bass never reacted to the Adhesive Elastic Bandage wrapped around the stitches. He turned to measure the large coloured man, standing on his left. His sizeable forearms were folded, revealing a parachute regiment emblem tattooed on his right arm. *"Ex-forces, here to be the muscle."* Bass, indicated.

"What are you doing here, Mr Sebastian?" Julian questions.

"Are you here to escort me to the Urgent Psychiatric Centre? I already said that I'd come voluntary." Jacks voice spoke of much dread.

"We have already met before, Jack. I just would like to ask you a few questions." Bass sat down on a visitor's chair, opposing the bed.

"Jack you don't have to tell this man anything." Julian states.

"You've been avoiding me, Jack. Now I have you here. This man can't protect you, he's as helpful as a rabid racoon."

The ex-armed forces man, unfolded his arms, stepped closer to Bass, ready to remove him from the premises.

Brooke cautioned her partner with a stare that could only mean "tread lightly here."

"Why did you slit your wrists, because you're a failure as a comedian? Or was it because you felt guilty after killing Jenny Woodfield?"

"Mr. Sebastian! That is quite enough!" Julian said, sternly.

"Come on you're out of here." The muscly ex-para, grabbed Bass by his arm.

Jack Mill burst into tears; "I never killed Jenny, I couldn't hurt her, I couldn't hurt anyone. I have always felt a lingering sadness but for some reason; her death was the final nudge off the cliff. I grew so tired. *So tired...*" The purple bags on his face felt like they were burning. His whole body became unresponsive, drool was soon to pour out of his slack jaw.

Everyone in the room, turned to watch The Comedian.

"... I don't know if I care about anyone, they don't care about me... And why should they? Who am I? I am no one."

Julian placed a comforting hand on his back. "It's going to be ok, Jack. Whatever it is you want to say, you can tell us, it's ok to talk." He never meant to speak in such a condescending tone.

"I got so tired, of putting on a fake smile to everyone. Every day I talk to people, ask about their day, but inside, I don't really care about their day. I tell my friends I like their ties, again, I couldn't give a shit about their ties. I know I'm supposed to care, but I don't really know if I do. I don't know if I feel anything anymore; What if my skin is just an outer shell for the emptiness within me?"

Julian states; "Feeling disconnected to your feelings, is a natural part of anxiety-"

Bass interrupts, "That's why it's best to just tell people; "you don't care." Rather than pretending. It's better than being two faced."

"Well, your one face, is just down-right miserable, Bass." Brooke states, defending the victim.

Bass looks surprised, he thought Brooke would be on his side. "Don't have a go at me! The person you should be interrogating; is this coward." Referring to Jack.

Jack felt terrible about as his actions already, hearing the word "coward," only cut further into the wound.

Julian gasped with shock. "Deciding to take your own life, is not the sign of being a coward, it's a cry for help."

"Well, he is! You have to face this world alone, like everybody else!"

"It's the ignorant people like you that prompt suicide in others." Julian declares.

"Let's talk outside." Brooke, storms out.

Outside the hospital, Brooke paces up the street, she spins around to scream at Bass. "How could you say that?"

"What?"
"That man in there needed help. You have said atrocious insults to people, but this is too far."

Bass pleads "Brooke-"

"Save it! You always claim; "you are on your own." Now, you really are. I am going to work on my own for a while."

"How long for?"

"I cannot say for certain, just give me some time."

Bass's guilty long face, watched with a broken heart, as Brooke walks away from him. There's a hammer pounding on the inside of Bass's head. Every time the hammer bangs, all that is imprinted on his mind is; "You've pushed Brooke away." "She hates you." "She's never coming back." His head is a shed, he doesn't know what to do. Now, walking down the street, his fast-paced feet are losing balance, unable to walk in a straight line, he nearly stepped into an unnoticed lamp post.

Bass knew what he said was wrong, but he believes in tough love; you "push through the pain." "Even when life gets tough, you still keep going." The reason why Carl Sebastian was more angry than sympathetic, is because he can't see why The Comedian has "given up" by "giving in" to the dark thoughts, while Bass is still battling his own.

Chapter 56

Carl Sebastian clears his head by walking down the dirt track to the home of Father Paul. Bass is now sat on a single green, cushioned, L-shaped, dimpled, sofa. Father Paul, slowly brushing past the sofa arm, holding a large woven palm leaf basket tray in his hands, it carried biscuits, two pink-flowered cups of tea in matching saucers. Bass lifted his hand from the knitted armchair sleeve cover, to collect the warm beverage. The Private Paranormal Investigator watched as the Father's faithful companion followed two inches behind, a lovely looking German Shepard, Bruce. Bass recalled the vicious barking Bruce gave, when he knocked on the door, The Vicar had to briefly lock the houses-defender in the kitchen, before Bass was welcomed inside.

Father Paul placed the tray on the small round coffee table, he sat down on the mirrored chaired, opposing Bass. One hand holding the tea and the other one is supporting his back.

Bass could see the agony in the older man's face, when he transacted from standing to the chair opposite. "*This man is not fit enough to tackle a seventeen year old athlete and break all of her bones.*" he suspected.

The vicar felt relieved, now sat down to relax, he broke a biscuit in half, dunking his portion in the tea before digesting it.

Bruce sat patiently waiting beside his master, his slavering tongue was out of his panting mouth. Father Paul saw his pets' eyes, desiring the other half of the biscuit. Father Paul gave into Bruce's cuteness and fed him the treat. The dog snatched it off his wrinkly hands, pointing his head down because he prefers to chomp at it closer to the acrylic carpet.

"After the way you spoke to me last time, I'm surprised to see you." Said The Man of The Cloth.

"If you didn't like how I talked to you, then why did you let me in?"

"My door is always open for my fellow man, especially when they are in need."

"Who says I'm in need?"

"It looks like you are hurting."

"We're not here to talk about me" Bass deflected. "I read a police statement saying; you were out walking the dog when you found Jenny Woodfield's body."

"Is that a crime?"

"Is your normal walking route ten miles away from your church? No offence but you are no marathon runner."

"You wouldn't believe me, if I tell you."

"You'd be surprised how often people tell me that. I am a Private Paranormal Investigator, my specialities in the supernatural."

"Though, not religion."

"I admit, recently I have seen something's, that have changed my mind, although, not enough to be totally convinced to believe the exact same thing as you."

Father Paul smiled. "One day, I was out walking Bruce, on the grounds, like normal. He started barking at me, then ran back and forth into the woods. He continued to bark until I followed him, he led me through the trees and to the cornfield. Leading me to a fox, in the middle of this cornfield. A farmer had shot it, after it trying to eat one of his chickens, it was still alive but in a lot of pain."

"Did Bruce ever tried to rip the foxes head off?"

"No, he just sat beside me, while I had to-" Father Paul had paused in deep thought.

Bass assumed, he was remembering the terrible burden, of having to put the fox out of its misery. Bass could tell he was the sort of man, who would give it a proper good burial afterwards.

The vicar carried on; "I know a dog's sense of smell is much stronger than ours, but this was miles away."

"Are you telling me, this mutt had smelt Jenny Woodfield's body, ten miles away?"

The dogs' ears pointed up and stared at Bass with his big, soft, black eyes.

Father Paul stroked his companion on his head; "I'm saying the lord had guided me, through Bruce."

Bass continued to stare at the dogs eyes, while Bruce returned the look, into Bass's sad green eyes. Unsure if it was God telling Bruce, but Bass was sure *something* did.

Bass placed his tea down on the coffee table, sat back down to ask; "How long have you worked in Holders Bridge, Father?

"Oh, it must have been over twenty two years."

"So, was you around during the murder of Billy Lane?"

Father Paul's face became sullen, "I did his eulogy, so tragic He was one of my best friends and a good man. To this day, no one has found his murderer. I pray for his soul."

"Who's? The victims or the murderers?"

"Billy's, of course. The only redemption that brute will receive, is when he or she will confess their sins. I myself cannot forgive, but our lord is of the forgiving kind, not the vengeful one, as some prophets believe."

"How did you know him?"

"We worked at a youth centre together in Birmingham." Father Paul pointed to a picture on the wall.

Bass stood up to get a closer view of an old black and white photo, protected in a wooden circular frame. A patrolling Bruce stood closer, maintaining a watchful eye on the stranger in his home.

Bass lifted the photo from the nail on the wall.

There was three men and one woman standing behind a gang of ten children outside a white door.

"Which one is Billy Lane? I bet it's not the one with the ponytails, wearing a white mini-skirt and white kinky boots."

The Vicar chuckled politely, even though he's really unamused. "The one with the moustache, glasses and the flat cap." He identified.

"I see." Bass hangs the photo back on the wall. "Why would anyone want to hurt him?"

"There were nasty rumours. Billy was really good with the children. He had a natural talent for being an entertainer, a real show-man. He very much enjoyed making the children laugh, Billy would go to extreme lengths to hear the children laugh, a bit too extreme for the parents liking, especially when the tickling started-"

"Tickling?" Bass interrupted

"Yes, there was a lot of tickling and sometimes, it went on for too long, all innocent of course, but that's how the rumours started. There was also one or two serious allegations, none proven allegations.

Including from someone who lives here... Clive Dunscroft."

"He lives here, in Holders Bridge, where Billy Lane was murdered. He followed him here?"

"Clive Dunscroft moved here, one year after Billy did. Of course he had motive, but Clive was cleared of all charges. That's one of the reasons why the poor soul is tortured by the locals. If he was really guilty, he wouldn't have stayed in town."

"Unless he wanted to look innocent." Bass ponders while rubbing his chin. "I need to call Brooke." Bass secretly hoped that this new information would get her to talk to him, she has been ignoring the five apologetic text messages he has sent her. This time, if Bass calls her with genuine information, Brooke would talk to him again, then he could make it up to her, she'd forgive him, and they'd be friends again. With an optimistic smile on his face, he called her from his old flip-phone...

Chapter 57

Tired of walking from one place to another, Gail Brooke drove to Clive Dunscrofts' house. To purse her own intuition. Not normally a judgemental person, but she can't shake-off the strange vibes. After knocking on the door, Brooke can see a large figure approaching the door window. Then she heard a shuffling of keys, two key locks unfasten, three bolts undone.

Clive pulled open his door, partially, leaving the latch on. The man stood far too close between the small gap that it was impossible to peep past his head.

Brooke can see the one eye, measure her up and down, and she should could hear his slow heavy breathing.

Feeling uncomfortable, Brooke took a step back, away from him. "Mr. Dunscroft, I was wondering if I could have a moment of your time, please."

Clive Dunscroft, was eerie silent, eventually he spoke "Why?"

"Perhaps we could discuss it further, if you let me in? It is rather cold out."

Clive skipped back, slammed the door shut, and then unbolted the latch. He proceeded by holding the door wide open, keeping his head bowed, avoiding contact, a familiar stance.

Brooke was cautious about going inside his house, but there could be evidence inside. "Thank you" she said behind nervous laughter. To her left, was some stairs behind the wooden stair bannister, at the very top step was a toy truck, parked on the edge. Underneath her, there were black marks and stains on the red carpet, she could guess, if she had no shoes on, Brooke would feel some-kind of stickiness. To the right was a pile of boxes.

"Are you moving, Mr Dunscroft?" Brooke asked.

"Yes." He replied, treading behind her. "I'm having a hard time, in this town, nobody likes me."

"I have heard rumours that, some of the children have been most unpleasant towards you."

"I think a change is much needed."

"For you and Bradley?"

He never replied.

As they enter the living room, Brooke sits down on his blue settee. Brooke found it strange, this man is being too reserved about his own son, so she pushes; "Where is he?"

"Upstairs. Playing."

"I see."

Clive stood rigidly over an awkward Brooke, he hadn't spoken for a few seconds, but with Brooke now anxious, it felt like an eternity. While flexing his neck to turn his head to the side he offered; "Would you like some tea?"

"Yes please."

Clive's thick-rimmed glasses stared at Brooke for a moment longer, before entering the kitchen.

Brooke scanned the living room. There were no toys insight, the room was very tidy, which is quite strange for a single parent looking after a toddler. *"Perhaps most play-toys are boxed up."* She then assumed.

Brooke turned to look out the open door that leads to the hall, behind the wooden staircase is Bradley, both hands held on a round banister, his shy face peeping through the gap.

Brooke politely waved.

The boy ran back upstairs, not saying a word.

Clive returned with a tea in a cream mug that had a crack on the rim.

Brooke kindly took the drink off his hands, though she never intends to drink it. *"He never even asked if she'd like sugar."* She noticed.

Mr Dunscroft sat on the single blue sofa, his respiratory rate was slow, inhaling powerfully. His sausage fingers tapped the fringe of the sofa's arm. "Why are you really here, Gail?"

"Please, call me Brooke. I have been working with a Private Investigator..."

Brooke noticed Clive gulped, when she mentioned "Private Investigator."

"... Trying to solve the murder of Jenny Woodfield."

"I have told Chief Inspector Simon Cole, I was at home."

"I suppose, Bradley was your alibi."

Clive nodded. "I could not hurt another child, especially one as young, as kind and as beautiful, as Jenny Woodfield. Children should be allowed to remain pure and unharmed. They should not be forced to feel the full-pelt of the worlds' cruelty, at such a young age. Children have to gently ease into the adult world. Yes, Purity is something that cannot be returned, once taken away, or even stolen."

"I have to agree with you there. Albeit, Jenny was a very mature teenager, I taught her myself. She was kinder than most people. Though, I cannot describe her as totally innocent."

Clive Dunscroft turned sharply at Brooke, he stared daggers at her through the thick rimmed glasses.

Brooke, was petrified, wishing Bass was here.

"I have to check up stairs." Clive eased off the sofa, he plodded out the room.

Brooke could feel the gaze, and was curious to know; why he still had his hat and jacket on, while he's inside; *does he ever take it off? Is he going out soon?*

Brooke's mobile began to ring, the screen displays says' "Bass calling" Unwilling to speak to that egotistical, horrible, narcissist. The call might be an excuse for her to leave, or call for help.

At Father Paul's house, Carl Sebastian is calling Brooke from his ancient mobile phone. Agitated to either Brooke would answer the call or not. On the inside he prays she accepts the call in a forgiving mood, though on the outside, he won't let Father Paul see his distress.

"Carl, what is it, you want?" Brooke answers in an unyielding tone.

"Brooke, I have some information, Clive Dunscroft, the weirdo you mentioned before. Apparently he was raped by Billy Lane."

"The man who was murdered twenty years ago?"

"It gets weirder, he moved to Holders Bridge a year before Billy crocked. Despite being found innocent, suspicion has constantly followed him, like a crazy ex-girlfriend."

"Wait, if Billy Lane did force himself upon Clive as a child, I now understand his surreal harangue."

"I don't know what that means?"

"He has just violently ranted about how children should remain innocent. This explains his shielding, watchful and solicitous parenting method. He is not wanting Bradley, to receive the same fate."

"YOU'RE AT HIS HOUSE? GET OUT OF THERE." Bass ordered.

"He's not going to hurt me, not while his son is here."

"Don't be naive. You don't know what people are capable of. Leave now, I'll meet you at the coffee shop. Text me the address, immediately." Bass hangs up.

Brooke begins to message the address, unaware that Clive Dunscroft is now standing by the living room door to over hear the following conversation and to block the exit.

"Carl, my son, Clive Dunscroft is a troubled man, I don't know if the allegations are true, but I don't think he'd intend to bring harm to your friend." Father Paul, tried to comfort Bass.

The phone rings, after Bass receiving the text message, sent by Gail Brooke.

"Don't worry *Father Ted*, he's not going to kill anyone while his sons in his house."

"Who?"

"Bradley, his son."

Father Paul's face turned from relaxed to look deeply disconcerted. His ageing body, unsettled.

"What's wrong? Is dementia seeping in?" Bass retorts.

"Carl..." His perturbed eyes shot up to fix on The Private Investigator, "... I've known Clive Dunscroft for a long time, he doesn't bare a son named Bradley, or any other child."

An alarmed Bass reaches for his phone, the panic-stricken thumbs and finger, have been too clumsy to work the keypad on his phone effectively, accidentally jabbing the wrong buttons and yells; "Come on!" Whilst scanning through the phone book for Brooke's mobile number.

As the phone rings, he runs out the house, as fast as he could.

Father Paul calls the police, with his landline.

Brooke, looks down at the ringing phone, unknowing of Clive's presence behind her, listening in. "Hello." Brooke could hear the heavy breathing and heavy feet hitting the ground, she could tell he's running.

"Have you left the house yet?" Bass said rapidly, in-between puffing and panting,

"No-"

Bass cuts in "Bradley is not his son."

The news jolts Gail "What?"

"Clive Dunscroft does not have a son!" Bass musters some energy whilst running, so it sounds like he's screaming at her.

Jaw dropped, Brooke slowly pulls her phone away from her ear, hanging up. Her head spinning to the left, her frightful green eyes notices Clive, and he's using his large build to block the way out the door.

Brooke planned for another exit. *There's the kitchen, I hope to god, there's a back door.*

"Thank you for the tea, Clive. That was my partner on the phone, he has found new evidence, I have to get going." Brooke lies.

She goes to walk out, past Clive, however, he does not budge. "I'm sorry but I can't let you go."

Brooke's body quakes with fear.

Simon Cole is sat in his office, when the phone rang. "Hello, Chief Inspector Simon Cole, Speaking… Father Paul?" F.P. tells him Gail Brooke is at Clive Dunscrofts house, she's in danger and Bass is on the way.

Simon Cole hung up the phone, now disturbed. Panicky, but not for the sake of Gail or Carl, it's because Clive Dunscroft knows a secret that could ruin his reputation and diminish his respect. He runs as fast as his short legs will allow, to the nearest police car. Once he rang the sirens, he dangerously drove, swerving around corners that causes other on-coming vehicles to slam their breaks.

Brooke sprints through the kitchen, to the back door, she pulls hard on the back door. It won't budge. She tried pushing the door, still unmoveable. Clive Dunscroft, did not run to the kitchen after her, he leisurely walked. Once he stepped onto the stone floored kitchen. Brooke tried her hardest to break the door down. She ran into the door with her shoulder, the door merely wobbled. She bellowed while attempting to shoulder-barge the door down. Clive slowly moved closer, picking up a kitchen knife, admiring his reflection on the silver edge.

"Somebody help me." Brooke shrieked. One more "Help" from the bottom of her lungs, praying someone nearby will hear.

"I'm sorry, Brooke, you seem pretty nice, but I can't let you take Bradley away from me. He needs me."

Brooke cries "I won't, I won't tell anyone, I promise."

"If I go to jail, he'll be on his own. Vulnerable to the paedophiles, rapists and murderers. I can keep him safe. I'd never hurt him, not in the way you think. You must understand." Clive tries to justify his actions, stepping closer to Brooke, wielding the knife up in the air, ready to strike.

Brooke grabs a handle of a sauce pan to her left, swings it once as a warning, then with great force, she hits his arm, pushing the knife away from her. With an almighty uppercut, she slams the cookware into Clive's face, shattering his thick rimmed glasses. It was a perfect opportunity for Brooke to slip past. The English Teacher, ran to the front door, noticing the door is overloaded with locks, and luck was against her, Clive has already sealed them all. Unbolting two was simply not enough, Brooke had to move, Clive was chasing her behind, his face was red with rage. His clamorous hands blindly punching the walls and the air, with malice. His vision was impaired, which is the only thing beneficial to Brooke right now. The directionless fists draw closer to Brooke, she panics and runs up the stairs.

Bradley heard all the shouting, screaming and banging. Terrified by the noises, he steps out the room, crying, clutching his ears shut with his hands, tears pour from his sobbing face, snot and drool seep out down his red, chubby face. He yearns to his bellow to be heard, horribly, frustratingly, no matter how hard he tries, his tiny vocal chords will not make a screech.

Gail flew up the stairs, just bypassing the toy truck on the top step. She could see how frightened the poor boy was, she knelt down and took him in his arms. "Everything is going to be alright." she said to him, attempting to assure the lad. She picked up the boy and took him into his room, slamming the door shut, behind her.

Bradley jumped behind his *Spiderman* duvet cover, wrapping himself up inside to remain invisible.

Brooke barricaded the door by tipping the wooden wardrobe over.

Clive Dunscroft crept up the stairs.

Brooke pressed her ear, closer to the door, she could hear the heavy breathing from the other side, it was close he was behind the door, standing there. *What's he doing?*

"OPEN THE DOOR" Clive shouted, making Brooke jump out of her skin.

The teacher leapt over the toys over the floor, to join Bradley in bed, Brooke pulls out her phone and just as her shaking hand is about to dial triple nine-

-THE FRONT DOOR CRASHES DOWN

"CLIVE!" Simon Cole howls.

"We're in here!" Brooke calls.

Clive Dunscroft unemotionally perched solid-still at the top of the staircase, looking down at the Chief Inspector

"Let the girl and the boy go, it's over." Simon orders.

"He needs me."

"No. You need him."

"His family are a pair of washed up junkies, they won't love him like I do. He's better with me." Clive clarifies.

"That's not your call to make." Simon states, while he slowly starts to make a cautious ascent up the stairs.

"Don't forget I know your secret." Clive warns.

Simon slides his alarmed pupils to the right, hoping Brooke hadn't overheard the blackmail.

Brooke did over hear, now curious to know; what is the secret? Believing she could help Simon, she lifted the wardrobe that's shielding the door.

Clive heard the motion, as he spun to his left to get Bradley, Simon rugby tackled the behemoth in front of him.

Clive gave an almighty roar but he did not go down, instead, he grabbed hold of the smaller and inferior Chief Inspector, then used him as a battering ram, to shatter the door at the end of the corridor.

Simon was barely conscious, on the floor, pieces of wood around him. His vision matched Clive's blurred sight. It took a while before Simon woke up from his concussion, he groaned in agony, trying to get back onto his feet, he noticed the room was painted in photographs, not just ordinary photographs, they were all of children, at the park, the swimming pool, at a back garden birthday parties.

"What is all this?" Simon puzzled, holding onto the wall for balance.

"It's not what you think, I just wanted to capture their Purity." Clive, tried to explain.

Simon noticed a particular photo, it stood out from the rest, one of Jenny Woodfield, running down the dirt track.

Gail strives to smuggle Bradley out the house from behind Simon and Clive.

Clive spots the two figures escaping.

"Run." Brooke shrieks as she drags Bradley down the stairs.

Clive chases after them, on the corner of the corridor, before the declining steps. The Chief Inspector grabs hold of his arm, the brute spins around, misplaces a backward step, onto the toy truck that's hazardously parked. Clive Dunscroft, slid backwards, his arms flapped in the air, yelling, his body broke through the wooden bannister, then his head takes a fateful blow on the edge of the wall, sitting between the living room and the dining room.

Simon gazes down the stairs, to notice Clive's red baseball cap is now covering his face, underneath blood is pouring out of Clive's bald head, further staining the red carpet.

Chapter 58

The out-of-town forensic team returned to Holders Bridge, to retrieve Clive Dunscroft body. An out of breathe, sweaty, on the verge of collapsing, Carl Sebastian used his last ounce of strength to push his way through a herd of inquisitive neighbours. He overheard one gawker say "What is happening to this town?"

"BROOKE" Bass panicked, he was already out of breathe, fearing the worst for his partner, a new serge of adrenaline flowed through his body, he quickened up the pace, almost knocking the probing bystanders into each other. The Private Investigator spotted Gail Brooke, bringing Bass a sigh of relief.

Over the line of yellow tape, Brooke was sitting on the side of a police car bonnet. Little Bradley was wrapped around a blanket, beside her.

Bass rushed towards her, a policeman halted him, "Sir, you can't go in there."

"It's ok, you can let him through. He's with her." A voice ordered.

Bass turned to see who gave the order.

It was Chief Inspector Simon Cole, looking woeful, slowly writing a statement on his yellow legal pad.

Bass tilts his head, to express gratitude.

A few yards from Simon, a young teenager, goes to take a photo with her mobile, Simon runs over to her, blocks the lens with his hand. "Anyone caught taking photographs will be apprehended and taken to the station, where your phones will be confiscated!" He threatens the congregation of towns' folk.

This time, it was Bass you grabbed Brooke, he reeled her in, hold on so tightly, afraid to let go.

Brooke embraced him.

"I'm so sorry, Brooke, I shouldn't have let you gone on your own. I shouldn't have said those things that pushed you away." Bass apologised.

"Too right, you should have not spoken of such ghastly things. Saying-that, I am glad you're here."

"I can be a dick at times, but the last thing I want to do, is upset you. You make me not want to say horrible things because you make me want to be a better person."

They both released each other from their comforting grasp. Bass turned to glance at the timid boy sitting next to Brooke.

"Is he alright?"

"Clive Dunscroft never sexually abused him, he was not a paedophile, I suspect the forensic examination will provide proof of that."

"I don't understand, why did he kidnap him?"

"I assume he wanted someone to play with, and he wanted to see himself as a child again, through the eyes of another child. Does that make any sense?"

"The narrow minded people of this town won't believe any of that."

"It will be hard to change their minds."

A brief case carrying, large woman, wearing a black blazer, a matching knee length shirt, tights and high heels, approaches Bradley. "Hello Bradley, my name is Amanda, I'm from social services-"

Bass interferes "Where are you taking him?"

"I am taking him to a place where he can receive the care he needs."

"What about his mother or father? Are they not worried?" Brooke asks.

"They were deemed... *unfit.*" Amanda delicately puts.

"You're putting him into care, aren't you?" Bass expects.

"Just until we find him a good family. Come on Bradley, it's time to go." Amanda reaches out her brief-case-free hand as an offer.

Bradley accepts, they walk to a police car together. The social worker opens the door for Bradley, before he enters the vehicle, the boys diffident face turns around to look at Bass and Brooke.

Bass could see the frightful tears pouring from the faint-hearted boy. As he looks empathetically towards the boy. Bass spoke softly, "Don't cry kid." still hoping Bradley would still hear.

Brooke overheard, yet she did not say anything, offered a comforting hand, rubbing against Bass's large right arm.

"He'd be better off with Clive." Bass surmised.

"You never know, times have changed since we were young. You never know, he could be adopted by a family in the foreseeable future."

Bass can sense Brooke is remaining hopeful, but all he can remember is the beatings and isolation. "I hope for his sake, you're right. A shy, skinny, lad like that is going to be eaten alive."

A member of the press approaches Simon Cole, "Chief Inspector Cole, James Marshal from Holders Bridge Guardian can I get an exclusive?"

Simon paused, to gather his thoughts.

The young lad in a drench coat, eagerly waiting, hoping to make it to the big time, with a ground breaking news story.

"Yes, you may. But no pictures I'll forward you some appropriate photos." Simon reluctantly agreed.

Bass whispered to Brooke "I bet he'll send a picture of himself when he had a full head of hair."

Brooke laughed, "A topless one, in a hero's stance, while sticking out his chest, with a facial expression that looks as if he is smug or caught in a profound thought."

Bass chuckles "High five."

Young James was jumping with glee, "Can you tell me why you are here? I noticed a body pulled into an ambulance, was that Mr Clive Dunscroft?"

"It was. He had kidnapped a young six year old boy, whose name I will keep disclosed from the public. We believe it was not of a sexual nature, but we are waiting on the forensic report for conclusive evidence. He was a troubled individual and mainly wanted to act out his childhood fantasies."

"Mr Dunscroft was victimised of sexual assault when he was younger, by Billy Lane." Reporter Marshal avers.

"Billy Lane was taken to trail, though the jury found him innocent."

"There was speculation he murdered Billy Lane, twenty years ago."

"He was cleared of all charges, I was the officer that found evidence of Clive Dunscrofts innocence, at that time."

"What happened to Mr. Dunscroft?"

"Accidental Death. Holders Bridge's secondary schools, English Teacher, Gail Brooke, was a guest at Clive Dunscrofts house and once she heard the child in the house was not a relative but a prisoner, she tried to save him. Gail and the young boy fled down the stairs. I tried to apprehend the suspect, on the scene, he resisted and we tussled. Mr Dunscroft fell down the stairs, suffering a fatal strike to the back of the head." Simon stated, like it had been another rehearsal.

Bass looked at an embarrassed Brooke. Her shameful head was down in her hand.

"I thought he was his son."

Bass put his arm around her shoulder, "You weren't to know."

"Is there any link between this and Jenny Woodfield's murder?" James enquires.

Simon cessations "Yes, after I was physically thrown through a door, I landed in a room full of photographs of children, many pictures, covering the entire wall. One of those pictures were of Jenny Woodfield, running down the dirt track..."

There were gasps among the crowd of proximate observers.

"... We are still searching the house, but we have already found Jenny Woodfield's missing running clothes. I believe I have found the murderer of Jenny Woodfield. Thank you. No more questions." Simon Cole disappears into a cheering crowd, a man offers him a handshake, a respectful appreciation for his service. Followed by a random woman grabs Simon and hugs him.

Bass and Brooke turn to give each other a look.

Simon has never felt more complacent, the people of Holders Bridge see him as a hero, and the secret that he helped cover up Billy Lanes murder has died along with Clive Dunscroft.

Chapter 59

Raymond Woodfield ran into his house, leaving the front door open, he ran upstairs, leaving shoe prints on the cream carpet.

Janet Woodfield was sitting on the edge of the bed, exhausted from the cleaning. She noticed some of her eyeliner ink had spilt on her white make-up desk. "Bollocks to it" sick-to-death of having a cloth in her hand, she let it pass and the weary eyes gradually close. Just as she is about to drift off completely, Raymond almost kicks down the door.

Janet's blood shot eyes stare at that ridiculous bright white smile of his. "I cannot remember the last time I loved you." She put bluntly.

Her husband, runs to her and bends down on one knee, like he did when he proposed. He held both of her hands, fingers interlocked. "Janet, honey, sweetie, they have found our Jenny's killer."

The shock caused Raymond's wife to open her eyes and jaw. It took a few moments for the news to sink in. "Is this true?"

"Clive Dunscroft, and now he's dead as a doornail." He spoke in a jolly tune.

"Why?"

"Something to do with wanting to be a child, I can't be a surely sure. But now it's over-roonie."

"Raymond, I'm glad it's over but there's still a hole here."

"Then let's us take flight and leave this joint." Raymond leaped onto the bed beside his wife, still with their fingers intertwined, he became all giddy.

"What?" She heard him, but she still asked again.

"We were lovey-dovey once, why can't we be like that again?"

"You have possibly gone mad."

"You're right, I have been mad, for that I am sorry. I should have been here when you needed me the most. Something came over me." He waved his flat hand over his tall, fluffy black hair.

"I had been bored stiff for what feels like a decade. When Jenny was going to turn eighteen, I was to leave you both..." He put up his hand, in defence "With the house and my money, of course."

"And what was you going to do? Hit the brothels and the open road?"

"Those sort of seedy places are not my cup-of-tea. I was going to hit the open road, with my new red, 2017 Mercedes-Benz AMG Roadster, with the roof down along the way." Raymond waved his palm in the air, in front of Janet's eyes, as if it were to help envision the dream.

"You still could go?"
Raymond pleaded to her blue eyes, he stroked her red curly hair and offered "I want you to come with me?"

"What?" Janet gasped.

"None of us are getting younger."

"What about the house? Your job?"

"Oh, buggers to my job, boring meetings and nit-wits. I can't stand it anymore. We'll sell the house cheap to the bank, and make some easy money on the road."

"How?" Janet doubts.

"I don't know, part time work in shops, hustle at pool-"

"You are terrible at pool, Raymond."

"I don't care, it's not like we can't afford to lose a bit of cash. The cars outside waiting."

"Raymond, did you forget, I'm a woman, I need to pack some clothes, and I detest re-wearing the same outfits weekly."

"We'll get what we need on the road." Raymond picks up his wife.

Janet wraps her arms around Rays' fake-tanned head, bites into her red lipstick, smiles with such joy, and giggles with amusement.

Raymond carries his wife down the stairs, praying his backs not going to give-way anytime soon.

Outside Mrs. Woodfield is astounded to see the red, 2017 Mercedes-Benz AMG Roadster, in her front drive. "Raymond, did you buy the car without telling me?"

"I sure did, after I sold our old car." He grins.

Janet liked how cheeky and assertive he was being.

They both hopped into the roofless car, Janet by the passengers' side and Raymond at the front, with his sunglasses on.

The car reversed out the drive, Raymond's' left hand on the gear stick, Janet's right hand on top his thigh. The re-kindled couple drove out of Holders Bridge, without turning back.

Chapter 60

Shelly Jane is sat in her shop, Goforcoffee, alone after shutting early. The news that Clive Dunscroft murdered her friend, and is now dead, had brought her to tears. In a moment of blind rage, she scrunches up her apron into a ball and throws it to the floor.

Shelly walked over to the sweet counter, and "pigged-out." "Forget about the figure for now." She thought.

After binge eating a tub of sweets, she reached the *love hearts*, instantly recalling the time on the school playground, when she was eleven and Simon had brought her one. Even though all the other kids on the football team made fun of him, he still carried on playing. *He's a persistent little fighter.* She was his first love, maybe she shouldn't have left him for Richard Dirking. Yes, he was handsome, successful but did she really love him? Shelly suspects he slept with different people on his long business trips, but she'd be a hypocrite to complain. Now, Simon had caught Jenny's killer, he's a hero to her now, and no one else loves her as much as he does.

"I'm going to do it, I am going to leave Richard and be with Simon, something I should have done a long time ago."

Chapter 61

Mark Bell was topless, barefooted, in fact, the only thing he was wearing was his light white jogging bottoms. On the wooden floor of his living room, the young fit lad had just done his thirty press ups, a set of ten burpees. Now half way through his set of twenty sit-ups, the door knocks. He ignores it because ten more sit ups are needed to be completed. "Ten... Nine....seven."

The knocking on the door gets louder. He is torn between finishing his set and doing the polite thing, and answer it.

"Six." *grunts in agony.* "Five."

The knocking reoccurs but from the side door.

"Damn it." Mark jumps up to his feet and answers the door.

Chelsea Heart is standing by the side door, with her arms folded.

"What are you doing here?" Mark said in an irritable tone.

"They've found Jenny's killer."

"Shane?"

"No, he's disappeared, I've been trying to track him down, the last two days but I can't find him. It was Clive Dunscroft."

Mark rubbed his fingers through his thick brown hair, gracing his hands with wet gel. Unsure what to make of the information, a mixture of wanting to cry and smiling, caused a strong ambivalent feeling was overwhelming, but before he had the chance to do either...

Chelsea scanned Mark, she saw his pectorals flow in and out while he's regaining his breathe, and the sweat pour down his tight, wet, six pack and the trimmed hips, it made her own breathing difficult. Chelsea involuntary licked her own red lips and ogled Mark with her light blue lustful eyes. "I've come to tell you two things..."

Mark gaped at Chelsea.

"One: I'm sorry about accusing you and shit like that..."

Mark was startled but that's probably the best apology he'll receive.

"... Two: I'm going to have you Mark."

Mark began to panic, realising that was not a question.

Chelsea jumped him.

Mark was on the floor his body was on the cold kitchen floor. Chelsea hauled down his jogging bottoms so they were now wrapped around his ankles. The overly-keen woman grabbed hold of his phallus, playing with the tip of her toy. Once erect, she placed it in between her miniskirt.

Chelsea moaned, closed her eyes and showed Mark no mercy. Her body moved in a passionately violent way, scratching Marks hard body and lean hips with her nails. The Minx bites into his neck until he had a hickey; informing the other girls that he belong to her now.

Mark's body is bound to be aching in the morning, when he was with Jenny, it was delicate, and at times; awkward. Nothing compared to this.

Chelsea's screams of pleasure began to get louder, as she dominates Marks hands and rubs them against her small firm breast.

All the muscles in Marks body begin to tense, he was yelling, prior to Chelsea shoving her tongue down his throat, they kissed, wildly. With one hand, Chelsea sunk her clawed down the strong jaw-line, the lovers stared intensely into each other's eyes.

Mark raptures, now taking shorter and quicker breathes. "I'm sorry, I didn't mean to finish so quickly." Hoping he hadn't disappointed her.

The minx kisses him softly on the lips, then reveals a naughty, playful, grin "Don't matter..."

The seductress scratches down the side of his right pectoral again. "... Because we're going to do it again."

"Oh, boy." Mark whimpers.

Chapter 62

After making love, both enervated, dripping warm bodies of Carl Sebastian and Gail Brooke, laid in bed, close together. Brooke was on her side, fingers toying through Bass's dark chest hair.

"Let's go out for dinner." Bass suggested.

"Are you asking me out on a date?"

"Only if you say yes."

"Are you not going? Now the case is solved, is there a reason for you to stay?"

"I'd like to stay, if you'd have me?"

Brooke smiles "It sounds perfect. I should be able to move back home now."

"Do you have a spare bed or a settee, I can crash on?"

"You can sleep in my bed."

"I'd rather not, you snore." He jokes.

Brooke hits Bass in the face with a pillow, playfully.

Bass looked upon his goddess, green eyes and frizzled blonde hair, he rolled on top of her. Brooke's two hands rubbed his goodly triceps and his sweaty shoulder blades. Bass kissed Brooke, he had to, he couldn't look at her smiling face and not. The man moved his lips downwards, tenderly and tastefully kissing Brooke's even stomach along the way. Pressing further down, Bass used his tongue to lick the walls of a more sensitive area. When Brooke wanted to kick out her legs, she could not, for Bass had wrapped his strong arms around her thighs, pressing the finger tips on the inside. Brooke resorted to realise her exhilaration by wrapping the bed sheets around her hands, pulling the mattress sheet away from the corners. Her light head spun with pleasure so much, it tilted from side to side. The more Brooke groaned, the more vigorous Bass got with his tongue, because knowing he was satisfying her, also made himself more aroused.

Brooke was panting, she released the grasp of the bed sheets, to caress her bosom with one hand, and the other one held her man's head in place.

A while later, Carl and Gail, were getting dressed, Bass was buttoning up his white shirt. Brooke was changing into her purple dress "I cannot wait to change my attire, I'm tired of constantly wearing the same clothes."

"Well you should be able to, now you can go home. We'll check out, go for dinner and then go to your place."

"Maybe, you can use your tongue again?" Brooke beams.

"Next time, why don't I handcuff you to the bed and put a blind fold on you?"

"No." Brooke refused "I abhor being restrained and I like to have my vision at all times."

"Ok, I respect that."

"Do you think Clive really committed such an audacious and heinous crime?" Brooke asked, changing the subject to the Woodfield murder.

"I know we haven't been haunted the last two days, that's a good sign. He had her running gear in his house and pictures of her."

"Why did he choose Jenny?" Brooke enquires.

"A nice pretty girl, being friendly to a sad loner, might be easy for him to become obsessed with her."

"Do you speak from experience?"

Bass almost ignored the question completely, "Perhaps, if you do become obsessed with someone or something, you should have the self-awareness and strength to move on."

"It can be hard."

"Life is hard." Bass turned to the mirror to knot his black tie. "Do you want to eat at that restaurant, where we first went on a date?"

"What about: The Man with No Face? How does that correspond with Clive Dunscroft?" Brooke ignoring the previous question, remaining on topic.

"When I went in the house, I never saw a mirror, not even in the bathroom, maybe he renounced his own reflection, due to self-hatred or shame."

Brooke, fell silent, contemplating the possibilities.

"One last time. The restaurant where we went on our first date?" Bass asked again.

"Yes, that sounds nice."

"Great, I'll see you there." Bass joyfully skips out the room.

"Wait. Where are you going?" Brooke interrogated.

"I've got an errand to run first. Don't worry, I'll be there, Eight PM sharp." Bass conservatively answered.

Brooke shook her head in disapproval, hoping that they would walk down together.

Shelly Jayne returned home, yearning to dispose of her green uniform, and to replace it with the comfortable pyjamas. Closing the front door, the aroma of minced lamb resonated from the kitchen. "Richard, what's for dinner, it smells lush?"

Chief Inspector Simon Cole, awaited for his lover in the kitchen, wearing an apron over his uniform, using a spatula to stir the vegetables in a heated pan.

Shelly was startled by his surprise, "I didn't expect to see you here?" She found it peculiar, because she could have sworn she had noticed Richards Lamborghini outside. "Where's Richard?"

"He's gone out with some friends for the night, it's just me and you tonight."

"It's a little bit risky, then I suppose, the verge of being does arouse us."

"I am cooking your favourite, Shelly. I'm in a pretty good mood today"

"You should be." Shelly smiles with admiration. "You caught Jenny's killer, I'm so proud of you."

"Dinners not quite ready yet, so I've ran you a bubble bath, upstairs."

"You really are the best, Simon. I'm going to leave Richard, I'm going to announce to the whole town that we are together, I don't care what people say."

Simon paused, dropping the spatula in his hand "It's all I've ever wanted to hear."

Shelly's heart-felt, soft eyes began to cry tears of joy. She wraps her arms over Simon, while he buries his head in her chest, wrapping his short arms tightly around her skinny ribs.

Gail Brooke, sat down by the table covered by a navy blue cloth, the folded white napkins, three long candles, and a celebratory bottle of Champaign rests with in an ice bucket. Brooke is growing impatient for Carl Sebastian to arrive, constantly checking her phone for any news of his whereabouts, and the time. Her flat stomach ruptures, indicating the hunger.

The smartly dressed waiter uncorks the Champaign bottle, upon request and Brooke chugs her entire glass, the waiter happily poured her a second.

A tall, familiar face, eagerly draws closer to the beautiful English Teacher, in an arrogant stride.

"Gail." He shouts "It's me, Brad."

"Hello, Brad" Brooke smiles, though just out of politeness.

"Do you mind if I sit here?" Brad asks, despite already sitting down, beside Brooke before she answered.

Brooke secretly wished he hadn't joined her, "I am actually waiting on someone."

"Oh, don't worry, I'll make myself disappear when he's here." Brad intrusively says, even though he's now taken off his blue suit jacket, and wrapped it around the back of the chair. Brad is secretly wanting to sleep with his colleague again. "So, who is the lucky guy?"

"Well, he is new to the town, he is a Private Investigator, who helped solve the murder of Jenny Woodfield-"

Brad abruptly interrupted "That guy! He's absolutely off his nut." Brad leans over, tapping his fingers onto the table whilst telling the story "I heard while he was looking for you, he accidentally went to the Primary School, there was a three years old student's birthday party, she offered him a slice of her mums home-made birthday cake. He had some without saying thank you, SPAT IT BACK OUT, ON THE FLOOR, he told this horrified little girl that her mum should spend the tax payers' money on cooking lessons rather than wasting it on her nine 'o' clock Gin."

"I am not sure either to believe that or not… it does sound like him." Brooke knew what this snake was after, he's hoping to steal her away from the date. First, it'll start by making Bass look bad, next he'll start bragging about himself, to make himself look good…

"… I was told I was the best striker on the field…" Brad was bragging.

"Oh really." Brooke nods, really, she isn't listening. Regretting ever sleeping with him, she was vulnerable at the time of her father's passing, and wanted to feel some easy comfort, on the lonely, quiet nights. Brooke knows it was wrong to use him, notwithstanding, Brad didn't seem to mind. The notion of making love with Brad now, makes her want to vomit, with his goofy face and daft blonde hair cut, which makes him look like *Biff* from *Back to the Future.*

Carl Sebastian was approaching the restaurant, holding a bunch of flowers. Appearing through the window, he noticed Gail was talking to someone who looks like *Biff Tannen?* Who is this guy? Why is he talking to Brooke? The green eyed monster consumed Bass, his fist clenched, crushing the stem of the flowers. An urge to pummel his arrivals face, respires out from his tight chest. *Play it cool, or you'll scare Brooke.* Bass poised. After steadying himself, Bass grabbed hold of the door knob, returned his glance to Brooke and her friend, something dawned on him, this moment represents all of Bass's life, on the outside, looking in. No matter how hard he tries he'll never connect to anyone. Bass's heart began pounding, his palms sweat, the happy face reverted back to the natural repulsive frown, unable to open the door, his eyes depress. *I'll just scare Brooke anyway, she's better off with that idiot, than me ...NO... STOP... THOSE ... THOUGHTS ... You are a drifter... You do not get attached to anybody on the job... You have finished with this town... It's time to move onto the next.* Bass assured himself, to remain phlegmatic. The Private Investigator stolid away, disposing the flowers, along the way.

Gail Brooke's attention turned towards the door, having believed there was someone at the door, viewing through its window, no one was there.

A naked Shelly Jayne steadied herself into the warm bath water, instantly feeling the hot water on her feet. Easing herself into the tub, the bubbles rubbed amongst her wet, silky skin. She took a gasp caused by pure relaxation. Shelly smiled, astonished by the lovely gesture from her caring boyfriend. The sexy mood lighting was created by the dozens of candles around the bath tub.

The door opened slowly, Simon crept in.

"Is everything to your satisfaction, my lady?" He asked

Shelly's grin was suggestive "Why don't you join me? The waters fine." She flicked some bubbled water onto his shirt.

He laughed and picked up a sponge.

Shelly fancied, her back being rubbed, so she leant forward for him to do so.

Carl Sebastian was alone in a hotel room, just off the motorway. Sitting on a white bed, drinking whiskey to repress his feelings even further until he becomes impassive to the name; Gail Brooke.

Bass's bare feet felt the softness of the grey carpet.

There was an urge to listen to sad songs but Bass knew that would make him cry, and grown men shouldn't cry, they need to be strong.

Now, Bass's feet felt wet.

The drifter looked downwards, there was no water, his hairy clown feet looked dry, and so he returned to downing his sorrows.

Bass's face looked more puzzled, because now his feet were not just slightly wet, it felt like he was standing in a puddle.

The private investigator looked down again, the grey carpet had vanished; his ankles were standing on water, not *in* water, *on top* of water.

A panic-stricken Bass rushed to his feet. As soon has The PI stood up, he was no longer in the generic hotel room, his body was transported to the calm sea…

With her eyes closed, Shelly Jayne purred like a cat, while Simon Cole was rubbing her back with a smooth soaked bath sponge.

"This is great." She spoke, whilst in a state of tranquillity.

The coffee shop owner opened her eyes again, smiled at Simon, who returned one. She glanced towards the right-hand-side of her beloved, peaking at the sink and bathroom mirror. A troubled feeling was in the waters, something was amiss.

She scanned back and forth from Simon and the bathroom mirror, she scrutinized the man by her and surveyed the mirror; it was fogged up so it was more difficult to be sure...

Simon noticed an inquisitive expression on Shelly's face, making him anxious.

Mrs. Jayne rescanned the mirror and examined Chief Inspector Cole's position. Shelly's body became stiff, the dread has turned the waters temperature from hot to freezing cold. For what she has spotted was impossible, Simon Cole has no reflection...

Carl Sebastian is ankle deep in the middle of the sea. It's not humanly possible, to stand still, ankle deep *on* water. The Private Paranormal Investigator slapped his bare arm, where the rolled up sleeves didn't cover. "Not dead yet." he said.

With the water being the purest of blue, Bass assumes his body had been elevated to The Garden again, but why?

Standing rigid, petrified to step anywhere, Bass swept the area with his eyes, unable to sight any land, he resolves to remain perfectly still. Not being a strong swimmer, he could easily drown.

The Gardener appeared beside him, he too was *up on* the calm visible ocean, crouched, fiddling with his hands anxiously, looking deeply concerned. He spoke, low and fearful; "Do not turn around."

Bass disobeyed his warning and peered over his shoulder...

Shelly Jaynes' body shivered with fear, cuddling her bare legs with drenched arms, she found it hard to take control of her breathing, falling silent, thinking of excuses to get out the bath, where she'd be less vulnerable.

Shelly gulped before she spoke "So, *emmm,* where did you say Richard was again?" Her voice quivered.

"I told you, out with his friends." Simon lied.

Shelly doesn't know, Richard is laying in blood soaked bed, with his face and skull smashed to pieces.

Simon's back rubbing was becoming faster, unbridled and fiery.

Shelly can feel the sponge scratching down her bare, saturated back. "Go easy, ok?" she has an uneasy, fake giggle. "Do you remember about the love heart sweets?"

Simon responds "What about them?"

Shelly's heart pulsated, her watery eyes frightfully looked up towards the sinister grin, over shadowing her.

"You're not Simon."

The man pretending to be Simon pulled Shelly's blonde hair down.

Shelly could feel this almighty strength of Simons short arms force her under the bubbly water, the desperate need to scream was mere gargling, as Shelly Jaynes' lungs, throat and mouth filled up with bath water. The liquid was snorted through Shelly's nose and into her brain, her eyes stung as she opened them to see Simons face laughing at her. She kicked her arms and legs in the air, splashing water and tipping candles into the bath with her, killing the flames.

If that weren't enough, the imposter posing as Simon, pulled out a Stanley Knife from his pocket, to stab Shelly's naked body repeatedly, causing the blue water to gradually turn red.

The pour woman screamed in agony as the small short blade impales her flesh, the attempt to yell caused her lungs to fill up with water more quickly. She tries to fight back but is not strong enough, during the struggle Shelly kicks the plug, draining the bloody water down the sink.

...Carl Sebastian did not heed The Gardeners warning, he peered over his shoulder, watching blood raise up from the clear blue water and spread to its surface.

Chapter 63

The following morning, Carl Sebastian woke up on the floor in the hotel room. The sun radiated through the window, sprinkled its heat onto Bass's dazed and half-conscious state. He used his hand to block out the sun, as its brightness were marring to his sensitive eyes.

The mobile phone began to ring.

Bass staggered towards the phone, resting upon the hotels desk. He noticed lots of missed calls and text messages from Gail Brooke, though his thoughts were too muddled for it to register at this moment in time.

He answered the call "Hello."

"Carl. It's Chief Inspector Cole. There's another body."

"What?" Bass shouldn't be so surprised, after what he saw last night, the blood flowing into the garden, must have been a sign.

"Meet me at the dirt track, where Jenny Woodfield was murdered, and don't tell anyone."

"I won't."

"Not even Gail Brooke." Simon ordered.

There's a good chance of that, she's the last person Bass wants to see. "I'm actually just out of town, so I may be a little while."

"I'll wait, be as quick as you can."

The phone hung up.

Carl Sebastian, quickly drove down to Holders Bridge, as fast as he could, parking at a cul-de-sac, closest to the bowl. Power walking heavenwards to the top of the bowl. On the opposite side to The Private Investigator, over the dip, stands Simon Cole, alone, hands in pockets, waiting.

Where's forensics? Where's the other officers? Where's the horde of probing civilians? Bass can't elude the feeling that something's wrong. He treads cautiously, towards Simon, as he makes his way down the dip, he notices that The Chief Inspector is wearing a thick blue winter coat, with a furry rimmed hood.

Bass paces up hill, he notices Simon is wearing dull grey work trousers. *"Why are you not in uniform? Is there even a body?"*

"Oh yes, there's going to be a body here." Bass suspicion was right, he was being set-up.

"If I'm going to die, I'm taking you to hell with me."

Simon chuckles.

"Why did you do it? Why did you kill Jenny Woodfield?"

"It was nothing personal, I just wanted to kill someone to get you here."

Bass appeared confused, "Why me? Why would you want me here?"

"I hired you because I wanted a worthy adversary." When Simon spoke, it was in the voice of Janet Woodfield.

"You were the one that called me, pretending to be Janet Woodfield."

Simon spoke in Janet's voice again; "That's right dear."

"You are a good impressionist, convincing, I'll give you that."

"I'm so much more than that." Simon told, sounding like his usual self. He placed the furred hood up over his head, turned his back away from his opponent.

Bass watched the man opposite, spin back around, Bass was bewildered, Simons face has now changed to Janet Woodfield's. "What are you? Some-kind of shape-shifter?"

The creature disguised as Janet orates, though it's in Simons voice "I was a man once, I knew that I was meant to be somebody, someone who was supposed to do great things. But people saw me as a nobody, I was nothing to them, then I actually became *nothing*. An entity that can take the form of anyone or anything."

"You tried to kill Brooke in the hotel room?"

"Yes, also at her home and in the hospital. Both attempts foiled by the ghost of Jenny Woodfield."

I've been alive for centuries, killing people wherever I go. I was known as: *Jack the Ripper, Zodiac Killer, The Moonlight Murderer,* and so on. I have never once had a ghost stop me, until now."

This sick-o's been doing this for years. Bass imagined.

The entity continued to tell its tale; "It's fun killing, taking the lives of others and not getting caught. After a while, I got a taste for something else..."

"Is it by any chance; Ice cream?" Bass mocked.

"I disguise myself as other people, to frame them for murders they didn't even commit, such as *Steven Avery or "The Hurricane" Carter.*"

"You could have chosen to do something more productive with your time, I heard paintings good for the soul." Bass remembered; fire normally kills ghost that could work, he pats down the pockets of his jeans, but he failed to bring a lighter or some matches, *shit.*

"There's nothing that compares to enriching feeling of power, you get from your victims screams or blood. Or that feeling of invincibility, you get from not being caught. I could choose who lives and dies..."

Bass is disgusted by the way Janet/not-Janet was liking her lips.

"... I used to make people suffer, keep them alive for day-"

"Enough!" Bass suspended, placing his body into a defensive stance, fists up in the air, muscles tenses, shoulders curled, the right leg stood in front of the other. "If you going to kill me then do it, just as long as you stop talking. You like to gloat, is that why you wrote a song about yourself?"

"I merged myself into parents, teachers and into other children, to spread the word about The Man with No Face, in order to bring fear into the hearts of others."

"I could write a scarier nursery rhyme whilst watching porn." *My mouths going to get me killed.*

The entity overheard; "I couldn't kill you, because I am you..."

The woman that looks like Janet, digs her sharp claws into her face, twirls around, with the hood still up. When the entity turns to face Bass, it was like looking in the mirror.

Carl Sebastian was facing the exact resemblance of himself; same height, same face, but its eyes were not full of dejection, and the imposter carried such a smirk, that the real Bass couldn't wait to wipe-off.

"I am you, Carl Sebastian. From the future, you are the nothing that I'll become."

Bass shook his head in disbelief, muddled thoughts spun through his chaotic head. "You're just trying to mess with my head."

"It's true, I am you, and the barrier between worlds is wafer thin. Thanks to you I can become anything, anywhere at any time."

"No." Bass assures himself, "I'm messed up, moody, angry and down-right fucking miserable. There's no way I'd murder innocent people. I took this lifestyle to stop cunts like you."

"You're right." The Fake Bass re-joins, "I meant what I said earlier, I was hoping you'd make a rather good adversary, someone who is one step behind me, close on my tail, keeping me on my toes, but never actually catching me."

"Because the fear of getting caught arouses you." Bass recalls what Simon once telling him.

"But I was wrong, you're not the man for the job. You'd rather spend your time with Gail Brooke." The copy of Bass pulls out a Stanley knife and moves towards the real Carl Sebastian.

"I'm going to take that off you, jam it in your neck." Bass promises.

The entity slowly approaches his enemy, mockingly laughing, as it changes its skin again. The entity is now morphing into another familiar face.

Bass's defences drop.

"What's the matter honey? It's me, Brooke." The entity spoke in Gail Brooke's voice, to taunt his foe even further.

In the back of his mind, Bass knows it's not really her, but all he can see *is* Brooke. He's vulnerable around her, there's no barricade, protecting him, "Stop." murmurs Carl Sebastian. With his red eyes, he just watches, as the Brooke impersonator slowly punctures his tight blue woolly jumper, perforating his abdominal wall and cutting the right common iliac artery. His body collapses to the ground.

The deceiver crouched over his victim, taking the phone from his pocket. "You won't need this."

Bass is laying on the floor, in agonising pain, clenching both hands over the wound, putting pressure to reduce the blood loss, but it's no use, the severed artery is pouring blood out, thick and fast.

"Goodbye Bass." The pretender smiles menacingly.

The sun beamed behind Fake Brookes' head, and with the delusional state Bass is in, he doesn't see an evil clone, he just sees Gail Brooke, the girl he's met, got to have known and truly cared about, smiling down at him, one last time.

The entity walks away.

Too busy focusing on his breathing, a dying Carl Sebastian is incapable to say anything, he raises his weary, shaking, right blooded hand to call her back. Although, Bass can feel the colour fade from his skin, and the cold. *So cold. I just... need to... close my eyes...*

Part 4 – Death comes to us all.

Chapter 64

Carl Sebastian rouse on the same grass he had slept on. With his body numb, Bass was thankful the pain had gone though, it was as if his form was floating.

Hundreds of grass blades underneath, began to carry him along the field. Surfing his numbed star-fished body onto the calm, smooth surface of calm water.

Carl Sebastian's eyes rested, a relaxing smile softened his ruffled face. The waters gentle motion soothed him to sleep like a baby in its mothers arms. His mind has never been so serene, his body has never been so collected. Re-opening his untroubled dark green eyes to the dark. Even though there is virtually nothing around him or the undisturbed waters, there was nothing to fear.

Stars began to appear, so close and so bright, the only time you'll ever get to see them like this, is when someone stands mountain height, unlit and above sea level.

Carl Sebastian knew he was going to a better place...

The Private Paranormal Investigator woke in The Garden. Confused to know why he has been taken here, Bass grunted. Purposely provoked the pain receptors in his arm, by slapping it with a bare hand, there was nothing, despite not feeling as ease as two minutes ago.

"That's it then." Bass accepted.

"Hello there." A voice greeted, from behind.

Bass turned around to see a man, an unfamiliar though handsome face, similar height, dark black hair, dressed in a sharp suit that fitted perfectly. *"Tailor made"* Bass considered.

The man gave a clear, radiant smile.

Bass returned with a frown, he walked towards him, noticing the unilluminated eyes.

Bass recalled Frank Mill finding a man, naked behind his pub, saying he had the darkest of eyes.

This must be him, but how did he get here? Bass wondered. "Who are you?"

The man replied vaguely; "I have gone by many names."

"I guess helpful, wasn't one of them." Bass sighed. "What are you doing here?"

"I could ask you the same thing?"

"I don't know why, but I have a feeling you do."

"You are here, because of a creature, disguising itself as Simon Cole, murdered you."

"You've been in Holders Bridge for the past two weeks, how did you get from there to here?"

"It's easy for me to travel between worlds."

"What was the purpose of your visit?"

"I've done many bad things in my time, all I ever wanted was to return home." The man silently gazing into the distant, magnificent, uncompromising beauty of The Garden. "Have you done things you'd like to be redeemed for?"

Even though he believe he does, Bass never responded, not needing to tell a stranger his life-story, although sensing that the well-suited-debonair already knew.

"I'm sorry for breaking the rules of nature, I have taken Jenny Woodfield's' soul to a better place, that's why you and Gail haven't seen her spirit for the last two days. A lovely innocent, like that, should not have suffered the way she did, before her time."

"Why am I here and not in Heaven?"

"Is that what you call it? Heaven?"

Bass, still never responded.

"All you have to do is walk through that door." The man tilted his head to the opposing Investigators left.

The P.I. turned around to see a door, *his door.* A dark brown, solid oak, wooden one with a golden knob. Appeared from thin-air. Bass reluctantly walked towards it, feeling the cold stare from the man's unlit pupils, along the way. Taking a firm grip of the gold round nodule, Bass turns it to the left, knowing a tsunami of pain and sorrow will follow, but with being dead, he thought; *what was there left to lose?*

As Carl Sebastian pushed the door open, his soul transcended to another world...

Bass ended up on a train, he scanned the surroundings; it was empty train and a very quiet one. None of the blue seats or the bright white hand-rails rattled, no wind seeped through the single glazed windows, and there was no sound from the railway tracks, it was as if the train was floating.

Bass looked out the window, the train was riding in-between an astounding view of snow-topped glaciers. No clouds in sight to ruin the spectacle. Bass returned to view the opposite seat, and across the table was Gail Brooke.

Tears of joy sprouted, to swim beneath the lower eyelids of Carl Sebastian, the overwhelming feeling of defenceless, safe jubilation returned, brightening Bass's insides and beam.

Brooke placed her arms on the table, Bass leaned in and held her soft hands.

"Brooke, I'm so glad you are here. Where are we going?" Bass asked, with a twinkle in his eye.

"Does it matter?"

"No." A lump in Bass's throat made him choke on the words that are trying to escape. He can feel his eyes dampen and turn red, not feeling the need to hide his emotions, a joyful tear leaked out, ran down his cheek.

When Bass's emotional dark green eyes, matched her lighter pair, he decided to stay here forever.

Like all dreams, you had to wake up and Bass could feel himself waking up, "No, No. I want to stay! No!" He fought against his own body but everything, including Brooke enfolded inwards by a bright white light…

Carl Sebastian returned to the garden, on his knees, falling forwards onto his hands, digging his fingers into the freshly cut, green grass. The built-up rage poured out, giving Bass an utmost roar. Veins stuck out of his red face while screaming into the ground. His body now tensed, rose up and he gave another deep roar, his jaw opened so wide, it could have been dislocated. All the years of repressed tears came out, all at once, like an uncontrollable flood, falling from his eyes, down his red screaming face, waving down all the bones sticking out his neck.

Rolling on the floor, a wailing Bass used his hands to cover his heart weeping eyes, palms touching the twitching cheekbones, yearning to stop crying but the ache was too much. The heart-renting oppressed memories and feelings hit him like a ton-of-bricks. First it was the few faces of the people he lost, at the time he told himself "they were never really his friends, they were just clients. Life moves on." So he didn't have to face the pain of grief. Second was the bottled-up guilt, he should have felt, for the ill-treatment towards; colleagues, suspects, strangers and his only friend; Gail Brooke.

Still, sorrow danced its way out of the four chambers of Bass's heart, and escaped via the relentless surge of tears. He screamed into the dirt; "I can't do it anymore. I don't want to be on my own, but I hate other people. Who the fuck would want to be with me? *I'm so broken.*"

Relief gradually flowed back into the blood stream, as the breathing became more controllable, the whimpering was coming to an end. Bass regained posture, patted down his jeans and woolly top, even though no pieces of grass or mud were caught on his clothes. He was embarrassed, breaking down, crying his heart out in front of a total stranger, fearing the gentlemen would assume he's weak.

Bass noticed something in the distance, from behind a perfectly trimmed bush, an object, poorly hidden from sight. It was a pair of legs, the ends of two overalls and black boots... *It's The Gardener.*

Bass dashed defensively towards the strange, stylish man.

"Would you believe me, if I told you it wasn't me." The man told, as if he had read Bass's thoughts.

The Private Investigator's silence gave his response.

"We had a slight disagreement, like I said earlier, all I wanted was to return home."

Bass noticed the differing man looked dishearten.

"Now I know more than ever, I can never go home."

"Am I supposed to feel sorry for you?" Bass questions, rhetorically.

"This actually bodes well, in your favour."

"How so?"

"I can return you to Earth, I can trade a life for a life." The man indicates his hand to The Gardeners body.

"I don't want anything from you." Bass rejects.

"Are you sure? Because shortly, the creature who is posing as Simon Cole will pretend to be you, and murder Chelsea Heart, Mark Bell and Gail Brooke."

Brooke. Bass began to panic. *She has her whole life in front her, I have to save her.*

"Of course, you can do nothing, and the picture you just saw in your head, will be your reality in the next two hours." The dealer offered.

Bass isn't going to lie, it sounded very tempting, a dark, selfish part of him desired it, so much. Though, he couldn't let anyone hurt Brooke "Do it. Take me back down to earth." Bass agreed.

"Ok." He smiled. "You'll need this." The man reached into the inside pocket of his very expensive suit, pulled out a gold knife, and tossed it to the side of Bass.

The Investigator picked up the blade and begun to study it, words in Latin were forged along the rim. Assuming this is the only thing that can stop the entity.

"I believe, the entity is how he is, because of me." The refined gentlemen began to confess, "He made a deal with me."

"What else do you know about him?" Bass enquired.

"He has killed many people. It can revert back into the nothingness anytime it wants. It was locked away in a prison, outside the realms of time and space. For you humans it was a mere two seconds but for him it was centuries."

The room with the clocks, Bass recalled.

"I'm afraid, my uprising to earth caused a crack in his cell, allowing it to escape."

"What are you going to do now?"

"Return to the flames, I suppose."

Bass didn't fully understand, he doesn't want to say anything that would change this man's mind, as long as the demon disappears, than who cares?

Ten shadows spawn from beneath the well-polished being.

Bass watched in awe, as the shadows ran around the rigid dealer in a circle.

The man with no name clapped his hands…

Carl Sebastian returned on the field, where he died.

Chapter 65

Chelsea Heart, had heard rumours of a strange man making all-sorts of deals, impossible things turning true. Shelly had told Raymond Woodfield, and then he had told her father. Chelsea was going to do whatever it takes to get her friend back, not caring who she has to hurt.

Chelsea ran as fast as she could to The Balcony Restaurant, the smoke filled lungs and lack of stamina would only let her pale legs, only go so fast.

Chelsea finally arrived, the door wouldn't budge; something was blocking the entrance. Pushing as hard as possible with her shoulder, the door slowly jammed open, revealing pieces of wood and tool boxes were barricading the door.

The walls downstairs were being re-plastered, but that's ok. She knew that, this man was upstairs. Chelsea placed her hand on the gold handrail, instantly letting go, wiping off the bulk of dust on her miniskirt.

Reaching upstairs, entering to what appears to be an empty ballroom. The seats around the dance floor, had been chewed on by rodents.

Typical Chelsea thought, she should have known better than to get her hopes up. *It was all just fake news, of course it wasn't going to happen, nothing ever good happens to me.*

Just when she was about to break down and cry, a rat scurried from one side to another, returning to its nest, through a hole in the wall. Chelsea screamed the house down, and ran out as fast she could.

Chapter 66

Wishing he had his phone, Carl Sebastian, ran to the police station.

Once inside, the red headed receptionist looked pleased to see the tall, handsome, rugged, outsider, with muscular arms. "Hello *youuu.*" said in a flirtatious tone. "How can I help you today?" She asked while liking her lips, expressing sin through her naughty blue eyes.

"Where is Simon Cole?" Bass demanded, in a deep, immediate tone.

"Who?" She looked confused.

"I'm not in the mood to play games. Where is Simon Cole?" Bass slammed his fist on the desk.

Scaring, and slightly thrilling the luscious receptionist. "I'm really sorry, sir, but I don't know who you mean."

"You introduced me to him, a few days ago, when I first came to this town."

She was startled and confused, "I remember seeing such a handsome man as yourself, but I don't remember no Simon Cole."

"How could you not know who he is? He was Chief Inspector! In charge of the Woodfield investigation!" He yelled.

The red head appeared dazed; "They've caught the person reasonable for Jenny's murder."

"No, it was Simon Cole, he framed Clive Dunscroft."

Another police officer overheard the commotion, so he intervened. "Can I help at all, sir?"

"Yes, where is Chief Inspector Simon Cole?" Bass screamed.

"Sir, Simon Cole left about two decades ago. He's not been back since."

The delirium made Bass's head hurt; "That's not possible, he was in charge of Jenny Woodfield's murder."

"No sir, I was, I found Jenny Woodfield's belongings at the Dunscroft residence."

"This isn't possible." Bass denied.

"Why don't you take a seat? We can talk about this in a civilised manner." The other officer kindly rendered, extending a welcoming hand.

Bass abruptly pushed his proffer, "Stay away from me." Not knowing who to trust, he fled the station.

Carl Sebastian made his way to the building opposite, where the morgue and the room of broken clocks were. *How is he doing this?* He recollected the mysterious man in The Garden saying "He can revert back to nothing." *Does that include; erasing his own existence from other people's minds?"* Feeling exhausted and out of his death, there was no time to stop, he was on a mission, to find Simon Cole and kill him, before he kills Brooke and the others.

Bass entered the building and found the lift, the death machine that once wobbled and temporarily broke down mid-flight. He hesitated in walking in, terrified to have another experience like last time. Has the ascent begun, Bass clutched onto the handrail, preparing for the worst, taking steady breathes and braced himself for the impact. The ride went smoothly, the grey lift went to the floor without a glitch. Bass presumed the death machine that shook and rattled the last time, was a mere one-off.

The metal doors opened, to a dark and empty hall way that was habituated by a swarm of bees, the buzzing echoed throughout the narrow corridor. Bass could see nothing was at the end of the corridor, aside from a cleaning cupboard and a bee hive. Surmising that, trying to get to the other end of the corridor, would result in him being stung-to-death, Bass descended in the lift.

Chapter 67

Chelsea Heart and Mark Bell, were hiking along the dirt track, followed by a farmer's field. Telling her new boyfriend what she had heard and where she had just been.

"I didn't think it was closed." Mark said.

"I didn't neither, looks like it had been empty for years."

The couple approached a sign saying "No Entry. Private Road. Residence Only." Hanging from a fence.

"I wonder what's down this way." Chelsea wondered, whilst climbing over the fence.

"I don't think we're allowed down there." Mark hesitated.

"Come on, let's go somewhere different."

"We'll get into trouble."

"Only if we get caught."

Mark followed in trepidation.

The young woman's phone began to ring; she pulled out her mobile and stared at the screen. Debating on either or not to answer the call.

"Who is it? Mark asked.

"It's Bass. What the fuck does he want?"

"Answer it and find out."

She did. "Hello?"

"Chelsea, it's me Simon Cole."

"Simon? What are you doing on Bass's phone?"

"He's here with me, I have some belongings of Jenny Woodfield's, I thought you might like. Janet and Raymond are out of town. Where are you?"

"I've gone out with Mark."

"Whereabouts? I'll pick you up."

"No, I'm close to the school, meet there in an hour?" Chelsea suggested.

"Sounds good." The man who sounded like Simon Cole hung up.

Chapter 68

Carl Sebastian eventually found Gail Brooke's mid terraced house, he knocked on the door, though his head hangs in shame.

Gail Brooke opens the door, not welcoming him inside, she stares at him furiously. "What is it you want, Bass?" She said spiteful.

"Brooke, it's not over-"

Brooke interrupted "Why did you stand me up? I went back to the Bed and Breakfast, only to have found out; that you have left town. What is your problem? Do you hate me?"

"I do hate you..."

The English Teacher looked surprised while Bass welled up, consumed by an overwhelming emotion, the sobbing returned, no barriers to protect him, the unrelenting puling began.

It was the first time Brooke had seen him break down in tears.

"I hate how much I think about you.

I hate the fact, no matter where I go, or what I do, I'll never get over you.

I hate how one minute you make me so happy, and so sad the next.

I hate how no one else will ever make me feel the way you make me feel.

I hate how vulnerable you make me, but I always want you around."

His breathing quivered, Bass's tears and heartfelt words, now made Brooke cry.

"But you deserve better than me. I'm worse than the monsters I kill..."

Brookes hand on his sullen, rugged face, was a heavily touch.

"I just got so scared... Because...I love you, Brooke."

Gail felt sympathetic for her man, then gave Carl the biggest and tightest hug, ever shared.

"It's you." he serenaded in her ear. "...It's only you."

Bass kissed Brooke, like it was the last kiss he'd ever give her. His hands held her head, her blonde hair ran between his fingers. Brooke's hands ran up and down, caressing Bass's hips before burying her palm in his thick chest. They couldn't seem to pull away from each other.

Brooke's mobile rang, glancing at the screen.

Bass could see the puzzled expression on her beautiful face.

"It says that you are calling me." Brooke lifted her phone, to show Bass.

"It's him."

"Who?"

"Simon Cole is not who he says he is, he's some kind of shape shifter."

Brooke's heart stopped, she answers the phone, yet placing the mobile gradually to her ear.

"Brooke, I need your help! The killers still out there, meet me in the school, as soon as you can. Don't talk to anyone else on the way! Trust no one." The voice sounded exactly like Carl Sebastian.

Her eyes shifted between the phone and the person standing in front of her.

"I'm on my way." Brooke responds, before hanging up.

"He sounded just like you, but you are right here. What is happening?" Brooke shudders.

Bass tried to explain it; "Simon Cole is a shape shifting entity, the only way to kill him, is with this ancient knife." He taps his pocket. "Brooke, listen to me, he could be anything or anyone at any time. We have to be very careful, we have to stay together at all times, keep our eyes on each other."

Brooke shakes her head in disbelief.

"Hey. Hey. Look at me." Bass coups her soft cheeks and looks directly into her eyes. "It's going to be alright, I'll look after you. I won't let anything happen to you. We have an advantage here."

"How so?"

"It doesn't know that I am back from the dead..."

Chapter 69

Chelsea and Mark walked, hand in hand, past the bakery, where all the school children gathered, prolonging their return home, to hang-out with friends for a bit longer. Eating the pastry treats, that their parents forbidden.

A heard of screaming children were hurrying home, running past the newly beloved couple, almost breaking their chain. Mark laughed, though Chelsea looked annoyed. "Bloody kids." She said. They turned around the corner, the noise from the kids excitement had died. The empty street was filled with a ghostly silence, and one little girl in a bright red dress stood mischievously still. She stood still on top of a painted white line, her head bowed, so her pony tails dropped to the left. Her hands were held behind her back, almost as if she were hiding something.

An unnerving feeling came towards Chelsea, but her boyfriend appeared bewildered. The pair cautiously walked on the right hand side of the road, they noticed the little girls eyes had fixated on them. As they drew nearer the girl began to sing a nursery rhyme...

"Beware, beware the man with no face.

He cannot see. He cannot hear.

He is the man with no face."

Beware, beware the man with no face.

He doesn't sleep, he cannot smile.

He is the man with no face."

"PISS OF YOU LITTLE WEIRDO." Chelsea screamed.

Mark was appalled "You can't say that to a little kid."

"Well, what is she doing singing that creepy song?"

Mark shrugged his broad shoulders.

"Come on let's go." Chelsea ordered.

Chapter 70

Carl Sebastian and Gail Brooke are in Miss Brooke's classroom, emptying all furniture from one room to the next. Bass carried the last three stacked singular chairs to the next room.

"I am still struggling to comprehend your tale, Bass." Brooke said whilst pushing a plain grey desk from out the room, into the room across the hall.

"Help me with this." Bass patted his hands on Brooke's teaching table.

Brooke went to the opposite side of Bass, and simultaneously they strenuously lifted both ends of the heavy wooden lectern.

"You have to believe me Brooke, apparently "this thing" is coming after you, disguised as me and it will kill you."

The pair hobbled into the second, identical room.

"And you have also returned from the dead?" Brooke questioned with a bemused tone.

"Well, It's not as bad as man-flu." he mocked.

"YOU CAME BACK FROM THE DEAD?" Brooke repeated.

"Here." Bass designated.

The Teacher and the Lazarus dropped the heavy load onto the floor, it's now sat with the rest of the furniture from Gail's school room.

"Brooke, if anyone threatened your life, I will instantly take it seriously, no matter how ludicrous it sounds."

Bass took a moment to regain his breathe, and to cherish Brooke "I couldn't let anything happen to you. You're the world to me." He started to cry, if he were to shed tears, he'd best do it now, before the beast approaches. *What if he fails to protect her?* It had only just started to sink-in; the thought of losing her.

Brooke will, and always, admire his protectiveness. "You are more courageous than in one way."

"What do you mean?"

"You are brave to stand up to your enemies, but you are now bold enough to express your emotions."

Bass changed the subject, "We still have some more work to do; he'll be here shortly."

The schemers walked back into Gail Brooke's work room, Bass reached into his bag and pulled out a crowbar, jimmied it between the wall and the chalk board.

"Does that have to go as well?" Brooke questioned.

"Everything must be out this classroom, not one item, not even a stone on the floor."

"Could it really turn into anything? A curtain perhaps?"

"Yes, it could. Remember, if something should go wrong, then lock yourself in this room, do not let anyone in. No matter what they say, if an object, *any* object should appear, you know it'll be him."

"That explains the figure in my hotel room."

"Luckily, Jenny Woodfield came to warn you."

"I cannot recall feeling "lucky" at the time." Another notion came to Brooke. "Motion detectors."

"Motion detectors?" Bass overheard.

"When I was in the hospital basement, something unseen followed me, though the motion-detecting lights picked it up."

"Brooke, you're a genius. I might have some in my car, I'll go and get them." Bass then pulled off the black board from the wall.

Bass carried the long chalk board, awkwardly into the other room, now there is nothing in the room expect for the blue and brown, Victorian, diamond shaped, floor tiles, and beige wall paper.

Bass ran out to the car, to gather motion detector lights from the boot. Meanwhile Brooke is running up and down the study-hall, using her keys to lock all the other classrooms in the room. Thankfully it was a small school, so it was not as time consuming. The only room in the secondary school, that is accessible, is Brookes' vacant one.

Chelsea and Mark enter the school, heading to the Headmasters office, "Miss Brooke? What are you doing here?" Mark enquired.

Brooke was just about to lock the Headmasters office, but before inserting the key into the lock, she became distracted "Mark. Chelsea." She whispered. The mature adult detected scratch and bite marks all over Marks neck, also down his exposed chest from the low-cut top. "Oh my word, are you alright? Have you been attacked?"

Marks awkwardly shifted to and from Chelsea "It was... wolves." he badly lied.

"You have to leave, right now." Brooke told.

"Why? What's going on?" Chelsea involved.

"It's not safe here." Brooke whispered, pushing the love birds, hurrying them to leave.

Chelsea stood still, with her arms folded, "I'm not going anywhere, until you tell me the truth."

Brooke admires, (and loathes) her stubbornness, "Simon Cole murdered, Jenny Woodfield." Mark and Chelsea were profound by Gail's improbable statement. "That can't be true, he's The Chief Inspector. He was like, in-charge and stuff." Mark asserts.

Brooke didn't want to mention the fact, it was not really Simon Cole but an imposter, because the truth would only appear more implausible. "I do not have time to explain, he is on his way. Myself and Bass have prepared a trap."

"I never liked that short prick." Chelsea supported Brooke's claim. "If this son-of-a-bitch killed my friend, I want to help."

Brooke refuses "I cannot let yourself get killed, we can handle it. Go home and I will call you when it is over."

The adult uses her soft hands to push Chelsea, but the rebellious youth shrugs it off. "Me and Mark ain't going nowhere."

Around the corridor Bass's voice shouted "Brooke! I've set up my two motion detectors along the north entrance and the other by the east wing. I've paid the cleaner thirty quid to stay at home for the evening. P.S. I owe you thirty pound." Carl Sebastian appears from the corner, noticing Brooke standing with Chelsea and Mark. "What are they doing here?" He furiously spoke.

"We got a call from Simon Cole saying; he was going to meet us here." Chelsea explained.

"Yeah, to give us Jenny's stuff." Mark aided.

Bass pulled out the golden knife.

Mark and Brooke flinched.

Chelsea turned defensive, ready to fight.

"Put that down!" Brooke demanded.

"Brooke, come over to me."

"Not until you put that down, you know whom they are; Mark and Chelsea."

"You don't know that."

Brooke ran to Bass's side, trusting it was the real Carl Sebastian, because only he has the sacred gold blade.

Bass held Brookes' arm with his left hand, using his right hand to point with the edge of the knife. Directing the sharp blade to and from a guarding Chelsea, and a petrified Mark.

Chelsea discerned the wall behind her, the only way out is being blocked by a mad-man with a knife.

"It's ok, we're just leaving." With his held up against his panting chest, Mark took a step forward.

Letting go of his girls ar, Bass obstructed Marks exit. "Have you been together the whole time?" The private Investigator interrogated.

"What on earth are you on?" Chelsea said defensively.

"Since the phone call and the walk to school, were you constantly by each other's side?"

Mark nodded his sweaty head.

"You never separated? Not even for the toilet?" Bass probed.

"It's true what the towns been saying, you really are insane." Chelsea confronted Bass.

Bass was unsure how to prove that the two youngsters are who they say they are. If he had taken the time to get to know them, then he could have asked personal questions, only they would have known. Regretting not probing into the suspects

lives even further, Bass conjured up another idea...
"Give me your arm."

Mark retreated to the wall behind him.

"NO FUCKING WAY." Chelsea screamed in protest.

"What are you doing?" Brooke was concerned, not only for her friends sanity, but for the opposing kids.

Bass's intention was to cut the flesh, to see if the wound would appear different to the entities. It was a long shot, but what else did he have.

"I said give me your arm."

"We're going nowhere near you, psycho." Chelsea resisted.

Brooke attempted a civilised solution; "Chelsea, how did you and Jenny meet?" She spoke in a rational manner.

"School." Chelsea replied.

Bass turned to Brooke "Do you know if that's true?"

"It could be."

"Anyone could have guessed that, you need to ask something deeper." Bass tried advancing the situation.

The two youths appeared puzzled.

"We need to know if it is really you." Brooke explained.

Bass's imagination ran wild *What if they're in it together.* His head was hurting, *No, don't theorize that. You're over complicating it, and you have no proof.*

The sound of the main entrance opened...

"Hello, is anyone here, it's me Chief Inspector Cole."

Brooke panicked, "No, he's here." words of dread slid out of her trembling body.

"Help! Help! We're over here! He's trying to kill us!" Mark yelled, pleading to be saved.

Bass and Brooke immediately hushed him, Bass sprinted and covered Marks mouth. The boy's screaming was now just muffling. The taller man cringed, as he felt saliva spat all over his large hand. Mark attempted to elbow The Private Investigators over-weight stomach. In spite of his efforts, Bass is tough enough to take the blows.

"Shut up." Bass quietly urged.

Another voice echoed through the halls, a familiar one "Brooke, it's me Bass. I'm here with Simon."

Mark restrained himself, no longer struggling to break free from Bass's clutches. His dopey eyes peered to the man behind him. Though the real Carl Sebastian, didn't release his hold just yet.

Chelsea disbelieved her ears, "That sounded like you, but you're right here."

"Mark, Chelsea, go to my classroom, right now, it's nice and empty. Do not bring any objects inside and do not let anyone inside. Not even if it appears to be myself or Carl." Brooke adjured, giving Chelsea the keys to the school.

Gail's phone rang, she ignored it.

Bass let go of Carl, pulling out his knife, "That'll be him."

Mark was baffled "I'm still confused by everything."

"It's some sort of shape shifter, it calls himself; The Man with No Face. Even made up his own song, *because only cool people do that*." Bass sneered.

Chelsea frowned, proceeded to swear in slang, that's cryptic to the adults; "That shit cray"

"Still, it can transform into anyone or anything. Go now, stay together and do not be seen by anyone." Bass enjoined.

Chelsea grabbed Mark's hand, before leading him away she told Bass "Kill that cretin before I do."

"I will." Bass assured.

Gail Brooke approached a Carl Sebastian, but it was not *thee* Carl Sebastian. Its back was turned, still from behind it looked like Carl Sebastian, the clothes were identical, a plain blue woolly jumper, with the sleeves rolled up, jeans and brown shoes. It even has the same height and figure; broad shoulders, wide upper back, thick arms and pot belly. Brooke had to steady herself, knowing that she has to act normal, her thumping heart is causing sweat to break. "Bass, it is so good to see you." She attempted to speak clearly, but there were some nervous jitters.

"Brooke, it's so good to see you." The creature posing as Bass grinned. It feels superior and smarter than the deceived English Teacher. Assuming the inferior human girl, doesn't know that he's not really Bass, made him feel more powerful.

Brooke can see it's smugness in its imitating dark green eyes. "Where's Chelsea and Mark? You told me they were here?"

"Where is Chief Inspector Cole? They went to find him."

"He's had to go."

"Shelly's husband Richard, murdered her in the bathtub, then he killed himself."

Brooke didn't need to pretend when she broke down in tears, it was devastating news about Shelly. The grieving friend knelt down on the floor. Banging her pretty blonde head on the lockers behind her.

"Hey it's going to be ok, I'm here now." The Entity placed Carl's hand on Brookes shoulder.

She was nauseated by its touch, Brooke's spine shivered. "Thank you," placing a fake smile before asking; "Can I have a hug?"

"Of course you can have anything."

Brooke stood up and hugged the man posing as Bass, from the back of its bold head, she watched carefully as the real Carl Sebastian tread stealthy, holding the gold blade, ready to use it on the shape shifting deceiver.

The real Carl Sebastian will not hesitate to do what needs to be done, taking shorter and steadier breathes, as each light step draws him closer to the dupe.

Just before Brooke pushes the impersonator towards its death, the hoax whispers in her ear... "I know Carl Sebastian is behind me."

Brooke's confounded, light green eyes shot open.

The Entity grabbed Brooke, spun her round, and with such strength, through her into the real Bass.

Bass saw Brooke come flying towards him, instantly dropped the knife, before her body knocked him onto the shiny school floor.

"I've been doing this for centuries Bass, you won't get the better of me..." The creature gloated.

Bass groaned, he reluctantly pushed Brooke off himself, searching for the gold blade.

"... I saw your motion detectors by the entrance, also *your car*."

Bass felt stupid at this point, though he spotted the Latin engraved knife. Running towards it, the pretender tackled him out the way. The real heroes head hit the lockers, The Copy went to punch his enemy in the face, but he ducked, and the fist made a vast dent in the grey door.

The actual Bass went to grab the opposing clones jumper, though there were nothing to grab, it felt like grabbing skin.

The imitation laughed at his failure.

Brooke woke up rubbing her dazed head, stumbling on her way up, watching two Carl Sebastian wrestling on the ground. Thankful for her love of shoes rather than heels, she was able to run to the blade. The impartial teacher seized the gold handle with both her hands.

The two Carl Sebastian's stiffened, mounting up from the floor, simultaneously. Placing both hands over their hands over their identical heads, concurrently. It was a perfect mirrors image, the two versions of Bass were symmetrical "How do I know which one is which?" she cried.

"It's me, Brooke. I'm Bass." Said the one on the right.

"Don't listen to him." The left one protested.

"I know you better than anyone." Claimed, the left.

"We don't really know anyone." The right, conjectured.

Brooke swung the knife to the direction of the left.

"He's right." The left Bass dropped sullen. "Stab us both."

"Ok, I'm not afraid of dying." The right one agreed.

"I am not going to kill you, Bass." Brooke declined.

The right clone spoke "Remember when I kept playing heavy metal music to annoy you-"

The left clone interrupted "Remember when we danced in The Garden."

"Anyone could have seen that?" the right, protested.

"But no one could have copied how I felt."

Brooke swung the direction of the gold blade to the right replica.

"Wait, our clothes." The right image, suggested. "We'll take off our jumpers and Brooke could inspect our bodies."

"I'm not taking my clothes off in front of you." The left twin protested defensively.

"I grabbed his clothes, it was like it was stuck onto him."

Brooke pointed the deadly instrument to the left "Do it."

The left replica of Bass was hesitant, feeling all the eyes were on him, reluctantly dropped his hands around the neck line

Brooke watched how guarded this Bass was.

The left Bass stared at his mirrored image, returned his gaze towards Brooke.

Brooke inched forward, feeling out of patience.

The left clone took off his jumper and shirt off, eventually.

Now, Brooke edged the knife closer to the right replica.

The right one lifted his jumper and shirt off.

The Bass on the left hand side looked astounded "How are you doing this?"

"Do what?"

Brooke scanned back and forth between both identical bodies.

The right-hand sided Bass, had a notion; "Cut our flesh, remember, just a scratch on the arm. To see if we bleed differently. *If it bleeds we can kill it.*"

"Like in *Friday the Thirteenth*?" Brooke referenced.

Both Bass's looked disapproving; "No, *Predator!*" They equally corrected.

"Let's get it over and done with." Brooke stared at the right clone "You first."

The duplicate on the right stuck his left arm out, he cringed from the pain that's carving into his bare flesh.

The English teacher watched blood pour from the forearm, but hadn't noticed anything indifferent.

The second look-alike lifted his right arm, mentally preparing himself for what's to come.

Gail ran the cutter along the arm, tearing the skin, though the results were the same. "What am I going to do now?" She worried.

Chapter 71

Chelsea was pacing up and down, on the blue and brown, diamond shaped, Victorian, floor tiles, in the naked classroom. Mark has his arms folded, leant up against the beige wall. The setting sun falling on his pretty face and jet-black air.

"I can't wait in here any longer." Chelsea explodes, sick of being locked in the room, and kept in the dark, she's turned stir-crazy.

"We have to wait here."

"Something's up, they're taking too long."

"We gotta stay, they'll be back soon. If we vanish, then return, they might think we are the proper killers."

"You don't really believe this crap, do you?"

"Well encase it is, someone should stay."

"That's a good point; you stay here."

"We should create a code; one that only we know, so we can I.D. ourselves."

"That's the smartest thing you've said in ages." Chelsea agreed.

"What's gonna be our code?"

"Four, Eight, Six, Two, One. Twelve" Chelsea conjured up.

"I'll remember that." Mark believes.

"I'll be back, as soon as poss.' I'm gonna "leg-it" round the school." She goes to leave.

"Chelsea." Mark halted.

"What?" She speaks abruptly.

"Be careful."

Chelsea smiles, "You big softie. Lock the door behind me." She instructed.

Mark rushes to lock the door, the second his girlfriend leaves.

Chelsea made her chary way around the school corridor; sticking close to the walls edge, feeling the locker doors brushing against her pale arms. As she drew nearer to the corner, Chelsea could hear two voices; Gail Brooke and Carl Sebastian. As Miss Heart peered around the corner, her prying blue eyes saw, not only *one*, but *two* Carl Sebastian's. Both men knelt on the floor, with hands behind their heads. In between is Brooke deciding which one is real.

"What the hell's going on?" Chelsea bawled.

Brooke whirled round, "Chelsea, get out of here!"

While the teachers back was turned, the clone of Carl Sebastian on the right hand side, leaped up, shoulder-barging Brooke, taking the opportunity to disappear. The creature vanished in the blink of an eye. A bewildered Chelsea leaped back, completely afraid of her surroundings.

The real Bass stood on his feet, ran to Brooke. "Are you alright?"

"I am ok, I still have the knife." Brooke reassured.

Bass took the knife from her, then he screamed at Chelsea; "We've lost him now! Thanks to you."

"Bass, please don't blame her." Brooke proceeded by linking arms with Chelsea; "We have to get her out of here."

Bass held Brooke's hand with his available left one. His right hand, still gripping the gold blade.

"What about Mark?" Chelsea feared.

"Is he in my classroom?"

"Yes."

"We'll go back for him. If he has any sense, he will do as he's told, and remain there." Bass said, whilst resentfully looking directly at Chelsea.

Brooke was relieved by the young girls intrusion, she'd have never forgiven herself if she had stabbed the real Carl Sebastian "Hopefully, he shall not let anybody inside."

The heedful trio, cautiously step towards the main entrance, mindful of every little object. Gail Brooke gazed at the water fountain, maintaining a wary eye on it, doubting it's origins, unsure if she had seen it before, Brooke mentally prepares for the water fountain to come alive and attack her and her friends.

Chelsea walks past fifteen lockers, observantly looking at the unoccupied coat hangers, hinges on the doors, to see if one is out of place.

Bass too, is alert of the surrounding environment; "Don't touch anything and do not let go of each other."

Eventually the triad reached the main entrance, only to discover a thick metal chain wrapped around two pull handles.

Chelsea pulled the door, as if some miracle would occur, and the door would open.

"Is there another way out?" Bass puts a question to Brooke.

"Yes, the fire exit, on the west wing."

"What if we smashed a window?" Chelsea considered.

"The windows are made with protective glass."

Bass looked up, noticing a motion detecting light, he installed earlier had been destroyed, assuming the other one, on the east wing, had been violated too.

"We cannot let *The Thing* escape; we might be trapped in here, but so is it. If it leaves the school, we might never get a shot at killing it again." Bass stated.

"We're trapped in here we 'dis thing?" Chelsea blustered.

"Chelsea, if this thing escapes, it'll just carry on murdering people, like your friend. Forever getting away with it."

"You're right, let it come for us."

"That's what I'm counting on."

"Shall we rendezvous with Mark?" Brooke suggested.

"I think that fire exits closer, if you wanna check it out, before." Chelsea proposes.

The threesome retraced their steps, carefully striding past the water fountain, the uninhabited coat hangers and fourteen lockers…

Eventually the gang made it to the fire escape, Bass pushed down on the metal handle, to open the door, but it would not budge, something on the other side was blocking the escape. With the door slightly ajar, Bass peeked through the tiny gap, a police car was parked directly in front, so there was no escape.

"Mark." Chelsea panicked, urging to run back.

The sound of the tannoy system turned on, the sound of a muffled microphone echoed throughout the school halls..."Hello, this is your headmaster speaking."

"That's not the headmaster." Chelsea inferred.

"Chelsea Heart, Mark Bell, Gail Brooke and Carl Sebastian. You have all been very naughty..."

"It's the naughty corner for us, then" Bass mocked.

"... You will need to be put in time out." The voice of The Headmaster began to deliberately garble and sedate its words, *"I'mmmmm commmmiiiiiinnnnnnngggg..."* His Voice grew deeper, sounding like a computer's dying voice gradually losing power before shutting off *"forrrrrrrrrrr yoouuuuuuuuu."*

"Where's the tannoy system based?" Bass requested.

Brooke recalled; "I forgot to lock the headmasters' room."

Bass saw the nervous stare on The Teachers gorgeous face; "What does that mean?"

"There's another set of keys in there that could unlock all of the rooms."

"Including your classroom?"

Brooke nods her head.

"It bet it was that thing that announced Jenny's death, over the tannoy system. Who else would do that?" Chelsea suspected.

The sound of the tannoy system returned... "Help me. Help me. Is there anybody out there?"

Bass didn't recognise the person speaking, he noticed that a trembling Chelsea, knew who it was.

"That's Jenny." She described. A mixture of rage and dejection ran through her body.

"It is not Jenny." Brooke assured, placing an arm around her shaking body, in order to bring comfort.

Chelsea pushed off Brooke's arm; "I know it's not her, but how dare he use her voice."

The entity carried on speaking, by imitating Jenny Woodfields voice; "Chelsea. Chelsea. You have to help me. You're my best friend..."

Bass put his hand on Chelsea's shoulder "Do not listen."

This time, she didn't shrug off the offer of consolation. Tears appeared through her eyes, brought by fury, not grief.

"... I'm dead because of you, you with your coke addiction. You with your self-absorption. You with your bad relationships and failures, bringing me down. YOU, YOU, YOU RUINED MY LIFE..."

Chelsea pressed her hands over her ears, so hard it felt like she could crush her own skull. Despite her attempts to suppress the ridiculing noise, the din still penetrated through the barriers of her pale palms.

"... I'M DEAD. I'M DEAD. I'M DEAD. I'M DEAD. I'M DEAD. I'M DEAD. I SNAPPED MY NECK AND NOW I CAN'T GET UP AGAIN."

Only Brooke and Bass heard Jenny laugh, her laughing was meant for mocking the tormented ears of the two women. The scorned laughter derided into the sound of a high pitch, jack-in-a-box -clown, type of chuckling; *"HAHAHAHAHA."*

"I bloody hate clowns n'all." Chelsea added, with dismay.

"I'm going to the Headmaster's office, to end this." Bass vowed. "You two go and get Mark."

Just as The Pupil and Teacher separated from Bass. The power is cut off, causing a blackout in the school...

Chapter 72

In the darkness, Mark Bell paces his way to the square window on the door. Thankfully there's nothing in the room otherwise he'd be tripping on chair legs and all sorts; like tripping over guide ropes, drunk at a festival. The young man pressed his head against the glass, buttoning his nose, scanning what little of the corridor he could see. Left to right, noticing the lights were off at the rest of the school. Constantly worrying, his friends had been a long time since he last heard anything, and that horrible message over the schools-speakers. *"What kinda sick-o would do that?"* He thought. Taking a step back to scratch his head...

BANG! BANG! BANG!

Mark jumped up to see Bass banging his arm on the door. "Mark, Mark, let me in." Scrambling to get the door open, "Come on, it's me, just let me in." He's yanking on the circular knob hard, almost pulling it off.

Mark noticed blood dripping from his bare arm, leaving a print of smeared red on the windowpane. "How do I know it's you?"

"I got separated from Chelsea and Brooke during the blackout."

"You told me not to let anybody in."

Bass yelled; "Now, I'm telling you to let me back in." his tone was getting more aggressive.

Mark steps further back, away from the door "I'm sorry, I can't, not without the password."

"I'm not in the fucking mood for this."

Mark's uneasiness kept him silent.

Bass vigorously strikes his fist against the door; "Mark, you have three seconds to open this door." He warns.

"One."

Mark begins to consider opening the door; *what if it is just Bass, and he's just his usual pissed-off-self?*

"Two."

"He's bleeding, he needs help." Mark contemplated.

"Three."

Mark lightly treads forward, he stops when he notices Bass laughing.

That's not Bass, he never laughs at anything

"Marky, Mark. When I get in there, I'm going to gut you like a fish. I'm going to hang your body upside down. Then I want you to see your own guts, and blood pour out in front of your very own eyes." The person that appears to be Bass, grins, and then cackles.

A fearful, intimidated Mark pins his eyes shut, hoping when he opens them again, the person who looks like Bass will have disappeared. His wish came true. The entity vanished, leaving a blood stained glass window. It was a relief, although he was still affright.

Seconds later, Chelsea Heart rapidly thumps the door with the sides of her fists. Her hair was a mess, frantically shouting "Mark, Mark, you got to let me in, I lost Brooke, I don't know where she's gone."

"Chelsea." Mark ran to the door, their hands mirrored, almost touching, if it weren't for the windowpane in-between.

"You have to let me in, please Mark. I'm scared."

Mark prayed it is really Chelsea, but he had to make sure; "What's the password?"

"Four, Eight, Two, Ten, Twelve."

"That's not it." Mark stepped away, fearing the creature had returned to "gut him like a fish."

"No, No, it's; Four, Six, Ten, Twelve, Two."

Mark shakes his head; "You're not Chelsea. It's not the right password."

Chelsea looks confused "What? Yes it is." She insists.

"No it's not."

"It is, it definitely started with a Four, then went up in twos'."

"It had a five in."

"It never had a five in!" She yelled.

"I can't really remember." Mark admitted.

"Neither can I, I've just been crazy out 'ere."

Their youthful faces fixated to each other's, their eyes stared through the glass, so lovingly, and nothing else could distract them.

Mark felt disgruntled, he close to his girlfriend; they could almost touch. Yet, so far away. He could see the desperation in her piercing blue eyes; "Stuff it." he said, proceeding to unlock the door...

Chapter 73

Carl Sebastian took longer to get to the Headmasters' office than he would have liked, not only had he tread in the dark, he couldn't maintain his balance by grabbing hold of something, encase it grabbed him back. He did take a gamble, going in the little-boys-room, wrapping tissue around his knife wound, to stop the bleeding. He had to, because anyone or *anything,* could follow the drops of blood, right to his location.

Before he opened the door to walk in, Bass heard footsteps running towards him, he spun around, knife-in-hand.

Brooke instantly halted, raising her hands, once she saw the sharp blade. "Bass. It is me."

"Stay back." Bass bellowed. The last time he hesitated when the creature posed as Gail Brooke, this time he won't repeat that mistake.

"Bass, it is me, I am here in all honesty."

"How do you know it's me?"

"You have the knife." Brooke pointed out.

That creature, that fiendish, despicable miscreant-" A lump in her throat paused her quivering words, and the tears begin to rain out of her light green eyes.

Bass desires for the opposing woman to be genuine, longing to give her a tight hug, but until he's curtain, the Private Investigator must remain vigilant.

"The monster has killed Chelsea and Mark."

The news startled Bass, previously; when he's lost people under his care; it's never affected him. Before he used to say; "I never really knew them." Today;

grief as affected him for the first time, saddened by the news, a tear escapes from his tear-duct.

Brooke moves in to give Bass a hug.

Her efforts causes Bass to jolt backwards, "Stay back! I don't know if it's you." He begins to interrogate; "How did you lose Chelsea?"

"It was a blackout, and then, not only lockers, but walls began to change. Separating myself from Chelsea, I deduce; the creature killed Chelsea, disguising itself as her to deceive Mark."

Bass noticed the woman never used abbreviations whilst talking, just like Brooke. Be that as it may, The Investigator isn't fully convinced. "Tell me something, I would have only told you."

"You arrived late to the pub once, and your poor justification were; "I am sorry, I am late, I forgot my safe-word and my mistress would not untie me.""

Bass recollected telling her that sarcastic excuse. "Brooke, thank god it's you."

Bass squeezed his girlfriend in his loving, masculine arms.

"I just want this nightmare to end, How can we ever tell their families what really happened? How would they react to our statement?" Brooke said.

Bass looked at her beautiful blonde face; her light green eyes and the same lovely smile. Still... The birth mark on Brooke's left ear had gone. *This isn't Brooke.* Bass concluded. Carl Sebastian perforated her heart with the Latin inscribed blade.

The creature imitation of Brooke stumbled backwards, digging its forged finger nails around the painful, penetrated wound. The entity that posed as Bass, Simon Cole, Brooke, screeched. Its cries of pain dissolved into laughter "I knew you would make a great adversary."

Bass would never admit out-loud; that piercing this fiends heart, feeling its blood trickle onto his hands, felt satisfying.

The creature fell to its knees, and then leant it's head on its ever-changing right arm, its altering left arm grasped the trauma. It appeared as if the entity was having a seizure in the recovery position. The shrieking face is constantly remoulding, morphing into different colours, shapes and sizes. An estimate of seven to ten different faces breach the barrier of skin, all at once. The carcass, which lacked a skeleton, melted into the ground, the remnants evaporated in the air.

"Brooke!" Bass sprinted; no touch of tiredness arrived. His chunky legs bounced down the corridor, skidding around corners, needing to know if she was safe.

Carl Sebastian made it to the safe room, the door labelled; Miss G. Brooke. There was blood on the door, fearing the worst, his heart raced. He viewed through the windowpane, and saw a sight, that brought nothing but jubilation. The real Gail Brooke was on the floor, holding an unharmed Chelsea and Mark. In her natural care-giving arms.

Chapter 74

Frank Mill is closing up The Dive; Ten PM is the earliest he's shut, in a long time. Business has been slacking since his brothers' breakdown. He's certain it'll pick up again. When exactly? Remains unclear, though, it'll happen.

The oldest of Mill brothers placed the last seat on the table, whilst wiping the bar, he hears the doors open.

"We're closed!"

Frank turns to see a tremoring couple, two pale teen's, who had left their complexions from where they'd just been. The look of horror had clouded the young eyes of Chelsea and Mark, causing them to appear exhausted, however, it'll be a long time before they sleep.

"You both look like you need a drink. I can't serve you any alcoholic drinks, mind."

Mark and Chelsea sluggishly walk to the stools, facing the bar. Once sat, the pair slump their bodies on the wooden surface.

"You look how I feel." Frank commented.

Chelsea looked bemused.

"What happened to you guys?"

"You wouldn't believe me, if I told you." Chelsea sounded distant when she spoke.

"Well, at least you have each other."

Mark and Chelsea look at each other, simultaneously their arms drop in between the gap, as they hold hands.

Frank smiles "What will it be?"

Mark replies; "Two diet cokes, please."

"*Errrr* Mark, I can answer for myself, thank you very much. I'll have a full fat coke, thanks."

Mark rolls his eyes.

Frank pours the requested drinks, placing the pints on the beers mats. "It's on the house."

Mark takes sips from his pint glass.

Meanwhile Chelsea is just staring into the blackness of her liquid, lured by the darkness. It's so easy to sink in, but she's not going to give in, she raises her fizzy drink into the air, and proposes a toast; "This one's for you, Jenny." Necks it down in one. The sugar perked up Chelsea; "How's Jack?" she asked the bar man.

"I don't know, he has no contact with the outside world at this moment, and he's currently not allowed any visitors."

"I'm sorry to hear that."

Frank hung his head in shame; "He tried to warn me, and I saw it coming, but I didn't listen. I feel so guilty. Crap, I should have done something." The bar owner appeared distant, "Mum and Dad always said; it was my responsibility to look after him, and now I've failed them too."

Chelsea wish she was a huger, than she could cheer him up.

LUCKILY, Mark is. He leaped off his stool, ran round the bar and held Frank tight.

Believing to be a man's-man, Frank would never show affection in public, and a hug from another man would make him uncomfortable. Now, he brightly smiled, returned his open arms and patted the young lad's muscular back, "Do you think he'll forgive me?"

"I think he will, family always come through in the end." Mark guaranteed.

"Thanks, that means a lot. I am going to get everyone in Holders Bridge to sign my card, contribute to some flowers and that, to show that we do care about Jacky-boy. Also the next charity concert will do to raise awareness for *Depression and Anxiety,* to make more people aware. Will you be the first ones to do the honour of signing the card?"

"Sure." Chelsea asks; "Can you call my father, and ask him to pick me up? I just need to tell him; I love him and I'm sorry for being such a cow."

"Sure." Frank walked to the landline.

Mark grinned, and playfully tugs on the hand he's holding; "Chelsea Heart, are you really going to apologise?"

"Don't get used to it, shit-head." Chelsea told, just before she puts her head on his broad shoulder.

"I love you."

"And so you should, you'll never get another girl like me."

"I'm not sure, if that's a bad thing." Mark jokes.

She gently taps him on his cheek, "I love you too, sexy boy."

Chapter 75

The sun filled morning has stopped the day from being cold. Carl Sebastian and Gail Brooke walk down the dirt path, to the river's edge together. Brooke's arm is linked around Bass's, probably to stop him from running away. The English Teacher smiles and tells her man; "I am so proud of you."
On the other hand, Bass appears apprehensive, "What if I don't deserve this?"
"Everyone deserves a second chance." Brooke supports.

Bass leers at Father Paul standing, all in white, knee deep in slightly murky river water.

"Why do you look so scared?" Brooke enquires.

"I'm not sure, I feel a bit anxious about it."

"I believe in you."

"Will you come with me?"

"And get my trousers wet? No way. I will wait here for you." Brooke replies.

"I thought girlfriends were meant to be supportive?"

"I can be supportive on dry land."

Bass chuckles, he takes off his brown shoes, rolls up his jeans, then placed his hairy feet in the freezing cold water. "Bloody hell!" he shivers whilst making his way towards The Man of The Cloth. The Private Investigator pauses half-way, turning to face Brooke.

Brooke realises he looks frightened; "Nearly there, it should only take a few seconds then it will all be over."

Bass wades towards a grinning vicar "I thought Pride was a sin."

"I'm merely happy for you, my child."

"Yeah, yeah, let's get this over and done with." Bass rubs his hands together.

Father Paul placed a hand on Bass's forehead, and began to read a passage from the bible.

Bass crossed both of his hands over his chest, not listening to the spoken verses being read to him, too busy focusing on the amazing, beautiful blonde woman, gazing upon him, from the river bank.

The next thing; Carl "Bass" Sebastian's head is pushed underwater, washing away his past. So, to begin again...

Acknowledgements

First I would like to thank you- The Reader- I hope you enjoyed the book.

Whitney Sweet at TROU Lit Magazine.

Sprotbrough Library, Doncaster, England.

And to all my Friends and Family for their support.

Printed in Great Britain
by Amazon